PENGUIN BOOKS

THE GATES OF IVORY

Margaret Drabble was born in Sheffield in 1939 and went to the Mount School, York, a Quaker boarding school. She won a Major Scholarship to Newnham College, Cambridge, where she read English. She was awarded a CBE in 1980.

She has written several novels: *A Summer Bird-Cage* (1963), *The Garrick Year* (1964), *The Millstone* (1965, filmed as *A Touch of Love* in 1969), *Jerusalem the Golden* (1967), *The Waterfall* (1969), *The Needle's Eye* (1972), *The Realms of Gold* (1975), *The Ice Age* (1977), *The Middle Ground* (1980), *The Radiant Way* (1987) and *A Natural Curiosity* (1989), all of which have been published by Penguin. She has also published a short critical book on Wordsworth and many articles, as well as *Arnold Bennett: A Biography* (1974), *The Genius of Thomas Hardy* (1976, edited), *A Writer's Britain* (1979) and *The Oxford Companion to English Literature* (1985, edited).

Margaret Drabble is married to the biographer Michael Holroyd and lives in London.

D0230331

MARGARET DRABBLE

———————

THE GATES OF IVORY

PENGUIN BOOKS

PENGUIN BOOKS

Published by the Penguin Group
Penguin Books Ltd, 27 Wrights Lane, London W8 5TZ, England
Penguin Books USA Inc., 375 Hudson Street, New York, New York 10014, USA
Penguin Books Australia Ltd, Ringwood, Victoria, Australia
Penguin Books Canada Ltd, 10 Alcorn Avenue, Toronto, Ontario,
Canada M4V 3B2
Penguin Books (NZ) Ltd, 182–190 Wairau Road, Auckland 10, New Zealand

Penguin Books Ltd, Registered Offices: Harmondsworth, Middlesex, England

First published by Viking 1991
Published in Penguin Books 1992
3 5 7 9 10 8 6 4 2

Printed in England by Clays Ltd, St Ives plc

For Joe Swift

For Chhiek Ieng That

For all those on the border

I would like to thank all those who helped me with the background material for this book. I hope they will not disapprove of the fictional use to which I have put their facts. It is not possible to name them all, but I would like to give particular thanks to Susan Balfour, Anthony Barnett, Elizabeth Becker, Jack Emery, Rosalind Finlay, Stanley and Romaly Harper, Tony Jackson, Judith Jacob, Mary Kay Magistad, Amanda Milligan, Chris Mullin, Minh Phuoc, William Shawcross, Nicki Sissons, M. R. Smansnid Svasti, Chhiek Ieng That, and the Manager of the Oriental Hotel.

Dreams, said Penelope to the stranger, may puzzle and mislead. They do not always foretell the truth. They come to us through two gates: one is of horn, the other is of ivory. The dreams that come to us through the traitor ivory deceive us with false images of what will never come to pass: but those that appear to us through the polished horn speak plainly of what could be and will be.

Homer, *The Odyssey*, Book XIX, 560—65

The Gates of Ivory

This is a novel — if novel it be — about Good Time and Bad Time. Imagine yourself standing by a bridge over a river on the border between Thailand and Cambodia. Behind you, the little town of Aranyaprathet, bristling with aerials and stuffed with Good Time merchandise, connected by road and rail and telephone and post office and gossip and newspapers and banking systems with all the Good Times of the West. Before you, the Bad Time of Cambodia. You can peer into the sunlit darkness if you wish.

Many are drawn to stare across this bridge. They come, and stare, and turn back. What else can they do? A desultory, ragged band of witnesses, silently, attentively, one after another, they come, and take up the position, and then turn back. A Japanese journalist, an American historian, an English photographer, a Jewish survivor of the holocaust, a French diplomat, a Scottish poet, a Thai princess, a Chinese Quaker from Hong Kong. For different reasons and for the same reason they are drawn here. That young man with curly hair is the son of the British Chief Prosecutor at Nuremberg. That broad-shouldered woman in the yellow Aertex shirt is the daughter of a discredited Oxford-educated Marxist scholar. Here they come, here they stand. They are asking a question, but there is no answer. Here too Stephen Cox will stand.

Good Time and Bad Time coexist. We in Good Time receive messengers who stumble across the bridge or through the river, maimed and bleeding, shocked and starving. They try to tell us what it is like over there, and we try to listen. We invoke them with libations of aid, with barley and blood, with rice and water,

3

and they flock to the dark trenches, moaning and fluttering in their thousands. We are seized with panic and pity and fear. Can we believe these stories from beyond the tomb? Can it be that these things happen in our world, our time?

The dead and dying travel fast these days. We can devour thousands at breakfast with our toast and coffee, and thousands more on the evening news. It would be easy to say that we grow fat and greedy, that we thrive on atrocities, that we eagerly consume suffering. It is not as simple as that. We need them as they need us. There is a relationship between Good Time and Bad Time. There are interpenetrations. Some cross the bridge into the Bad Time, into the Underworld, and return to tell the tale. Some go deliberately. Some step into Bad Time suddenly. It may be waiting, there, in the next room.

*

While opening her post one dark morning, Liz Headleand was surprised to come across a package containing part of a human finger bone. It contained other objects, but the bone was the first to attract her attention. She could feel it before she saw it, through the scruffy layers of envelope and battered jiffy-bag. She shook the bag, and out it fell upon her desk, wrapped in a twist of thin cheap grey-green paper. She prodded it curiously with her own fleshy finger, and immediately and correctly identified it as kin.

On closer inspection, she discovered that she had before her two bones, the two middle joints of a small digit of a small hand, tied together with dirty fraying cotton thread. They took her back to anatomy lessons of yesteryear. A hundred years ago, she had studied bones and muscles, articulations and connections. She had learned the names of the small bones and of the large. This knowledge was not much use to her these days. But from a hundred years ago dry words whispered to her. The radius and the ulna, the carpal, metacarpal and phalangeal bones.

4

She regarded the missive without alarm but with respect. She touched it gingerly. She gazed at the rest of the package. There were envelopes within envelopes. Wads of paper, notebooks, newspaper clippings. A complex presentation. It had come from abroad, and the stamps were unfamiliar. Was it, she wondered, a gift of leprosy? Was a fatal illness lying there before her? The bones looked like an amulet, a charm against evil. Did it bring her good or ill? Which was intended? And by whom?

Liz, as a healer of hurt minds, was professionally familiar with distressing post. She knew the handwriting and the notepaper of derangement. She had received objects before now: once a used condom, once a dried purple rose. But never before had she received a human bone.

The ensemble exuded craziness, from string, from dirty peeling adhesive tape, from large crudely printed address. DR E. HEAD-LEAND, 33 DRESDEN ROAD, LONDON NW8, it requested. It was quite substantial. Manuscript size. Was it perhaps an unpublished and unpublishable novel, from a leper in the Congo? From a burnt-out case, shedding his unwanted thoughts and fingers on Elizabeth Headleand in St John's Wood? She wondered, half seriously, if it would be safe to touch it. She recalled the public library books of her childhood which had carried health warnings about contagious diseases. This looked a dangerous package. If any package could kill you without explosives, this would be it.

Liz thought of rubber gloves, but dismissed the notion as absurd. She picked up the bones, wrapped them up again in their wisp of creased paper, laid them to one side of her large leather-topped desk, and applied herself to the package.

First she extracted an airmail envelope of unfamiliar design, with her name upon it in an unfamiliar hand, written, like the address, in wandering capitals. She opened it. A piece of lined bluish-grey paper mysteriously informed her I ASK SEND YOU THIS GREAT CRISIS GOOD BYE! BYE! BYE! No date, no signature.

She moved on. Was she bored, was she intrigued? She could not have said. Everyday craziness is dull, but grand craziness compels attention. Could this be craziness on a grand scale? She eased the string from a brown envelope full of paper, and found the handwriting of her old friend Stephen Cox.

So, it was a novel. Stephen was a novelist, therefore this was a novel. She read its first sentence.

'And he came to a land where the water flows uphill.'

Stephen's script was small, hesitant, but tolerably legible. He had used a ball-point pen. She could have read on, but did not. She looked again at the finger. Was that Stephen's finger lying there?

She pushed the papers back into their envelope, noting that it had once been sealed with string and sealing wax. She approached another, smaller envelope. It too contained bits of script in Stephen's hand, some of it laid out in what looked like stage instructions and dialogue. Was it part of a play?

She remembered that Stephen had vanished to the East to write a play about Pol Pot. Or so he had said. Two years ago? Three or four years ago? Something like that.

There were cuttings, paperclipped together, indented with rust. News stories, photographs.

She realized she should treat these messages with the care of an archivist. Their order and disposition, once destroyed, would vanish for ever. Already she had forgotten precisely how, within the package, the finger had been placed. Posthumously, as an afterthought? But she had to look further. Now. Curiosity compelled her. She had to see whether there was a message there for her, for Liz Headleand, for herself alone.

She found picture postcards, unscripted. Of a shrine, of a pagoda, of a boat on a wide river, of a lake with reflected drooping trees, of Buddhist monks robed in saffron, of a smiling carved face in a jungle, of dancing girls, of a marble mausoleum. Some were glossy, some were old and faded, some were new but poorly tinted. She found a long document with official stamps in an unknown language. She found a laundry bill from a hotel in Bangkok, and a currency exchange form, and a receipt from a hotel safe. She found two more little notebooks full of jottings and sketches. She found a quotation from John Stuart Mill, and a poem by Rimbaud. She found a scrap of orange ribbon and a flake of brittle pearly shell, and a tiny photograph of an ethnic child sitting on a buffalo. But her own name she did not find.

Was it there, somewhere, hidden, coded? Why had Stephen selected her? What obligation had he laid upon her?

She felt important, chosen, as she sat there at her desk. At the same time she felt neglected. Why had he not enclosed a note saying 'Good wishes, Stephen'? He had sent her postcards from foreign parts before, with brief messages. She had received a couple from this long absence, this long silence. From Singapore or Penang or Bangkok. Or somewhere like that. Why was he now so sparing with his signature?

Here was his story. Perhaps he was telling her that she would have to read it all.

Or perhaps he was dead, and this was all that was left of him.

Liz gazed at the array of relics and records. Her bell buzzed. Her first patient would be waiting for her. She could not look more closely now. But, as she left for her consulting room, she locked her study door. She did not want the Filipino cleaning lady to see Stephen's bones.

*

'A finger bone?' echoed Alix Bowen, Liz's first confidante, with disbelief, impressed.

'That's right. Well, two finger bones really. The two middle joints of a little finger, I think. They're too small to be Stephen's. He had quite *long* hands, didn't he?'

'Yes, he did.'

They had both fallen, instantly, into the habit of speaking of Stephen in the past tense. Wordlessly they acknowledged this and decided to strive against it.

Liz continued, into her new cordless telephone, to describe to her friend Alix the other varied contents of the package. The prose manuscripts, the attempts at a play, the diary notebooks, the postcards, the sketches.

'Sketches of *what*?' Alix wanted to know.

'Oh, all sorts of bits and pieces. Buildings. Temples. Styles of oriental architecture, labelled. Straw huts. A monkey. A cooking pot resting on three stones. A butterfly. A skull. A boat.'

'I didn't know Stephen could draw,' said Alix.

'He can't,' said Liz, restoring him to life. 'Or not very well. But he's had a go.'

'And there's no message, no instructions about what you're supposed to *do* with all this?'

'Nothing at all. Or not that I've found yet. There may be something hidden away in there. But I'm going to have to go through it all very carefully to find out. Why ever did he send all this stuff to *me*?'

Alix was silent, wondering the same thing. She had been responsible for introducing Liz to Stephen, and had at one stage hoped and feared that a middle-aged romance might blossom, but they had remained Good Friends. Not such good friends, however, as Alix's husband Brian and Stephen had been. Brian and Stephen had been buddies, comrades in arms, comrades of letters. Brian would surely have been a more fitting receiver of literary goods. Why had Stephen selected Liz? Should Alix and Brian feel offended, excluded?

Both Liz and Alix appreciated, without mentioning it, the element of sexual innuendo in the sending of a bone. This might in some way be an act of courtship. Stephen would surely not have sent a bone to Brian Bowen.

'Maybe, of course,' said Liz, '*he* didn't select me at all. Maybe somebody else did. The wording of the message to me is ambiguous. Maybe they just happened to come across my address.'

'Maybe,' said Alix, mollified.

'I suppose I'll have to try to read it,' said Liz, with a mixture of pride, perplexity and reluctance. 'I suppose, if there's anything publishable in there, it might be quite valuable? Do you think?'

'Yes, perhaps,' said Alix cautiously. She did not like to say that if Stephen were dead, it would not be *very* valuable. Stephen had been a successful writer, after a fashion, and had made, latterly, a good living from his trade. His manuscripts no doubt resided in some North American university, in carefully controlled atmospheric conditions. This package could go and join them, if it proved authentic. But it would not fetch a very high price, if known to be the last. Stephen was — or had been — at that mid-stage in his career where his value depended upon a prospect of output, of *œuvre*. He had had more years of work ahead of him. A last message and then the silence of death would do his prospects no good. It would create a momentary stir, and no more. His publishers would not like it at all. Unless, of course, this last manuscript proved to be a masterpiece. But if it were, who would be able to tell? It sounded from Liz's description as though it needed a good deal of editing. Alix knew, from the complaints of friends and from her own experience in the role, that editors these days are not what they were. It would take an exceptional editor to deal with this Do-It-Yourself Novel Pack that had landed up on Liz Headleand's desk.

Liz, following this unspoken train of thought, inquired, 'Did Stephen have an agent?'

Alix reflected.

'He was rather keen on negotiating his own affairs. He was quite good at it, for such a vague sort of person. But I think there was somebody. Wasn't that dotty woman he knew some kind of agent?'

'What dotty woman?'

'That drinking woman. Isn't she in his flat in Primrose Hill now?'

Liz was silent. She had not known, or had forgotten, that there was a dotty drinking woman in Stephen's flat.

'Yes,' said Alix, 'I'm almost sure she was some kind of agent. You could always contact her, I suppose. He'd just changed publishers, with the last book. And anyway, he had two lots of publishers, one for his serious work and one for his thrillers.'

'What was her name?'

'I think she was called Hattie. Hattie Osborne.'

'Hmm,' said Liz, smelling a rival.

'I say,' said Alix. 'Does it look a . . . *newish* sort of bone?'

And they continued to discuss severed bones, heads, feet and ears for some time. The use of, in the taking of hostages and the threatening of nearest and dearest. The use of, in emotional blackmail. They mentioned Van Gogh and Alix's murderer-friend Paul Whitmore. They discussed jokes about finger bones found in soup in Chinese restaurants, about greyhounds discovered in the deep freezes of curry takeaways. And were there not stories, Alix wondered, about American soldiers in the Vietnam war collecting bags full of Viet Cong ears and sending samples back to their appalled girlfriends?

'But those are just *stories*,' protested Liz. 'Like the Viet Cong playing Russian roulette. Atrocity stories. That thing on my desk is real. I promise you.'

'You must ask Brian when he last heard from Stephen,' she continued, modulating her tone to indicate seriousness. 'We must try to work out who heard from him last. Can you remember when he left?'

'I've no idea,' said Alix. 'Was it the year we came up north? I know he came up here to see us at least once. But he knew all sorts of people we don't know, who may have much more recent news. Like that woman Hattie.'

'I never went to his flat,' said Liz.

'Nobody ever went to his flat,' said Alix. 'He was the mystery man.'

'Do you think I ought to *report* this package?'

'I don't see why. A bundle of manuscripts isn't an offence, is it?'

They both laughed.

'Well,' said Liz, 'you're right. I'd better read the stuff. But I don't know where to begin. Which bit did he mean me to read first?'

'The finger bones.'

'Yes. Of course,' said Liz.

'And after that, I guess, you can choose. Let me know how you get on.'

'He should have sent it to *you*, really,' said Liz, provocatively. 'It's you that's good at cataloguing and deciphering manuscripts and that kind of stuff.'

'And it's you that's good at crazy people,' said Alix, refusing to be drawn, and trying not to think of the letters of her late employer, the poet Howard Beaver, which she was struggling, slowly, to collate. Come to think of it, the last thing she ever wanted to see was another heap of handwritten, ill-assorted papers. Liz was welcome to the lot.

'But you will come and *look*?' asked Liz.

'Oh yes,' said Alix, insincerely. 'Yes, I'll come and look. But you must have the first crack at the code.'

'Yes,' echoed Liz, a little hollowly. 'Yes, at the code.'

Somehow she knew that Alix would not come. Alix never came to London these days. Alix, Liz suspected, had better things to do.

*

Neither Liz nor Alix found it easy to remember exactly when Stephen had departed. Their own lives were so busy and so piece-meal that markers disappeared into the ragged pattern. Neither kept a journal, so each, separately, was reduced to looking through old engagement books to see if Stephen's name was mentioned. Liz, poring over the notation and logging of old dinners, parties, theatre visits, committee meetings and foreign trips, marvelled at her increasing ability to forget whole swathes of time. That great gap in the middle of the autumn of '86, what on earth was *that*? She seemed to have done nothing for a month. Had she been in the USA, or Australia, or in hospital? She had no recollection.

At last, working backwards, she was rewarded with an entry in the January of 1985 that read 'Dinner Stephen Bertorelli's Notting Hill 8.30'. She closed her eyes and tried to summon up the restaurant, the meal, the conversation. Yes, that had surely been the occasion when she and Stephen had talked about Alix's murderer, and Pol Pot, and whether it was partly a sense of failure that drove people into aggression. *Does a sense of inferiority breed violence? Discuss.* And this they had discussed, at length, if she remembered rightly. Alix's adopted murderer Paul Whitmore had been cruelly rejected by his mother and taught to believe himself a burden, and, as an unfortunate result, had hacked the heads off several North Londoners within a mile or two of the spot where Stephen and Liz were quietly and peacefully devouring their *fegato alla salvia* (or had it been King Prawns 'Grilled'?). Pol Pot's problems and solutions had been less personal, more generic. He had not distinguished himself at school in Kompong Cham, at technical college in Phnom Penh, or at the École Française de Radio-électricité in Paris, where he had failed all his examinations. But this had not prevented his political ascent. Had a million Cambodians died to avenge Pol Pot's defeat at the hands of the French educational system? Psychologically, Liz thought she had conceded to Stephen, this might have been possible. Overkill, she had murmured, but *something* must have tipped him over. Hitler's parents had been held responsible by some historians and psychohistorians for his eccentric excesses. *Something* must have caused even Hitler.

Had this, then, been the dinner when Stephen had announced, half as a joke, half as a self-challenge, that he was determined to try to get into Kampuchea or Cambodia or whatever the wretched country then called itself? He had already been rejected by the Vietnamese Embassy, and was pursuing a visa through Oxfam or the Red Cross. He was off to write a play about Pol Pot. Or so he said.

She looked for more signs of later dinners with Stephen, but could find none. This did not mean they had not existed. She had quite probably conflated several dinners'-worth of conversation, for Pol Pot was a subject to which Stephen frequently returned. He had told her about Pol Pot's Paris days with the Marxists and café revolutionaries, about his wife and sister-in-law who had also studied in Paris. He had asked her if she had read Hannah Arendt. He had expressed a desire to go and see for himself what really happened. She had asked him why he had picked on Cambodia, when the world was full of atrocities waiting for novelists, poets and screenwriters to descend upon them like vultures, and he had smiled his gentle, quizzical little smile and said, 'Because it's so extreme, I suppose. He had a great project, you know, P-p-Pol P-p-Pot. The greatest reconstruction project of the twentieth century. He was going to take Cambodia out of history, and make it self-sufficient. He was going to begin again. I suppose I want to find out what went wrong. Of course, everybody now blames P-Pol P-Pot. Pol Pot killed my father, Pol Pot killed my son. That's what they all say. But Pol Pot still has 40,000 supporters. He's still represented at the UN. And Sihanouk says he's a man of great charm and charisma. He must have more to him than a radio-electrician *manqué*.'

'Paul Whitmore didn't have any charm or charisma,' said Liz.

'No. But he was a private killer, not an official one.'

'So you think Pol Pot's really a hero?' Liz had asked, dipping her Amaretto into her strong black coffee and sucking on the moist dissolving almond crumbs as she waited for his reply.

'No,' said Stephen, carefully rolling himself a little cigarette. 'No,

I don't think that. You know I don't think that. But I'm interested in what happened. How did he get such a bad name? Such a *big* bad name? Such a big, bad, *difficult* name?' And he had smiled, at his own difficulty.

'Because he was such a big bad monster and was responsible for the death of a nation?' suggested Liz, placidly.

'Do *you* believe in monsters?' Stephen had asked. 'Single, self-generated monsters?'

Or something like that he had said, on one of those evenings before he disappeared. He had gone off to see if he could find out what had happened to the dreams of Pol Pot. Out of curiosity. To write a play, about the Rise and Fall.

'Look, Liz,' he had said, 'you are curious about human nature. And so am I. So why should I not go?'

'There's plenty of human nature here at home,' Liz had offered, in a tone and with a gesture that embraced the restaurant with its office-outing birthday table, its assorted couples, its solitary elderly diner with his book, its family gathering, its amiable smiling proprietors: the street life outside of dreadlocks and strollers and buskers and cruisers and crooks and drifters: the enshrined Campden Hill dignitaries to the west, the Bayswater backwaters to the east: the brutal and grand dwellings of Czech and Soviet and Indian diplomats: the Peking Ducks and Pizza Parlours of Queensway, the terrorist hotels and bed and breakfast doss houses of the dangerous shabby fire-gutted North Kensington squares, and the mean streets extending north to the grim terraces of the Mozart Estate and multiple murder, to the converted terrace houses of first-time first-baby double-mortgage young buyers.

And Stephen had taken all this in, and had shrugged his thin shoulders, and had said a little wistfully, 'There is nothing to keep me here.'

Liz had not thought that Stephen really intended to write a play. He did not write plays, he wrote novels, and they were not, in her

view, particularly strong on dialogue. All this talk about a play had
been just talk. A blind, a screen, an act of bravado, a dramatic
gesture. That was what she had thought then, and that was what
she thought now, as she tried to force her mind back over old
history. But he had meant to leave, and he had done so. *'There is
nothing to keep me here.'* That is what he had said. Those had been
his very words. They rang in her ears. What had he meant by
them? It came back to her that she had thought then of saying
something rash and blind like, 'You could stay for me.' But neither
the invitation nor the inclination to do so had been strong enough,
so she had said nothing.

She was glad now that she had said nothing. If he would not
stay for Hattie Osborne, who was allowed to live in the flat on
Primrose Hill that none had ever entered, why should he stay for
his dining companion Liz Headleand? Let him go, let him depart.

Memory is treacherous. How could they have discussed Alix's
murderer and his mother? At that stage he had not been Alix's
murderer at all, Alix had not even met him, and nobody had heard
of his monster-mother. If the murderer had belonged to anybody in
those days, he had belonged to their friend Esther Breuer, who had
lived in a flat beneath him in a house at the wrong end of Ladbroke
Grove. Paul Whitmore, Pol Pot. Paul Whitmore's house was demolished now, and Pol Pot's country in ruins, and Liz's memory
was full of gaps and inconsistencies. They disturbed her. Was there
some clue that she had forgotten, some reason why Stephen Cox
was now appealing to her with a bundle of old papers and bones
and string?

Alix Bowen was able to be more precise about dates than Liz,
because she had Brian and her son Sam to confirm them. Yes, Brian
and Sam agreed, Stephen had been to stay with them in Northam
in February 1985, not long after they had moved up from London.
He had been the first person to sleep in their spare room. It had
been very cold and he had been given a hot-water bottle. He had

praised the room and the hot-water bottle highly, nay excessively. One never knew quite when or why Stephen was taking the piss. Sam's view was that Stephen was giving a lecture on the historical novel at the uni. Alix had not remembered this but did not dispute it. She thought they had had *osso buco* for supper. What had they talked about? The disarray of the Labour Party, council-house sales, the failure of Marxism Today? Had they also talked about Pol Pot? Yes, Alix thought they had. There had been some jokes about Pol Pot and Northam's council leader Perry Blinkhorn and the red flag. Stephen had said he was off to Phnom Penh, but they had not known whether to believe him. He'd only stayed with them one night, and then he had vanished.

Brian had had a letter from him in Bangkok, but he had lost it. He couldn't remember what it was about. Or when he had received it. He looked for it in a half-hearted manner but was so depressed by the junk he turned up that he abandoned the search. 'To think I've accumulated all this in three years!' he said, irritably, as he stuffed the papers back into his desk.

It was Brian's view that Stephen had taken himself off for artistic reasons. Stephen had abandoned his last novel, half-finished, in a fit of despondency, and was looking for a new theme. He had thought the Orient might jog his failing creative powers, as Rome had jogged Goethe's. And the Cambodian theme was a grand one. The death of a nation, the death of communism, the death of hope. It had not yet been written to death. It was unresolved. Pol Pot was still alive, lurking in the bushes. Stephen might well embrace the fatal ghost of such a challenge.

Over the years, since the mid seventies, Stephen and Brian had discussed the Cambodian question over many a pint. Vietnam had been a relatively simple issue; it had been easy for both of them as young men to cast the Americans as the villains in this protracted epic. When the Khmer Rouge had entered Phnom Penh in 1975, Brian had tended to take their side, and was tempted to dismiss as atrocity stories the tales of refugees who informed the Western world that their new leaders were ignorant child-peasants who killed anyone who spoke French or English or wore spectacles. But the evidence had swelled from a trickle to a flood and had borne Brian before it. The mysterious assassination in Phnom Penh of British fellow-traveller and friend-of-the-revolution Malcolm Caldwell had convinced him that the Khmer Rouge were almost as black as they were painted, and he had watched the unfolding retrospective horror story of skull landscapes and killing fields with revulsion and dismay. Had Brian identified with Caldwell, the gullible leftwing scholar? Perhaps. Brian had been so disillusioned that he could not even cast the invading Vietnamese as heroes when they defeated the Khmer Rouge in 1979. This was a story without heroes and without salvation. It had only victims. The exodus of the Vietnamese Boat People spoke for itself, if one were willing to listen. Brian had listened. Brian had been instrumental in persuading Northam's ideologically committed red-flag council that it would not be betraying its colours if it set up a resettlement project for Vietnamese refugees. But some had been curiously hard to persuade, some had been reluctant to abandon their old allegiances. None of them, needless to say, had ever been to Vietnam.

Stephen had been less distressed because more sceptical. He tended not to believe anything he was told. He stuck to the view that there were more than two sides to every story, and that it was almost impossible to tell what was happening. The Vietnamese and Cambodians alike were secretive, evasive, paranoid. Stephen pointed out that they had good cause to be so.

Yes, said Brian to Alix, Stephen might well have thought that Cambodia would kick-start his imagination.

Kill or cure, you mean, said Alix, and then wished she hadn't.

Alix accepted Brian's diagnosis. Brian knew Stephen better than anyone, and if he thought Stephen had gone off in search of artistic renewal, then he was probably right. It seemed to her a somewhat flimsy reason for fleeing to the far side of the world, but then she was a woman, and she had no creative imagination, so she wouldn't be likely to see the point of it, would she?

Alix missed Stephen Cox and wished he had not gone away. One does not have so many adult friends in a lifetime, and she had liked Stephen. He was a delicate, reticent, honourable man. He was Brian's friend. She hoped he was still alive.

*

The more Liz looked at the package, the less she liked it. She took her duties seriously and purchased various plastic wallets to try to preserve the contents in their original order, but when it came to reading them she discovered in herself a deep resistance.

She started with the piece of prose that began 'And he came to a land where the water flows uphill.' It continued in portentous but lyrical style for a page or two, describing an oriental landscape, a broad river, and a young man on a boat travelling upstream into the heart, she supposed, of darkness. Liz found it rather boring, though she did not like to say so, even to herself. Notes in the margin directed her to 'The Miracle of the Tonle Sap', a phrase which meant nothing to her at all. Impatiently she abandoned the young man on his allegorical voyage and turned to the diaries, which were more fun, though unsatisfactorily enigmatic. She puzzled over 'Miss P. on good form tonight with brothels and tales of Opium King' and 'Met S. G. at Press Club and talked of cannibals'. She was introduced to a character called K. V. who told Stephen about his grandfather's estate in Norfolk, and another called H. A. who was the daughter of M. A., a fact which Stephen had thought worthy of underlining.

Then she flipped through the fragments of drama, but they too were non-starters. They consisted of sketches for a series of tableaux outlining the careers and confrontations of the principal actors in the Cambodian tragedy, Prince Sihanouk and Pol Pot. They were much crossed out and about. One read:

1. Paris, Latin Quarter. 1950. Double wedding of Pol Pot, Ieng Sary and the two Khieu sisters. A huge set-piece banquet prepared in rented ballroom by Thiounn Prasith. Dancing. Jokes. Thiounn Mumm toasts the two couples and pledges the over-throw of Sihanouk. Laughter. Lighthearted. Khieu sisters both strikingly beautiful, stylish, worldly. Champagne.

2. Paris, 28 rue St André des Arts. Domestic scene. Thirith with baby on knee. Her sister Ponnary bitching about why Sihanouk wouldn't marry the Thiounn girl. Again, much laughter. [1951?]

3. Phnom Penh, September 1960. First Party Congress of Cam-bodian Communists convened in empty railcars at Phnom Penh Station. The Return of the Three Ghosts. The Three Ghosts speak. The Naming of the Party. The Beheadings on the Tennis Court.

4. Kompong Cham, 1970. Queen Mother's Palace. Queen Kos-samak consults the augurs and draws the tarnished sword of defeat from its scabbard. She reproaches her son Sihanouk: They use you as a buffalo to cross the waters. [NB she died in 1975? Check.]

5. The march of Lon Nol's army to the Holy War. He Black Papa. Amulets, tattoos, sorcery, talismans, magic scarves. The casting of the horoscope. [NB The Khmer Rouge militant atheists? How militant?]

6. Ratanakiri, 1974. Pol Pot and wife Thirith in camp. She weeps for the children she has not seen for ten years, she demands return to city. [Some reports say they had no children? Check.]

7. Phnom Penh, September 1978. The Feast of the Undead Intel-lectuals. Fail not our Feast. The starving eat the food prepared by Thiounn Prasith of the Hôtel Royale.

8. The Jungle, 1980. Number One Jungle Actor Star drinks from skull.
9. United Nations Reception, New York, 1987. Thiounn Prasith and Ieng Sary drink blood.

Liz Headleand ran her eye down all this stuff and much more. She recognized Pol Pot and Sihanouk, the principal protagonists of the Cambodian tragedy, and correctly surmised that the Khieu sisters were the two Paris-educated Khmer women who had so intrigued Stephen. Had he not told her that one of them had studied English Literature? Was that his excuse for all his Shakespearian references?

Thiounn Prasith was a name that meant nothing to Liz. There was little in the package to indicate that he was one of the official representatives of the non-existent state of Democratic Kampuchea at the United Nations, and that he had been one of the architects of the Communist Party of Cambodia and of the Khmer Rouge. He was and is one of the most eloquent apologists for the Years of Zero, 1975–9. He does not let go. He wears a suit and a tie and he lives in New York. But Liz was not to know this.

Muddled, confused, irritated by her own ignorance and by all these foreign names and meaningless dates, Liz moved on, and came at last across something that she understood. It was a small booklet headed 'Atrocity Stories'. These made sense. They also confirmed that she and Alix had been speaking on the telephone about a real person, about a Stephen who had really existed and whom, in the real world, they had really known. He had thought some of the thoughts that they had thought. She read one or two of the entries. Yes, it was easy enough to see what Stephen had been up to in this section. She took his point, and saluted it. She heard, for a moment, his clear light voice speak.

But then she lost it again in scraps and scrawls and jottings. Where was the story in all this, where was the glue that would

stick it all together? Her fingers ached with impatience, with irritation. 'Really, Stephen,' she said, aloud. But he did not answer.

She distrusted her own impatience. She had always wanted to
make sense of things immediately. She had a tendency to leap to
conclusions, to cut Gordian knots. She would never have made a
scholar. How much she now regretted the impetuosity with which
she had burned her mother's old papers! She had destroyed them
through fear, and, though curiosity had long since devoured fear,
she could no longer recover them, for they had been consumed by
the Ideal Boiler. She was not afraid of Stephen's papers (was she?);
there could be nothing *personal* lurking there?

In one sense at least, Stephen's papers somewhat resembled
her mother's. Her mother had collected newspaper cuttings about
the Royal Family. Stephen seemed to have collected ageing
yellow items from court circulars. She came across a little wad of
them, stapled together, with some items picked out in fluorescent
pink. He had highlighted the movements of various aircraft of
the Queen's Flight, had saluted the General Committee Dinner of
the Kennel Club and the reception at St James in aid of the
Racing Welfare Charities, and had noted royally attended events
in aid of the NSPCC, CARE, MIND and Mencap. As Stephen
had been a known republican, his intentions could not have had
much in common with those of the late Rita Ablewhite. Except,
perhaps, madness. Collecting newspaper cuttings is a well-known
sign of derangement. Why on earth should anyone have wished
to note that the *Annual Newsletter* of Moxley Hall School would
be published in May of 1984 with full details of Old Moxleian
Day? What *junk*, Liz found herself thinking, what a waste of
time!

Atrocity stories, Parisian revolts, Mumm champagne, Kennel
Clubs, Pol Pot's baby niece, John Stuart Mill, they add up even *less*
than Hestercombe and Oxenholme on a silver wine cooler. At least
the Hestercombes and the Oxenholmes had inhabited the same

country and spoken the same language. This stuff was all over the place.

On her third evening of study, she came across the photograph of Mme Savet Akrun. It was cut out from a newspaper, and the reproduction was not good, but nevertheless it had a power. The image looked hauntingly familiar. Had she seen it somewhere before? The caption was 'Where is my son?' Mme Savet Akrun, erect and dignified, her hands folded on her lap, sat on a low chair and stared at the camera. Her eyes were large, her face thin and wasted, her lips gently curved. She wore what looked like a slightly Westernized sarong. Her greying hair was neatly pulled back into a bun. Her expression, adopted perhaps for the camera, was of grave suffering. It was a posed shot, slow, expressive. (If Liz had thought to look for a credit, which at this stage she did not, she would have seen for the first time the name of Konstantin Vassiliou.) Liz read the story, which told her that Mme Savet Akrun, mother of four, was held in Camp Site Ten, on the Thai–Kampuchean border. She had walked over the border in 1979 with her three younger children, from the countryside of Siem Reap province, where she had been living and working in a village. Her husband, her parents, her parents-in-law, her sisters, a brother and several of her nieces and nephews had all died in the terror, some of illness and some by violence. Her husband had owned garages and a small cinema in Phnom Penh. She had taught in an infants' school and was now employed in the camp by the Khmer Women's Association Centre for Adult Education. 'I am one of the lucky survivors,' she was quoted as saying, 'but my life can give me no joy until I find my son.' She had last seen him in a small village near Battambang. He had been marched away by a group of Khmer Rouge soldiers, the article said. 'Is he still alive? How can I find him?' she asked. The journalist went on to say that she was one of thousands trying to trace lost relatives through the International Red Cross and other agencies.

A human interest story, not a hard-news story, and as such it interested Liz. She understood it. She had a displaced tremor of feeling for Mme Savet Akrun, sitting there so patiently with the sorrows of thousands resting on her thin, unbowed shoulders, asking, 'Where is my son?' Liz hoped very much that he was alive, but had to doubt it. How could he be, amongst the more than a million dead?

And if he were alive, searching for him would be like looking for a needle in a haystack. A needle in the haystack of the wide, wide world. She leafed through the pile of cuttings. Khmer refugees had spread to far corners of the earth, to Canada, France, New Zealand, Australia, the United States, even to Britain, to any country with the space and generosity to take them. They came from families fragmented over ten years by war and violence, and many of them did not know whether their relatives were alive or dead. Tracing was difficult, for the Khmer language was little known and hard to transcribe, and the spelling of names varied widely. Many had changed their names many times, for many reasons. For safety, for policy, to forget the past, because they carried forged papers. Where, indeed, was the son of Mme Akrun? Did she believe he was alive, or had she offered herself for this photo opportunity in a sacrificial spirit, as an emblematic figure for her nation?

Liz, until this moment, had not given much thought to the displaced people and refugees of the world. She had noted horror stories from the PLO camps, from the Afghan camps, from the Sudan. She had read of the Vietnamese Boat People. She had known of the existence of the Thai–Kampuchean camps, although she had not known they were so large. One of them, Site Two, with its population of over 170,000 people, was said to be the second largest Khmer city in the world, larger than Sisophon, larger than Battambang, nearly as large as Phnom Penh. Liz had, like many middle-class British citizens, given money to Oxfam for years by banker's order, and had very occasionally, and against her better judgement, allowed herself to be moved to particular donation by a particular appeal for a particular catastrophe. She was surprised to find herself spending so much time gazing into the two-dimensional newspaper eyes of Mme Savet Akrun.

That same week Liz, her attention newly alerted to all things Kampuchean, was informed, along with the rest of the media-fed world, of a new atrocity in the west of America. An archetypal, all-American atrocity. A lone gunman in Darlington, California, had run mad and attacked an elementary school. He had killed five, and wounded dozens. Bad enough, one might say, too cruel anywhere, but the secondary wave of background information managed to compound the horror. For these children had been the children of Khmer refugees, who had escaped the terrors of their own country, who had escaped the Year Zero and the dreams of Pol Pot, and who had reached the land of the free. They had settled there, in the small town of Darlington, and they had been greeted with special schooling, special language tuition, special resettlement officers to advise them. And there they had died, in the school playground, amidst the smell of hot tarmac and jelly beans and popcorn, mowed down by a 24-year-old dressed in military fatigues wielding a Chinese-made AK47 assault rifle. He shot more than a hundred rounds at them. And then he blew out his own brains.

One of the mothers was quoted as saying of her daughter, 'I brought her all this way to die.' Irony had kept this woman company until the end. Or had the words been placed in her mouth by a newsman with an ear for a good line? Can one believe anything one reads in a newspaper?

The young gunman, it emerged, was the son of a soldier who had been on active service with the United States Army. Some reports said the father had served in Vietnam, others denied this. Some said he had died in a psychiatric hospital. Some said he had been honourably discharged 'on mental grounds'. The killer son had been a fan of Libya and the PLO, said one paper. He was a copycat cretin, said another.

Since the war ended, 60,000 veterans have committed suicide, more than the number killed in combat, one of the stories claimed. 'From generation unto generation,' suggested another. We survive the ordeals of bunker and jungle and bombardment and Diarrhoea-Aid of the East to run amok amidst the fair fields of the West.

It makes one think. And Liz thought.

She came, at the end of the week, to the conclusion that she was making no progress with Stephen's dossier. She did not know enough about Indo-China to tackle it. (Somebody told her that the very phrase, 'Indo-China', was no longer acceptable. She was so ignorant that she could not see the objections.)

Maybe there was some message in there for her, but she began to doubt it. Perhaps it had arrived at her address by accident? She needed help.

She thought of ringing Alix again, or their old friend Esther Breuer, or her ex-husband Charles, or her ex-husband Edgar Lintot, or her new half-sister Marcia Campbell. Any of them would lend an ear and some understanding. Then she thought of her stepsons Alan and Aaron, and her daughter Sally. They too would listen with sympathy. (Stepson Jonathan and daughter Stella had defected: she rarely dared to ring either of them now.) Or perhaps she should ring Charles's friend Melvyn Stacey, who worked for the International Red Cross and knew about the Thai–Kampuchean border? She thought of ringing the Vietnamese Embassy, or Oxfam, or war correspondent Hugo Mainwaring, or Peter Bloch at the embassy in Bangkok. She even thought of ringing Stephen's brothers, but had no idea where to find them. He had been a private man, a disconnected man. After a while, she settled on Aaron, as she wanted to speak to him anyway about tickets for his new play. He was out. Success had purchased him an answering machine, and she heard his voice informing her that Aaron Headleand was unavailable. Slightly offended, she rang off, swallowed her pride, and did what she knew she should have done earlier: she rang Hattie Osborne.

*

I've never much liked Liz Headleand. I've no reason to. For one thing although I've been introduced to her a hundred — well, at least a dozen times, she never has the slightest notion who I am, and always looks quite blank and bored at the very sight of me. That is not ingratiating. For another thing, she strikes me as a very bossy woman, and, as I am in some moods quite bossy myself, I naturally wouldn't be expected to get on with her. Would I?

I can see these reasons are a bit flimsy. Actually, I hardly know the woman. I know her friend Esther Breuer a bit better, and I like Esther. Esther is an oddball, like myself. Liz Headleand pretends to be normal.

As a matter of fact, I didn't really know Stephen Cox all that well either. Although he was one of my closest friends, and I one of his. Although I've known him for ever. Well, nearly for ever. I don't think anyone really knew Stephen well. Perhaps those Bowens knew him. He always talked about them with a kind of sentimental fondness, probably because he'd known them such a hell of a long time. I only met Brian once, and I thought he was a crashing bore. And Alix Bowen is one of those women who always make me feel really uneasy. I mean, she is so fucking *nice*. She really *is* nice too, which makes it worse. Not that I know her well either. Though I remember having quite a good chat with her at Otto Werner's Twelfth Night party. About death, as I remember. I think her father-in-law had just snuffed it, and Otto was about to go off to Washington. I think she was a bit in love with Otto, in those days. I haven't seen her for years.

Anyway, Liz is the one I distrust most, so you can imagine how annoyed I was when she rang me and told me this rigmarole about Stephen's papers. She got me at a bad moment too. So the whole thing got off to a bad start. I'd just had this row with this Natasha person about Siddhur's screenplay for Partext and to comfort myself

I'd gone out to buy a chicken korma, and on the way back to the flat I was sort of swinging it up and down in my basket in a brave and cheering sort of way when the lid came off one of the boxes and I got korma all down my skirt. It was an Indian skirt, so it sort of went with the print, but I wasn't best pleased. I'd just wiped it off and put what was left in a soup dish and was settling myself down in front of the telly to eat it when the phone went and it was Liz. With this saga about papers.

I couldn't work out what she was getting at, at first. She kept asking me if I was living in Stephen's flat and if I was Stephen's agent. I was pretty cautious to begin with because Stephen wasn't really allowed to sublet, and then again I'm never really sure if I *am* Stephen's agent. For some things and not for others, I think I said, in an offputting kind of way, because frankly I thought she was being a bit nosy. And then when I heard what she'd got I wished I'd been more forthcoming. I can't remember quite what I said, but I think I claimed to be Stephen's literary executor (which, after a manner of speaking, I am) and I said I'd have a look. Actually, I think that's what she'd wanted. So that's how it began.

It was strange, having to think about Stephen again. I'd behaved so atrociously on that last evening that I'd kind of blotted him out of my mind. Even though I am living in his pad and sleeping in his bed and I'm sorry to say drinking up his wine, even the bottles that said KEEP UNTIL 1992. I suppose I'd been hoping he wouldn't come back *too* soon. He was well out of my way, and I was beginning to ingratiate myself with the landlord. (Mr Goodfellow, he's called. A nice man.) Not that I wished Stephen any harm, of course, but he'd always been a bit of a wanderer, and I wasn't at all surprised not to hear from him for a year or two. He sent me a postcard, and that was quite enough for me. I'm a very undemanding woman. It was of a sleeping Buddha, if I remember rightly. Which I do. I have it still. It's on the mantelpiece.

But when Liz rang, I realized it was more than a year or two. It was more like a year or three. Time flies. I checked in my rent book, and it was indeed over two years since I took over his modest establishment. And then I did begin to feel a little anxious. Maybe something really had gone wrong?

I'd arranged to meet Liz in a couple of days, and during that time I made a few inquiries. He'd arranged for his royalties to be paid through his accountant, who'd been left in charge of the VAT and all that nonsense, so I rang them to ask when they'd last had any instructions from him (I was quite proud of that word, 'instructions', it sounded pretty professional, I thought). They said they couldn't say. I asked where he was when they last heard from him, and they said they didn't know, and I said who were his bankers, and they said they couldn't tell me, very unhelpful. They said they thought he had a bank account abroad. I asked where, and they said it was nothing to do with me, and rang off.

Then I tried to remember if anyone had seen him or heard from him lately, but I drew a bit of a blank. And it wasn't until then that I began to think it was a bit funny that he hadn't published anything at all about his travels in all the time he'd been away. On previous trips he'd either been earning his keep by giving lectures, or he'd covered his airfare by printing bits and pieces for the papers. Maybe he didn't need to do that any more? Maybe he'd passed the point of hack work? He must have made quite a bit out of his last couple of novels, since he won the Booker. Then I thought that perhaps he'd just got pissed off with old England, and had really wanted to disappear. If anyone might take it into his head to do a bunk, it would be Stephen. And if he wanted to disappear, who were we to try to stop him?

But Liz Headleand's phone call nagged me. She'd sounded a bit rattled, which wasn't like her, or not what I thought of as her. I'd always seen her as Super Competent. Offensively competent. With that big house, and all those children.

I had a feeling that somebody I knew had bumped into him within living memory in either Singapore or Bangkok, but I couldn't for the life of me remember which or who, or when, or what they'd said. I *tried* to remember, but how on earth does one *will* oneself to remember? I mean, how does one make the memory brain cells work? Mine have all gone funny, I'm afraid, and I'd never have got the name back if it hadn't been for a programme on telly (it sounds as though I watch a lot of telly, which I do) about the Opium Triangle and Burma, and suddenly, as I was watching this shot of little child soldiers marching up and down in the jungle with some donkeys, it came to me. John Geddes, that's who it was. And it had definitely been Bangkok. I was so pleased with myself that I poured myself another Scotch, which might have been a mistake, but wasn't — odd how drink sometimes makes the memory work better, when most of the time it buggers it up. Anyway, it all began to come back. John Geddes had been out there looking for locations for Carlo's script of *Victory* and had run into Stephen in a bar in Bangkok. Stephen had been looking pretty good, according to John. Flush, I think was the word he'd used. Not flushed. Flush. So whenever *that* had been, Stephen was still doing fine, and wasn't languishing in a Khmer Rouge prison or a fever hospital or a leper colony, or wherever it was that Liz thought he'd ended up. A bar in Bangkok. I rang John, to check, but not surprisingly he wasn't in. He never is. His lover (who, rumour has it, is HIV-positive, poor bugger) was there, sounding pretty glum, which he would be, and he said John was in Peru trying to find locations for a movie about the Shining Path (not another Vargas Llosa adaptation, he said, wearily, an *original* screenplay). I asked if he could remember when John had been in Bangkok, and he said which time, for the Rain Forest movie or for the Khmer Rouge movie, and I said neither, it was for the *Victory* movie, and he said was that the Vietnam movie, and I said no, it was the Conrad movie, and he said he hadn't the faintest idea. He sounded so sad that I arranged to meet him for a drink, but that's another story. Well, almost another story, because when we met at the Spoils of War we worked out (but this is jumping ahead a bit) that John must have met Stephen in late '85, in the Hotel Nirvana, which didn't tell us anything much. The lover (he's called Indra) said John said that Stephen took him to a very up-market brothel, but Indra thought he might have been saying that to annoy him, that is him, Indra. Anyway, that's jumping ahead, or back, and anyway it was a dead end.

The next thing that really happened was my meeting with Liz. I'd wanted to arrange to meet on neutral territory, but failed. I didn't want to ask her round to Stephen's old flat and I haven't really got an office at the moment, so I suggested lunch at the Escargot but she said she was too busy for lunch and could I come round to her place at six for a drink. I didn't really want to get sucked into her orbit, but didn't see how to get out of it, so I said I would. She's moved house. I remember going to a huge party of hers in Harley Street in the days when Charles Headleand was making documentaries, donkeys' years ago, but they've sold that house (they must have been mad!) and now she lives in this very nice but rather suburban Edwardian maisonette in St John's Wood. Actually I shouldn't be rude about it, it's very nice really, 'tis only envy that speaks, and I must say she poured me a very satisfactory slug of Scotch, none of that half-a-finger drowned-in-water ladylike nonsense you sometimes get from people old enough to know better. We had a bit of polite chit-chat about this and that and then she got down to business. She keeps the package in a large rectangular cardboard box (I think it had had a video machine in it, I don't know why I mention that, just to be circumstantial I suppose) and she took off the lid with a sort of abracadabra look on her face, and there was this tatty jiffy-bag and these little plastic folders of stuff. I must say my first thought was that it didn't look very publishable in its present condition, and I think I said as much. I thought she wasn't going to let me get my fingerprints on it, but, after making it quite clear that it was still in her custody, she did let me have a look. It was at this point that she produced the finger bone, which she hadn't mentioned on the telephone. She keeps it in a special little plastic money bag, the sort people produce in the bank, full of coppers on Monday mornings, while the queue gets longer and longer. She didn't know what to make of it, but it seemed to me quite obvious that it was a joke. I mean, knowing Stephen, of course, it was a joke. I *still* think it was a joke, actually, though I agree I can't explain how it got there, or why the package was sent without any instructions. Perhaps he was ill? Delirious? Dead? Or gone away? I suggested all these possibilities, and she said she'd thought of them all, but thinking of them hadn't got her anywhere. I saw her point.

She said she'd tried to read the papers, but hadn't made much headway. I said I'd have a go at them, if that's what she wanted. She said she was worried about letting them out of her safekeeping. I said we could take photocopies. She said how would we photocopy the bone. Then we had quite a good laugh, so I suppose you could say the joke had worked. Stephen's joke, I mean. We had a little chat about radioactivity and whether you can catch diseases from using word processors. I don't know how we got on to that, something to do with having your feet X-rayed, I think. Apparently they used to go in for X-raying children's feet to make sure their shoes fitted, in the old days, until they discovered it made their bones rot. *O tempora, O mores.* A whole generation of rotted feet.

We had another drink, and I admired her cat. I have a very good cat of my own, though I have to keep it out of sight of Mr Goodfellow, but I have to say her cat is quite a fine-looking cat. It's a tabby. As we chatted, I was leafing through one of the little diary-booklets (Ryman's Memo, coil back, lined, $8\frac{1}{4} \times 5\frac{7}{8}$, red cover) and I could already see that there *were* a few things I probably could decode better than anyone. Indeed I was afraid I glimpsed some allusion to our horrible Last Supper. Thank God it looked

31

pretty incomprehensible to an outsider. But it made me all the keener to get my hands on the stuff, and find time to go through it all without her standing over me.

We agreed that I could have a photocopy of everything that looked worth copying, including the laundry list. Laundry lists are very important to biographers, I told her, quoting an article by Victoria Glendinning in the *TLS*. I think she was impressed by that evidence of unexpected scholarship on my part. She said her secretary would do it in the morning and send the stuff round on a motorbike. Then we had a terminal conversation about who had last seen Stephen where and when. She said she thought someone called Peter Bloch in the embassy at Bangkok had had some kind of contact with him, and should she try to get hold of him. I said wait a while. Then I told her about John Geddes and the film of *Victory*. She'd never read *Victory*, so I found myself telling her the plot. In case you've forgotten (tactful, aren't I?), *Victory* is that one about the lone mysterious Swede called Axel Heyst who mooches around the South Seas dwelling on the ineffable and eternal until he hitches up with a dancing girl (actually it's a musician in a ladies' orchestra, but we made her a dancing girl) at the Oriental Hotel in Bangkok, and runs away with her to a remote island. He is pursued by an aged British conman–playboy, his sidekick the evil and greasy Ricardo, and a Naked Savage, who are convinced he is hiding away with a lot of loot. The real villain of the piece is the Oriental hotel manager, a fat German. It's a wonderfully racist piece and it would have made a bloody good movie, but it came to nought, as such projects usually do. I must say I think Carlo's screenplay was brilliant, the best thing he's ever done. But that's beside the point.

The laundry bill was in fact from the Oriental Hotel. I didn't point this out to Liz Headleand. I didn't see why I should make things easy for her. I don't think she's ever been to Bangkok.

If Max von Sydow had been twenty years younger, he'd have been wonderful as Axel Heyst. But that's beside the point too.

Anyway, we agreed that I should have a look at the photocopies before either of us made any further official inquiries. It's not as though it's a message in a bottle, or an SOS calling for a search party, is it, I said, and then we both looked at one another and though we didn't say anything I could see that we were both thinking that perhaps it might, after all, be precisely that. I was still clutching the little red memo book, and I suddenly plucked up courage and said, 'I say, do you think I could take this one with me now? Just for a look? I promise I'll be ever so careful, but I really would like to start on it straightaway, I can see all sorts of fascinating things in there.' I burbled on like this for a bit, and I could see she was embarrassed to say no outright. (People usually are. This is one of life's more useful secrets.) All right, she said, but don't lose it, will you. I swore I wouldn't, and slipped it into my bag, thanked her for the drink, and away I went.

I must say I had an odd evening, reading Stephen's orts and fragments. You see, I was with Stephen on his last night in London. It was ghastly. Really ghastly. I don't like to think of it at all. He must have had an appalling flight. I can't think what came over me. No wonder he ran away. Though of course he was on his way out anyway. It wasn't me that drove him off. I must try to remember that. Whatever happened, it wasn't *all* my fault.

*

It was a terrible evening. March 1985. Picture Stephen Cox and comrade Hattie Osborne, on their way to their elderly friend Molly Lansdowne, in the back of a taxi. They are to dine with her, *à trois*, before moving on to the seventieth birthday party of another friend, Marjorie Kinsman. Neither of them can remember how this arrangement stole upon them. It has just happened, and they have surrendered to it. They have to go to Marjorie's, for over the years, severally and together, they have drunk many pints of her whisky and vodka, and they must turn up to celebrate her unlikely survival.

But why add Molly to the evening's jaunt? She must have added herself.

Hattie is already very drunk. She is high-pitched, fast-talking, feverish. She lets her hair down, in the back of the taxi, telling Stephen about her last lost lover, who had split from her for ever the week before over an incident involving his wife and his eldest daughter and a piano lesson. He is, she tells Stephen, a two-faced, double-crossing, feeble little shit of a liar who wants to have his cake and eat it. She loved him, she tells Stephen, she still loves him, she must be mad. Stephen utters soothing nothingnesses, as they roll past the opulent golden shop fronts of Knightsbridge. He is worried, a little embarrassed. He is used to confidences, for he is the kind of man in whom women choose to confide, but Hattie seems determined tonight to go over the top. He sits back, and decides to let her roll over him. Tomorrow he will have vanished. What does it matter?

The abuse continues, as Stephen, Hattie and Molly settle down to a little picnic of not-quite-defrosted potted shrimps, rubbery smoked chicken, random salad and unripe Camembert, washed down by gin and water. The conversation becomes more and more *louche*. The setting invites it. Molly's flat has the air of a crumpled love nest. It is all bijoux and trinkets and tapestry cushions and French furniture. The plates are French china, chipped, pretty, non-matching. The glasses are dusty. Molly no longer sees as well as she did, but is too vain to wear spectacles. She is a handsome woman, with deep sharp blue eyes, and a delicate skin, and soft grey pompadour hair swept back into a coil tied with a blue velvet ribbon. Stephen had always admired her looks, but, as the evening wears on and the tone sinks yet further, he begins to see her as dyed and raddled, farded with the pink and the white and the blue. She is wearing rustling silver. Picture her, in her blue and silver, an English rose, dried and dyed and perfumed. Picture Hattie Osborne, a striking huge-eyed painted forty-year-old with a great headful of snaky falsely frizzed Medusa curls, and a long gold dress with a plunge neckline revealing glimpses of a naked bosom. Picture Stephen Cox, polite in his everlasting white suit. He sits neatly between them like a mascot, like a eunuch, as they tear to pieces the men that they have known. Bedecked and bedizened with jewels, they screech with tongues and talons.

Impotencies, meannesses, cowardices, treacheries, bad manners in and out of bed, all are hymned, bemoaned, indicted. Offences twenty years old are held up to the light, shaken, and savaged. Stephen thinks, this is the kind of dreadful conversation I quite enjoy, but it is going too far. The lipstick, the mascara, the oh so saddening march of merciless age upon them all, there, then, even then, as they sat there eating their salmonella-charged cold platter of treats from the delicatessen. 'Pour réparer des ans l'irréparable outrage.' The line from *Athalie* goes through and through his head. Jezebel, with her borrowed glory. They are all worn and used, they are on their way to the *danse macabre*, the leper's ball, the bitter end. Hattie, frenzied, recoils in fear from her mirror image in Molly's eye, and plunges on recklessly like a mad horse. It is of sex they sing, of the wrongs and pains of sex, and of its disappointments. Mad women, demented women, voracious, demanding, insatiable women.

'Buggery may, of course, be the answer,' says Molly, dabbing daintily at her lips, staining her old-fashioned damask napkin with deep sticky pink. 'For satisfaction. After a certain age. Have you ever been buggered, Stephen? No? Have you, Hattie? I never have, and it's too late now, I suppose. Is it the fashion, these days? One seems to read a lot about it. It wasn't done, when I was young. Is buggery in, Stephen?'

She looks at him, demanding a response, but he is unable to answer, for the invitation in her eyes is too alarming. But Hattie careers on, unstoppable, taking this fence in her stride, the bit between her teeth.

'But of course!' she cries. 'Of course! Many, many times! Orlando always preferred it! But then that was because he had such a tiny prick. And he wasn't much good at buggery either!'

In vino veritas. She spoke the simple truth. And as she spoke, she suddenly unzipped the back of her gold dress, and let it fall forward from the waist over her turquoise-rimmed gold-plate and debris of cheese and biscuits. She sat there, topless, her excellent firm breasts eloquent over the Camembert. Stephen and Molly stared at them. Molly's eyes filled with tears.

'Yes,' said Hattie, in a high-rhetorical trance, gazing into space like a priestess. 'Yes, buggered, poked, screwed, raped, you name it, I've had it, and was it ever, ever enough, any of it? No, it was not,' said Hattie. 'It was never enough. It will never be enough. Never!'

Defiance blared from her nostrils, and she was breathing quickly and noisily, as though she had been running or violently making love. Her face was flushed with passion. She looked wonderful. She looked appalling. Stephen was frightened out of his wits. At any moment a breeze might blow upon her and she would turn grey and fall apart and crumble into ash before his eyes. This too too solid, this too too vibrant flesh would melt. Molly had already melted. Hattie hung on there, panting. Molly Lansdowne blew her nose, firmly, on a lace-edged handkerchief plucked from her own bosom, took another gulp of gin and water, reassembled her features, and heroically took charge.

'There, there, my dear,' she said, in her droll social voice. 'You'd better fasten yourself up again, Hattie darling. You can't go to Marjorie's looking like *that*.' She paused, and gallantly added, 'Unfortunately.'

Hattie smiled, and descended from her height, and struggled back into her gold. Stephen helped to zip her up. The smooth skin of her womanly back tingled beneath his fingers. She was charged with electricity. She had a dark mole on her left shoulder. She was still dangerous, but for the moment docile. And off they had all gone, to Marjorie Kinsman's birthday party, where there had been more drinking, more talking, more excited provocations. He had lost Hattie in the Circean throng of toads and pigs and monkeys and foxes. She had been sucked into the revelry, but he remained conscious of her presence throughout the long evening, catching her voice, her laugh, from beyond the alcove, from the tiny terrace, from the drawing room upstairs. He had made no commitment to depart with her, and she was accustomed to getting herself back from parties, but nevertheless she continued to beam towards him through the chatter and cigarette smoke and smouldering of idle passions, and at about half past one in the morning, as he was thinking he really must leave, as he hovered in the hallway trying to detach himself from Selina Mountjoy and Bruce Gibbon, he heard her cry out from the stairway. She cried out, but not to him. She cried to the world. 'Oh *shit*,' she cried, as she fell forwards, tripping over the hem of her long gold gown, caught by the ready arm of squat little Ivan Warner, always at hand whenever disaster struck. And Stephen had known that he could not leave her there, to be torn to pieces by her enemies, and he had gone to the rescue in his white suit, and for the second time that night she put herself together again, and they had made their farewells together and staggered out on to the cool pavement beneath a racing moon to look for a taxi. She took her shoes off and stood barefoot as they waited. 'You'd better come back with me,' said Stephen, who never said such things, as he gave the driver the address of his one-room flat on Primrose Hill. She held on to his hand in the taxi, and rocked and swayed. He made her coffee when they arrived, and she turned suddenly ice sober, and sat there calmly as though a storm had passed. 'You're a good friend, Stephen,' she said. 'You're a pal.' And they had cuddled together in the narrow bed, and whispered of little things. They recalled their first meeting, a hundred years ago, in a dubbing studio off Wardour Street, and a party at the Round House, and the time when Hattie had in her turn rescued

Stephen from the clutches of a voracious bejewelled Italian journalist. They spoke of the moment when they had become friends. Hattie, observing Stephen romantically lunching alone in a self-service Italian restaurant near the British Museum, and struggling incompetently with a plate of spaghetti and some galley proofs, had boldly advanced upon him and his table with her tray, and sat herself down, and offered him a glass of wine from her carafe. He had not resisted. The proofs had snaked all over the floor, and Hattie, rescuing them, had offered her services as personal organizer. They had laughed a lot, over that, and over the years.

There was no way they could ever make love to one another, these two. They were saved from that. They had remained good friends.

And that was how Harriet Osborne came to take possession of Stephen Cox's apartment. In the small of the night they arranged it, and, both being mad, in the morning they kept their bargain. 'We mad people should stick to our agreements,' said Stephen, as Hattie thanked him in the green dawn. And off he flew to Bangkok, and vanished from her sight.

It is not surprising that Hattie looks back on this night with horror. She cannot remember all of it, but she remembers enough to know that she behaved atrociously, even for her. But then, Stephen is a gentleman, and will not tell. And she has got a very low-rent flat out of it. And maybe he is dead and will never be able to tell. Molly Lansdowne is dead, dead of a heart attack in a hotel in Spain. Only Hattie remembers. And she will never tell.

*

Stephen Cox sits strapped into his Club Class seat at Charles de Gaulle Airport waiting for take-off on the Air France flight to Thailand and Vietnam, with his new discreet professionless passport in his pocket. He does not regret handing over his key and his rent book and his last will and testament to Hattie Osborne. One should

THE GATES OF IVORY

obey impulses. His impulses had not enabled him to comfort Hattie in the way she most needed, but an empty apartment, however small, was an acceptable offering. He wondered how she would get on with his mysterious and philanthropic landlord, the aptly named Mr Goodfellow. And would she remember to give the bank the note he had scribbled requesting cancellation of the standing order for rent? It did not matter much, one way or the other. The rent was very low, and Mr Goodfellow was too honest to allow himself to be paid twice over.

He had told Hattie he had no idea how long he would be away. He said this to everybody. It was the truth.

He was feeling surprisingly well after his white night. Alert, light in the body, fancy free. The flight from Heathrow to Paris had been on time, and now, on the main leg of his journey eastward, he had happily been allocated a place near the Emergency Exit, with extra leg space, and the seat next to him was still free. He stretched and spread himself and began to browse through the copy of *The Times* he had purchased in London. Already the British news seemed irrelevant, parochial. Who cared about phone-tapping and Swiss takeover bids for British firms? Who cared if the Queen Mother had attended a ceremony in Nuneaton or the Countess of Snowdon a luncheon in Leith? Who cared that Lady Philippa Carlisle was six years old today, or that Princess Anne had tinted her hair red? Even the long slow diminuendo of the defeated miners' strike and the rise of the new star Gorbachev failed to interest. Stephen read on, complacently, already half elsewhere, noting in passing that Paul Whitmore, the Horror of Harrow Road, was to appeal against his sentence, and that little Sophal May, an eleven-year-old Cambodian refugee, had been reunited with her parents in New York after a decade of searching.

His attention was caught only when he came across the obituaries of two of his acquaintances. It seemed a dangerously high body count. Both had died prematurely. One had once been his publisher.

He had died, though it did not say so, of the drink. The other had been a fellow-scholar at Oxford. Cancer had killed him. Stephen paid a silent tribute to Michael Rowbotham and Stuart Cross, and registered the fact that Death was already his companion. Death had joined the caravan early, even though Stephen's visa would take him only as far as Bangkok.

An announcement in French followed by English declared that the plane would take off in twenty minutes, and that the name of the captain was Commandant Parodi. Stephen was pleased by this. Who better to fly one into the unknown? We live in the age of parody, reflected Stephen. He had known another Parodi, years ago, in Normandy. He had been the manager of the Grand Hotel in Cabourg, the hotel of Balbec, which Proust had made his own. Stephen had arrived there on his bicycle, and the manager had been at first suspicious of his credentials, then appeased. *Monsieur Parodi.* Was it a common name, were these two related? Stephen did not know. The curving wide beach of Cabourg returned to him, the blue-grey watercolour sky, the yellow sands, the girls forever on their bicycles. He had walked from his hotel room across a marble foyer into the sea, wearing a white bathrobe. And in the evenings, he had played roulette in the casino, and eaten from little oval platters of *fruits de mer*, silver platters heaped with oysters and winkles and urchins and prawns and razor shells and mussels and green weeds of the sea. Good Time, he had then inhabited. He had been young enough to lay his chips for luck upon the number of his own age. Now he had long since left the board, and played roulette no more.

But luck was still with him, and the seat next to him was still empty. He appropriated it with his books, his briefcase, his plastic-bagged purchase of a small duty-free radio. He thought himself free from company, for Captain Parodi was already beginning to taxi towards the runway, but no, here at the last moment was a fellow-traveller, invading and claiming his space. He scooped up his belongings and redeployed them beneath his feet. As he did so, he took note that Death had been joined near the Emergency Exit by Lust.

Lust was extremely attractive. She was also tiny, and the extra leg-room was wasted on her, but Stephen did not grudge this. If the seat must be occupied, let it be by such an apparition. She settled herself in, clearly a practised last-minute traveller, without fuss, with a comfortable little rustling and patting of pillow and blanket. She seemed to have no baggage: perhaps the attentive steward had disposed of it in some privileged secret store? Stephen observed her covertly, as Captain Parodi swooped upwards to the skies. Of her legs he had a good view, for her tight emerald skirt rode high above her knees, and her ankles were extended, neatly crossed. Her little green lizard-skin high-heeled shoes were impractical fetishes. Her feet made Stephen's feet look enormous. Her hands were neatly folded in her lap, and she wore large rings with flashing stones. In her lap reposed an absurdly small, soft, kingfisher-blue bag with a golden clasp and a golden chain. Her breasts were high and showy under a trim white silk shirt. She wore a lavish quantity of cosmetics upon her brown and flawless skin. She twinkled and jittered with light, although she sat so still. Fire leapt from her emeralds and her diamonds. She smelt of musk. She was infinitely composed

Champagne was served, and Stephen and petite Lust each accepted one glass, then another. She seemed to be well known to the steward. They journeyed eastwards.

Caviare was served, in small glass pots. Black aphrodisiac. Petite Lust from time to time examined her even white teeth in her pocket mirror to make sure that no unsightly soft damp dark sea eggs adhered. Into the back of her gold powder-case a goldsmith had hammered a black enamel orchid. She drank half a bottle of white wine with her meal, and then calmly embarked, with her cheese, on half a bottle of red. Stephen stared in admiration. How could so much liquid accommodate itself so gracefully in so small a frame? She did not flush or fumble. She remained calm, cool, brown, self-possessed.

Over coffee, she announced to Stephen that her name was Miss Porntip, and that she lived in Bangkok and was Beauty Queen of Asia.

During the in-flight movie they exchanged further information. As gangsters and drug-dealers on the small silent screen raced and tumbled and cheated and sweated and fell over cliffs in fast cars, Stephen Cox and Miss Porntip told one another little stories about their lives. He admitted to being a writer and an adventurer. She claimed to be a woman with many assets as well as her beauty. They spoke of Thailand, Indonesia, the Pacific Basin, the New World. Miss Porntip was derisive about Vietnam and China and Kampuchea. 'This plane,' she said, 'it fly on to Ho Chi Minh Ville. Is ruined, Ho Chi Minh Ville. Was fine city. Saigon was fine city. Café Continental, Rue Catinat. Dancing. *Thés dansants.* Is all ruined now.'

'It must have been ruined long before your time,' murmured Stephen, politely. She could not be more than thirty, he thought, though he had no way of judging the bloom on an oriental skin. Certainly, the Vietnamese who had boarded the plane in Paris had looked far, far older than his new friend. They had belonged to another epoch.

She wanted to know why he was interested in Indochina. He was hard pushed for an answer. 'Is mainly the French and the Americans come there,' she said. 'Is not for the English. English did not fight there. No English missing soldiers to collect.' She asked if he planned to stay in Bangkok, and if so at which hotel. He named his hotel. She wrinkled her nose in disgust. 'Is old and not so nice,' she said. 'Many fine hotels in Thailand now.'

She spoke as though she owned half of them. Perhaps she did.

'Writers do not stay in nice hotels,' he tried, tentatively, more for his own benefit than hers, and realizing as he spoke that he was talking rubbish. The Grand Hotel in Cabourg had been one of the finest hotels in the world. She treated his remark with the contempt it deserved.

'Is not necessary stay in horrid places,' she said, firmly. 'Is not necessary see poor people and horrid places.'

'What if they are one's subject?' he suggested.

'Why choose subject? People not want to read of horrid things and poor people. People like nice hotels and jewels and nice things. And if poor people necessary, use . . .' (she searched for a word, and, triumphant, found it) 'use invention. Is correct, invention?'

'Yes, correct. Invention. Imagination. But these things have their limitations. They cannot make something out of nothing.'

'Why not? Films and stories make out of nothing. Look.' She gestured towards the silent screen, where a bronzed and derivative hero ran through long corn beneath a lowering, circling pursuing helicopter. 'Look, is nothing. Is no person and no-thing and no place.'

He laughed. He was entranced by Miss Porntip. She was surely no thing herself, she was surely a dream. Commandant Parodi flew on, five miles high over the Euphrates, towards the lopsided melon moon of Karachi.

*

The New Trocadero Hotel, Surawong Road, does not strike Stephen as particularly new. Surely it must be the *old* Trocadero, with a new neon sign? But it is new to Stephen, as indeed is the whole of this strange city, this City of Angels. He is not surprised that Miss Porntip had disapproved of his hotel. He is half inclined to disapprove of it himself, but checks himself sharply. He is not here to enjoy himself, after all.

His room (executive style with bath) has a certain authentic greyness that makes him seem a little more authentic himself. The window looks out on to a vast grey cylindrical water cooler dripping ceaselessly on to a gravel-clad roof. Stephen reflects that it must be spreading legionnaires' disease throughout Thailand and half wishes he had bothered to make time to visit his GP to inquire about hepatitis and malaria and meningitis. One can carry the Death Wish too far, and anyway what is the point of succumbing to illness in a foreign hotel? There is no story in that, no copy to file, no message to send home.

He unpacks his clothes, hangs up his white suit and his blue, places his rolled socks tidily in a drawer. He examines the contents of his vast old-fashioned brand new refrigerator and reads the notices by the ill-placed mirror. They inform him that if he wishes to purchase any of the room's fittings, the prices are as indicated. He looks around him. There is no way he could want to purchase any of these objects. They are all either old or unattractive or both. A bedside table, a bed, two chairs, a sheet, two pillows, an ashtray, a small wooden tray with a glass and a Thermos of purified water, a pair of flimsy and ill-fitting curtains, a doubtful rug. Each item is priced, even the grimy and slightly torn shower curtain in the bathroom. Door knob, 150 baht. As this is what Stephen paid for a taxi from the airport, it does not seem a bargain. A bedside light is listed, but does not exist. Should he report this to the management, lest he be charged for its removal?

There is a new television set, still encased in thick fleshy semi-transparent grey polythene. He switches it on. It responds, but there is no picture, only a white blare. He switches it off. He will play with it later. It is priced at 11,000 baht, which seems quite cheap. The only misspelling on the list is a handwritten addendum, 'Bath Mate' for 'Bath Mat'. The phrase reminds him pleasurably of Miss Porntip, with whom he has a date for the evening in the Oriental Hotel. He wonders whether she will keep it. He has no way of knowing. She has drawn him a little map, showing him the pedestrian's route from the sombre Trocadero to the gay Oriental. It is, she says, a short walk. They have an assignation in the Authors' Lounge at seven thirty.

He lies on the bed and stares at the ceiling. The room is basic, but it works. It is cool and air-conditioned. He has slept in worse rooms, far worse rooms than this. His own room, in Primrose Hill, currently occupied by a weary Hattie, is nearly as basic as this.

He wonders what on earth he is doing here. Is he in search of a story or of himself, or of an answer to the riddles of history? Or is he merely trying to colour in the globe?

He thinks of Joseph Conrad, whose own adventures in the South Seas began here in Bangkok. It was here that Conrad received his first command. Stephen Cox admires Conrad. He is drawn to his loneliness, his restlessness, his temptation to despair. He likes the possibly apocryphal tale of the young Conrad, pointing at the atlas and putting his finger 'on a spot in the very middle of the then white heart of Africa' and vowing to see it for himself. And so he had gone, into the unmapped quarter, amongst cannibals and savages. Stephen, like Conrad, had nourished his boyhood dreams with travel books, with Mungo Park and Marco Polo and Captain Cook and Pierre Loti and Gide in the Congo. Dreams of escape, dreams of distance. He had wanted to see, before he died, the whole wide world.

The bare light bulb dangles. The machine hums. A tap drips. Stephen fills in the turning globe, patch by patch. At prep school, in what was called Geography, he and his classmates had been taught to surround islands and continents with a blue edging of sea. A useless, harmless exercise. There were strict rules governing the angle of the blue pencil. A wide, rayed fuzz was not allowed. Little, even, horizontal strokes alone had been permitted. No reasoning for this had been provided. Prep school, like the army, had been without reason.

He is feeling very tired, but he dares not close his eyes lest he fall asleep and miss his rendezvous with the improbable Miss Porntip. He picks up a copy of the *Bangkok Post* purchased in the lobby below, and runs his eyes over news stories about Ronald Reagan and the Ayatollah and the King of Thailand and a logging concession. In this paper he will find no deaths, or none that he can call his own. He finds an item about the deployment of Vietnamese troops of the People's Army in the Phnom Malai area of Battambang, an area briefly reconquered by the Khmer Rouge three years earlier. There is a picture of a young Khmer Rouge soldier in a denim jacket, sitting on the ground, smiling broadly, casually and proudly cradling a gun. His head is wrapped in a chequered cloth, on top of which perches what appears to be an American cowboy hat. His smile gives no indication that he is in any way aware that the Khmer Rouge are the folk monsters of the modern world. The author of the article speculates that there are 40,000 trained Khmer Rouge soldiers active on the frontier and inside Kampuchea, and that Pol Pot himself is in a hideout in the Cardamom mountains.

Stephen Cox's own army experiences had been peaceful. He had lazed about in the Dorset countryside (during his National Service) with his friend Brian Bowen and a suspected shadow on his lung, and then had been transferred to a Russian language course in Cornwall. He could still speak a little Russian. He wondered if the People's Army spoke Russian. The Soviet Union was Vietnam's only friend. It was strange that while the world reviled the Khmer Rouge as mythical monsters, they also reviled the Vietnamese who had liberated Phnom Penh from the Khmer Rouge. Khmer and Thai and Vietnamese Stephen did not speak. There had been no National Service courses offered in these languages.

Stephen has never seen a war, never heard a shell explode. An American plane had crashed into the shallow waters of the Levels near his childhood home in Somerset in 1942, but that was as near as he had come to death by acts of war.

So why does he lie here? Is he looking for trouble?

He gets up, looks again in the refrigerator. There is no mineral water, only beer. He does not want a beer, but decides to have one nevertheless. Why not? But there is no bottle opener. The previous guest must have extravagantly purchased it. Feebly, he lies back, and waits for the time to pass.

*

The Swan of Ice

A swan of ice drips upon the chequered marble floor. A white-suited slave discreetly mops. Little naked oysters lie obediently in silver spoons, raying outwards in a spiral from a huge, spiny, not-quite-dead lobster. Its feelers struggle and waver, its maxillary palps feebly panic and tick. Tiny swans of cream-filled light-buff puff pastry float on a silver sea. Teeth bite, flash, smile. There is black caviare, and prawns of dangerous radiant coral pink. There are jewels, silks, perfumes. This is the gorgeous East. Conrad was here.

This, in Stephen's handwriting, on the back of the torn-off front page of Staff Briefing Paper for the International Committee for Resettlement of Displaced People, folded in half and tucked into the memo book I'd nicked from Liz Headleand. I like it. Stephen's high style. Well, it's a parody of Stephen's high style. Well, Stephen's high style is parody. But what can you do with half a page? It sounds like the Oriental to me. I stayed there once with John Connell when he was making *The Princess and the Talisman*. It *was* a bit swan-of-ice-and-dying-lobster. Wonderful prawn soup. John was on good form that week. Ah well, never look back. 'Conrad was here', eh? Stephen always had a thing about Conrad, which is odd when you think that Conrad was such an amazing racist old reactionary, and frankly Stephen has always been somewhat to the left of Pol Pot.

There were quite a few notes about Conrad jotted about, though you'd have had to know your stuff to spot some of them. 'The Violin of the Captain of the *Otago*', for instance. The *Otago* was Conrad's first command, and its previous skipper used to play the violin to himself mournfully all over the high seas. Conrad was haunted by ghostly water music. The old skipper was mad. Then there were quite a few notes about *Victory*, which Stephen must have been reading. Such as 'Query: Portrait of hotel manager libellous?' I should think so. Conrad had to print an apology, saying that of course he knew not all Germans were quite as ghastly as the appalling Schomberg. Not that I was all that interested in whether Conrad or Stephen had libelled a hotel or a hotel manager. I was much more keen to find out whether he'd libelled *me*, and if so, to destroy the evidence. I was sure I'd seen my own name jump out of the pages as I flipped through it under Liz's nose. As one would expect one's own name to do, if it were there. But when I looked more closely I was damned if I could find it. Had I gone and brought the wrong memo book, I wondered? Was Liz Headleand even now amusing herself with a description of my naked tits, while I was stuck with naked oysters? Maybe I'd imagined it, in a paranoid sort of way.

There was a lot of stuff about a character called Miss Porntip. She seemed to be some kind of erotic fantasy of poor old Stephen's. Nothing very consecutive, just notes and scribbles. Jottings about her clothes and sayings. The wit, wisdom and wardrobe of Miss Porntip. To tell the truth, I don't think Stephen ever got much further than fantasy. I think he was one of those men who put sex in a compartment and never let it get out. Not that I blame him. When it does get out, it *is* a menace. To tell the truth, I don't think Stephen liked women, as such. I think they nauseated him. In the flesh. I'm only guessing, mind you, from putting two and two together from clues in his books. It's funny really, because he was always a good friend to women. People like Marjorie and Molly adored him. And he was a good friend to me. I wonder if *I* nauseated him?

I don't see why people shouldn't be celibate if they want. It would certainly make life easier. I wish I did want. But oh alas I go on wanting the other thing.

I got quite excited when my eye lit on something that looked as though it might connect up with me. There were my initials, HO, written several times over, in red ball-point, and underneath them were the names of several London hotels and restaurants adorned by queries. The Carlton, Claridge's, the Dorchester, the Ritz, the Troc and the Cri, Stephen inquired of himself. Then he had written DICKENS? NEW ZEALAND HOUSE? And again, HO?

At first I thought Stephen was trying to remember some do I'd been to with him, or at which I'd met him, and I did manage to dredge up a dim memory of a reception at Claridge's, for Richard Burton (or was it Mrs Gandhi?) – and another on the Martini Terrace of New Zealand House where I had a good chat with Monica Dickens when she was one of the Authors of the Year. I think I behaved quite nicely on that occasion. But then as I read on I realized I was on the wrong tack altogether. HO wasn't Harriet Osborne at all, it was Ho Chi Minh. Silly me. There was a lot more HO later on in the diary. Though what he had to do with Claridge's or the Carlton or New Zealand House remains obscure. I'm sure he never went to parties at such places, did he? Did he ever come to England at all? I've no idea. Perhaps Stephen was planning to employ a little artistic licence and introduce a scene into his play with Pol Pot and Ho and Chairman Mao all dining in Claridge's with Richard Burton and Mrs Gandhi and Monica Dickens. Why not?

He was at least *half* planning to write a play. I found one page laid out as a sort of screenplay, with camera directions. It was set in a Paris apartment, rue St André des Arts, 1952. POV Khieu Ponnary, POV Saloth Sar alias Pol Pot, that sort of thing. They were talking about regicide and how to get rid of Sihanouk. This Ponnary person appeared to be Pol Pot's fiancée. I didn't know Stephen knew the lingo for TV plays. Point of View, and all that. He never let on about it. I used to try to talk him into doing TV scripts, all those years ago, back in the seventies, when we both needed the ready, but he never would. He wasn't interested. He said he'd had his bellyful of the cinema, translating subtitles when he was Down and Out in Paris in the sixties.

The rue St André des Arts rings a bell. I wonder if it's where we went to see Maxence and Claudine. Bill and me. Or was it Harold and me?

Stephen seems to have been reading *Macbeth* as well as *Victory*. There were quite a few *Macbeth* quotes dotted about. Some in red ink. Very pretty. Bleed, bleed, poor country. Blood will have blood, they say. The unmentionable play. Was Ponnary a sort of Lady Macbeth figure, perhaps? Screwing Pol Pot to the sticking post?

They said Aaron Headleand's new version of *Coriolanus* is worth seeing. I really ought to make an effort and get to it. He's one of the up-and-coming. I liked his *Squeaking Cleopatra*. The boy Cleopatra. Bit Stoppardian, but not bad.

> And from the blown rose, many stop their nose
> That kneeled unto the bud.

I don't know why those lines of Cleopatra haunt me. Well, no, that's a lie. I know exactly why, and I don't like the reason. I read a stupid article in the paper today by that ghastly skinny short-skirt skeleton Cassie O'Creagh about why men continue to be attractive in their fifties, when women go off in their forties. All to do with reproduction. Sexist crap.

I did find the reference to me, in the end, in Stephen's diary. The one I'd subliminally glimpsed. It says, in a sort of scribble, 'Hattie in her gold dress. Trumpet and kettledrum.'

Well, I like it. Better than a blown rose, anyway. I think it must be some sort of quotation, but I can't place it. Dear God, how we all live in quotations. Trumpet and kettledrum. It makes me sound quite dignified. Shakespeare? Marlowe? Chapman's Homer?

Oh well, plough on, I suppose. At the very least we can get some bibliographical collection in America to make an offer. Isn't there a library in Austin, Texas, with a room full of Erle Stanley Gardner's hats? They'll like a finger bone.

*

The swan of ice drips. Stephen, waiting in the Oriental for the doubtful arrival of the hallucinatory Miss Porntip, sits on a chintz cushion in a rattan chair in a quiet corner confronting the Trimalchian cocktail party into which he has wandered. He had not expected the Authors' Lounge to be so fully occupied, and was surprised to be admitted without invitation. His white suit is his passport. Is that the manager, that handsome lean-faced Scandinavian gentleman, shaking hands on the threshold? Is he the successor to the disreputable Schomberg and the disappeared silk merchant, eaten by tigers? He had let Stephen through without a murmur, and now here Stephen sits, as a novelist should, observing.

Conrad was here. And so, it seems, was Stephen's old friend and rival Pett Petrie, best-selling author of the runaway upmarket success, *Ziggurat*. Stephen has discovered his name in the Authors' Lounge menu. Various writers have given their names to cocktails. Conrad and Somerset Maugham one might have expected, and Morris West and Peter Ustinov and Gore Vidal he is not surprised to find. He salutes with respect the presence of the old seafarer William Golding. He notes that Barbara Cartland has given her name not only to a cocktail of pink champagne but also to the Dish of the Month, a confection of fillet of sea bass with mousse of rhubarb. All this, though strange, is acceptable to Stephen. This is the Oriental, not the Trocadero. But the sight of Pett Petrie's name jolts him. How has Pett, his contemporary, joined this international literary jetset, this self-promoting sybaritic elite? Until ten years ago, Pett was nobody. A struggling author, a minor Wimbledon short-story writer and poet who had never been further afield than a poetry reading in Rotterdam. And now he is a world-famous novelist and has given his name to an oriental cocktail of brandy, vermouth and candiola juice.

What the hell is candiola juice? Stephen feels outsmarted. He smarts.

He conjures up the sombre Trocadero, with its serious clientele, the haunt of war correspondents and international relief workers. He tells himself that he is a serious person, not a best-seller. He is the Graham Greene character in a dingy corner with a cockroach. Not for him the fleshpots and the transient glitter of hype. (He peeps, surreptitiously, to see if there is a Graham Greene cocktail, and is relieved to note that there is not. Or not yet, not yet.)

He sips his glass of free-flowing champagne, and gazes round at the motley of hotel guests. Japanese, German, Thai, American, Korean, French, Swedish. Some chatter, some wander lonely through the crowd, nibbling and grazing. Stephen does not look out of place in his white suit. His white suit is made of miracle material. It never creases or crumples. It never picks up dirt. Stephen's face and accent do not crease and crumple. He is the English public-school product, the mad Englishman abroad. He is an asset, a decoration. He is a man for whom doors glide open. So he reassures himself, as he sits alone.

Will Miss Porntip be admitted? Has she perhaps an invitation?

A large blond Nordic bronzed film-star or mountaineer is speaking to a small gleaming Malaysian statesman or industrialist. Are they speaking of holiday-making or drug-smuggling or gun-running or Hollywood? An elderly European woman with an ebony silver-topped cane and an air of minor royalty is listening patiently to an excited girl in a flame-coloured mini-dress who may or may not be her granddaughter. A handsome middle-aged Thai in white uniform with gold braid addresses a dark-suited Japanese gentleman. A lonely drinking Dutchman, rawly clad, towers above the throng. Two little Japanese girls in immaculate sailor suits dart nimbly through the knee-level forest. The little one is chasing the larger. They are identical except in size, their hair cut in straight and solid carved fringes, their perfect features lucid and bright, their little white ankle socks flashing, their polished black pumps twinkling. They are enjoying the party more than most. They are extraordinarily beautiful. Their sailor suits remind Stephen that he is in the great port of Bangkok, on the Gulf of Siam. So far he has not seen a glimpse of river or of sea. As he watches the little sisters, a wave of emotion pours through Stephen. He knows not what it is, but it makes the hair rise on the nape of his neck. It is a tremor from the globe itself, and from its many peoples.

But now the party is disturbed by a small commotion. It is, of course, the arrival of Miss Porntip. Here she is! She is greeted with smiles and salutations. The suave manager bows deeply from his great height, and kisses her hand. Slaves cluster, proffering titbits, silver-haired gentlemen bend with deference over her small body. She makes a royal progress. She is now robed in floor-length dazzling cyclamen-shot-pink, trimmed with gold. Her hair is full of purple flowers. From her brown arm dangles a small magenta bag. She flits, laughs, twirls neatly on her slender heels, accepting greetings from the very air, accepting from a specially presented silver tray a specially elegant glass of bubbly. She is making her way towards Stephen, fluttering, indirect, the butterfly's way, but here she is, and, with a smile and an outstretched hand, she gestures that he should not rise, and she sinks beside him, upon the rattan couch.

The slaves melt discreetly away. The swan melts. The children laugh in the undergrowth.

'So,' says Miss Porntip. 'It seems here is party. This is not nice quiet rendezvous as planned. You enjoy party?'

'I enjoy watching the party.'

'There is often party. These not real people, these mostly passing people.'

'Birds of passage.'

'Yes. Is so. You have drink?'

He lifts his empty champagne glass.

'Here,' she says, and offers him hers. She waves her hand, and, as he takes his first sip, another materializes as if by magic at her elbow. They clink glasses, smile, and pledge one another.

'So,' she says. 'And how is hotel?'

'Dim,' he says. 'Dim, but serviceable.'

She laughs. The swan drips. It is losing its glassy essence.

'We will not stay here long,' she says. 'We will go eat. You hungry?'

'Yes,' he says.

She laughs again. He smiles, more slowly. She places her little brown hand upon his knee. He notices that she has changed her rings to complement her costume. Gone are the emeralds. She is now sporting amethyst and ruby and sapphire. She is a symphony of hard reds, hard pinks and blues. She taps his knee with small light fingers.

'Welcome,' she says. 'Welcome to Bangkok.'

Her lips are a glossy, varnished, violent pink. Unnatural, delightful. Her nails are painted a bluish pink.

'Stephen,' she says, experimentally, affectionately, a little smugly. She seems surprisingly proud of him. He wonders how, amongst all these rich travellers, he has managed to catch her fancy. He wonders whether he should reply with a murmured 'Porntip', but cannot quite make it. She seems to acknowledge that her name might ring oddly in his ears, and to pay this possibility no attention. She has assurance, she has dignity. She is a sophisticated woman, Miss Porntip, a woman of the world. Is she to be trusted? (He supposes he ought to ask himself, trusted for *what*?)

Trusted for dinner, anyway. That is agreed. She leads him out of the party, scattering little nods and thanks as she goes, a compact princess. She takes his arm, and trips beside him, propelling him firmly through high rooms furnished with antique furniture and gilt mirrors, and pushing her way through a white curtain woven of ropes of fresh white jasmine. Now they are in a perfumed garden, twinkling with Chinese lanterns of orange and deep iris blue. She

leads him on, towards the river. They stand, on the parapet, overlooking the Chau Praya. They stand where Conrad stood. They
gaze at the broad heaving swell, at glittering bedecked barges, at
buzzing hydrotaxis, at water ferries, at dark slow moving hulks, at
twinkling lights and reflections, at a whole city on the move.
'Come, come,' she says, and leads him further onwards, to a swaying
landing stage of wood. They stand there, rising and falling to the
irregular rhythm of the water. Green and purple water hyacinth
float and suck in the current. The flood slaps and tugs. Miss Porntip
takes Stephen's left hand, and kisses each of his fingers, and then
sucks, gently, upon the smallest of them. They both stare at the
water.

Miss Porntip sighs, happily. 'Yes,' she says. 'Now we go eat, and
I tell you more about my poor childhood and my business success.
Yes?'

'Yes,' says Stephen. He is struck into docility by this strange
little woman, by this warm night. She can suck him dry if she
wants. If she can. The water sucks at the wooden legs of the
landing stage. A smell of burning diesel and rotting vegetation
mingles erotically with the scent of jasmine and the vinous musk of
Miss Porntip.

'Come,' she says. And they go.

They walk through dark narrow streets full of people, through the
smell of noodles and soya and oil, and knock on an unlikely door let into
a wooden building on stilts over water. They are no longer by the wide
river. This is a backwater, a hidden way, a secret canal. 'Klong,' murmurs
Miss Porntip, mysteriously. 'Klong.' They make their way past alcoved
diners to a low table on a wooden terrace overlooking the reflections. A
flowering tree bends over them from an inner courtyard. 'Sit, sit,' she
says, and he sits, a little creakily, as the seats, though prettily cushioned,
are low. He looks around him with keen interest. Is he about to be
murdered? Is Miss Porntip about to produce from her person a tiny
jewelled dagger and slit his throat? He really does not care.

Does the whole terrace move and sway a little, or is it his head that swims? It seems to him that there is a slight, almost imperceptible motion, a giving, a non-resisting. The wooden walls of the building behind them are a deep polished red brown. They slope and incline, tapering upwards and inwards, slightly off true. He has left the Bangkok of right angles and marble and cement. Silk hangings portray temples, bamboo groves, little goddesses. A calm stone head smiles serenely from the depths of thick foliage. A little spirit shrine adorned by candles flickers in the leafy distance like a magical dovecot. It is hard to tell whether they are indoors or out. The table at which they sit is elaborately lacquered in red and gold. The only discordant note is the clash between its rich flamelike tones and Miss Porntip's harsher metallic pinks. He half expects her to click her fingers and change colour like a chameleon, but it does not seem to cross her mind to do so.

Pretty pickings. Electric spoils. Is this the Thai equivalent of high Victoriana?

A small silk waitress approaches and sinks to her knees beside Miss Porntip. They converse, quickly, briefly, in a foreign tongue, with many smiles and nods. She vanishes. Miss Porntip smiles at him with confidence.

'I order meal,' she explains.

He nods acquiescence.

'And now I tell you more of my sad story,' she says, 'and you tell me more of yours.'

'It's a deal,' he says.

For the first time in their acquaintance she looks very faintly disconcerted.

'A deal?' she echoes, as though she has never heard the word.

'A deal,' he repeats. 'You know, a bargain. Your life for mine.'

This time she gets it, and she smiles, radiant again.

'Is my life first, then yours,' she says.

He is glad of this small hesitation, this retreat and advance. It

56

proves she is not an automaton, a musical doll. She can understand most of what he says. Can those be real gems around her little throat? A bird sings from the spirit house. It is not a real bird. It is a jewelled toy.

'Yes,' she says, as a thin tapering glass of pale straw wine appears at her elbow, at his. 'Yes, my sad story.'

They sip the wine, nod approval. A person less formed for sadness it would be hard to conceive.

'I tell you more of the village,' she says. 'The hard life, the poor land. My parents were farmers. Like your grandparents. But not good land. Very poor land. Your grandparents very rich fields, many cows, farm subsidies, you tell me. For us, not so. Our land is very poor. Very porous soil, hard to store water, and saline deposits also. Many droughts, then floods. Very primitive farming. Low yield farming. My family own twenty acres, but very poor crops. Only 750 kilograms per year of paddy we produce. We have no mechanism, only buffalo.'

She smiles, nostalgically, and from her tiny bag produces a tiny square photograph. A small child in a limpet hat sits on a water buffalo against a green sunset. Miss Porntip when young, or a favourite niece?

'For many years my family farm this land. Once we had been more rich. Our house was good house. Teak house. But many bad harvests made many difficulties, and my grandfather sold land. So we had only twenty acres. We gathered also food in the forest. Bamboo and toads.'

She smiles, dazzlingly.

'Delicious toads.'

She pauses, dramatically, and continues.

'And then came Americans and the new roads.'

She looks at him interrogatively, to see if he is paying attention. He nods. He follows her.

'I was born 1955,' she says. 'I was little girl when the Americans come and build highway. They build highway, airbase. They chop forest. They take the women. My aunt, she live with American man in town. She keep his house and cook his food. The Americans bring much money to our district. But not to our village. We too far away in hills. My aunt, she go live in town with American man. With Uncle Mort.'

She sips her wine, reflectively. Little bowls and dishes begin to scatter themselves upon the table.

'Uncle Mort eat a lot of meat,' she says. 'It is true that Americans eat much meat, much more meat than Thai people. Thai people like meat, but Americans more so. American meat. It arrive in deep-freeze. Airloads of meat. Also ice-cream and maple syrup. Is also true about ice-cream and maple syrup.'

Piquant little sauces cluster in shallow vessels. Green herbs float in a watery pool. The aroma of lemon grass rises.

'Uncle Mort give me much ice-cream.' She shakes her head, pulls a slight face. 'I did not so much like the ice-cream. But he kind man, he nice man, he good to auntie. She good to him. Auntie, Uncle Mort and me, we sit in bed and eat ice-cream. His face red. Big and red. Whiskers, also. He was from Idaho. I-da-ho. He tell us many stories about Idaho. In bed with ice-cream.'

He cannot tell if this memory is sweet or sour. Her narrative tone is light, neutral, quizzical. With her chopsticks she picks up a carved star of radish and a green frond, and nibbles, delicately, with her small even white teeth. He imitates her, less elegantly. He feels large and red like Uncle Mort.

'The village change,' she says. 'The population grow. More and more babies. No contraception, in hills. My mother have six babies. More and more farmers sell land. More tenants. The people are still very very poor because the land is bad and no investment. Harvests very bad in 1960s. Forests disappear. Toads disappear. Bamboo is cut back. More and more poor people. No money to buy machinery. Bullock and buffalo is only labour. One pair of bullock cost 10,000 baht.'

She pushes a dish of rice towards him, helps herself to a piece of fish.

'Average income, annual, per household, 10,000 baht.'

She pauses, lets him try to work this out.

'Emerges,' she says, 'Ricardian rent.'

He is arrested with a morsel dangling from his chopstick somewhere near his chin.

'Excuse me?' he says.

'Emerges,' she says, firmly, 'Ricardian rent. David Ricardo. British economist. Theory of rent and wages.'

'That's what I thought you said,' said Stephen, returning the morsel to his plate in order to reorganize himself.

'Yes,' she continues. 'No capital for development. My brothers work for wages. They work like buffalo. There is no money, no work in village. My auntie makes good money. Is now the time of the women.'

'The time of the women?' he echoes, stupidly.

'The time of the economic power of the women. I watch, I learn. When fifteen years old, I win beauty contest. I very pretty child. The children in our village not so very pretty, but my family very pretty. My auntie very pretty when she young.'

This calm self appraisal is clearly part of her lesson in the economic development of north-eastern rural Thailand, but nevertheless Stephen feels it requires some acknowledgement. He gallantly remarks that she must indeed have been a very pretty child, as she is now a very beautiful woman. A fleet little sequence of expressions dimples rapidly over her face in response: pleasure, coquetry, a bridling modesty, an irritated dismissal of a diversionary tactic, and a renewed pleasure and amusement.

'Yes,' she says. 'Very pretty. An asset, prettiness. My capital. At this time, the girls begin migration. To the big cities. To Bangkok. In 1974, Americans leave. My auntie, she go to Bangkok. The girls work in coffee shops, in massage parlours. Big business tourism begins now. These girls send big money home. The villagers buy bullock, they build new houses. The men labour like bullock. The women labour like women. There are stories of great riches. Fairy stories, like this fairy story I tell you this night. Eat, eat, you do not eat.'

'I am too enraptured by your story,' he says, but at her persuasion heaps more little titbits into his porcelain bowl. She continues to pick, lightly, with her imported lacquered Chinese chopsticks, as she speaks.

'My auntie very clever woman,' she says. 'She give me good advice. She teach me accounts.'

'Excuse me,' Stephen again interrupts. 'May I ask you a question?'

'Please.' She smiles graciously, but manages to imply it would be better if the question were pertinent.

'I just wanted to know how many years' schooling you had,' said Stephen, humbly. The question is acceptable.

'Four years elementary,' she says. 'Education good investment, but slow return. No time to wait. So only four years elementary. Then I learn from Uncle Mort and Auntie.'

'Did they teach you about Ricardo?'

'Of course not, Mr Stephen Cox, of course not. They peasant people. Uncle Mort also peasant person. And not very intelligent. Auntie very intelligent, but peasant person.'

Suddenly she giggles, relents, changes demeanour, strokes his hand.

'You storyteller, you say. You know how to tell stories. Not to hurry. But you want me hurry. You want me tell story quickly. All right, I tell you. You want to know how I know Ricardo? You want to miss five years' story? Okay, I tell you. I meet Ricardo with American economist. He writing book on Thai economy. He interview me. I get to know him very well.'

A look of nervous distrust must have entered Stephen's transfixed gaze, for she adds quickly, 'But he gone now, gone long long ago, gone back to University of Princeton. He finished. He very nice man, very useful man, but he finished now.' She pauses, reflects. 'Very useful man,' she repeats, 'but not rich. Not like business clients. He count change, he bargain. He — what you say — he make deal.' She laughs, a clear, delighted laugh. 'He *economist*,' she repeats, inviting Stephen to share her enjoyment of this eccentricity.

'I get it,' says Stephen.

'You spoil story,' she says. 'I try to tell with much suspense. My days in coffee shop with auntie, my days in massage parlour, my days in own parlour. My beauty queen titles. Miss Banta, Miss Udon Thani, Miss Thailand, Miss Asia, Miss World, Miss Universe. My empire. My business investments. I make much money now, Stephen. I wear diamonds and rubies and sapphires.'

'You mean those *are* real?'

'Oh yes, they real.' She flashes them at him. 'I like real. I like real things. I not like pretend.'

'And how long did this economic miracle take you?' he wants to know.

She tells him he wants to know everything too quickly. She recommends a little more of the prawn. She decides, generously, that it is his turn to speak, and asks him about his own career. Has he too won prizes?

'Oh yes,' says Stephen. 'I too won a prize. The beauty prize of novelists.'

'And are you rich?'

'Well,' he says, 'by my standards, by British standards, let us put it this way, Princeton economists earn good salaries.'

His response is too oblique for her. She ignores it.

'Britain is poor country,' she informs him. 'Post-industrial country. You import from Japan, from Korea, from Thailand. You no more manufacturing. You cooling, we heating. You protectionist now. You senile now.

'So, you are poor man, Mr Stephen Cox. You Trocadero man, not Oriental man.'

Stephen protests, mildly, for his own honour rather than that of his nation.

'No, I am not poor,' he says. 'I have enough money for what I like. I like to be here, so I am here. I am a free man. I can choose. Freedom is riches.'

She looks at him as though he has missed some basic point of logic.

'What your income?' she asks. He evades, elaborates.

'I have no family, no wife, no children, no dependants. I own no house, I spend little money. I am a success.'

She looks unconvinced.

'I am a celebrity,' he continues. 'Of a sort.'

She raises, very slightly, both plucked and arched eyebrows. He sits before her, a man in a white suit, from an old, old country, far away.

'Yes,' he says. 'I am not as much of a celebrity as Joseph Conrad, Somerset Maugham, Barbara Cartland and Pett Petrie, but I am a celebrity nevertheless.'

'Explain these people, please,' she says. So he explains the celebrity ratings of the Authors' Lounge. She has never heard of Pett Petrie and Barbara Cartland, but Conrad and Maugham have, like David Ricardo, entered her personal Hall of Fame. She expresses indignation at Stephen's omission from the Drinks of the Month, and says she will have a word with the manager. She proceeds to suggest ingredients for a suitable cocktail. Juice of toad, essence of opium. As they converse, another little flotilla of tiny porcelain vessels sails gaily on to the table. Stephen had thought the meal was over, but finds he is still hungry, so continues to pick and toy. The delicate morsels melt away without trace. The evening lasts for weeks, for months. Little medicinal bitter liqueurs arrive in golden thimbles. The lights bloom softly on the oiled canal.

He wonders if he will be able to pay the bill, but there is no bill. It is all arranged, the little waitresses murmur. Perhaps this restaurant is one of Miss Porntip's many establishments? Now she is suggesting they move on to sample the delights of others. He wonders if he will be able to stand up. His legs have stiffened and will not uncrumple. He is not as young as the supple, the super-flexible, the supremely adaptable Miss Porntip. He has pins and needles as he stands, stretching. Carved dragons and many-armed warriors surround him. Three-legged, three-toed birdmen form a guard of honour as they move towards the door. The whole building is surely moving slightly, it sways and gives. Thai people very flexible people, Miss Porntip had informed him. They like to please. They like to be pleased, but they like to please. Stephen and Miss Porntip, arm in arm, leave the dark scented sloping teak house over the water.

*

The Bridal Brothel

The street dazzles. Night life, Western Thai style. Neon lights burst and splatter. Red, purple, green, orange, blue. Acid, metallic, harsh. The hot street smells nauseously of cooking, of French fries and onions and ketchup, of Oxford Street in the tropics, of pizza and beer. Giant cocktails shake in the sky, naked breasts jut at the moon. The blandishments of Babel fizz and the polystyrene cartons fly. Japanese, French, Austrian, Mexican, Swiss, Vietnamese, Lao, Indian, Cantonese, Pekingese, Spanish, Polish, Turkish, Sinhalese: the base cuisines of the world jostle for attention. British pubs with shamrocks and tartans and Union Jacks and Irish whiskey, American hamburger joints with giant plastic tomatoes and six-foot-long fibreglass gherkins. From one doorway blares a jazzy version of the 'Londonderry Air', from another Pink Floyd. Sex shows and Thai masseuses invite. A street trader offers Mozart's Greatest Hits! *Others flog fake Rolex and fake Benetton and fake Beatles. Buoyant mystical brand names bespatter the street market of the world in an orgy of commerce. This is the Nite Spot of Nightmare, the pedestrian precinct of Porn. A shyly smiling little prostitute with a paint-brush clasped in her vagina begins to inscribe* WELCOME TO BANGKOK *on a white sheet of paper over which she squats. Her hips rotate. Her expression becomes more and more tense with concentration. She forgets to smile, until she has triumphantly finished her task. Then, like a good girl in class, she smiles once more, waits for approval, for applause.*

WELCOME TO BANGKOK. *They wander through brothels Red Indian style, brothels Honolulu style, brothels geisha-girl style, brothels in the style of the Kingdom of Old Siam. They wander into a brothel full of brides, dressed in white and cream and ivory lace, in satins and silks and sprigged muslins, with white and cream roses in their hair and pearls around their throats. A discreet and restful place this is, with a seven-tiered iced white wedding cake as centrepiece, topped with an icing-sugar bride and groom, he fully dressed in Western morning suit, she naked but for her veil. Organ music plays softly, and little white leather-bound hymnals and prayer books fall open to display portraits of gentle rosy erotic brides clad in ecru underwear. Champagne stands in ice buckets, and bridal bouquets flow from silver chalices. A couple of brides play cards at a low table. White chocolates are offered upon a silver tray.*

*

Hattie Osborne is right to suppose that Liz Headleand has never been to Bangkok. When Liz comes across purple passages describing the City of Vice and Angels, she has no way of testing them against reality. Unlike Hattie, she does not pick up allusions to the Oriental Hotel. She has never heard of the Oriental Hotel. She does not know whether prostitutes who write messages with vagina-propelled paint-brushes or brothels full of brides are the porno-graphic equivalent of atrocity stories, or whether they are com-monplace tourist attractions. They seem at once excessively fanciful and all too plausible. She has heard that blasé Californian and

Japanese couples these days choose to marry in the strangest venues: in underwater caverns, in department stores, in floating hotels moored to the Great Barrier Reef, in ski-lifts halfway up the Matterhorn, in the catacombs of Sicily. Why not a brothel bride, a rent-a-bride, a fake wedding with cakes and lilies? Everybody loves lace and confetti. Well, almost everybody.

Liz Headleand struggles with Stephen's struggles with genre. She is whisked from the overwritten spun sugar of Bangkok to the plain man's trip up the Mekong, from Sartrean dialogues about the Strong Man to adventure story scraps of Conrad and Buchan and André Malraux. She does not congratulate herself on identifying these sources, as they are plainly identified by Stephen himself, in asides and footnotes. She has never read any Malraux, and is not quite sure who he is. Or was. She intends to ask Esther Breuer or her ex-husband Charles. It is the sort of thing they might know.

She rings up Hattie Osborne, and they compare notes on progress and discuss plans of action. Liz is in favour of chasing up the accountants for further disclosures about recent transactions. Hattie is in favour of pursuing Peter Bloch at the embassy in Bangkok. But both agree that they are reluctant to do anything suggestive of setting the police or the law or even the Inland Revenue on to Stephen. Therefore, for the time being, they do nothing. They carry on with their own lives, dipping from time to time into the Cambodian packet.

But from now onwards their lives are and will be different. Stephen has altered them. He has posted Cambodia to them, and now its messages are everywhere. Like a cancer, like the Big C itself, it spreads. They may not yet have caught the disease, but their cells are predisposed to receive it. They seem to hear the mysteriously self-transforming name of Cambodia-Kampuchea-Kambuja-Cambodge wherever they go. They hear it whispered in Sainsbury's and on the 24 bus. It flickers in the headlines of newspapers glimpsed over the shoulders of others, and repeats

subliminally in the afterglow of zapped documentaries. They are
solicited by posters from Oxfam and reports from the Save the
Children Fund. References to Nixon and Kissinger and Sihanouk
and Sean Flynn glob up at them from the fermenting sludge of the
seventies. Liz happens upon an old copy of *Time* magazine at the
dentist's, and finds herself gripped by a prize-winning article by a
young Australian woman who claimed to have spent a week with
the Khmer Rouge in their hidden headquarters.

Hattie takes herself for a cocktail to Claridge's in search of the
ghost of Ho Chi Minh. Liz is visited by the sad features of Mme
Savet Akrun, asking in endless replication, 'Where is my son?'
Hattie patrolling the Isle of Dogs, by the cormorant-haunted
Thames, sees a slogan on a wall which she knows in her quick gut
is written in Khmer. Liz receives a new patient who works with
Khmer and Vietnamese orphans. Hattie meets someone who filmed
with John Pilger and prompts him to retell some of the stories of
the Horror. Liz meets someone who knows William Shawcross, and
promises herself that she will read Shawcross's books.

It is as though that small, expendable country, that hole in the
map of the world, were trying to speak to them. Liz, one morning,
impulsively rings the Vietnamese Embassy to ask how to get a visa
to go to Kampuchea. She has tried this before, but got nowhere.
Again, she gets nowhere. They laugh at her request. They do not
laugh like officials, they laugh like human beings in a homely
desperate house. Kampuchea does not exist. Officially, it does not
exist. No, she cannot get a visa. No possibility. She rings the
Foreign Office. The Foreign Office tells her that Kampuchea does
not exist. It has not existed, for Britain, for many years.

Liz is discouraged, but not dismayed. She knows that more lights
will flash up on the dark screen, that more connections will be
made. She will remain on alert, with the power switched on.

It is in her second week on alert that she finds herself attending
an evening function as the guest of her ex-husband Charles. It is the

annual dinner of the International Archaeological Commission, and there is to be an address by the King of Brandipura. According to Charles, it is something to do with UNESCO and an appeal for funds for temple restoration. Most events these days seem to involve appeals for funds. Liz, zipping herself stoutly into her yellow dress, wonders why on earth she agreed to go and why she is still so willing to humour Charles, but an hour or two later finds herself rewarded by a glimpse, across the crowded auditorium, of her old friend Esther Breuer, whom she has not seen for some time. Esther is sitting between the Hon. Robert Oxenholme, Minister for Cultural Sponsorship, and a bearded white-robed Arabian. Liz catches her eye, and Esther smiles and waves as the king launches into his speech. This is a good sign: they will pick up their old, somewhat lapsed friendship, Esther's smile tells her. Maybe they will be able to sit at the same table, if the *placement* permits. Maybe Robert has arranged the *placement*. Robert arranges a lot of things.

The king is a small and well-braided gentleman with a round scholarly owl face and glasses. He is a Buddhist and a man of peace. He speaks eloquently and in excellent English of his country's great architectural heritage. He speaks about international tourism and the protection of the environment and the forests. He alludes to the Olympic Games which will shortly take place in Korea and delicately regrets the closed frontiers of North Korea, Burma, Kampuchea and Vietnam. He applauds the new spirit of openness in China. He quotes a line or two in French from a poem on the ruins of Angkor Wat. Black poppies, flowers of night, dreams of eternity. Liz suddenly sees before her the little temple sketches inexpertly drawn by Stephen Cox.

The audience is as attentive as a London audience can be on a warm night. Some doze, some fan themselves with programmes and appeal forms, some pinch themselves to stay awake, some wonder what there will be for dinner. There is strong representation from the Far Eastern embassies. Ladies in ethnic dress shimmer and twinkle.

Esther Breuer lets her mind drift towards the furnishings of her new little flat in Kilburn. It is very near her old flat, above which the murderer Paul Whitmore had spent much of his time chopping up his neighbours. The old flat has been demolished, but Esther is busy re-creating its ambience. She has painted one room red, another dark blue. She has rearranged her collections. Some pieces have returned in trunks from Bologna, others have been reclaimed from friends. Will she ever get her little Roman fountain with doves back from Peggy and Humphrey in Somerset? They are loath to part, although they will not openly admit it.

Robert Oxenholme is thinking about Esther Breuer, whom he had asked to marry him, and who has not yet given him a final refusal. Now she is back in London and freed by death from her demonic Italian lover, will she consider him more favourably? And does he hope that she will, or that she will not? He has been courting her, he has been taking her to parties, to galleries, to the opera, to the theatre. (He is a man with many free tickets.) He has enticed her into his own high-ceilinged apartments at the better end of Holland Park. Sometimes she has settled there for a whole night, but in the morning she is always off again, her small bag of possessions hanging from her small shoulder. Robert is beginning to think Esther is excessively territorial. But here she sits by him, captured for the evening, in her black silk trousers and her green taffeta shirt. What is she thinking of? Is she thinking about him? Is she thinking about Angkor Wat? Shall he tempt her with a honeymoon in Egypt, with pyramids and with Petra and Palmyra and the pleasures of ruins?

There is polite and good-natured applause as the king ends his address. He is a well-mannered chap and the audience likes him. He flatters its ignorance and he has not spoken for too long. Released, off it surges for its wine and orange juice and Perrier.

Robert has indeed arranged that the Headleands shall be at his table, and the four of them settle down together, in the company of an Indian shipping magnate, an Indonesian cultural attaché, a British diplomat and an austere sallow late-middle-aged French woman of mysterious provenance. They exchange pleasantries, and over the salmon it emerges that the British diplomat had been much moved by the king's poetic reference to Angkor. 'I was there, you see,' he says, 'in the old days. What a wonderful country! What a tragedy!' Such a peaceful country Cambodia had been then, such a quiet, sweet, gentle, good-natured people! Nothing was too much trouble for them! Such simple people, but so kind!

His watery innocent blue eyes film a little, misting over as he recalls that heroic journey of his youth: the bridge from Aranya-prathet bravely crossed on foot, the Cambodian border guards playing boules, the farmer who gave them a lift, the mayor of the village who arranged for them to sleep above the post office, the refusal of payment, the hospitality, the indifference to visas. The hired bicycles, the silence of the ruins, the water-lilies in the moat. The hornbills. Happy days.

The French woman has also been to Angkor, but she does not share the diplomat's view of the Khmer character. She asks, rhetorically, whether he believes a nation can change its character overnight? Her father, she tells them, had been killed by guerrillas on the Saigon–Phnom Penh highway in the 1950s. A discussion of the legacy of colonialism and the brutalization of native populations ensues. The tone is less apologetic, Liz notes, than it would have been ten years earlier. It is not comfortable. Diplomatically she tries to return her neighbours from politics to the slightly less explosive subject of the ruins. Was the jungle really full of tigers? How overgrown were the temples? How sophisticated were the carvings? How base the bas-reliefs?

(Very base, mutters the French woman, *sotto voce*. Crude. *Primitif*.)

Charles volunteers the information that an enterprising tour operator, undeterred by the Khmer Rouge and the country's continuing economic troubles, is offering visits to Angkor Wat even now and Liz can go and see it for herself if she wants.

('Panthers,' murmurs the French woman.)

The Indian shipping magnate says that a team of Indian archaeologists is currently working on its restoration. The French woman looks sceptical and gazes haughtily at the guests at the next table. The Indonesian cultural attaché murmurs of the immense monuments of Borobudur in central Java, which represent the centre of the universe, but nobody listens to him, for none of them have been to Java, and none of them save the Indian have heard of Borobudur. It is not yet upon the tourist itinerary of the world, though it will be before the decade is out.

Robert Oxenholme has not been to Java, but he has been to Angkor, as he now admits. 'Yes,' he says, politely refilling the French woman's glass, 'I was there with Prince Sihanouk. Odd chap, Sihanouk. Quite a character.'

The Indian shipping magnate embarks upon a description of the great Temple of the Sun at Konarak, with its mystic wheels and erotic carvings. He is more persistent than the Indonesian, and makes his voice heard.

Robert does not listen. His memory drifts. Angkor had seemed to him demented, a folly on a godly scale. The smooth face of the endlessly repeated mad-god-king Jayavarman had stared blandly down, as the more lively yet equally enigmatic features of his successor Prince Sihanouk had egged Robert and his chums on to follies of their own. Water-skiing, home movies. It had been quite a party. Sunglasses, saxophones, flutes and dancing girls. Sihanouk had been obsessed by his home movies. Robert had been prevailed upon to play the part of a Cambodian deity, a disguised monkey prince, courting a giggling royal damsel in high-heeled Gucci shoes, a scarlet silken robe, and a flame-tiered medieval head-dress inset with real Pailin rubies. Mad, they had all been, and probably sacrilegious, but it had been many years ago when they were all young things, and now Angkor Wat and the Bayon were returned once more by violence to the jungle, and Sihanouk was said to be in Peking, striking devious deals with his enemy-allies, the Khmer Rouge.

Jayavarman had been many-faced, a mild and modest man of peace who mercilessly tortured his enemies and engaged slave labour to carve his face a thousand thousand times. Sihanouk too was a man of many faces. The Playboy Prince who had once been the Playboy King (he had demoted himself, like Wedgwood Benn, for political purposes), the fixer who had wheeled and dealed and turned and turned again in his efforts to preserve himself and his small country. His faction for the liberation of Kampuchea from the Vietnamese occupation is called FUNCINPEC. What an acronym! The National United Front for an Independent, Neutral, Peaceful and Co-operative Cambodia! What a slogan! FUN-SIN-PECK!!

Pol Pot's face has not been much repeated. Pol Pot's image is shy and obscure. He is not known to be fond of home movies.

Now Sihanouk is said to want to return to the old country, to die at home in style. He had certainly lived in style. A hybrid, cross-bred, well-fed, jetset style. Sihanouk has planned menus for dinners at abortive peace conferences around the world. He prefers Paris as a meeting point, for obvious reasons. Under Pol Pot, Sihanouk lost five children and fourteen grandchildren. He has a son, Prince Norodom Ranariddh, who teaches law at the University of Aix-en-Provence. Sihanouk is willing to deal with the Khmer Rouge.

Robert, eating a raspberry, idly wonders whether any reels of that old movie still survive, and what they would be worth to a blackmailer. They had showed figures more illustrious, more news-worthy than himself rashly disporting themselves amidst the tumbling slabs and twining creepers, upon the terrace of the Leper King, beneath the orange Indo-Chinese moon.

The Leper King, who was neither King nor Leper. The Monkey

71

Prince, who was neither Prince nor Monkey. The King who was no King. The country, which had made itself into No Country in Year Zero.

In his flat in Holland Park Robert had a carved stone fish and a smiling lizard which he lifted all those years ago from the ruins of Angkor. With his own hands he had picked them from the crumbling masonry at Ta Prohm, and pulled the suckers of the creeper from them, and brought them home. He is no orientalist, but he cherishes them. He keeps them in an oriental corner, with bonsai-trees he has grown himself, from seed, from stone. He is good with bonsai. His little peaches bear tiny, useless, gemlike fruit.

Robert Oxenholme the vandal. At least no Cambodian Minister of Culture will start a campaign for the return of Robert's modest pickings. Cambodia has other things on its mind. It will take a mighty act of sponsorship to rescue Angkor Wat and Angkor Thom from the jungle, from mutilations heaped upon mutilations. The armless, the legless, the leprous. The Khmer Rouge are said to have blackened the cloisters with their camp fires, and the antique trade on the border flourishes still. The Khmer Rouge blacken, and the Indians pour in new grey-white cement. Like the sallow French woman, Robert doubts if the Indians are doing a good job, though unlike her he is too polite to let a shadow of this cloud his pleasant social face.

At least he had been a vandal in a great tradition, in the buccaneer footsteps of André Malraux, French Minister-of-Culture-to-be. Sihanouk had pointed to the empty niches from which Malraux had hacked his spoils. Robert is glad to have seen these things, in better days. How would Esther have responded to the caparisoned elephants, to the palanquins, to the golden turrets and the emerald gloom?

Would she have taken to the saxophones and the water-skis and the many-flavoured water-ices?

His thoughts return to his suit of Esther. Why should she accept him? He is not a serious person. He has been a dilettante all his life. He has been too fastidious to make an effort, too afraid of failure. His glance flicks across the table to Charles Headleand, that ambitious hard-working middle-class meddler, who had failed once and twice, and picked himself up, and driven on. Nobody had thought the worse of him, and now he was on a winning streak again, with his fingers in more pies than ever. And what of Fun Prince Sihanouk? He was still trying to outwit them all, he was still hoping to die in his own palace in Phnom Penh. Had Sihanouk feared failure and ridicule, he would have been dead long since.

I am a small person in a small country, thinks Robert Oxenholme. (He is in fact over a foot taller than Sihanouk, and a not unprominent figure in a country with a population more than ten times that of Cambodia, give or take a million or two dead.) But although I have never written what could be called a book, I have written a useful scholarly monograph on an Italian painter. And I have asked Esther Breuer to marry me. I am not totally without talent and without courage.

As he gazes thoughtfully at Esther across the table, watching as she crumbles and rubs the remains of her bread roll into a heap of unsightly, friendly little pellets, Liz Headleand suddenly breaks in noisily upon his musing. She demands to know if he ever knew André Malraux.

He starts, slightly, as the plates of his mind reconnect. Is Liz Headleand a thought-reader? He has never trusted shrinks.

Yes, he admits, as a matter of fact he had met him, several times, back in the early seventies. In Paris. And they had played tennis together, one winter, in Morocco. In Marrakesh. What makes her ask?

'Oh,' says Liz. 'I was just wondering about all those stories about his plundering Angkor Wat. Are they true? When was it? Do you know what really happened?'

Robert tries to remember. It had been the early twenties, he thinks. Malraux and his wife Clara, in their early twenties, had set off into the jungle and returned with crates full of priceless statues, wrenched from the living walls. Iconoclasts, thieves, blasphemers. They had been arrested, detained in Phnom Penh, tried, convicted, fined. It had been a great scandal, a cultural sensation. The artists of Paris (well, *some* of the artists of Paris) had sprung to their defence, and they had been released on appeal. Yes, he agrees, he had been quite a character, Malraux. (He keeps one eye on the French woman as he speaks. Where do her sympathies lie? She gives nothing away.) Malraux, the amateur intellectual who wanted to be a man of action. Dabbling in architecture, dabbling in crime, dabbling in Indo-Chinese politics. Terrorism, communism. Has Liz ever read *La Condition humaine*? No, neither has he, but it was a sensation in its day. And in later years, Malraux had become more Gaullist than de Gaulle. He had become Minister of Culture and had expiated his crimes against the buildings of Cambodia by cleaning up the buildings of Paris.

'Is that not right, broadly speaking?' he asks of the disapproving French woman. Reluctantly she concedes that it is.

Robert confesses to his stolen fish and his stolen lizard, and Esther nods: her nod implies she knows them well. Liz, watching the interplay of familiarity between Esther and Robert, is distracted, intrigued. What are these two plotting? Esther has already been back in England for a month, and has bought a new flat. Nobody, she had told Liz, as they moved towards their table, had seen it yet. Does nobody include Robert? Is he the privileged secret guest? Does Esther spend time with Robert Oxenholme in Holland Park?

'Ho Chi Minh,' says Robert, still on the subject of the French passion for the Orient, 'used to work in an antique shop in Paris, in the sixième, just by the École des Beaux-Arts. Touching up fake oriental antiques.'

'Really?' says Liz. 'What odd things you do know, Robert.'

'And before that,' says Robert, 'he used to work in London.

Sweeping a school playground. And washing dishes at the Carlton. Or was it the Dorchester?'

'I think Robert's really a spy,' says Esther, smiling enigmatically at the table at large. 'He knows such *very* peculiar things. And such unlikely people. And his job is an obvious front. I mean, how could anyone be a Minister for Sponsorship?'

The French woman looks affronted. She does not care for the British sense of humour. And she happens to know that Ho Chi Minh did not work in a hotel, he was in the merchant navy before he took up politics. (She also happens to be a spy: though that is irrelevant.)

Chatter chatter glitter, munch munch, chatter chatter munch. Coffee and mints are served. Chatter lick and munch. The King of Brandipura wipes his glasses on a large old-fashioned blue silk handkerchief. Far away across the long room, Charles Headleand's second ex-wife, the Lady Henrietta, laughs her high-pitched neigh of a laugh. Saharan scholar Frances Wingate tries hard to catch the soft murmurs of a modest but relentless Sinhalese monk. A pregnant television announcer dressed in navy-and-white spots turns faint and is carried out. Film-maker Gabriel Denham flirts heavily and a little automatically with the daughter of a Pakistani general. A Swiss banker pockets the card of a Japanese industrialist. An elderly bearded goat of an architect advises a shocked young actress on how to fiddle her income tax. The Brazilian-born wife of an American conglomerate thinks she will die of boredom if her neighbour does not stop talking about the ecosystem. A Scottish laird informs a pretty Dutch archaeologist that his son is dying of drug abuse in a hospice. A New Zealand animal rights activist harangues a Korean airline operator about the eating of cats and dogs.

The United Nations are at play. The world goes round.

Pol Pot lurks in his tent in the Cardamom mountains.

Pol Pot lies ill of cancer in a Chinese hospital.

Pol Pot waits like a fat tiger in a suite in the Erewan Hotel in Bangkok.

Pol Pot has 40,000 armed men.

Pol Pot is dead.

Chinese whispers. The world goes round.

On the way out of the institute, Charles cannot avoid a brief encounter with Henrietta. She waves and swoops. Charles darling, Liz darling, Robert darling. She kisses them all. Liz responds stolidly, allowing her cheek to be brushed. Henrietta does not introduce them to the tall dark stranger she has in tow. She walks him off into the night.

On the pavement, in the sultry London air, Charles and Liz, Robert and Esther, linger to exchange words of parting, but as they pause a large black limousine rolls smoothly up beside them. Its driver salutes Robert. 'May I offer you a lift?' Robert inquires of the Headleands. Charles shakes his head. It is beneath his dignity to get into another man's chauffeured vehicle. But Liz, who is tired, who has as ever an early start the next morning, who knows that Charles is parked a good six minutes' walk away, accepts. Charles bids them farewell. Liz thanks him for a pleasant evening. Very civilized, they all are, and very comfortable is the large dark upholstered leather interior. They sink in, thankfully. 'What luxury!' says Liz, as the driver takes instructions, and shuts his little glass window, and swims off through the heavy autumn night of Regent's Park.

'It's so nice, being with Robert,' says Esther, only half mockingly, sitting small and neat in the middle of the wide back seat. 'It's so nice, always to have a lift home.'

'If you were to marry me,' said Robert, 'you could always have a lift home.'

Esther stiffens. Liz cannot believe her ears.

Robert appears not to notice these reactions. He appeals to Liz, leaning across Esther.

'Why won't she marry me? I've been trying to persuade her for months. She can't have anything serious against me, can she? She doesn't really think I'm a spy, does she?'

His tone is light, playful, teasing, a pleasant party tone, but his remarks are received in a shocked silence. Esther covers her face with both hands in embarrassment. Liz is taken totally by surprise. The moment of silence, with all its implications, lasts and lasts, as the car glides round the Inner Circle. Robert puts an arm round Esther, and says, 'You see, my sweet? She simply can't believe you won't have a nice cheerful eligible chap like me. She's struck dumb.'

'Indeed I am,' says Liz, rising a little too late to the challenge. 'I would marry anyone who would take me home in such style. Well, almost anyone. And I am a great convert to what we might I suppose tactfully call late marriages. Look how well Ivan Warner seems to be getting on with Alicia!'

And they prattle harmlessly on about Ivan and Alicia, Charles and Henrietta, Henrietta's tall dark stranger (could he represent relief to some of Charles's alimony problems?), until Liz is delivered safely to her doorstep. And then the silence resumes.

Robert and Esther are both shocked, Robert by the revelation that Esther had not gossiped about his proposal to Liz, Esther by the revelation that he had assumed that she had.

Robert Oxenholme is accustomed to regarding himself as a figure of fun. An acceptable, by no means ridiculous figure of fun. An entertainer, a lightweight, a might-have-been. He had been sure that Esther would have laughed about him with Liz. Does the fact that she has not mean that she takes him, after all, seriously?

Esther is appalled by Robert's low opinion of her discretion. She is ashamed. Perhaps his tone implied that he had never meant to marry her at all, that she had been a fool even to consider accepting him? Perhaps the whole thing had been an incomprehensible upper-class joke?

In the silence of profound uncertainty, they are conveyed magisterially through the back streets of Kilburn.

Liz dreams of temples and monkeys and tigers, of chattering and screeching, of jungles and ruins and an ambush on an ill-made road.

Esther dreams she is drowning in the Seine in a large limousine.

Robert dreams that he is travelling through India in an old-fashioned wagon-lit with his first wife Lydia and her second husband Dick Wittering, eating chicken sandwiches.

Charles Headleand dreams that a large blue life-size Chinese ceramic horse is standing in his office. It has been placed there by government regulation, and must not be removed.

Hattie Osborne dreams that Stephen Cox has come home and wants his bed back. He is standing by her bedside, saying, 'Get up, get out, get up.'

*

The dreams of the world suffuse and intermingle through a thin membrane. The thin silver-blue beating pulsing globe turns and they shift like a vapour with the darkness. Mme Savet Akrun dreams of the thud of spade on skull. It is like no other sound in the world. It repeats and repeats and repeats. In a dry sweat, dreaming, she wills herself to wake.

Khieu Ponnary dreams of blood and brains, through thick Valium stew. Her husband Pol Pot dreams about his bank account in Zurich. All over Kampuchea the bereaved and the survivors (and all who survive are bereaved, all) dream of the thud and the skull, the blood and the brains, the corpses by the wayside, the vultures and the crows.

Stephen Cox dallies in the soft beds of the East with Miss Porntip, unable to cross the frontier through the gates of horn. He dwells in the land of lotus and poppy and orchid and ivory. Miss Porntip, sweet succubus, sucks him and makes him flow away into the thin sheets of warm repose. She feeds him on lilies, then sucks his strength away.

Miss Porntip has already sucked dry and cast away a Princeton economist, a film-producer, an agro-business chief, a top official at the United Nations High Commission for Refugees, a diamond merchant, and a general in the Thai Army. A British novelist will now be added to her closet of husks and bones. Stephen is almost unresisting as she weaves her spells and mixes her potions. He is fascinated by her. She lectures him upon the booming Thai economy and upon her own business triumphs. She has fingers in every pie. She tells him of the girls she has rescued from the concrete mixers and construction sites, girls who now work for Miss Porntip for good wages in hygienic conditions. She tells him of her logging concession and her interests in the management of tropical rain forests. She is interested not in conservation but in profit. 'You conserve, you in old country,' she tells him. 'We make money. Is our turn now.' She tells him of her pineapple-canning concern and her prawn farm and her project for preserving candiola fruit through judicious radiation. She tells him of her plastic box subsidiary and her television satellite stakes and her plans to launch a new Asian mini-tampon. Her empire is vast. She is insatiable. She is the New Woman of the East. He cannot but admire.

'We make new history,' she tells him, grandly. 'In old days, was only one story for woman in Thailand. Is called Village Maiden to Beauty Queen. Sometimes tragedy story, sad lover lost, massage parlour, ruin, return to village, sometimes ill, sometimes crippled, sometimes disgrace. Sometimes family forgive, sometimes not, sometimes death. Is sad story. Other story, same story, but happy story. Beauty Queen, much riches, fame, glory, TV-star, Hollywood, bridal Western style with seven-tier cake and white icing. Now is new story. Now is success story of the woman, the independence of the woman. Is New Plot.'

Stephen at one point dares to ask her if she happens to know her own IQ.

'Is very very high,' says Miss Porntip. 'You surprise? You think no Thai ex-beauty queen intelligent? You think no woman intelligent? You think no Thai intelligent? You sexist and racist, perhaps?' Stephen flinches from this bull's-eye battery of questions, but she presses on. 'Most of family except for auntie very very stupid,' she says. 'So, I am convergence towards norm. Is statistically correct.'

Stephen ponders this.

'A very *sudden* convergence,' he ventures.

'And why not sudden? These sudden times. Quick change. Heating economy. Huff puff all hot hot now.'

And Stephen sighs, defeated.

Miss Porntip is illuminating on the subject of Thai culture. She tells him that one of the intellectual tasks she had to perform to become beauty queen of her village was to name three varieties of garlic. 'On national level, questions more difficult,' she confides. 'Name President of United States. Name star of *Rambo*.' Other features taken into account, as well as intellect, had been 'Face, shape, hair, movement, feet, bottom.'

'Bottom?' Stephen echoes, slightly shocked.

'Yes,' repeats Miss Porntip firmly. 'Bottom. Arse. Bum. Bottom. Is great asset, good bottom. More important than breast, is bottom. Is good, my bottom?'

Miss Porntip tells him her stories, and occasionally she allows him to tell his, though she is forever interrupting him with pertinent or impertinent queries. He tells her of his aged mother, now in her nineties, lying senile and speechless in an old people's home with a fine view of the Quantocks, and even as he speaks he can see her working out how soon the lengthening life span of the Thai population will make investment in old folk a profitable affair. He tells her of his last night in Knightsbridge with Hattie Osborne, but she tells him it is bad story, anti-woman story, and will not listen. He tells her of his younger days in Paris in the heady sixties, sitting alone at a restaurant in the rue Léopold-Robert, eating cassoulet or stuffed cabbage with his books propped up against a water carafe. Stephen has eaten alone all over the world, but this was his formative period, this was where he acquired the habit. He tells her about the married woman, wife of a finance minister who picked him up one day as he was reading the poems of René Longuenesse. She had picked him up and played games with him in her husband's bed and manned the barricades with him and climbed down fire escapes with him and swum naked with him in a little lake in the forest of Fontainebleau. She had taken him to the races and to clandestine political gatherings, she had introduced him to Marxists and Algerians and Vietnamese, to friends of Frantz Fanon and acquaintances of Ho Chi Minh. She had showed him the house in the rue Compoint where Ho had lodged and studied and read Dickens and Dostoevsky and written poetry by the midnight oil. Then one night, trapped in the marital bed by the approaching footsteps of the finance minister, she had pushed him out of a high first-floor window into a rose bed.

'You see the scars,' says Stephen, delicately raising one corner of his trouser leg, showing a white streak on his slim ankle. 'There's metal in there. She left me a metal pin as a billet-doux.'

Miss Porntip laughs.

'You like bad girls,' she comments.

'Yes,' says Stephen.

'And then?'

'Oh, then came others. Other wild women. Other adventures.'

'More windows? More jumpings?'

'Well, yes, more of that kind of thing. But no more broken bones. I learned to land with more care. It's all a question of relaxing as you fall.'

'And me, am I wild woman?' she wants to know. 'Am I bad girl?'

'You must answer that,' he tells her. 'You're certainly not the kind of girl my mother wanted me to marry, that's for certain.'

'So you never marry? No children?'

He agrees, returns the question. She concedes that she too has never married, she too has no children.

'And what for you here in Thailand? What you do here in Bangkok?' she asks.

He tries to explain not for the first time that he is here – well, to be crude, he is here looking for copy. He repeats his old alibi, that he is trying to write a play about Pol Pot. Once more she wrinkles her nose in disgust. She tells him Khmer people of no interest, she tells him communism and socialism are dead, she tells him his copy is here, here in Thailand. This is where the action is, she says. She tells him how and with whom to open a tax-free bank account. She says Pol Pot old hat. Is a time of trade now, she says. He says, if it is a time of trade, why is it so bloody hard to get a visa for Phnom Penh? She says he can buy visa anywhere, but she does not advise to.

Miss Porntip is Stephen's Oriental self, but he retains his Trocadero self. Sometimes he sleeps with Miss Porntip in *grand luxe* in her lofty modern apartment in a condominium overlooking the temples and palaces, but more often he sleeps in his own grey room. And, as he sits there of an evening adjusting his television set, or as he eats alone in the gloomy restaurant, he asks himself what he is here for in Thailand.

There is no easy answer. Here he is, but for no good reason. There had been nothing to keep him in England, but is that a good enough reason for being, in particular, here?

It is true that it is Pol Pot that has brought him here, though his plans to write a play are notional. He has, as Liz would confirm, long been taken with the prospectus of the Khmer Rouge and the plan to return to Year Zero. Stephen has a bleak view of human nature as it exists in its known manifestations, and an ecstatic view of its possibilities if ever it were to be released from them. He is that dangerous creature, a dreamer of ideological dreams. He does not much like the human race, with its chitter chatter munch munch aggressive acquisitive competitive pettiness. He is as guilty as anyone of chitter chatter petty mutter petty bitty bitch bunch bite and suck, but that doesn't mean he *likes* it. Or himself.

He thinks the species is capable of something better. It is holding itself back, it has taken a wrong turn, it 'could do better'. It is afraid of the big risks. It clings to a shabby past. It needs a Big Idea. A *really* Big Idea.

Stephen carries a text in his wallet, photocopied from the works of John Stuart Mill. It is a key text, and this is why he carries it. It reads thus: 'If the institution of private property necessarily carried with it as a consequence, that the produce of labour should be apportioned as we now see it, almost in inverse ratio to the labour – the largest portions to those who have never worked at all, the next largest to those whose work is almost nominal, and so in descending scale, the remuneration dwindling as the work grows harder and more disagreeable, until the most fatiguing and exhausting bodily labour cannot count with certainty on being able to earn even the necessaries of life; if this or Communism were the altern-ative, all the difficulties, great or small, of Communism would be but as dust in the balance.'

This great and classic text would be endorsed by many with less eccentric views than Stephen: by his old friend Brian Bowen, by Brian's wife Alix, by Perry Blinkhorn of Northam City Council, by Liz Headleand's youngest stepson Alan Headleand, and by many defenders of variant forms of socialism and the egalitarian society. But he parts company from most of these in his view that the test is as pertinent now as it ever was. He does not see, as they do, the slow march of bloodless reform, which qualifies Mill's fears. This slow march to Stephen is a slow poisoning of hope, a slow accept-ance of defeat. Stephen believes that a deep, violent, volcanic shift is required to change the way things are. After this cataclysm, human nature, purged and pure, will find its own sweet natural level, freed from 10,000 years of exploitation, encrustation, sediment and stratification. It will flow forth free and clear, from the crystal skull of Pol Pot, from the pure well of Cambodia, and fill the world with joy.

The flaws in Stephen Cox's logic are blindingly obvious. A child could spot them, let alone a democratically elected back bencher.

Stephen Cox can spot them all too well himself. He lost faith in Paris in 1968. He has already written one highly successful, cynical novel about that loss of faith. Yet, as he rolls himself a little cigarette while waiting for his bowl of soup in the dark and arctic restaurant, and listens to the hum of the world's cooling machinery, he admits that he is still curious. Communism has failed and capitalism has triumphed and John Stuart Mill's hypothesis has been rendered otiose. But had Pol Pot known that? Stephen has come here to try to find out. He is still curious.

A fatal curiosity. He remembers invoking that phrase once while dining with his friend Liz Headleand in Bertorelli's at the beginning of the year. Her memory of this conversation is vague and defective, and so is his, and so is mine, but it had nevertheless taken place, and it lingers on in both their recollections and in the limbo of my old Amstrad word processor like a formative shadow. They had talked of Pol Pot and Kampuchea and atrocity stories. Stephen had expressed his interest in his curiosity about a country which had tried to cut itself off from the forward march of what is called progress. It had refused all foreign aid. It had turned its back on electricity, electronics, mechanics, postal services, medicine. It had returned to People Power. Men yoked with oxen pulled the plough. Men and women with bare hands built dams and dykes as in the dawn of time. They had dosed one another with bitter leaves, and given one another transfusions of coconut juice.

A sort of original *Green* party, Stephen had suggested to Liz, with his dubious little smile.

'Yes,' Liz had said smartly, thinking she had indulged him far enough, 'and they had slaughtered one another with their bare hands too. With sticks and spades. And what about your hero, the charming and charismatic Pol Pot? He was probably living on champagne and caviare, while the slaves toiled.'

'Probably,' Stephen had conceded. 'Yes, probably. But we don't *know* that, do we?'

'I sort of think we *do*,' Liz had insisted, frowning over her coffee, dunking her little Italian macaroon.

'Anyway,' Stephen had said with gay bravado, 'perhaps I shall go and see.'

'You'd better be *careful*,' said Liz.

'Why should I be careful?' Stephen had more or less memorably said. 'I have nothing to lose. There is nothing to keep me here.'

And, looking back, as he rolls his little cigarette, he reflects that this was probably the moment at which what had been fancy had hardened into purpose. Everything had unrolled from there. And now he sits here, nearer but not very much nearer his goal, waiting for his soup.

Be careful, Liz had said. But he has nothing to lose. Except his life, except his life, except his life.

Stephen Cox's thoughts about human nature are deeply lonely. He is a lonely man, as you can at once perceive if you see him sitting there, his book propped up against his bottle of Singha beer, thinking visibly about the turpitude of man. Loneliness comes off him like a cloud of gnats. Yet he is a romantic figure, a mysterious and sympathetic figure, in his white suit. As he perhaps intends to be. He may be a rolling stone, but he does not look demented, dishevelled, dulled. An observer might well wonder (might well be intended to wonder) if the man in the white suit is not perhaps a person of distinction? And even as he sits there, he is approached by a young man much slung about with cameras and bags, who pauses at the corner of Stephen's table and says, 'Excuse me, but am I right in thinking you're Stephen Cox, the novelist? I'm most awfully sorry to intrude, but I just thought I had to say hello, and to tell you how much I've liked your books.'

Stephen, being human, is delighted. Such words are balm to one outshone in the Orient by Pett Petrie and Gore Vidal. He smiles, admits that he is, he thinks, himself, invites his new friend to join him.

His new friend is blond, tall, handsome, open faced, brown, with unfashionably long hair held back by a sweat band. He wears shorts and trainers and a khaki shirt. He has a gold chain round his neck. He sits down with Stephen, and tells him that he is a photographer and that he has just got back from the border camps. He too is staying at the Troc. His name, he says, is Konstantin Vassiliou.

*

Well, that *is* what I call a coincidence. A whole day full of coincidences. It makes you think, doesn't it? I mean, I hadn't heard *from* Stephen or *of* Stephen for years, and suddenly his name is everywhere. Suddenly Stephen is the buzz. The hot property. It won't come to anything, of course, but never mind, there might be an option in it somewhere. The first thing that happened was a call at seven fourteen this morning from a chap who said he was Marlon Brando, and I said do you know what time it is, piss off, but it actually *was* Marlon Brando his very self, and he was interested in the rights for Stephen's French novel. He went into this great spiel about how the bicentenary of the French Revolution was coming up and everybody would be making French Revolution films and didn't I think *Barricades* would make a wonderful movie and who had the rights and where was Stephen and could I give him some contact numbers, and I said Stephen was abroad but as far as I knew the film rights were negotiable, and to get in touch with Derry & Michaelis, and then I suddenly realized what he was on about and said but you know Stephen's novel isn't about the French Revolution at all, it's about the Paris Commune, and he said wasn't that the same thing, and I said oh I suppose so, sort of. But frankly the man's a fool. Of course it's not the same thing. Wrong bloody anniversary. Anyway, I left him to chase it up himself. I'll be interested to know if D. and M. claim to have had any recent dealings with Stephen.

Anyway, that early morning call stimulated me to ring Stephen's accountants again, but I was a bit more devious this time, I said I was a Miss Price calling from Customs and Excise about an irregularity in Mr Cox's returns, and they went away in a fluster and came back and said what was I talking about, he'd deregistered eighteen months ago. So I hung up, before they could retaliate with any tricky questions. But that was interesting, wasn't it? Perhaps I could embark on a new career as a detective.

I don't suppose it was exactly a coincidence that the man sitting opposite me on the tube on the way to Romley was reading *The Road to the Killing Fields*. After all, it was a best-seller, and a lot of people must have been reading it up and down the country, if sales and best-seller lists figures mean anything at all. (Which I'm told they don't.) There were a lot of spin-offs from that movie. Well, that's not quite fair, you could argue that the movie was a spin-off from some of the real-life stuff that's begun to come out of Kampuchea recently. Art and life, life and art. I wonder if Stephen saw *The Killing Fields*? Maybe it hadn't been released, when he left. Somebody rang me up the other day with an idea for a script about that Scottish fellow-traveller who got himself murdered in Phnom Penh in 1978. Malcolm Caldwell, was that his name? One of the last Westerners to see Pol Pot alive. I poured cold water on it, told him all that had been done, but in fact I don't think it has, and the more I think about it the better it seems as an idea. Ah well, we all make mistakes. He's probably sold it to Warner Brothers or David Puttnam by now.

This chap opposite me on the tube was an odd-looking guy. Not what you might call a reading man. Black leather, skull and crossbones on his T-shirt, earrings, punkish black hair. But his boots were the most scary. They had high heels and these weird silver metal square toes. Really kinky. I've never seen anything like them. Must have been custom-made. One couldn't help thinking his interest in the Killing Fields was hardly wholesome. But then, whose is?

The tube is hell. I hate it. But how else do you get to Romley?

Why go to Romley at all, you might well ask, and the answer is that I was on an errand of mercy to see my friend Angus who's filming *The Lillo Story* out there in a nice cheap warehouse. Well, mercy and business combined, to be honest, because I had a little proposition of my own to put to Angus. I'd hoped I'd get a nice lunch at the Caprice out of him, but he said no, he hadn't time, come and have a bacon sandwich in Romley, and you can have a look at the real Grace Lillo and tell me how to stop her annoying Sally Beeton.

Mercy, business and curiosity. I couldn't resist a look at the real Grace Lillo. You remember the Lillo scandal? Remember the Harrises, who abducted Grace Lillo when she was sixteen and kept her as a sex slave in a back room for three years in Sevenoaks, of all places? She wrote her life story, or rather she had it ghosted, and now Angus is turning it into a nice piece of cheap intense erotic British domestic 1950s claustrophobia, with every hair of every hairstyle and every gleam on the Formica, a period gem. The only problem is that Grace, now in her fifties, keeps wanting to come and watch the filming, and pesters Sally Beeton night and day with weird phone calls. Sally is playing Grace-chained-to-the-bedstead. Angus says Grace is dotty, which I must say wouldn't be surprising after all she'd been through. Apparently she was in love with both the Harrises. They'd completely brainwashed her. If *brainwashed* is the word.

I personally think Sally Beeton is a pain. Nor do I think she looks very 1950s. Sexy girls in the fifties still managed to look sort of clean and healthy, and Sally looks completely decadent. Those lips. Too much, really. Red Tory lips, I call them. Anyway, that's all beside the point. She can act, and she's beautiful, and she's box office, and she's only twenty-two, and she doesn't want to be pursued by obscene phone calls from her alter ego. I can see that.

I don't know what Angus thought I could do with Grace Lillo, and, as it turned out, I didn't get the chance to do anything as she didn't turn up. I watched an hour or two of boring retakes of a scene with Mrs Harris frying bacon in a sort of allusive Kitchen Sink manner, then I had a heart-to-heart for ten seconds with Sally, which was about all I could take, and then Angus and I slipped off down the road for a bite. I must say England's an odd country. Would anywhere else in the world have been able to invent the workman's caff? We had cheese and pickle and strong tea in those weird thick semi-translucent hardboiled-egg-white cups, and a chat about Firebird Holdings and pornography and *L'Histoire d'O* and suchlike matters, and I told Angus I'd had a phone call from Marlon Brando himself at the crack of dawn and how I'd told him to piss off before I realized it really was him and not some prankster, and he told me some similar tale about being invited to a party by Marlene Dietrich or was it Racquel Welch, and not going because he thought it was his mates having him on. Then we had another cup of shudder-making tea (you should have seen the chap serving, tragic, dear God, tragic, a chap with the shakes like that shouldn't be allowed near a teapot, poor old boy) and Angus told me about his budget most of which seemed to be going on Miss Beeton, and I said would he ever want to make a really exotic film in some desperate location, and he told me that he's heard that John Geddes had been frightened out of his wits in Peru because two British hikers had been assassinated by the Shining Path in the next village, and that he (John that is) was on his way home to Fulham Broadway. I asked if there was any news on the grapevine about Carlo's *Victory* script, and he said PDJ had got cold feet because of David Lean's *Nostromo*, which in his view would never get finished either. Or started, come to that. And then if I remember right we returned to the subject of Grace Lillo and Sally Beeton, and how strange it must be to have your own past self portrayed by some total stranger when you were yourself still alive and kicking. I don't know what the legal situation is, really. I mean, if somebody decided to make a film about Harriet Osborne, would they have to pay me for it? Could I stop them? Could I sell them my life? Is my life story a *property*, or does someone have to write it up first?

I think it was at this point that Cambodia came up. I said I'd seen this weirdo reading the *Killing Fields* book on the tube, and I asked Angus if he'd ever met Dith Pran, the real life hero, or come to that Haing S. Ngor who played Dith Pran in the movie. Dith Pran's a journalist and Haing S. Ngor isn't really an actor, or he wasn't until he made the film, he was a doctor of sorts, I think, and now he's a writer as well or at least a ghosted writer, and frankly his life and survival story is just as harrowing as Dith Pran's. They could make a movie about Haing S. Ngor and Dith Pran could play him. Except that obviously Dith Pran can't act, or he'd have acted himself, wouldn't he? Alter ego, ghost-person, shadow-self, which-is-the-hero, which-the-impostor. I could tell Angus wasn't really listening to my philosophical ramblings, even though they were highly pertinent to the problems he was having with Grace Lillo and Sally Beeton, because he suddenly interrupted me and said it was funny I'd brought up the subject of Cambodia, it was rather on his mind too, he'd had dinner the night before with an old school friend of his who'd just got back from Phnom Penh. From the White Hotel, *figure-toi*, in Phnom Penh. (I wonder what happened to *that* movie?)

I could tell that something was suddenly weighing on my old friend Angus's spirits so I went and got him another cup of tea and a Kit Kat and told him to tell. You should know that Angus, although he makes movies about erotic bondage, was once (well, maybe still is) a man with a conscience who wanted to make serious documentaries about housing estates and famines. The clue to Angus is that he went to a Quaker school. You need to know that. It explains a great deal. It certainly explains why unlike many movie men he was willing to spend an evening in a vegetarian restaurant being harangued by this woman who works for Médecins Sans Frontières. Angus didn't actually *say* that she harangued him, and I don't suppose she needed to. The contrast between Angus's glamorous life eating cheese sandwiches and Kit Kats out in Romley and hers living on boiled rice and boiled water in Kampuchea must have been telling enough without her pointing it out. As a matter of fact Angus clearly *did* have a lot of admiration for this woman, Marianne, and says he's kept up with her better than with anyone else from his school days. But that's not the point of the story. The point of the story, from *our* POV, is that she produced this portfolio of photographs for him, of life in the north-west, and of her field hospital, and Angus was stunned by them, and said who took them, and she said this young man called Konstantin Vassiliou. Angus said who is he, and she said she was going to ask him, because that was the kind of thing *she* expected *him* to know, but as far as she knew he was an English freelance photographer who'd won various photojournalism awards, and she'd like to catch up with him if she could.

Now the name Konstantin Vassiliou didn't mean anything to me until I saw it in Stephen's papers, where it appears quite a lot, particularly in the diary bits. But when Angus brought it up, naturally it caught my attention like a red flag. All I could get out of Angus was the info that he'd taken the photos a couple of years or so ago and that Vassiliou had been one of the nicest people Marianne had ever met in her life. He must have been *quite* nice or he wouldn't have sent her the photos. In my experience photographers are always promising to send photos to their victims and subjects, whose time they waste for hours on end, but out of sight out of mind and never do you hear a word or see a contact sheet from them again. They flash you, print you, fix you, sell you, and vanish. So young Konstantin had got past square one of niceness simply by sending the photos. And what were they like, what were they of, I wanted to know. Oh, amputees, cripples, people in a workshop making wooden crutches and primitive wheelchairs. Not very jolly. But great photographs, Angus said, great.

He found it hard to be more specific than that. He's not really a word man, our Angus.

He told me that Marianne at school had always wanted to study French and German, and had done just that, but then had gone off to some African country for the VSO for a year, and had come back and decided to be a doctor. She had to start from scratch, with Chemistry and Physics A-level. Dear God.

Being a photographer is a lot easier than being a doctor. Being a journalist or an actor is a piece of cake.

I thought I'd better try and get in touch with this Marianne, or with Konstantin Vassiliou himself. One or the other of them could surely give an update on Stephen. So I thanked Angus for the delicious lunch and packed him off to his warehouse, then I whizzed back on the tube to Primrose Hill and started with that elementary tool of research, the telephone directory.

Well, in the London phone book there are a dozen or so Vassilious, none of them with a K, and most of them living in the lesser known postal codes of North London, so I started with the more promising regions and drew a few blanks. But on my fourth or fifth attempt I got this woman's voice, from N22. Excuse me, I said, I'm trying to reach a photographer called Konstantin Vassiliou, do you happen to know where I can contact him? And *she* said, I only wish I did. So *I* said, you mean that is his number? And she said, no, not really, not any more. She said this in such a – well, I don't know how to describe it – such a sad but stalwart kind of way, not like an abandoned wife, anyway, that I thought in for a penny, in for a pound, and I said you mean it *used* to be his number, and she said, well, yes, I'm his mother. Then she asked what I wanted him for, and I said I was trying to contact a friend of his and mine, last seen in Bangkok, and she said that Konstantin was still out there but she hadn't heard from him for a long time. There was a sort of irritable motherly tremor in her voice as she said this, as though all were not well. Frankly, I didn't know what to do. I could hardly cross-question this total stranger, could I, especially as I'd no idea what to cross-question her *about*. So I said, sorry to have bothered you, and rang off. I think I left my name and number. Or rather Stephen's number. But I'm not sure. To tell the truth I was feeling a bit uneasy about the whole business.

The more I think about it, the more I think the name Vassiliou sort of rings a bell. Of course, if you think about any name for long enough you can make yourself think that, I know. But there really is some sort of echo. Wasn't there some scandal, back in the sixties, about a stolen baby? An heiress and a stolen baby? Or have I made it all up?

*

Konstantin Vassiliou and Stephen Cox, despite or perhaps because of the disparity in their ages, take to one another at once over their lunchtime beer and chicken. Konstantin, while modestly claiming not to be much of a reading man, expresses his admiration for Stephen's work. He is tentative and polite, as though aware that he may have captured Stephen off guard in deep incognito. Stephen responds warmly. There is something very pleasing, very disarming, about young Konstantin's manner. He looks as though he has modelled himself rather too consciously on some kind of Easy Rider, but his laid-back grace has a sweetness, an innocence, a deference which takes Stephen in and seduces him. If this young man is playing at being a hero, he is playing with finesse. He seems to know his way around the world. Stephen instantly sees in him a passport not only to the other Bangkok, the city which Miss Porntip disdains, but also to the frontier and the gates of horn.

And so it proves to be. Konstantin, settling back into his old rooms in the Trocadero annexe, invites Stephen up for a drink that evening. Stephen, leaving his bare dangling bulb and torn shower curtain, his grey bath mat and spartan bed and view of the cooling tower, makes his way along the corridor, up two floors, along another corridor, past a billiard table and a child's cot and various bundles of laundry and a plate of curry, and taps on Konstantin's door. Konstantin opens it upon a room that looks rather more like home than most of the pads that Stephen has, over the years, lightly inhabited. There are shelves of books, heaps of magazines, cushions, posters on the wall stuck up with Blu-Tack, a pot plant, a music system, glasses, bottles, a guitar, a typewriter, a rucksack, a small embroidered elephant, and other accoutrements of semi-permanent living. It is a young man's room, untidy, heaped, busy. Stephen settles into the corner of a settee, and begins to ask questions.

Konstantin claims to have been based in Bangkok for some months. He is a freelance photographer with a sort of semi-contract with Global International, or so he says. With fitting diffidence, when requested, he shows Stephen some of his work. There are landscapes, trees, temples, mountains, and shots of buildings both whole and blasted, but the majority of the pictures are portraits of people. Single figures, solemnly grouped families, children in a row. The tone is formal, grave, dignified. Peasants in Kampuchea, street people in Saigon and Hanoi, displaced people in the Thai border camps, refugees in Hong Kong stare a little reproachfully at the camera, in suspension, in a prolonged and questioning silence. Stephen gazes at the prize-winning portrait of Mme Akrun. It is a high-quality, 5 x 8 reproduction, without text. Here, she has no caption. She does not here ask, 'Where is my son?' She is silent. She speaks. She seems somehow familiar to Stephen, as she will seem also to Liz Headleand and, later, to Alix Bowen.

He pauses over her image, and is about to ask about her, when there is a knock at the door, and another visitor arrives and is greeted with a beer. Then another knock, and another visitor. News of Konstantin's return has got around. In his room they gather, the journalists and aid workers, the displaced people of the West, accepting beer and whisky and coffee, nesting down in corners and on cushions, exchanging news personal, news international, news trivial, news professional. Konstantin smiles and welcomes. He is the special friend with the open door. He is the special friend of everyone. The room hums with chatter and laughter, with light background music. Stephen is introduced discreetly, as Stephen from England. Mme Akrun, propped up on the bookshelf, watches them all.

These are by Stephen's standards young people, in their twenties and thirties. A Dane, two Americans, an Australian, a woman from Cheshire, a Japanese—Canadian. What has brought them all here? They tell tall stories, they boast and demur. They speak of dengue fever and Chomsky and Lacouture and Oxfam and broken gaskets. They speak of Thai Rangers and border passes and the Leper's Ball at the Siam Hilton. In-jokes, camaraderie, oneupmanship. It is a pleasant evening, an impromptu party. It makes Stephen feel a hundred years old. Casual drifters, hard workers. They gossip and drink and nod. As Stephen watches and listens and takes stock, he begins to recognize hotel habitués, familiar types and faces. That curly-haired fast-talking small bespectacled American, Jack Crane, surely he is the man glimpsed from time to time in the room on the second floor with the photocopier? And sombre Piet the Dane, the oldest of the group, he has observed drinking with a soldier in the bar. This is a society within a society. Shall Stephen join it? Is he acceptable? Does he carry the right cards? Will these people be of use to him?

When he gets up to leave, Konstantin follows him to the door, and lays a hand on Stephen's arm. It is an intimate, soft, placatory gesture, a pledge, an apology for the intrusion of others, a promise of more exclusive future meetings. 'I'm so very pleased to have met you,' says Konstantin, with impeccable good manners. 'Thank you so much for coming round.'

Stephen stands there in the doorway and smiles at his host.

'Thank you for inviting me,' he says.

Konstantin smiles, and brushes back his hair. His eyes are a very pale, light, clear grey blue. They insist on looking. They insist on eye contact. They instantly establish complicity. Why is this attention so flattering? The hand on the arm lingers into meaning, into a special relationship. Stephen allows himself to be enchanted. He is overcome. He submits. He departs to his dull and empty room.

The enchantment lingers, and Stephen, to his own surprise, finds himself watching and waiting for Konstantin and news of Konstantin. Konstantin is, it appears, a local hero. Stephen picks up allusions, rumours, Chinese whispers. Konstantin is a multi-millionaire. Konstantin is the most brilliant photographer of his generation. Konstantin has entered zones that none has ever penetrated. Konstantin has visited the secret base of the Khmer Rouge and photographed the mad wife of Pol Pot. Konstantin knows not fear. Konstantin is a mystic. Konstantin has the ear of kings and princes. Konstantin was left as dead on the battlefield and rose again.

Rumour speaks no ill of Konstantin. Stephen wonders at this marvel. Has he enchanted and seduced the whole of Bangkok's aid-worker society? Has he laid a hand on every sleeve? Or is it the free-flowing beer, the open door, that has subdued them all? To know Konstantin is a privilege, a blessing, a rare piece of luck. He spreads good fortune.

Konstantin's own version of the legends surrounding him is modest, prosaic, but none the less seductive. Over dinner one evening he admits to Stephen that he has private means and does not have to worry about money. His grandfather left him a small fortune, which was, says Konstantin, 'unsettling'. He had been unsettled, and had been through a period of profound depression, during which he decided he didn't care whether he was alive or dead and nearly got himself killed in Korea. 'It's quite easy to be a hero,' says Konstantin, ruefully, 'if you don't care if you die.' Recovering from the near-death and the depression, he took up Buddhism and photography, and now considers himself a properly reconstituted person, working more or less regularly as commissions come up in

South East Asia. He says he is particularly interested in Kampuchea. Why? Because he likes the Khmers so much. Because it's all such a bloody awful mess. Because it's there. Because I watched *Blue Peter* with my kid sister when I was still a kid myself. Because it's so difficult to get people interested in it these days. After all that excitement in '79, all that holocaust and famine talk, says Konstantin, now nobody wants to know. But I do, I still want to know.

Konstantin's answers to Stephen's questions are not very ideological. He is much less ideological than Miss Porntip or than Stephen himself. He seem to be a holy innocent, without side or guile. People gaze without fear into his lens and speak secrets to his receiving ear. Unlike Miss Porntip, he is a good listener.

Stephen does not mention Miss Porntip to Konstantin. He keeps her in another compartment.

Konstantin has a whole network of acquaintances in Bangkok. Stephen meets them, becomes part of them, pondering as he does so the way in which Konstantin keeps everybody happy. There are no outbreaks of jealousy or possessiveness, for everybody believes himself or herself to have Konstantin's own private personal attention. Stephen believes this himself, although he knows it cannot be true. Is it some sleight of hand, some trick? Or does this magic well from some more profound, more generous source? Stephen even finds himself buying a couple of books on Buddhism, as he searches for clues to Konstantin, but they are not very helpful, though he is quite taken with the imagery of *The Tibetan Book of the Dead*.

Stephen is half in love with Konstantin. Stephen tries to keep this to himself. It gives him pleasure to talk about Konstantin to Jack Crane, the American who works for the ICRDP (whatever that may be), and to Jack's friend Piet the Dane who works for the Red Cross tracing agency. They tell him stories about the border camps and the war. They both love Konstantin. He is a special person, says Jack Crane, a very special person. This is a phrase that usually infuriates Stephen, but he finds himself nodding in agreement. Why?

Konstantin and Stephen wander the streets and temples of Bangkok together. They take a trip upriver and Konstantin takes photographs of family groups in temple gardens while Stephen (very badly) sketches. They take a trip downriver to the port and see the great grey rust-patched ocean-going container ships from Hong Kong and Panama and Kingston, some of them inscribed with strange hieroglyphics, others with familiar script. The *Sang-Thai Breeze*, the *Sang-Thai Jewellery*, the *Crown Prince*, the *Manchester Reward*, the *Primrose*, the *Uni-Handsome*. They see old wooden junks and laden rice barges and children swimming by a banana grove. A woman smiles at them while washing her hair in brown river water. A red hawk circles above.

They chat to schoolboy monks about Mrs Thatcher and Madonna and Maradona, and they win virtue by presenting neatly packaged plastic buckets of offerings of rice and tinned milk and Ovaltine to older monks. They fly up to Chiang Mai for a few days to visit a monk who meditates on the death of the forest in a sacred grove of crape myrtle and mango and trees bearing emerald-green strychnine apples. They speak to the villagers in the valley below who imbibe the monk's doctrine and with their bare hands dig water courses to save the forest.

They play squash and swim at the Otis Club. They watch boys playing kites. They watch a parade and a firework display. They smoke, not very successfully, a little opium, and Stephen regrets, too late, his life of alcohol. Konstantin often lays his hand in friendship upon Stephen's arm or shoulder. It is an innocent romance.

Bangkok is full of diversions. Stephen wonders whether to acquire a tattoo, or to have the ancient wart on the ball of his foot removed. He and Konstantin stare in admiration and alarm at a poster which claims BY SKULL EXPANSION MY CHARACTER RADICALLY IMPROVED, and decline to have themselves checked out at the Chromosome Center.

They visit a wat to have their fortunes told. Konstantin shows Stephen how to shake the wooden box of wooden sticks until one falls out upon the temple paving. Stephen shakes and shakes but no sticks fall. His fortune is recalcitrant. Shake harder, says Konstantin, who is practised, whose thin numbered wooden fate lies neatly at his knees. Stephen shakes harder, and lo, three fates fall before him, a multiple destiny. He selects the one he thinks fell first. Konstantin tries to dissuade him, but Stephen, arbitrarily, insists. They take the little paper fortune slips from the little wooden drawers, and offer them to a bilingual monk for translation. Konstantin's is Number Thirteen, and it is a Golden Fortune. All will be good health and prosperity for Konstantin. But Stephen has insisted on Number Four, the Number of Death. His fate is deadly. It is Bad Time for Stephen, says the quizzical monk. Time of obstacles and sorrows. Time to Retreat.

Konstantin, displeased on Stephen's behalf by this incident, insists that they consult a proper fortune-teller, a wise old man with a placard which promises PAST, PRESENT AND FUTURE PREDICTED. Sweet and wrinkled, he tells them that they will undertake a dangerous journey, but will be led to safety by a good spirit. And on the higher steps of Wat Arun, the Temple of Dawn, they agree that soon they will travel together to the border. And, who knows, beyond. It is a pledge, an assignation.

Konstantin is Stephen's good angel. Miss Porntip is his bad angel. She does not let go easily. She senses she has a rival, and she reinforces her attack, inveigling Stephen with erotic little offerings and lecturing him the while on the triumph of capitalism. She appeals to his better nature by demanding English lessons, although she cannot concentrate on her conjugations for more than three minutes at a time, and will clearly never improve: they pick their way slowly through Conrad's descriptions of Schomberg's hotel, with its Japanese lanterns and its ladies' orchestra and its white mess jackets, and she tries hard to follow, but cannot find the patience, although she chose the book. Conrad is racist sexist swine, she says, aligning herself firmly and problematically with Chinua Achebe and other literary intellectuals. Is horrible. How can he make so bad man, so good girl? Why *Swedish* guy such good guy? Why *Swedes* so much hero? Why so much 'white men catering' talk? Everyone know white man food bad, Thai food extra good. Hamburgers, Coca-Cola, pizza is rubbish food. Noodles is good. Lemon grass is good. Prawn soup is good. All agree this.

Bobbing up from these deep waters, she tries to ingratiate herself by imploring him to stop calling her Miss Porntip and to start calling her by her pet name, her nickname, which is 'O'. 'Miss Porntip my given name,' she says. 'Is silly name. Here is common, but for English and Americans silly name. Here in Thailand we use pet name. My real name Porntip Pramualratana, but that difficult name. My friends call me O.' Stephen has not the heart to tell her that to him, corrupted at an early age by that anonymous French pornographic masterpiece, *L'Histoire d'O*, her pet name is far more seriously suggestive than her given name: he tries out 'O' occasionally, at suitable moments, but finds himself drawn irresistibly towards the Miss Porntip for more formal occasions. He finds the name, and her, entrancing.

Another new ploy is the jewel game.

She has a fine collection of gems and jewels, and she entertains Stephen by taking off all her clothes and adorning herself with trinkets. She languishes upon the marble floor with a ruby and diamond necklace about her throat, a ruby pendant in her navel, and a honey diamond dragonfly brooch pinned into her pubic hair. She sits watching television clad in nothing but pearl, ruby and diamond ear studs, a pearl and diamond tiara, with an emerald bracelet round her ankle. She prances off to make coffee, lit by a little shimmer of fiery stones. Stephen, admiring, comments that she looks a lot larger naked than dressed: the clothed Miss Porntip is essentially neat and diminutive, but the naked Miss Porntip is curved, rounded, womanly, important. She smiles, accepting the compliment.

But she is annoyed with him, mildly, for not taking more interest in the jewels themselves. Her gemstone vocabulary is extensive, and she speaks to him of parures and sautoirs, of marquise shapes and pavé cuts, of briolettes and baguettes and claws and carats and brilliants, of cabochon drops and stones set *en tremblant*. Her most hideous possession is a gold brooch, *c.* 1939, representing a little cottage with an open door and a large heart stuck clumsily on its side: the smoke is of diamonds, the garden blooms with sapphires and garnets. Proudly she tells him that it is designed as *une chaumière et un cœur*: what this is in English she does not know. She speaks no French. Is jewel talk, she says firmly, confidently. Her noblest piece is a diamond parure with variously cut stones of (she quotes) 'yellow, cognac, champagne and brown tint': she can gaze at these happily for hours, and even Stephen can see that they gain a certain glory when laid upon her pale brown belly. 'Lick, lick,' she says, and obediently he licks, and they quiver.

But he is a disappointing scholar. He cannot learn to tell the difference between Burmese and Siamese rubies, however hard he tries. He guesses Burmese, of a bracelet she dangles over the copy of the *Bangkok Post* he is trying to read, but she shakes her head impatiently. 'No, no,' she says, 'these poor Cambodian rubies, these cheapo rubies of Pailin.' He cannot distinguish a cultured from an uncultured pearl, or an aquamarine from an amethyst. You ignorant person, she tells him, as she strokes him with fingers covered in rings that look like the spoils of empires, though she claims they were purchased on the black market, quite above board, in Hong Kong.

'I love the jewels,' she says, as she caresses him and them. 'They living things, they my friends. They my children, my pets, my darlings.'

She says this to provoke and tease him. Sometimes he rises.

When he rises, she garlands him with gold.

When he tires of the jewels, she lures him away from thoughts of Konstantin with her library. Stephen is a rapid consumer of books, and Miss Porntip's gleaming electronically operated apartment is, surprisingly, well stocked with reading matter. She allows him to wander freely, although there is one locked cabinet which contains material not fit, she says, for his eyes.

Her books are classified not by the Dewey decimal system but by lover. Stephen browses now in the refugee section, now in the economics section, now in the section dealing with the strategy of rural counter-insurgency in Thailand, now amongst glossy brochures on the exploitation of the pineapple and the cabbage and the potato, and now amongst old Sotheby's catalogues. He reads about the ancient enmity of the Siamese and the Cambodian peoples, the ancient despising of the Vietnamese by the Khmer Krom. He discovers magazines of soft sexual porn from Pattaya and hard military porn from the Vietnamese war. Pert naked Thai women on tigerskins lie side by side with disembowelled Viet Cong women with rifles up their vaginas: the Thai general seems to have had a taste for both forms of abuse. They make Stephen feel a little sick. What worse atrocities can the locked cabinet conceal?

For light relief he turns to the film section, which is full of illustrated sanitized coffee-table books on Siamese dance and temple architecture and celadon pottery and flower festivals and elephant processions. They conjure up a grand, ersatz, Hollywood dream world, a City of Angels in which authentic details merge inauthentically into a vast, multi-faceted, kaleidoscopic, multi-ethnic, glittering exotic mirage of an oriental culture that never existed and never will exist. The dreams of the gates of ivory. Miss Porntip's film-maker lover had been engaged in making a high-kitsch costume adventure movie set in the seventeenth century about a talisman and a lost princess and a battle with the invading Portuguese. He had picked and dipped, and insinuated a ruby here, a silk there, a religious fancy from elsewhere, weaving a tapestry of nonsense to delight the surfeited youth of many lands. And why not, Stephen wondered, why not? Perhaps Miss Porntip was right. Perhaps a future in which brightly dressed, well-paid film extras lounged idly around on call and overtime eating ice-cream and maple syrup and king prawns grilled was greatly to be preferred to a future of ancient enmities, to guerrilla warfare and foxholes and redoubts and ditches and Kalashnikovs and mortal terror and famine and fear and hate and death?

The worlds at times overlap and intersect. Stephen Cox meets a Kampuchean refugee who is playing the role of a Kampuchean refugee in an American semi-fictionalized documentary about Kampuchean refugees. He meets extras who have worked on *The Killing Fields,* some of them survivors of the killing fields. He meets a cameraman who worked on *Apocalypse Now.* He meets a man in the Press Club who knows a man who knows Marlon Brando. He meets a Balliol man working for COER who was once President of OUDS and gave a great performance as Marlowe's Tamburlaine. He meets a man who has heard of a man who is conducting a drama school in the jungle with disaffected terrorists. Jungle Actor Number One Film Star Man. The gates of ivory, the gates of horn. The shadow world.

Miss Porntip, he has to admit, is more articulate than the charming Konstantin, even though she cannot speak English properly. And occasionally she consents to listen to him. One night he tells her (among many interruptions) about his mother. He tells her about the pink house in Somerset, with the purple Judas-tree in the garden, and the eels and apples. (He watches her mind flick to the exploitation of smoked eels and apple wine.) He tells her about his three brothers, those giants of his infancy, Francis, Jeremy and Andrew. How he had looked up, how he had admired, how he had been made to feel small. 'Little shitty pants' they had called him, in their boyish way. They had come and gone, from prep school and boarding school and college, with studded trunks and cricket bats and blazers and boots and books; bronzed, brazen, braying their schoolboy slang. He, the baby, had been left alone with his mother. How he had come to loathe the English countryside! How he had loathed his brothers!

His mother, stout and complacent, had tied him to her Mothers' Union apron strings. He had been a delicate child, and without love she had coddled him. He had been a solitary child, reading books to keep out of harm's way, playing patience and solitaire, collecting stamps, until packed off to the communal hell of prep school. His mother did not like friends in the house. Increasingly, she elevated the family as sanctuary. He was the child of her menopause. The Coxes ruled supreme in a nest feathered with family jokes, rituals, catch phrases, memories. All other families were ignorant, feckless, ill-bred, over-bred. The Coxes laughed at other people. They laughed at other people because they were not Coxes. His mother was frightened, increasingly frightened, of other people. His father, a country doctor who left home early in the morning and came home dutifully for his supper, said nothing. He quietly paid the bills.

His mother was red-faced, solid-salt-of-the-earth, bitter, bad-tempered, coy, immature, self-sacrificing, and deeply, deeply self-centred. She was deviousness incarnate. She managed to persuade herself and her neighbours that Moxley Hall and its disgraceful preparatory school were superior not only to all the local schools but also to Clifton, Ampleforth, Harrow, Eton, Rugby and Gordonstoun. She managed to persuade her boys that all girls were dirty and dishonest. Herself sexless and shapeless, she poisoned all hope and all fancy. How she had laughed at girls, with Francis, Jeremy and Andrew! How she had conspired with cakes and little sneers to trap them in their boyish juvenile world of mother-dependent greed and fear! Little Stephen, watching, had seen it all.

And he tried to explain it all to Miss Porntip, with some success. She was quick on the uptake.

'Your brothers all homosexual now?' she inquired, politely.

No, explained Stephen. That was not quite how it had worked. Two had married respectably, replicas of mother, and sent their offspring to Moxley Hall. They lived a life of gumboots and dogs and dances and pig ignorance. The third, Jeremy, had broken brilliantly away and ended up in gaol. Drugs had been his downfall.

'And you?'

'Oh, me. Me, I became an intellectual. That was my exit. I escaped through university.'

'And then through bad girls and wild women?'

Stephen acknowledged this.

'I can't stick it all together,' he said. 'Sex, politics, the past, myself. I am all in pieces.'

'Who can stick these things together? Why expect?' she demanded.

'But in *me*,' persisted Stephen, 'the gaps are so *great*. I am hardly made of the same human stuff. The same human matter. There is no consistency in me. No glue. No paste. I have no cohesion. I make no sense. I am a vacuum. I am fragments. I am morsels.'

She shook her head, worldly-wise.

'Is not unusual,' she said. 'Is normal. Is naturally or common matter.'

'The people I like I don't approve,' he persisted. 'The people I approve I do not like. The women I like I cannot love. The woman I love I cannot like. The life I seek I could not endure. I seek a land where the water flows uphill. I seek simplicity.'

'Is no simplicity. Is only way onwards. Is no way back to village. No way back to childhood. Is finished, all finished. All over world, village is finished. English village, Thai village, African village. Is burned, is chopped, is washed away. Is no way backwards. Water find level. Is no way back.'

'But it is heart-rending, heart-rending,' said Stephen Cox, crushing out his little cigarette in an enamel ashtray. 'All this waste. All this wasted possibility. All this suffering. All these dreams. All this cruelty. All these dead.'

'No, is not so. Is better now. Is better life expectancy, more electrics, more saloon cars, more soap, more rice, more nice clothings and suitings, more ice-cream, more maple syrup, more Coca-Cola, more cocktails, more Ovaltine, more champagne, more cassette players, more faxes, more aeroplanes, more Rolex watches, more perfumes, more satellites, more TV, more microwave, more word processor, more shower fitments, more motorbicycles, more ice boxes, more chips, more tampons, more tweezers, more fridges, more air conditionings, more cabinets, more musical, more confections, more bracelets, more prawns, more fruit varieties, more choice, more liberty, more democracy.'

'You believe that?'

She nodded, seriously. 'It never roll back now. Is finished. Socialism finished, simplicity finished, poverty finished, USSR and China and Vietnam all finished. Liberty, is all. Growth, is all. Dollars, is all.' She smiled, encouraging. 'Is good. Is better. Equality and fraternity is poverty and sickness. Is men working like beast, like buffalo. Is men killing one another like beast, like worse beast. Is no good, Stephen. Is finished. Is new world now. Is failed and finished.'

'So you offer me nothing but desolation and loss. You offer me nothing but heartbreak.'

'I offer you riches, I offer you choice, I offer you freedom. You can take, if only you choose. Forget old ideas. Choose.'

'No,' he repeated, forlornly. 'You offer me desolation and loss. You offer me stones.'

*

Konstantin Vassiliou tries to enlist the help of his new friend Stephen Cox with an idea for a book. He will do the pictures, Stephen can write the text. Konstantin already has interest from a publisher, and with Stephen's name the thing will be a piece of cake. Konstantin would be honoured. Please help. It will be a book about peaceful life, about the village. An anti-war book. *Bitter Rice*. The book that Robert Capa never made.

Stephen demurs. He thinks Konstantin is being naïve, but does not like to say so. He can hardly plead over-occupation as an excuse, as he has already lingered in the soft beds of the East for seven times seven nights with nothing to show for his sojourn but scribbles and sketches. But he does not like the idea of a picture book. He does not want to write the text for a book of glossy photographs of tragic people, even if the photographs are taken by his charming new friend. He has already turned down many offers to write texts and introductions to non-books. When he won the Booker, such requests had flooded in, and he had agreed, feebly, to write a foreword to an architectural guide to Paris Métro stations. This he had much regretted.

He regrets too that Konstantin has suggested something as banal as a book. Surely he should be above such things? He needs Konstantin to be the spiritual hero, not the cobbler-together of objects to put on Miss Porntip's glass-topped coffee table.

He protests that he is not good at that kind of thing. He is an *old-fashioned* book person. Konstantin, the man with the camera, is the man of the future, the coming man. Why does he not write his own text?

Konstantin shrugs and smiles disarmingly and says he cannot write. He says to Stephen, I write like you draw. Stephen laughs. But does not give a firm assent. They will go along together to the border, he agrees, and they will see what happens. Jack Crane will give them a lift to Aranyaprathet in the ICRDP van.

Stephen continues to wish that Konstantin had not stooped to a commercial proposition, although he continues to be flattered by his attention. For some reason, he wishes Konstantin to remain beyond reproach and pure in heart. He tries to quell his doubts about photojournalism. Why, as a trade, should it be any worse than his own? Is he himself, hanging around on the edge of events, a parasite, a maggot on dying flesh, is he himself beyond reproach?

Sean Flynn and Tim Page, in the Vietnam war, experimented with a camera that could be attached to a soldier's rifle so that when the gun was fired, it automatically recorded the death of its victim.

Sean Flynn vanished in Cambodia. He drove off, Easy Rider, on his Honda, and was never seen again. He left a legend, but no bones. Maybe he is still alive.

Konstantin insists that he is not a war photographer. I photograph survivors, he tells Stephen. I photograph life, not death. Stephen wonders if this is so. If it is possible.

Stephen, sitting in the Bangkok Press Club on the twentieth floor of a luxury hotel, sips a candiola juice, and sinks back into his deep armchair. He is evading the choice between Konstantin and Miss Porntip, between the light and the dark. He is reading a copy of *Asia Today* which informs him that most of Asia has leaped straight from illiteracy to the Visual Display Unit and has cut out the need for books. Stephen is a member of a threatened species. He is unnecessary. He reads that 'Peasants in remote hill villages who have never mastered the art of reading and writing are quite at home with the electronic revolution. They have bypassed Gutenberg.' He gazes at these words with incredulity. What fantasy world is this? Where do they find the electricity, in these remote hill villages? Do they all have their own generators? Are they not always in danger of storm or flood or guerrilla warfare or opium armies? Back home in the UK, in Good Time, Stephen has friends who have lost whole screenplays, whole novels, whole treatises on Wittgenstein into the unreachable limbo of their machinery. Are the hill peasants really that much smarter than his friends in Oxford and NW5?

Well, of course, judging by Miss Porntip, they may well be.

But what do they use their computers *for*, up there in the hills?

Are they calculating the yield per acre of garlic versus cabbage, the profits of King Prawn versus Queen Porn, or are they rewriting the Tragedy of the Ravished Maiden?

It is the quiet hour, *l'heure verte*, when the spirit sinks. Other solitary figures slump in the gloom. Television screens flicker, and there is a hum of fax and telex. Stephen still writes with pen and ink, with pencil, with ball-point pen. The electronic revolution may or may not have reached Miss Porntip's village, but it has certainly reached the Press Club of Bangkok.

The Khmer Rouge dispensed with the new technologies. They returned to people power, to bare hands.

Angkor had not been built, as the text books claim, by Suryavarman or Jayavarman or Indravarman or Hashavarman or any other Varman. It had been built by the bare hands of slave labour. By despised mountain people, nameless, known to history only as 'Dog', 'Cat', 'Detestable', 'Loathsome' and 'Stinking Beast'. They had laboured and they had died. (Or this is what Stephen, erroneously, thinks, but his sixties' Marxist scholarship is out of date: Dog and Cat had been in fact, we now believe, quite privileged people, whose pet names were perhaps adopted to ward off the evil eye. The true slaves remain – well, yet more deeply nameless and undistinguished.)

Democratic Kampuchea had not been built by willing patriots, by workers toiling to create a shared vision. It had been built by Dog Doctor, by Cat Teacher, by Rat Banker, by Detestable Clerk. They too had laboured and died, and no revisionist historian has yet rewritten their fate. The evil eye had beamed full upon them. Stephen Cox finds this disappointing. Who now will rebuild? No aid reaches Vietnam, no aid reaches Kampuchea. The Vietnamese cry out for American dollars. They are starving. They will withdraw from Kampuchea if aid is promised. They have had enough of proudly eating stones.

Over Stephen's head dangles a TV monitor, relaying American

newsreel of another explosion in Beirut, an explosion that camera-men have risked their lives to film. It is followed in rapid psyche-delic succession by photographs of an adopted child in Denver, bruised and battered by its middle-class parents: by famine in Mozambique: by a report of a new method of making calorie-free cream cakes.

Stephen is depressed. The green hour is very green. He sinks into its subaqueous wash. He is about to go under. Who will save him? And suddenly, there before him, smiling and extending a hand, is Simon Grunewald, ethnologist, homosexual and adventurer, exclaiming with his habitual eagerness, 'Stephen! I say, Stephen, is that really you? What luck!' Stephen knows that he is, if not saved, reprieved.

*

Liz Headland was invited to be one of the witnesses at the marriage of Esther Breuer and Robert Oxenholme. The marriage had followed quickly upon the limousine declaration. Robert, that night, had repeated his offer, and Esther had said, 'Yes.' Just the one word, 'Yes.' It had hopped out from her mouth, unexpectedly, like a toad or a diamond.

Liz was informed the next day. It was suggested that she, as party to the incident, as precipitating factor, would be blamed if the marriage were to founder. She took this as a compliment. She expressed her astonishment at length on the telephone to Alix, Aaron, Sally, Marcia and Charles. Who would have thought Esther would ever marry? Esther and Robert had assured Liz, Liz hastened to assure others, that they had no intention of having a very orthodox marriage. They did not intend to live together, or anything old-fashioned like that. Esther would continue to redecor-ate her Kilburn flat. But, nevertheless, married they would be.

Alix Bowen was not invited to the wedding, although she was forewarned. Esther, Liz suspected, suspected that Alix would not approve of Robert Oxenholme, and did not wish to expose him thus early in the day to her friend's fierce blue northern eye. After all, Robert was a Tory, and, although Alix had flirted with the Social Democrats, she had now returned to her roots. It would take a lot of social engineering to bring Alix Bowen and Robert Oxenholme comfortably into the same room.

The wedding was a quiet affair, without lilies, confetti, hymnals, or a seven-tiered wedding cake. It took place in North Kensington Register Office on a Thursday morning. The other witness was Robert's half-brother Simon Grunewald, invited on the principle that as he spent most of his time abroad with the head-hunters of New Guinea he would not be much of a trouble to the Oxenholmes in the future. The autumn sun of a fine Indian summer shone auspiciously, and the bride wore green and ivory striped silk Indian trousers from Mysore, topped with an ivory Cacharel shirt from Liberty's. The groom wore grey trousers, a yellow shirt, a white jacket and a pink tie. Both parties sported untidy button holes provided by the Best Woman from her own garden. The wedding breakfast was taken in Liz's garden also, where the four parties sat round a little white wrought-iron table drinking champagne and eating cold trout with dill and mustard. It was unseasonably hot. The sun beat down fiercely, and the bride had to put a table napkin on her head to keep off the glare. The groom and his half-brother wore dark glasses. Liz wore an old panama hat.

The conversation was not at all suitable for a wedding breakfast, for Simon Grunewald hijacked it. He insisted on describing in vivid detail the appalling habits of his friends in Irian Jaya. Liz tried at first to steer him towards something more seemly – the garden's glories, the Glory of the Garden, the newts in her pond, the unlikely couple's prospective honeymoon journey to the grouse moors of Ballinluig – but was routed by the loquacious Grunewald, who chattered on about ringworm and elephantiasis, about rotting corpses and embellished skulls, about nose ornaments and the ritual exchange of semen, about homosexuality and *mariages à trois*, and about the proud day when he ate a putrefying morsel of the brains of the grandmother of his friend and lover, the thrice-bangled killer Assaji. He describes the Bone House and the cassowary. Liz, pouring a little more double cream on to her gooseberry fool, and nibbling a thin vanilla biscuit, had been unable to resist these exotic revelations, and in the end abandoned all attempts at decorum as she quizzed Grunewald about his exploits in the wild. The newlyweds sat quietly in the sun in St John's Wood like two sleepy cats, as Headleand and Grunewald ran riot up the rivers on the far side of the world, to the music of a neighbouring lawnmower.

'But tell me,' said Liz, an hour later, addressing herself now to the Honourable Robert, 'this brother of yours that you've produced so unexpectedly, is he a fantasist, or is all this the truth he tells us?'

'Eh? What? Sorry?' said Robert, who had tilted his chair back and nodded off behind his shades.

'Of course I'm not a liar,' said Grunewald. 'I'm an ethnologist. Sort of. I've written a book. I'll send you a copy.'

'No, he's not a liar, he's a collector,' said Robert. 'He goes out there and beds down with the natives and buys their precious artefacts and paddles back down the river and sells them to the Museum of Mankind and the Metropolitan.'

'Truly?' asked Liz, of them both.

'Well, the artefacts are real enough,' said Robert. 'I've seen them. They must come from somewhere. Paddles. Daggers, spirit masks. If he makes them himself, he's even cleverer than he claims.'

Simon smiled, blinked, sneezed.

'Why have I never heard of you?' Liz demanded.

'Better to keep quiet, in my line of business,' said Simon.

'He's a pirate,' said Esther, emerging from her siesta.

'And anyway,' said Simon, 'I'm not totally unknown. Some people have read my book. It got quite a good review in the *New York*

Review of Books. And . . .' (he searched for further identification) 'and I know a friend of yours. Stephen Cox. I met him while I was on my last trip.'

'Stephen? You met Stephen? Up a river in Irian Jaya with the cannibals?'

'No, certainly not. I met him in the Press Club in Bangkok.'

'Really?'

'Yes, really.'

'And how long ago was that? And what was he doing?'

Liz feels she is on the verge of illumination. But the news is old, the trail is cold. Simon Grunewald frowns, calculates, and says, tentatively, 'A couple of years, perhaps? A year and a half? I was on my way out, on my last trip.'

'And what was *he* doing?'

'I think he said he was on his way to Phnom Penh. Or was it Hanoi? Somewhere in that direction.'

'And what was he doing in the Press Club?'

'What *does* one do in the Press Club? He was having a drink and a gossip and watching TV.'

'And you're a friend of his?'

'Oh, I wouldn't say that. We've met a couple of times. But out there, you know how it is, one gets chatting.'

'And what did you chat *about*?'

'Head-hunting, of course.' Simon had the grace to laugh at himself. He always has the grace to laugh at himself. Like his half-brother Robert, he is a graceful man. He is a handsome, Semitic caricature of Robert, product of Robert's mother's third marriage to a delicatessen-owner from Stoke Newington.

'Yes, we talked about head-hunting. Which led us on, as I recall, to the question of our friend Esther's lodger. The decapitator. The infamous Paul Whitmore.'

'He wasn't my lodger,' murmured Esther, for the record, but only the lawnmower paused to hear her.

'And he told me the story of how you and Esther were besieged by the police. It was, I have to admit, a good story.' Simon nods, one good storyteller paying respects to another, then continues, with a gallant narrative salute, 'Little did I think then that the famous Esther Breuer would become my half-sister-in-law. On this splendid sunny afternoon.'

They all smile, politely. Esther yawns. She is beginning to think she has had enough of her own wedding party and the engaging Simon. A little of him, as Robert had warned her, goes a long way. But Liz is not ready to let the subject of Stephen Cox drop. She knows that at any moment she is going to be compelled to produce her package. The Text, the Sacred Text.

'How *was* Stephen?' she wants to know.

Simon shrugs. 'Fine. Fine. Haven't you seen him lately?'

'Nobody's seen him,' says Liz. 'He's vanished. You are the last person to have seen him alive.'

She now gets Simon's sudden attention, though Esther and Robert are on their way out.

'Oh, really?' he says, looking a little alarmed by this new light.

'What was he *wearing*?' Liz demands.

'He was wearing a white suit,' says Simon, promptly. 'Just like on his book jacket. He looked just like that photograph. It's a Snowdon, isn't it?'

Liz is half satisfied.

'And what was he *drinking*?' she then wants to know.

'Is this an interrogation?' asks Simon. 'What happens to me if I get it wrong? Do I go to gaol?'

A menacing robin advances upon them, its head on one side. Liz throws it a placatory scrap of bread.

'He was drinking,' continues Simon, with defiant panache, 'a gin and candiola juice.' Then truth gets the better of him (for he is, despite all appearances, a scrupulous narrator), and he adds, 'At least, I *think* it was candiola juice.'

114

'What on earth is candiola juice?' Liz, momentarily diverted, wishes to know.

Simon begins to explain. Their wedding out of all control, Esther and Robert slip quietly away. They nearly forget to take with them the ill-wrapped newspaper parcel that Simon had dumped upon a window ledge at North Kensington Register Office. Murmuring thanks, backing quietly out of the garden, clutching their wedding present, they humbly make their escape.

*

Liz and Simon Grunewald stare at the finger bone. Simon, expert in bones, says confidently that it is not Stephen's for it is far too small. He thinks it is a ritualistic bone. He pokes around amongst the plastic wrappers, listening to Liz's explanations and speculations. He does not seem to be very interested in Text. He demands to look at the original brown paper wrapping, at the broken seal and the original stamps. Liz produces them from the video box with a feeling of slight guilt: she had meant to examine these more carefully herself, but the very idea of philately bores her to distraction and she has hardly given them a glance. Simon is not bored by philately, and he inspects them with a lively curiosity, producing from his pocket a small lens, which, he explains to Liz, is an essential tool of his trade.

The postmarks are illegible, but there is a blurred red-stamped message in an unknown script. There is a colourful array of stamps: three large, three small, stuck untidily at angles. Simon stares at them 'Fascinating,' he says, 'fascinating.'

'What's fascinating?' says Liz, intrigued by the way Simon has latched on to the dullest part of the whole mystery.

'Well,' says Simon, 'these *are* an odd lot. What does that look like, to you?'

Liz, who has not bothered to give the stamps a very close inspection, takes the lens and peers.

'Well,' she says, 'if I didn't know better, I'd have to say it looks like Prince Charles and Princess Di. A slightly oriental Prince Charles and Princess Di.'

'Exactly. A commemorative stamp. And look, this is a 1984 Correggio madonna and child. Plus two cattle egrets, a Hispano-Suiza and a view of Angkor Wat. Kampuchean, definitely Kampuchean. That's where this was posted. I didn't know they did a Charles and Di. The North Koreans did a beauty, you know. A real beauty.'

Liz stares at the stamps with a new respect. Her ignorance in this field is so total that she does not mind admitting to it. So after a pause she ventures, 'Well, I can understand the cattle egrets, they're quite sweet, aren't they? And Angkor Wat. (Is that an *aeroplane* flying over Angkor Wat?) I mean, they *are* all local. But I really don't get the others. Why on earth Correggio?'

'It was his anniversary,' says Simon, as though this explains everything. '1984, the 450th anniversary of his death. Lots of countries did commemorative stamps. The Hispano-Suiza's probably commemorative too.'

'But,' says Liz. 'I thought the country had been reduced to mud and rubble. I thought people were starving. I thought Angkor Wat had vanished back into the jungle. And you tell me they go on producing stamps to commemorate European artists who painted Christian religious motifs 450 years ago?'

'People will produce stamps through anything,' says Simon.

Then he pauses, rethinks, and says, 'Well, almost anything. As a matter of fact I don't think the Khmer Rouge *did* produce any. I think they cut out postage altogether. Along with hospitals and banks and shops and discos and foreign embassies. I'm not sure they printed any stamps at all. I'd have to look it up. But then, when the Vietnamese took over, they got things going again. Most people keep the postal services going. The Khmer Rouge were very extreme, you know. Probably still are.'

'Yes,' says Liz. 'I do know. So you're quite sure this package was posted from Kampuchea itself?'

'Well,' says Simon, 'almost sure. They're a nice set of stamps, anyway. Collector's items. Don't lose them, will you?'

*

Back in Esther's flat in Kilburn, Esther and Robert cautiously begin to unpack the clumsy parcel with which Simon Grunewald has burdened them.

'It's probably some ethnic object made of sago palm and human spittle and pig dung,' says Robert, with amused fraternal pride.

But it is not. It is a round Italian majolica dish, portraying Romulus and Remus suckled by their wild mother, in a pastoral landscape of painted greens and blues and golden yellows. A water god with a fish tail and a trident pours forth the Tiber from an urn. Little fishes swim in the rippling shallow ceramic waves. Robert and Esther gaze at it, then Robert, even more cautiously, turns it over, taps it, gets out his lens, inspects it more closely.

'Urbino?' he hazards. Esther nods.

'1531,' Esther remarks, less hazardously, for the date is inscribed for all to read.

'Oh dear,' says Robert.

'But it's beautiful,' says Esther.

'Oh yes, it's beautiful all right,' says Robert. 'And what one might call appropriate, for two Renaissance buffs like us. Very thoughtful of him. It's not the object that worries me. It's the provenance.'

'Oh,' says Esther. 'I see.'

She picks up the dish and gingerly touches its fine glaze.

'Perhaps,' she says hopefully, 'it might be a fake?'

'Not a chance,' says Robert. 'Just look at it. Not a chance.'

And they gaze at the river god and the wolf and the babes.

'I must say,' says Esther, 'the Renaissance really *was* rather a good period, wasn't it? I mean, I'd *rather* have that than a decorated skull or a pig's bone. Wouldn't you?'

'Yes, indeed,' says Robert. He puts his arm round her shoulders.

But seven hours married, are they already incriminated receivers of some £50,000 worth of stolen goods? Surely not. Perhaps Simon had picked this piece up for a song in a dusty antique shop in Penang or Shanghai, and had decided to present it to those whose eye deserved it? Perhaps Simon is madder and more generous and fonder of his brother than even Robert has suspected? Perhaps Simon is, quite simply, rich beyond Robert's wildest dreams? There is big money to be made from ethnic artefacts these days, and maybe Simon has cornered the market?

The river god smiles at his own bounty.

*

Stephen Cox and Simon Grunewald in the Press Club of Bangkok had discussed Simon's quest for the Noble Savage of Irian Jaya and Stephen's for the ignoble Khmer Rouge of Cambodia. They discussed the brotherhood of man. Simon described the extreme simplicity of the lives of the people he loves. They have fire and fish and sago palm and wood, but, although they are of the Stone Age, they have little stone, and what they have is imported. They have no minerals, no salt, no metal. Oil drilling has brought them violence and corruption. His people still hunt heads and eat their neighbours. They have eaten some of the oil drillers. They probably ate Michael Rockefeller, who disappeared in 1961. And serve him right, in Simon's view.

Logging is also a problem. The men do not want to chop trees and log for low wages, but they are terrorized, he said, by Indonesian slave traders. Just because they are jungle people with nose bones, these Indonesians think they can boss them about, said Simon, with a kind of buoyant boyish pathos.

'The Khmers,' said Stephen, 'are said to think themselves inferior to other Indo-Chinese people because they have darker skins. So

THE GATES OF IVORY

the books say. Even the Khmer books say so. Can it be true? Can we have got no further than that?'

'We don't want to get *further*,' said Simon, accepting another drink. 'We want to go *back*.'

They discussed the notion of progress and the cycles of history and its tragic empires rising and falling. My people are innocent savages, claimed Simon. They harm no one.

'They kill and eat one another,' said Stephen.

'Well, so what?' said Simon. And they both laughed.

'Eating people is wrong?' suggested Stephen. His words lacked conviction.

'Look around you,' said Simon, histrionically, 'look at this room full of sharks and spongers and liars and cowards and scoundrels. The gentlemen of the press. Are they any better than my lot? Are *you* any better? Am *I*?'

They spoke of Conrad. 'Now Conrad *was* a racist,' said Simon. 'He did not understand the savage mind. Or the savage body.'

'And do you *really* sleep with a cannibal?' asked Stephen, delighted by this adventure and this adventurer.

'Indeed I *do*,' said Simon Grunewald.

They moved on to the subject of ceremonial decapitation and Stephen, as Simon was later to recall at Esther's wedding, produced the story of Paul Whitmore. Both agreed that Paul's desires were aberrant. Still talking, they walked out into the dark warm night. Simon insisted that *his* people's desires were normal. 'There's nothing I'd like more,' he said, wistfully, 'than to take part in a head-hunt. You can't believe the thrill. The colours, the paint, the dancing. The ferment. They are all part of one another. It was like that when the world was young.'

*

Stephen has his pass from the military. He has dined at the embassy, and been indirectly briefed. It is his last night in Bangkok. Walking back towards Miss Porntip's, he observes a small commotion down a narrow side street, and pauses to look. There is much laughter, cameras, flashes. He approaches. It is a street of moderately ill repute, with a nightclub or two and a massage parlour. A knot of bystanders surrounds a pool of unnatural brightness. A camera crew is making an advertising film. Stephen is drawn towards the circle. He watches, appalled.

A scantily clad young dancer is holding by the arm a monkey. The dancer is wearing a jewelled bikini and a jewelled pagoda head-dress and high-heeled shoes. The monkey is wearing a short blue dress and red jewelled belt, and its hairy face is made up with white and blue eyeshadow and rouge and lipstick. It is standing on its hind legs, clutching a syrup-daubed microphone. The dancer is encouraging the monkey to lick the microphone. The monkey thus will give a passable photographic imitation of a nightclub singer. Cameras whirr, cameras click. Stephen stares. Around the monkey's neck is a collar and chain, cunningly disguised as necklace and beads. A poor beast in bondage. The dancer tugs at the monkey, to make it stand erect. The crowd giggles. The spectacle is obscenely, trivially distressing. The hairy legs and arms, the pink almost-human ears, the seductive pose, the almost-human appeal in those humiliated large-brown-dark-irised anguished eyes. You can't *do* that to an animal, is Stephen's first thought, to be followed instantly by its shadow, You can't *do* that to a human being. The girl and the monkey prank and ape and pose. By brothel standards, this is child's stuff, innocent stuff, and the girl is indeed little more than a child. Disgust and nausea well up in Stephen. Monkeys and girls, girls and monkeys. Where is the natural woman, where the man? Nose bones, penis sheaths, cassowary quills, shells, tattoos, face powder, rubies, emeralds, lipstick, unguents, paints and pastes and creams and lotions. Hattie Osborne and Molly Lansdowne and Simon Grunewald rise before him, Miss Porntip rises before him, his cruel stout unpainted mother rises before him. Stephen begins to sweat as he stands there in the street in the mocking crowd, in the hot, busy, narrow, noodle-serving street. A smell of mouse assaults him, a thick sweet smell of mouse. *Homo erectus*, ape *erectus*, sucking on a big black sugary phallic microphone in the city of angels.

Stephen staggers back to Miss Porntip and tells her about the monkey. She tells him he is drunk, he has drunk too much of the embassy's good French wine. He continues to rave about the monkey. She tells him the English are stupid about animals. He says this is not the point. She says English love animal more than human, what matter one monkey. He says what matter one person, any person, all humanity, what matter the whole boiling. She tells him to come to bed and sleep it off. He says he is going back to the Trocadero where he belongs, and will dally here no more. In the morning he is off, perhaps for ever. She says, beware well-known Thai proverb, 'Keep not cobra, monkey and diamond in one house.' He says, what the hell does *that* mean, but she cannot or will not say. She tells him he is dreamer and sentimental person who does not like real world. He tells her she is not real world, she is Cleopatra and Circe, and he is on his way with Konstantin Vassiliou to the *real* real world. In short, they quarrel, in so far as one can quarrel with a woman who does not speak proper English. Stephen goes back to the Trocadero and vomits her up. He leaves her and Bangkok and the Land of Never Mind and Mai Pen Rai for ever. He leaves her and sets out into the wilderness. He departs for the Promised Land, from which no traveller returns.

*

The Red Road

The dry red road unrolls. Peasants in limpet hats stoop over pale green fields in the early morning light. Beyond the fields is sketched a fringe of deeper and deeper green. Shiny decorated tin lorries make their way back from market. A child perches on a water buffalo. A boy chases a gaggle of geese. An egret stands hunched on one leg. A house perches on stilts. A water-lily swims on palest heavenly blue. A girl walks by the dyke's edge with a basket. A gold-fronted leafbird sings. An old man sits on a cane stool by a tamarind grove. A woman dips water from a large stone jar. Yellow flowers blossom by a creek. The land grows drier as we travel to the east. There is no way back to the village. There is no way back.

*

The red road to Aranyaprathet is a good road, better than the roads of India and Africa, better than the rutted red deep lanes of rural Somerset. The Americans and the UNHCR have spent money on these roads, and now relief workers travel regularly along them to the stranded victims of Pol Pot. The ICRDP van makes fair progress, although the driver likes to stop every hour or so for a snack. Jack Crane and Piet and Konstantin recount to Stephen plain tales of the border. There has been heavy shelling in one of the camps. The Khmer Rouge are hiding their casualties. They will not admit the agency workers.

The landscape on either side of the road looks peaceful, rural, eternal. It is hard to imagine violence. But slowly Stephen becomes aware that they are entering a new zone. There are fewer farmers, more soldiers. Stephen had seen soldiers on parade in Bangkok, toy soldiers dressed in canary yellow and apricot and powder blue and emerald green and shocking pink, with plumes in their helmets. But these are real soldiers, in khaki and camouflage, in tanks and lorries.

There are road blocks, inspections of passes. Stephen's indecipherable documents prove acceptable. He is glad to be in the company of men who know their way, with a driver who speaks Thai.

They stop for yet another snack. Stephen is not hungry. He gazes with displeasure at bowls of soup with little pale knobs of meat and bone. He rejects Coca-Cola. Stephen abhors Coca-Cola, and not only on ideological grounds. The sickly sweet fizzy liquid nauseates him. Crane and Piet and Konstantin and the driver drink theirs with pleasure. Stephen momentarily, guiltily regrets the sophisticated tastes of Miss Porntip, who in practice had shown a proper contempt for the stuff: though in theory, of course, she approved it. Is there a country in the world where Coca-Cola is not king? Stephen still nourishes hopes of Kampuchea and Vietnam. Stephen deserves to die of thirst. But he will not die for a while yet.

They arrive in the hot middle of the afternoon, at a group of wooden buildings outside the town by the side of the long straight highway. A board with handpainted lettering announces the ICRDP, an acronym which, as Stephen has at last learned, stands for 'International Committee for Resettlement of Displaced People'. Vans with the same lettering stand in a courtyard. A middle-aged Thai wearing a smart well-pressed cream semi-uniform suit comes out to greet them, shakes hands, smiles. Yes, he says, there is room for a visitor.

Stephen's room is small, simple, barely furnished, but clean and cool. A camp bed, a neatly folded blanket, a sheet, an electric fan, a wardrobe, a chair, a table. A Thermos of water, a mosquito net. Stephen lies on his bed and writes his diary.

In the evening they meet in the courtyard for a beer. Young men play table tennis and call and laugh. A transistor plays pop music, Western style, in the background. Piet has acquired a field radio, and speaks into it from time to time. They discuss the shellings, the moves and counter-moves of Khmer Rouge and Vietnamese. Stephen's presence is accepted without question, for this place is full of migrants. Reporters, photographers, politicians, UN officials, observers from other agencies come and go. The displaced people complain they are visited, fed and watered like animals in a zoo.

They take the van into the little town for a meal, and make a table with Piet and another group of Jack's acquaintances. Another Dane, a Swede, a Swiss, an Italian, and an English woman in a yellow Aertex shirt. They continue to talk politics and camp gossip. A certain mild competitive machismo emerges: who has stuck it out longest, risked most, had the worst illness, been nearest to death? Piet is silent, Crane talkative, Konstantin mediates. Stephen feels at

a great remove. What are they playing at, these workers for the
world? What has driven them from their own countries to this
outpost? Why are they sitting here eating noodles when they could
be making money in Hamburg or Gothenburg or Singapore or
Kuala Lumpur?

Were they out of step with their age, all of them, a ragged
hangover from the past, emotional cripples, nostalgic dreamers of
dreams, born out of their true time? Do they not know that the
sixties are over? (Konstantin's hairstyle suggests the possibility of
such an oversight.) Have they been unable to adapt to the eighties?
They are evolutionary casualties, huddled together for comfort, for
an illusion of purpose, while the powers and superpowers play their
ruthless, merciless, muddled, indifferent games. On the border, two
hours' drive away, are the camps of the displaced Khmers. Here in
Aranyaprathet are the camps of the displaced West.

Stephen sips his acrid tea.

Oxfam, UNBRO, ICRC, ICRDP, UNHCR, UNICEF, WHO,
FPP, FHH, WR, COER: these acrimonious acronyms cluster like
flies round the wounds of sick nations. The missionary, the priest
and the lady with the lamp have given way to the relief worker and
the photojournalist and the television reporter.

Capitalism and competition have triumphed, religion has withered
away, and there is no longer any place in the West for self-sacrifice,
dedication, brotherly love, compassion, community. In the sixties, it
had seemed that the West would soon be sated, that it would fall
sick of its own greed and glut. The agencies whose representatives
now clustered round Stephen had been founded to cure this excess,
to redress the balance, to purge the system and lance the deadly
swelling, to level the food mountains and to shake down the
superflux and to spread around the good things of the earth. But it
had appeared that they had all been misguided. They had acted on
false premises. For there was, it had turned out, no superflux. There
was no limit to man's greed. He could eat and eat and swell and

THE GATES OF IVORY

swell and yet want more and more. This was the lesson of the eighties. Avarice and greed have no natural limits. Man can eat on and on and never burst. His appetites demand rarer, more exotic fruits, fruits shaped likes moons and suns and stars and fishes, fishes shaped like fruits, and still he eats on and on. Appetites have no natural limit. They cannot be sated. There will never be a point at which men agree they have enough, and that the other lot can have the leftovers for free. The devil will always take the hindmost. This is what makes man great. This is what radiates the candiola, this is what sends him to the stars.

Stephen stares into his soup bowl as he contemplates this parody of progress. From the little town through the warm air drifts the sound of music, the hum of television, the buzzing of Isuki and Toyota and Nissan and Mitsubishi. Birds peck in hooped cages in the night market, and photocopiers and cuckoo clocks and Ritz crackers and US washing powder and processed cheese and Snoopy dogs and many varieties of ice-cream are on sale.

Is it common purpose or common disability that unites the members of this little band of workers? If he gets to know them better, will he distinguish in them the rapid speaking, the stammering, the displaced eye movements, the displaced egos, the bitten nails, the bitten words, the warts of the spirit that have driven them from their own countries to this border town? How can they be willing, after the Death of God, to spend their life against the grain, fighting against human nature, shoring up the impossible, trying to make water flow uphill? They do not seem to be here for death or glory, for their names on a byline, for their faces in front of the camera, for the hope of a Pulitzer Prize. They are not here for the money. What *are* they up to, here?

He finds his attention detached from its wanderings by the woman in the yellow shirt. She tells him she speaks Khmer, and is one of the few Westerners here to do so. She offers to give him an hour or two of her time in one of the camps. He accepts, gratefully, as yet unaware of the generosity of her offer. They make a date for the morning.

Her name is Helen Anstey. She is big, large-boned, red-complexioned. Her features are broad but shapeless, and her eyes are small. She is a plain potato-faced woman, the other end of the female spectrum from Miss Porntip and Hattie Osborne. Is this why she learned Khmer and now spends her time teaching teachers to teach the ever-growing camp population of small infants?

No, it is not, as Stephen learns on the way to Site Ten the next day.

Helen Anstey is the daughter of one of the most famous British fellow-travellers of the 1930s, the Marxist historian Michael Anstey. Stephen had briefly been taught by Michael Anstey, had attended his lectures at Oxford. He does not realize the connection immediately but it gradually comes upon him as Helen drives briskly along the red road in her muddy Isuki. The whiskers, the over-red lips, the spluttering enunciation, the open-necked shirts, the mottled bald head, the white chest hair, the dramatic forensic gestures begin to assemble, to form a floating mental representation (not unlike that of a descending Old Testament God) of the Grand Old Man as Helen recounts the adventures that have brought her to this place: and by seven a.m. (for they made an early start) Stephen is able confidently to accuse her of being her father's daughter.

She agrees that she is. Stephen admits that he had known him. Is this a coincidence? No, it is not.

The old man's passion is what brought them both here. It is because of his faith and his delusions that they find themselves sitting together on their way to a Displaced Persons' Camp.

Michael Anstey had been notoriously deluded. He had been an apologist for Stalin, a blind friend of the Soviet Union, long after most of his colleagues had admitted that all was not well in their chosen land. He had sworn that black was white and that red was green. By the time Stephen met him, in the 1950s, he was already

126

discredited in the academic world, but he had such bravura, such panache, such conviction, that he had managed to sail along proudly with a certain tattered glory. He was big enough never to appear small. Physically big, and grand of opinion; wrong, but magnificently wrong. Nobody could accuse Michael Anstey himself of self-seeking, of double-dealing, of the murder or betrayal of enemies. He was loyal to the death. He was, simply, wrong. He had got it all wrong.

Being the child of such a figure must have presented difficulties. Helen Anstey embodied them.

She had studied Russian, predictably, then less predictably had moved into oriental languages, six years at SOAS. Vietnamese, Cambodian. She had also learned a little Laotian from a private tutor. This much she confided to Stephen.

They do not discuss the old man's politics. They do not discuss their own politics. Yet here they are, exorcizing ghosts, repaying debts, settling old accounts, as they drive along beneath the rising sun. Freud would have had more to say to them, perhaps, than their more obvious begetter, Father Marx.

Add the glue of old white-whiskered Father Anstey to the Mother Glue of that senile old woman gazing unseeing at the Quantocks. Stick Stephen Cox back together again.

Helen and Stephen talk of other things, once the cord that joins them has been identified and acknowledged.

She tries to brief him about life in the camps. She repeats things he has heard before from others, things he has read in the *Bangkok Post*, but her perspective is her own, and he finds it sympathetic, familiar. As he would. She is one of the great army of the faithful disillusioned. How old is she? Younger than himself, older than Konstantin. The illusions that she has lost are those that had inspired him. They have reached the same point from different directions.

She speaks of the violence in the camps, the disaffected young. She speaks of the high birth rate. 'Though that,' she says, 'is a good sign, despite all the problems. There was a time when it seemed that a whole generation would be barren. You heard about the Women's Sickness?'

Politely, he shakes his head: although, of course, he has heard.

In the great displacement of the Pol Pot regime, she tells him, many women had ceased to menstruate. There seemed to be more at work than malnutrition. A death wish? A psychic disturbance? It hadn't seemed all that odd to her. If he'd heard some of the stories she'd heard from survivors, he'd be amazed that most of them functioned as well as they did. *I* used to go irregular just through worrying about examinations, says Helen, laughing heartily at the idle memory.

'But then they began to recover?' prompts Stephen.

Yes. They had become fertile again, and now the place was swarming with children – well, he would see for himself. When the United Nations Border Relief began to supply free food and water, they began to breed. It makes you wonder, about the Life Force, says Helen. They're not happy. How can they be happy? But they breed. They share husbands, like in Kampuchea itself. There aren't enough men to go round. But they breed.

Her tone is brutal but uneasy. A no-nonsense, managerial middle-class British tone, overlaid and underlaid with private anxieties, private desperations. What are these people to her, or she to them, that she should weep for them? She did not weep. She worked.

Simon Grunewald had said that 'his' people did not believe that other people were Real People. Their word for themselves meant 'Real People'. Other peoples were unreal. So you could eat them.

The UN, UNICEF, CIER, WHO, OXFAM, COER, etc., etc., usw., usw., had decided that *all* people were Real People. It was proving a difficult, an expensive decision. The Border Relief Operation costs more than half a million dollars a week, says Helen. And moreover it alienates the Kampucheans over the border, who resent the subsidies. But what can you do? You can't just let people die.

Why not, Stephen wants to ask, but does not, though some would, and will.

He finds Helen's bracing, abrasive tone interesting, after the fluid, graceful empathy of Konstantin Vassiliou.

Helen knows Konstantin. She is one of the only people Stephen has met who does not seem to be under his spell. She is suspicious of Konstantin's charm, perhaps because she herself is charmless. Perhaps because he comes and goes and takes photographs, while she stays and works long hours with slow and sometimes unwilling students. She mentions Konstantin's background, with disapproval. 'That young man,' she says, slowing down for yet another check point, 'has more money than is good for him. He's a nice boy, I grant you. Did you ever meet his mother?'

Stephen shakes his head.

'A remarkable woman,' says Helen, speeding up again. 'She kept giving all her money away. Said she didn't want to touch it. I don't know why, I don't think it came from anything very terrible. He wasn't an arms manufacturer or a drug-pedlar, her father. I think he was in cement. But she kept saying she didn't want the stuff. So when he died he left it to the boy. Cut out the other two children. Very British, eh? Primogeniture. The eldest son. Caused a lot of trouble in the family. The mother's divorced now. She works for the Africa Council in London. Or used to. Odd business. I don't know why Konstantin's got so hooked on this part of the world. Africa was his mother's patch. There's plenty of dying children to photograph in Africa.'

Stephen stays tactfully silent.

'And what,' she says, 'brings you to these parts? I take it that it's something more than idle curiosity?'

*

Pol Pot sits in his headquarters with a map and radio.

Pol Pot is in charge of the armed resistance forces.

Pol Pot is in Jakarta.

Pol Pot is in charge of a research institute on military affairs.

Pol Pot indoctrinates elite students in a villa called Zone 87 in southern Thailand.

Pol Pot is in Beijing with Prince Sihanouk.

Pol Pot has gone mad.

Pol Pot is dead. Long, long dead.

*

Ta Mok is in charge of the armed resistance.

Ta Mok has lost a leg.

Son Sen is in charge of the armed resistance.

Son Sen speaks well of Sihanouk.

Son Sen speaks ill of the Vietnamese.

Sihanouk plans the menu for the dinner in Jakarta.

Sihanouk writes to the Chinese Prime Minister thanking him for a tin of litchis.

Sihanouk is in Jakarta with Son Sann.

Son Sen is in Bangkok with Son Sann.

'Blood will have blood,' cries Ponnary. *'Encore de l'eau! Encore du Perrier! Encore de l'eau!'*

She rubs her hands and weeps and wails and laughs and sings and rubs her hands.

All these names are *such* a muddle, says the woman at the ICRDP.

*

Ho Chi Minh changed his name at least nine times while in exile, before he became Ho Chi Minh. He was known, successively and sometimes contemporaneously, as Cung, Nguyen Tat Thanh, Ba, Nguyen Ai Quoc, Vuong, Chin, Li, Tran and Cu Bac.

Pol Pot was once Saloth Sar. He has other aliases. Eighty-seven aliases. Some say 87 is one of them. In Paris, he wrote as 'Original

Khmer'. To the world he became, memorably, alliteratively, Pol Pot. At last the world remembers. He has made his point. He has entered History.

Noms de guerre, noms de plume, noms de théâtre.

*

All these names are *such* a muddle, says the woman. Stephen cannot but agree. Helen Anstey, who speaks Khmer, cannot see what their problem is. She finds these names just as easy to remember as Charles and Di, Liz and Charles, Esther and Robert, Brian and Alix.

*

Mme Savet Akrun has not changed her name, but she has good reason to fear that her son may have done so. He may have relabelled himself. He may by now be Jim or Pierre or Otto. He may be Smith or Nooteboom.

Mme Savet Akrun sits in her thatched hut at the Adult Education Centre and stares at the bamboo walls and the dry red dust of the floor. It is the quiet hour, the dull hour of the afternoon, between classes. She sits and thinks. She cannot leave this camp, now or perhaps ever, but her mind is free. Her mind moves.

Her mind can move to Phnom Penh, or to the village of her grandparents, or to Paris, or to images of cities she has never visited. Her mind can tread cautiously through the jungle, avoiding mines. Her mind can seek the living face of her dead husband. It can seek the faces of her three surviving children, who are here with her in this camp. It can show her horrors of horrors, or it can show her cities of Heavenly Peace. It can show her the fountains of Versailles, where her cousin trained as a horticulturalist and landscape gardener. Where are his gardens now? It can recall sidewalk cafés, dancing, boat trips, restaurants, festivals. She is blessed in the freedom of her mind and the rich store of her memory. But she has to take care. Some roads are dangerous. Some memories can kill. Some memories are mined.

She does not know how often she dare take the road towards her lost son. If she visits him too often, the pain is great. If she does not visit him, the pain is also great. She needs to conserve her strength, and the less pure pain is the less exhausting. She has to choose between the dead and the living, between her three living children and the many dead – husband, mother, brother, sisters. This is a simple choice. She avoids the sound of spade on skull. She turns away. Let the dead consort with the dead.

But what of the half-living? What of the disappeared? She has no way of knowing whether Mitra is alive or dead. If she abandons him now, will he die because she forgets him? She has thought herself a modern woman, she is not superstitious, she is not a worshipper of spirits or ancestors, she has been to Paris and studied theories of education. She no longer needs to conceal her once-dangerous knowledge. But something tells her that it is important to think correctly of Mitra. Some instinct tells her that she has the power. If only she can find it, if only she can use it wisely, the power will be in her. As once he was born from her body, so once again can she bring him back into this world.

She makes herself walk back, again and again, to that dark scene of confusion in the clearing. There he is, squatting by the fire, boiling water in a can, speaking words of comfort. She sees him quite clearly, his face in the firelight, his eyes white, his hair dirty and matted, but with that smile, that ageless smile of comfort and triumph, as he nurses flames beneath the little can on its three stones. He feeds in twigs and little branches. A small fire in a dark clearing. Her eldest child.

They have walked and wandered, a straggle of families, some kin, some companions of the road, obedient to meaningless directions that issue angrily from the lips of fierce armed children. They have laboured in one village, been moved on to another. They have rolled stones down a slope and carried dirt in baskets. They have lost all sense of direction. Is this a 10-mile space, a 200-mile space that they trudge and traverse? They do not know. Their salvaged possessions have dwindled to a few cooking pots, a few pages torn from a medical text book, a few garments, a hidden watch, a hidden pair of spectacles, a hidden gold chain, a bottle of unnamed pills. The father is already dead, stunned by a spade, then clubbed to death. Mitra, at eighteen, is head of the family.

They seem to be on their way south, to work on a dam, or so they have been told. For food they scavenge as they go.

They crouch round the fire. They have become jungle people, these city dwellers from Phnom Penh. They have learned to eat roots and catch frogs and fish.

She can see Mitra's face clearly. It is human and magic. There is something terrible and wonderful in his smile. He is proud of himself for outliving his father and taking on the burden of manhood in these unholy times. He is no longer the medical student, the fast talker with the motorbike, the boy with the Benetton shirt and the blue jeans. He is the man with the knife.

This is her last clear image of him. This is the last point where she can meet him. All the rest is confusion, noise, violence, uncertainty. A truck arrives, full of Khmer Rouge soldiers. Country boys, boys of sixteen, seventeen. Her little group cowers uncertainly. It is doing no harm, it is doing what it was told to do, it is moving southward along the trail. But doing what you are told is no protection. Instructions can change, suddenly, arbitrarily. The soldiers shout at them, in that loud hard-willed violent way that has become familiar. They demand to know who they are, where they are going. One or two of the older members answer, mildly, placating. Fear flickers and spreads. It is palpable. They are not yet immune to fear. She feels it in her bowels. These are ignorant children, these soldiers. They are mad with power.

Suddenly there is a burst of gunfire at the edge of the clearing. Mitra rises to his feet and moves towards it. There is shouting in the darkness. She thinks she sees a dangerous look on his face, a set and angry defiance. But maybe she imagines it. There is more shouting, more gunfire. She tries to back away into the trees with the younger children. She sees bodies being piled on to the truck, she sees men at gunpoint being forced on to the truck. Is one of them Mitra? The screen of her memory flickers, fades, blacks out.

Every day she goes over the possibilities, as she does now, in this hot dull afternoon.

He is dead. He died immediately, that night. He died of wounds received that night.

He survived, but died later, as did so many hundreds of thousands, from violence, torture, hunger, disease. He was detected, and killed, as his father had been. For having been, once, in another life, a medical student with a motorbike.

He is still alive, somewhere in Kampuchea, under Vietnamese-backed rule.

He has escaped and is in another camp along this same border. In Site Two, or Khao-i-Dang, or Greenhill, or Site Eight. Somewhere, his photograph is posted.

He has already been processed. He is in Bangkok. Or Los Angeles. Or Toronto.

If he is alive, does he ever think of her? He will not know whether she is alive or dead. Worse than that, he may not care. He may be anything, anyone. He may be a cook or a soldier or a thief or a mender of bicycles. He may be on a street corner in his own city, in his native land, selling cigarettes.

This is what he had pretended to be, during what is now called Pol Pot time: a vendor of cigarettes. He had been very convincing. He knew all the brand names, all the comparative prices. He could talk cigarette talk for hours, with the Khmer Rouge, with the old people of the villages. He was a good actor. Acting was survival, not play. He was proud of his arts of deception. He had told his mother to say she was a noodle-stall cook, he had taught her how to dissemble. She was not so good at it. He had advised her to keep silent. Not to speak. To cook.

Maybe now he sells cigarettes for real. Maybe now he is an actor for real.

Mme Savet Akrun is a realist. She does not permit herself to hope that he is pursuing his medical studies in a nice clean hygienic American hospital. She knows that life is not like the movies. She does not dare to hope. Yet she pursues him. She sends out messages, through the International Red Cross, through the ICRDP, through anyone who visits the camp. She send his name to the four winds, to the four corners of the earth. Her own picture has appeared in the *Bangkok Post*, it has entered the outside world as she cannot. She knows nobody in that other world except the French family with whom she boarded all those years ago while studying at the institute. She sends messages to them, but receives no reply. In twenty years, thirty years, they may have moved from the crowded, busy little suburban house that she remembers so clearly. Her letters pile up on the mat, are returned to the post office. She cries to the winds but there is no reply.

She works, she keeps herself occupied. She is on the Khmer Women's Association Literacy Committee. She tries to persuade the women of the camp that there is a purpose in learning to read and write. It is uphill work. She writes words upon a blackboard with pink chalk. She keeps her remaining family neat and tidy, in its little regulation hut on stilts. She and her younger daughter, Sok Sita, cultivate their plot. They grow vegetables, they keep chickens. The girl is a 'good girl', though not so bright. Suffering has stupefied her. The older girl, Am Nara, is married to a distant cousin. She too is a good girl. But Kem, her youngest, is a wild boy. He runs wild with the other wild boys. He swaggers and smokes and idles. She does not want to know where he goes at nights.

Life is slow, dull, hard. Sometimes there is panic and shelling, but most of the time there is waiting. She waits for the next visitor, to whom she can tell her sad story, through whom she may send out her hopeless pleas. Her story is sad, but all the stories round her are sad. Why should one be heard, and not another? Women sit in the dust and weep and stare strangely and laugh for no reason and sing snatches of sad songs. The camp is full of the interwoven tragedies of thousands and thousands of separate, lost, intercrossing lives, repeated in murmured tones, in endless susurration. Small lives, insignificant lives, nameless lives. The world knows they are there, these abandoned people, these survivors of the wreckage. She knows the world knows, for she has seen articles in French magazines, in American newspapers. She has seen her own photograph in the *Bangkok Post*. Her name is Savet Akrun. Her son is Mitra. She waits to tell her story yet again. One day her story will be heard. She waits, in the dull afternoon, for Stephen Cox.

She does not know that her photograph has reached Liz Headleand in St John's Wood. She does not know that her photograph has won a prize and made her and its creator famous, after a manner. She does not know that she has stared down from hoardings in large affluent cities to appeal for funds for the work of the ICRDP. She does not know that the chance artistic and worldly success and displaced ambitions of Konstantin Vassiliou have turned her into an icon. 'Where is my son?' she everlastingly demands, and Liz Headleand hears. But Liz Headleand is 10,000 miles away, in Good Time. It is Stephen Cox that approaches, and like Macbeth he has no children. When she asks her question of him, he will not hear. He hears other voices.

*

Liz Headleand, when she had recovered from the excitement of the Oxenholme wedding and the encounter with Simon Grunewald, returned with a renewed interest to the Text. The fact that it had been posted from Kampuchea itself lent it more urgency, more authenticity. At least Stephen had got there, as he'd wanted. Even if he'd come to a bad end there. This was comfort, of a sort.

She read and reread the fair-copy extracts she had entitled 'The

Swan of Ice', 'The Bridal Brothel' and 'The Red Road'. They seemed
to form a sequence. After them she placed 'The Turtle Lake', and
the less well-presented scraps called 'The Leper King' and 'The Fever
Hotel'. Did they tell a story? *Was* there a story?

She was rewarded as she inspected the diary pages by a reference
to an SG, which must surely indicate Simon Grunewald. A real,
outward reference, to a real person. (Well, *almost* a real person?)
And at long last, she found what she took to be a reference to
herself. Tucked away in a fine maze of script and scribble and
sketches, she found these words: 'Did Freud's concept of the super-
ego embrace the notion of common purpose? (KV, HA, JC, PD.) Is
the crowd always assumed to be morally inferior to the individual?
Ask Liz H. Is there something on this in Conrad's 'Outpost of
Progress'? I wish I had a dictionary. Crowd? Pack? Mob? Masses? *La
masse? La foule? La cohue?* History of evolution of words for crowd
and people power?'

Liz H., concluded Liz, could in this context only mean herself. So
Stephen Cox had thought of her on his journeys. He had wanted to
ask her a question, to have a conversation with her. It startled her
to find her own name, although she had been expecting it.

She looked again through the box, and found the picture of
Mme Akrun, asking 'Where is my son?' A simpler question than
Stephen's, but not unconnected.

She stared at the photograph.

In what time-scale do these two women now confront one
another? The paper woman, and the word woman?

Both exist. Both inhabit time. Can they ever meet? Are such
meetings possible?

This story could have been the story of the search for and
discovery of Mme Akrun's sun, Mitra: a moving, human-interest
story, with a happy ending, a reunion ending, with music. Or it
could have been the story of the search for and discovery of
Stephen Cox. This too could perhaps have had a happy ending:

perhaps, even, a wedding? You might well think that either of these two stories, or the two of them interwoven with a conventional plot sequence, would have made a much more satisfactory narrative than this. And you would have been right. Such a narrative would have required a certain amount of trickiness, a certain deployment of not-quite-acceptable coincidences, a certain ruthless tidying up of the random movements of people and peoples. But it should not be beyond the competence of a certain kind of reasonably experienced novelist. One may force, one may impose one's will.

But such a narrative will not do. The mismatch between narrative and subject is too great. Why impose the story line of individual fate upon a story which is at least in part to do with numbers? A queasiness, a moral scruple overcomes the writer at the prospect of selecting individuals from the mass of history, from the human soup. Why this one, why not another? Why pause here? Why discriminate? Why seek the comfort of the particular, the anguish of the particular?

Perhaps, for this subject matter, one should seek the most disjunctive, the most disruptive, the most uneasy and incompetent of forms, a form that offers not a grain of comfort or repose. Too easily we take refuge with the known. Particular anguish, particular pain, is, in its way, comfortable. Unless, of course, it happens to be our own.

Imagine Liz Headleand, whose profession is the particular, sitting in her drawing room in St John's Wood. It is a room we have come to know quite well, as we have come to know her. It is bright and newly decorated. It is a comfortable, Good Time room. Liz has a large box of papers on her knee (no, we are not so keen on them, but there they are) and on top of them is a prize-winning photograph. She is staring at the photograph blankly as she thinks of Freud, crowds, Stephen Cox, railway compartments, massacres, orphans, bereaved mothers, her own mother, her unknown father, and whether she has time to get to the shops before six to buy a

138

pint of semi-skimmed milk. These shadowy claimants jostle for precedence in her consciousness. She is on the verge of a connection. She is trying to read the text of the gaps between Stephen's shorthand. Imperfectly, warily, shyly, she waits and attends and invokes: and yes, there it is. It is a thought about Numbers. It is a thought about the Crowd, Genocide and the Numbers Game.

Somewhere in the box on her knee is a page full of numbers. It heads the 'Atrocity Stories' booklet. Yes, here it is.

Stephen begins at the beginning and records the victory of Merenptah, son of Rameses II, in his struggle with the Libyans. According to A. Erman (who he? wonders Liz), precisely 9,376 were slain, and in order to prove the numbers their private parts (or, if circumcised, their hands) were severed and loaded on to donkeys and carried home in triumph. (Or hands? Liz blinks, scratches her head, puzzles. Room for a bit of hanky-panky there, surely, or has she got it wrong?) Rameses III had also had a go at the Libyans, and had competitively notched up 12,535. Not for nothing were the Egyptians the fathers of modern mathematics.

The figures for the legendary monster Tamburlaine, credited to Toynbee's *Study of History*, are more impressive but less persuasive. The chroniclers of Tamburlaine had clearly not appreciated that readers distrust round figures. Tamburlaine, according to Toynbee, is remembered as 'The monster who razed Isfara into the ground in AD 1381; who built 2,000 prisoners into a living mound and then bricked them over at Sabzawar in 1383; piled 5,000 heads into minarets at Zirih in the same year; cast his Luri prisoners alive over precipices in 1386; massacred 70,000 people and piled the heads of the slain into minarets at Isfahan in 1387; massacred 100,000 prisoners at Delhi in 1398 . . . and built twenty towers of skulls in Syria in 1400 and 1401.'

Liz instinctively shares Stephen's scepticism about the precision of these numbers. Which is worse, the precision or the vagueness? She recalls a conversation with Alix and Brian Bowen about the

numbers of Romans killed by the Iceni at Colchester during Bou-
dicca's rebellion. Can death really have undone so many? There
weren't all that many *people* in illiterate Celtic Britain in the Year
Zero, Alix had protested. And what can the population of Asia
have been when Tamburlaine had finished with it? Minus ten
thousand, perhaps?

Did Stephen feel a need to rescue Tamburlaine as well as Pol Pot
from the hostile counting house of history? (He has added, for good
measure, W. H. Auden's anagram for Tamburlaine – A NUBILE
TRAM – but Liz is not good at word games and fails to recognize
it: she assumes it is merely a crazy jotting.)

Stephen then moves on rather rapidly across the centuries to the
Belgian Congo, where the Belgians had taken a leaf out of *The
Egyptian Book of the Dead* and improved upon it, their aim being not
so much to impress their supporters and posterity as to improve
efficiency and control expenditure on firearms: applications for further supplies of bullets to liquidate the native population of the
Congo Free State had to be accompanied by a suitable matching
number not of spent cartridges but of severed human right hands.

Despite this attempt at bureaucratic accountability, however, the
figures for what happened in the Congo are not satisfactory.
Stephen records that 'between 12 and 32 million' died there. He has
underlined the word 'between' heavily. He has also noted the
twentieth-century deaths of 800,000 Armenians, 6 million Jews,
about 3 million in Bangladesh, some 20 million in the labour camps
of the Soviet Union, 2 million in Vietnam, and between 1 and 3
million in Cambodia. In China, during the Great Leap Forward and
the Cultural Revolution, it is estimated that between 20 and 80
million died.

The words 'between', 'about' and 'some' are all underlined in red
ink. And with reason, thinks Liz. '*Between* 12 and 32 million killed' is
a phrase that cannot exist. '*Between* 20 and 80 million'? I mean, are
you *serious*? Do you call this *language*? What kind of history, what

kind of mathematics is this, what has happened to those spare tens of millions? Unnumbered, unburied, will they haunt the earth for ever, will they ever find a resting place? Do they not jostle us, do they not stifle us, are we not kept awake at nights by their squeaks and gibbering batlike cries?

Perhaps we can be proud of progress when we turn to the accountancy of non-human factors. Somebody in the Vietnam war was doing some pretty neat book work with explosives, according to Stephen's figures. He notes that the US dropped 14,400,000 tons of explosives between 1964 and 1974 on Vietnam. Also 400,000 tons of napalm and 19,000,000 gallons of herbicide, including 11,000,000 of Agent Orange; 257,465 tons of explosive were dropped on the Cambodian countryside.

A lot of ice-cream had also been consumed. Stephen notes that Meadowgold Dairies and Foremost Dairies had vied for the army's custom, and that in addition 40 (or, arguably, 41) smaller ice-cream plants had been set up in Vietnam to succour the troops. Stephen tots up numbers of dry cargo vans and refrigerator vans, cubic feet of pre-fab storage space, cubic square miles of hamburgers and cans of crackers, gallons of maple syrup and malted milk and carbonated beverages, cannage of meat balls and beans and tinned fruit cocktail and peaches. He records the fact the even under the most difficult conditions, 90 per cent of meals were served hot. He estimates the numbers of pre-cooked, freeze-dried Long Range Patrol Rations (LURPS) that had been devoured, and informs Liz that as well as an entrée, each LURP provided a sweet, cereal, sugar, coffee, cream, toilet paper, matches and a plastic spoon. He draws the audit to a close with an assessment of mortuary capacity (crudely speaking, not enough: Tan Son Nhut and Da Nang had overflowed off-shore to Japan and Thailand during the Tet offensive), and concludes with a guess at the number of golf balls personally autographed by President Nixon and presented as souvenirs to senior officers (about eight)?

Liz wonders where Stephen got all these figures from. She's heard of the US Freedom of Information Act, but this is crazy. Stephen had always veered towards what she herself considered a facile and fashionable left-wing anti-Americanism: had the Far East tipped him over into obsession?

The Numbers page ends with the words Good Time, Bad Time, copied out several times and adorned with doodles.

The next page is 'Atrocity Stories', headed by a quotation from William Shawcross's *The Quality of Mercy*, in which Shawcross notes that Allied propaganda in the First World War was filled with lies about widespread massacres, rapes and Belgian babies being slaughtered and turned into soap, and that in March 1916 the *Daily Telegraph* reported that 700,000 Serbs had been gassed to death. This was not true but was widely believed to be so. In June 1942 the *Telegraph* was the first paper to report the massive gassing of the Jews, and, as Shawcross comments, 'by awful coincidence the number given was once more 700,000. This time the story was not widely believed.'

Liz, safe in Good Time St John's Wood, can see for a moment the flickering ghost of Stephen's sardonic, cold, gentle little smile. It had always been a latter-day smile. She forces herself by its small illumination to read on, though she is squeamish about atrocities. They disgust her, which is, of course, what they are meant to do. This does not mean that they did not happen. Or that they did. (You may skip them, if you wish.)

There are extracts from Ho Chi Minh's writings for *Le Paria* published in Paris in 1922. They feature rapes, thefts, disembowellings, floggings, raw flesh, amputations, desecrations, firing squads. The French are the villains, the Annamese the innocent victims. In one incident, soldiers rape two women and an eight-year-old girl, then, 'weary', murder them, while they roast an old man alive at a wood fire. They cut off the girl's finger to take a ring, and her head to take a necklace.

THE GATES OF IVORY

There is a story from Clara Malraux's *Mémoires* about a group of convict-revolutionaries who were buried alive up to the neck by a 'certain D, the man responsible for the massacres at Pulo-Condor, and a friend of the governor'. Then their heads were devoured by ferocious red ants.

A similar story is told against Ho Chi Minh by an American journalist writing in something called *Missing in Action: Prisoner of War*, who claims that kind Uncle Ho had various enemies 'buried separately, upright and alive' in fields outside Hanoi, with just their heads sticking out. He then ordered harrows to be driven backwards and forwards over them, 'to scratch and tear and chop those living heads like many small tree stumps as the harrows went over them'.

(Liz finds this one hard to believe. The prose style is too flowery. But then Liz, like Lady Diana Mosley, finds it hard to believe that 6 million Jews were gassed to death. Six *million?* Surely not!)

There are many more anecdotes about boiled heads, devoured livers, rapes and bayonetings. The head motif recurs strongly in an unassigned quote which reads 'We Cambodians all knew the legend of the cooking stones. Long ago, Vietnamese soldiers took three Cambodian captives, and buried them alive up to their necks with just their heads sticking out. Then they made a fire between their heads and set a kettle on top of it.'

Heads and livers feature more than hearts, it would seem, in the Indo-Chinese mythology of revenge and death. Liz notes this with anthropological interest, and, as she turns the page, is surprised to find, like an answering echo, a scribbled note in Stephen's hand which reads 'As the heart to the Christian and the head to the Celts, so the liver to the Khmer?'

'Hey, Stephen,' says Liz, aloud. 'Hey, Stephen. Did you ever hear the end of the Paul Whitmore atrocity story?'

He does not answer. Aloud, Liz tells him. 'It was all his mother's fault, according to your friend Alix,' Liz says. 'His mother didn't love him, so he cut off a lot of people's heads. What do you say to that?'

143

Stephen says nothing.

'Paul Whitmore,' says Liz aloud, 'was real. Real but incredible. What do you say to that?'

Stephen says nothing.

Stephen's mother had not loved him, according to Stephen. Stephen's mother is still alive, in her nineties. She lies in a small room in a nursing home overlooking the Quantock Hills, and she cries out occasionally. 'Mummy, mummy!' she cries, in a little girl's thin voice. Her mother died half a century ago.

'I do think, Stephen,' says Liz, quite crisply, 'that you might have given me some kind of idea about what you wanted me to do with all this – this *paperwork*. I mean, I sort of get the point. But frankly, this is all just a mess. I give up. Do you hear? I give up.'

It is too late for the milk. Shall she get in the car and drive down to the late night superstore? Or will she be tempted there to buy more than her daily ration of cigarettes?

On the last page of the 'atrocity stories' booklet there is a curious little questionnaire, clearly doodled in a dull moment. Liz gives in, and rereads it. It consists of five questions, but only the first two have answers provided. It reads thus:

Q: What are the two most recognized logos in the world today?
A: The Red Cross and Coca-Cola. (Here follow various representations of red crosses and Coca-Cola cans: they are not quite up to the standard of Andy Warhol, but they make their point.)
Q: What happened to the liver of the brother of Lon Nol?
A: It was grilled in a Chinese restaurant in Kompong Cham and eaten by a jubilant crowd of Sihanouk partisans.
Q: Who described the Khmers as a 'conservative, easy-going' race, gentle mannered, leading lives of rustic simplicity and peaceful charm?
Q: What was the latest date at which it was possible for an English

writer to refer to foreign nationals as crones, yokels and smiling wenches?

Q: Whose work features a preponderance of brown hairy brutes, slaughtering savages, filthy scoundrels, noxious beasts, niggers, stupid animals, abominable idiots, poor devils, poor specimens, cannibals, murderous half-castes, cunning thieves, common desperadoes, and lying rascals?

Liz Headleand stares at these questions and thinks about milk. She gets up and nips a dying pink-brown nipple-bud from an azalea. Then she sits down again and rings her stepson Alan Headleand.

Alan is a sociologist and a political theorist. He is, like Liz, fond of quizzes. Once he won a blank cassette from Capital Radio for answering questions about TV personalities. He is also, unlike Liz, good at crosswords. He has been known to play chess.

He is in, and he is willing to play. When the first question is posed to him, he immediately comes up with Coca-Cola, and then, after a lot of deliberation, Mickey Mouse. Liz tells him that Mickey Mouse is not a logo, try again. Alan objects that Coca-Cola isn't really a logo either, strictly speaking. Liz says maybe, but that's not the right answer, try again. He demurs. She gives him the Red Cross, and he says yes, of course, fair enough, interesting, but I'd never have got it. He wonders, why not?

For the second question, he surprises her by getting very near Stephen's answer, for he guesses that Lon Nol's brother's liver was ripped out by his enemies. Liz supplies the given additional details, and congratulates him on his knowledge of the history of South East Asia. Alan says she should spare her praises, for the question was a leading question, and he is not a trained sociologist for nothing. He assures her that he knows nothing at all about Lon Nol, except that he sometimes features in crossword puzzles as the only palindromic leader of our time. Of his brother, naturally, he knows less. He hadn't even known he existed.

For Question 3, he guesses a travel brochure of the 1930s; for Question 4, he guesses 1929; for Question 5, he guesses (correctly, as it happens) Conrad. When told that there are no answers provided for these last three, he says, mildly, what a cheat.

'The next question,' says Liz, 'isn't part of the quiz, but I think it's connected. Do people in a group – no, sorry, he says crowd, not group – do people in a crowd behave worse than they do as individuals?'

'It depends what you mean by "worse", says Alan, predictably.

'Well, I don't know,' says Liz. 'I imagine he means more violently. More destructively. More stupidly. More savagely. That kind of thing.'

'Is this one of your barmy patients?'

'No, not really. Well, no, not at all. It's a question from Stephen Cox, about Freud and crowd behaviour. You've met Stephen, haven't you?'

Alan says he thought he had, and that he'd enjoyed his novel about the Paris Commune. *Barricades*, was that its title? That had been about crowd behaviour. And how was Stephen?

Liz finds herself telling Alan the story of Stephen's disappearance. She tells it in a light tone, not wishing to cause alarm or too much interest or concern. Alan is, accordingly, only mildly interested.

'Very Conradian,' he comments. 'Perhaps he's gone native, like Lord Jim, or that German chap I saw on telly the other night, trying to save some tribe in Papua.'

'I *hate* Conrad,' says Liz, with some exaggeration. 'Have you ever read "An Outpost of Progress"? Or *Victory*? Stephen keeps making these references to *Victory*.'

'Is that the one with the Caliban chap? The hairy apelike savage from the Amazon?'

'I don't think so,' says Liz. 'Surely it's the one set in Bangkok and the Gulf of Spain and the South Seas? That would make more sense, wouldn't it?'

Liz then asserts that she cannot face rereading the whole of

Conrad just to see what Stephen had on his mind while he was writing his diary. Alan sympathizes, as he is intended to do. He asks her if she has read *A Tale of Two Cities* recently? He's just been listening to it on cassette as he drives up and down the M6 to visit his girlfriend. And has she got round yet to seeing brother Aaron's version of *Coriolanus*, retitled *The Beast with Many Heads*? That's all about crowds and power. Dickens and Shakespeare are interesting on crowd psychology, offer Alan. Well, *quite* interesting.

'There must be a lot of books about crowds,' says Liz, vaguely.

Alan assures her that he will look some up for her, if she is really interested.

She says she is *half* interested. She appears to think deeply, and then she asks him, what is the population of the world?

Alan laughs and tells her she is mad, he is not a calculating machine, why on earth does she think he might know? And anyway, would she want it in European billions, or American billions? Plenty of margin for error there, says Alan.

He asks if he may try her with a conundrum of his own.

'Please do,' says Liz, eagerly. She likes talking to Alan, and she like conundrums.

'Why is it wrong — no, sorry, let me begin again — *would* it be wrong to pay somebody to undergo a death sentence on one's own behalf?'

'Sorry, say that again, I don't quite get it.'

'Imagine,' says Alan, patiently, 'that I am imprisoned in Penang on a drugs charge and given a death sentence. Imagine that I offer a sum of money — fairly *large*, I imagine it would need to be — to some local chap to get himself hanged on my behalf. He accepts. He dies. His family get the dough. I go free. Is that wrong?'

'I don't know if it would be *legal*,' says Liz, stalling. 'Do they allow that sort of thing in Penang?'

'I've no idea,' says Alan, even more patiently. 'Forget the Penang bit. I only put that in for local colour. Call it Erewhon. Or Nirvana. It's not the legality I'm interested in, it's the ethical question.'

But Liz has been sidetracked.

'Why ever did you make up that particular illustration? You wouldn't be so stupid as to try drug-pushing in Malaysia? Or anywhere, come to that?'

'Ma,' says Alan, slightly less patiently, 'forget drugs, forget Penang, forget me. Just try to concentrate on the issue. Can one sell one's own life, or buy the life of another? That's the issue. And if not, why not?'

'Isn't it kind of obvious?' says Liz.

'No, it's not obvious at all.'

'Then I'll have to think about it.'

'That's what I'm hoping you will do. Let me know what you decide.'

'You're not really going to Penang, are you? I hear it's very beautiful.'

Alan laughs. 'Of course I'm not going to Penang. I'm not going any further than the Chinese restaurant down Silver Street. But I've got to go now, I've got a date there with Sastri and Mayotte.'

'Now the Chinese,' says Liz, relentlessly, 'are they a nation of faceless collectivists, or are they a nation of individualist entrepreneurs?'

'I wouldn't know. I've never been to China. I sometimes think we should revise our concepts of national identity, don't you? Bye bye, ma, thanks for ringing.'

'Bye,' says Liz, faintly, much cheered, atrocities forgotten, as Alan goes off for his duck pancakes at the Opium Den.

*

Stephen Cox is given a guided tour of the camp by Helen Anstey, and then he is left to wander by himself on foot until curfew time. As he wanders, he begins a new notebook headed 'Survival Stories'. These are very like atrocity stories, of course, but they have different endings. For the narrator, that is.

He fills the notebook, during his week on the border.

Some of the stories are, frankly, appalling. The mother who crouches silent in the night and kills her baby lest it cry out and reveal her and its brother's hiding place. The woman who lies as dead beneath the corpses of her family, then staggers out at dead of night to a life of eternal night. The child who has lost mother, father, siblings, all, on its way to the camp, who stares at Stephen with fixed eyes and a snotty nose and says one word, 'Chuoy!', like a dull record. 'Chuoy! Chuoy! Chuoy!' it repeats, without expression. (It means 'Help, help, help,' says Helen.) The one-legged man who trod on a mine and crawled bleeding and delirious for days to safety. The rape victim left for dead, the man forced to dig his own grave and then buried up to his neck and left in the hot sun to die. There are many such stories. Stephen does not know whether they better illustrate the ingenuity or the monotony of human cruelty.

Some of the stories, mercifully, are less harrowing. Stephen likes the chap who says that he managed to convince the Khmer Rouge that he was a repairer of bicycles rather than a manager of a small jute factory. Helen, translating, says that he claims to be good at repairing bicycles. Bicycles were once his hobby. Now they are his trade. He repairs the bicycles of Site Ten.

Stephen meets the widow of a Lon Nol officer who passed as a street cleaner, and a Lon Nol officer who passed as a pedicab driver.

Helen says these are unusual cases. Most of the people here, says Helen, are peasants. Most of those with connections got out long ago and have been resettled. Only the powerless are left.

Stephen allows himself to be shocked. So even here, at the far end of the world, connections count? The connections that could have killed you, now count for you? Is that what she is saying?

Stephen wanders the straight red intersecting dust roads alone. Children cluster and stare, pigs and chickens scavenge. It is not pleasant, but superficially it is a great deal less unpleasant than the back streets of Calcutta.

On the way back to Aranyaprathet, Stephen questions Helen about connections. Did she mean to imply that all the middle classes, all the trained, all the wealthy had got out of here, that only the dross was left? When pressed, she admits that there are border-line cases. Cases of missing papers, missing links, disappeared relatives, whole family branches lopped from the tree. There are even some who say they prefer to stay here, who see themselves as working for a national future, for a restored Cambodia. The leaders, and the led. But they are all caught here, like fat rats in a well-baited trap.

On his third day, he is accompanied by Konstantin and his cameras.

Konstantin is a more receptive, less abrasive companion than Helen Anstey. He dawdles and idles and chats. He smiles and elicits smiles. He plays ping-pong with a group of boys and eats dubious fly-blown cooked offerings from the market, paying for them in dollars. He crouches in the red dirt with a group of wide-eyed children, who press round him to see what he has in his many pockets: he produces a tube of fruit gums, which he solemnly distributes one by one, and when they are finished he discovers some little cellophane packets of golden gummed stars. One by one, seriously, intently, he peels them from their white shiny backing paper, and one by one he sticks them first on his own forehead, then on the back of an offered hand, on an arm, on a knee, on a nose. The children laugh and laugh, emblazoned with their golden stars. Konstantin does not laugh: his role is to be magical. His expression is gentle, attentive. The children like him. He makes a mystery of the little stars. He puts his finger to his lips and says, 'Shh! Quiet!' The children do not understand English, but they fall silent, and look around, wondering. Konstantin produces from his pocket a little mouth organ, and plays them a tune. He plays 'Greensleeves', mournfully, not very well, but well enough. The children are silent, and then they break out into giggles and chatter.

Konstantin is popular. Stephen watches. It looks so easy, but it is not. It is very rare. It is special. Konstantin is on good terms with the strangest of strangers. He introduces Stephen to a tiny middle-aged widow with three pigs and a raucous amazing laugh. He introduces him to a blind monk and to a legless soothsayer. He introduces him to a dark-skinned tattooed ex-soldier with staring eyes and sharp teeth and a chain-mail jacket of small pierced coins of many nations, hung around with amulets and trophies and strange mystic tokens who in a jumble of many languages launches forth into a diatribe against Sihanouk and a hymn of praise for Lon Nol: 'Lon Nol he Number One Big Black Father! Sihanouk he Bad Father, from sky fall moneys, from sky fall foods, from sky fall bomb bombs, death death! Lon Nol he Number One man!' This figure presses upon Stephen a lucky charm, a precious package, two small finger bones wrapped up in a fragment of orange silk. 'You keep this, Englishman. This lucky bones. This lucky bones of luck person. *Bonne chance.* Cheers. Alleluia.' Stephen takes the package, reluctantly, and fingers it a little nervously: as he does so, the man's demeanour alters and darkens, and he thrusts forward at Stephen with a peculiar intensity and begins to speak very quietly and rapidly and rhythmically in what Stephen assumes to be Khmer. It is a curse, it is an incantation. He ends with 'Keep safe and No Death Come.' This is clear enough. Stephen smiles, politely, and waits for Konstantin to rescue him and lead him away.

Konstantin leads Stephen to Mme Savet Akrun. Had it not been for the icon of sorrow, the maimed Pietà, the mother of absences, Mater Dolorosa, he would not have been much interested in Mme Savet Akrun. She is a middle-aged woman, with receding gums and bad teeth, black from years of malnutrition; she is scrawny, scraggy, dried up, in her long drooping cotton print sarong. He would not have recognized her from her portrait. But she is pleased to see Konstantin. They converse, in poor French. You came back, she says to Konstantin. Nobody ever comes back. Konstantin gives her a folder of news cuttings and a cake of lavender soap. He gives easily, intimately. He introduces Stephen, as a journalist from England. She tells Stephen the bones of her story, her much-told story. She asks him to help to find her son. She thanks him, politely, for his attention. She says she will not give up hope.

Stephen is not interested in the story of her son. He wants her to tell him about her own survival, her escape across the border. He wants her to flesh out the dry bones. But he is too polite to probe, and she cannot speak of these things. She has formalized them into a ritual narrative, and cannot move over the borders of her tale. Dutifully she recites: the long walk, the minefields, the dirt, the forest, the mountain. Stephen is no good as an investigative journalist. He cannot think of any questions that will lead her beyond the beyond.

As he and Konstantin prepare to leave, she tells Stephen that it is a pleasure to hear such good French spoken. Does he know Paris, she asks him? Yes, says Stephen, quite will. She too knows Paris, she tells him gently. She often thinks of it. The Tuileries, the Luxembourg Gardens, Versailles. She says she has a cousin who trained as a horticulturist at Versailles. She wonders where he is now. She has not heard from him since 1975. He designed the prince's gardens in Phnom Penh, in French style. She writes his name down in Stephen's notebook. She asks Stephen to ask after him, when he is next in Paris. There is a Cambodian restaurant, in the rue du Faubourg du Temple, in the dixième. Near the canal. He should ask to speak to the proprietor.

Stephen assures her that he will. It all seems very unlikely. It seems more unlikely than the atrocity stories. A cousin, trained as a horticulturist at Versailles? A Cambodian restaurant in the rue du Faubourg du Temple? They shake hands, gravely. Konstantin kisses the thin woman on her brown forehead. She pats Konstantin on the shoulder. The hut is very hot. Her eyes are very dry. The world seems very still and small. A dry whisper rattles in the thatch. There is a silence, in which it seems that something is listening. But nothing is listening.

*

Mme Savet Akrun, schoolmistress, remembers. She remembers Versailles and the Petit Trianon of Marie Antoinette and her cousin with his mauve—maroon eyes. She remembers the café in the rue du Faubourg du Temple. She remembers the gardens of Phnom Penh, and the little lake where Mitra her baby threw crumbs for the great carp, where her girls made little shell borders and petal paths of red and orange marigolds in the sand. She remembers the jungle and the sound of spade on skull.

Imagine Mme Savet Akrun, schoolmistress, crouching, knees apart, arms round her knees, in the shadow of a palm-tree. She looks as though she is defecating, and attempting privacy as she does so, for ostrichlike she has tied her scarf around her head. Some have lost all modesty, some are inured to public distress: diarrhoea and enteritis and other undiagnosed disorders of stomach and gut have been great levellers. Others cling to what they remember as decency.

She groans, and waits. She is not defecating, she is waiting for the thick dark metallic gouts of blood that she knows will soon be loosed from her. She feels their formation, she awaits their passage. In the Old Days, the City Days of the Old People, she could not have timed this so well. Now she is in touch with her own rhythms, her own cycle. If she times this squatting carefully, the clotted blood will fall neatly to the dry earth, red to red, and she will wipe herself neatly clean with leaves.

Sanitary pads and towels are forgotten luxuries. Tampons she has never used, though they had, briefly, been obtainable in Phnom Penh. The Khmer Rouge are Green People. Menstrual blood runs down the legs of women who once took a butterfly pride in their appearance. Women smell. Women choose to cease to menstruate.

Here, ten years later, in the camps, sanitary protection of a sort is once more available, but she had no longer any need for it. She stopped menstruating prematurely, at the age of thirty-nine. Her daughter Sok Sita has never started. How can she speak of these things to Stephen Cox, journalist from England? She does not even speak of them to her own daughters. But sometimes she remembers. She remembers squatting. And wiping herself with leaves. She remembers shame and pride. Both are unclean.

*

Guess who I ran into yesterday? Polly Piper, of all people! In the new Sainsbury's in Camden Town. I haven't seen her for years. She and I had a rough passage once when we found we were both sleeping with that antique dealer gigolo from West Ken. She got Mondays and Thursdays, I got Wednesdays, his wife got the rest. Those were the days! There was a hell of a lot of blood, sweat and tears at the time, I remember, when we both found out we weren't the one and only Chosen Lover, but now it all seems a long time ago and not a very big deal. That poor chap, I sometimes find myself thinking, no wonder he looked *so* worn out. I bet Polly was pretty demanding, and I know I was, and I don't think his wife had signed off either. But that wasn't how I saw it at the time. I nearly took an overdose, I was in such a rage.

Anyway, there was Polly Piper, all six feet (well, nearly) of her, neatly turned out in a sort of short-skirted shoulder-padded navy two piece, looking spruce and powerful and businesslike, staring at the women's sanitary-wear counter. She had a basket full of nice healthy green produce, and I had this whacking great trolley with only a box of cholesterol-stuffed eggs in it. They weren't even free range. We could hardly avoid saying hello as we practically bumped into one another and did a sort of double take, and I said Hello *Polly*, long time no see, or something fatuous like that, and she seemed really pleased to see me and said Good Lord, Hattie, how are you, you look great. I'm fine, I said, thanks a lot, how's yourself. Well, she said, to tell you the truth, I'm suffering from *shock*! Then she laughed and showed her teeth and tossed her hair about in that commanding way of hers to show she wasn't serious, and I said Do tell, because after all I wasn't in a hurry, was I, you could *tell* I wasn't in a hurry because of the glazed way I was meandering around with the solitary box of eggs.

'I think it's *toxic* shock,' she said, and laughed some more, as though this were a new joke that had just occurred to her: which, it turned out, it was, because she then proceeded to tell me in a pretty snappy concise narrative style that she'd left her job as chief executive with a manufacturer of ladies' underwear and romantic fiction (this was the one she took up after she stopped being in women's prisons with Alix Bowen at the Home Office) and had taken up a career in sanitary protection. 'It's always been my passion,' she said, leaning against the lovely white rows of pads and fluffy packets and neat little cardboard packages, 'I think the tampon is the liberator of womankind, I've had this campaign going for years about removing VAT on them and I've great hopes of the European Court at Strasburg in 1992, but there's been this new setback, with toxic shock. Do you know about toxic shock?'

I said I'd heard of it, wasn't it quite popular in America, and if so would we get it soon? She said we'd got it already, a girl had died of it in Basingstoke only that week, wearing one of Polly's own company's tampons which she'd been foolish or unhygienic enough to leave in for forty-eight hours. 'I just don't know what to think,' said Polly, 'I don't know whether we should make a great song and dance about it and issue warning leaflets, or try to hush it up, or just plough on with the non-toxic research and pretend nothing much happened. Tell me, Hattie, if you don't mind my asking, what do *you* use and why?'

'Are you doing a survey?' I asked her, and she said no, not really, she was shopping for a small supper party for a Saudi Arabian diplomat, but she always liked to inspect what was on sale in the big stores and who was buying what. So I informed her (well, why not?) that I was at that very moment wearing a no-doubt highly toxic nice white super-size tampon backed up just-in-case by a delicate little non-biodegradable rubber-backed non-ecological panty-shield. 'Hmm,' said Polly, doubtfully, and asked me if I thought I and people dumber than me would accept grey unbleached tampons and grey cotton wool? Recycled, you mean, and she said well no, not *exactly*, I knew perfectly well what she meant.

'It's the onward march of progress,' she said. 'There's no way of uninventing the tampon. There's no way anyone's going to go back to washables and women's monthly sequestration from public life. But people are getting more ecology conscious, no doubt about it. How do we persuade the modern woman that the tampon is ecologically sound?'

'If it isn't, you shouldn't try,' I said, piously. I am *not* a fool.

'The sea is *abob* with the things,' she said.

'Surely you can make them biodegradable,' I repeated.

'Well, yes,' she agreed. 'They are already, they just take a hell of a time to deconstruct. And we have to worry about profit margins.'

'It's going to be fun in the future,' I said, 'with the greenhouse effect and all. We'll all be sitting beneath water level as all these tampons and the AIDS-activated swell of condoms float past our sandbagged windows. As we dine on lethal halibut and brain mad offal.'

'Not enough research has been done,' said Polly, 'into what primitive peoples think about menstruation and uncleanliness. I used to contend that if the tampon had been invented a few thousand years earlier, the whole history of womanhood would have been different. But now I'm not so sure.'

'And what do *you* use?' I asked, to divert her from these distressing doubts and speculations. And she laughed and said, 'Oh, I use our own brand, of course, I get free supplies, but I'm not entirely *happy* about it. Perhaps I should never have left the Civil Service. And what are *you* up to these days?'

'Oh, not a lot,' I said, vaguely, staring at my box of eggs for inspiration and wondering whether to bring up the name of that rotter Arnold whom she and I had shared in days gone by, or whether to ask her if she still kept in touch with her colleague Alix Bowen, when I noticed that her attention had left me and that she was gazing with interest at a shopper inspecting the well-stocked rows of sanitary superchoice. I could see at a glance why she was interested, for the shopper was sixty if she was a day, a little wizened Camden Town Bingo-style lady, the kind who cracks merry London jokes on the OAP bus routes, more like *seventy*, frankly, with slightly wrinkled stockings and boat shoes, but there she was hesitating between Lil-lets and Tampax and Dr White's as though she were a schoolgirl new to the Big Adventure. I don't know what Polly's first thought was, mine was *Jesus* life's a longer haul than I thought, but then she noticed us watching her and as we both looked away a bit on the embarrassed side to be caught staring she said, 'What's wrong, girls, is there a law against it?' and let out a terrible witchlike cackle and seized two packets of Nurse Allerfines (a *very* unusual brand) and made off with surprising speed into the high-tech distance.

Now Polly Piper and I are not girls. We are both over forty. I'd just like to point that out.

Polly said, as we moved on towards the bleach and household cleansing department, 'Do you ever regret not having children?'

I thought that was a funny question to pop at me at five forty-five on a Friday night in Sainsbury's. I began to wonder if Polly Piper was all there. I mean, was she going through a nervous breakdown or something? Had she been given the sack, or lost her wits, or was she suffering from an early menopause? I mean to say, her explanation for hanging around the tampons wasn't *wholly* satisfactory, was it?

'No, not often,' I said. 'Do you?'

'Yes,' said Polly. 'Yes, I do. I spent twenty plus years trying not to get pregnant. Then two years trying to conceive. And nothing. Nothing.'

'Bad luck,' I said.

'It's not bad luck,' said Polly. 'It's the judgement of the Lord.'

She was smiling as she said this, to make it clear that she was being ironic.

'It's toxic shock,' I said. And she laughed. And there we parted. I never managed to buy anything more than a box of eggs and the ladies' items. Silly I looked at the check-out with that great empty trolley. Polly put me right off. And when I got home I found I'd forgotten everything I'd gone for – the decaff coffee, the onions, the noodles, the Marmite, the lavatory paper.

You may wonder why I'm telling you all this. But it does link up. Believe me. Everything links up.

Have you ever read *The Black Swan*? I haven't. But I know what it's about because somebody told me. It's a novella by Thomas Mann about a woman in mid-life who is past the menopause, and who falls in love with this guy (and presumably vice versa) and starts to menstruate again when she takes up sex, and is very pleased by this sign of returning youth and fertility. Only it isn't menstruation, this new blood. It's cancer. I know this plot because I was once involved in trying to get Christopher Hampton to write a screenplay of it. I don't think he ever did.

The Black Swan and *The Swan of Ice*.

It was a full moon last night. I notice the moon. You get a good view of the moon over Primrose Hill from Stephen's flat. A Druid view.

Eggs, blood and the moon.

Oh yes, it links. You wait. If it doesn't link, I'll be very surprised.

*

How hard life was through those years when the French and the Japanese stripped us of everything! The rice fields of Nam Bo were immense, but the inhabitants lacked rice. My father's entire wardrobe consisted of a pair of trousers of thick, unbleached linen, stiff as cardboard. My sisters weren't better dressed. At the time of their menstruation, they had to take the canoe and hide themselves in the brush.

My father was killed by a French bomb. My mother died of old age.

When the French left, the Americans arrived.

We fed our child as the birds feed their young. Lacking rice, we went into the marshes to seek lotus and water-lily seeds.

Night on the Plain of Reeds *by Lê Van Thao, b.1939*

*

Every nurse's fear was being taken prisoner and not having any Tampax. You couldn't count on being in the jungle and using a leaf, because the jungle was defoliated. We were always told to have a suitcase packed, if we got overrun, we'd be lifted out. That was a crock of shit. I found out later that they never had any such evacuation plan. If we got overrun, it was just tough titties. In any case, we all packed the same things. We packed money, a camera, and we packed Tampax. My flak jacket was so full of Tampax that nothing could have penetrated it.

Nurse, quoted in Nam, *Mark Baker*

*

Mitra pushes a glittering articulated snake of super-trolleys down a gleaming corridor in Toronto, whistling as he goes.

Mitra bends over his medical text books in an attic in a Parisian suburb and late into the night he studies the names of the small bones and the large.

Mitra lies in a field hospital of delicate bamboo, delirious, with a newly amputated leg.

Mitra in a smart pastiche uniform of white and gold and green bows low at the gateway to the Shangri-La Hotel.

Mitra in a tattered uniform of camouflage and UN cast-offs sits on the earth with a group of children instructing them in the art of throwing the grenades which they have not got.

Mitra lies huddled in newspaper and a blanket beneath a railway arch.

Mitra strolls the green level lawns of Versailles and inhales the pungent aristocratic odour of box as he watches the crystalline play of the fountains.

Mitra crouches on his haunches and shreds chicken in the back yard of the Restaurant Phnom Penh in Montreal.

Mitra works as interpreter and resettlement officer in a refugee hostel in the Yorkshire Dales.

Mitra is dead and has been dead for ten years.

One among many. The Red Cross files are heavy. The tons of papers weigh.

*

Stephen Cox collects reunion stories to add to his atrocity and survival stories. It is a sentimental and suspect genre, Jack Crane warns him. The agencies make use of these stories in brochures and annual reports, but they do not always end as well as one might wish.

A child of seven identifies her mother's photograph on a scrap of newspaper, and is flown out to New York amidst the blaze of flashlight.

A boy of ten, survivor of shipwreck and cannibalism, wandering the Philippines with a distant cousin of fifteen, tells his story to an American journalist who uses it as copy in a 'human interest' piece. His uncle, survivor from the same wreck but washed to another shore, reads the piece in Sydney, and sends for his nephew. The cameras flash.

Families are reunited by chance sightings, by bizarre loops of conversation, by encounters in hotel lobbies and airports and hospital wards.

A mother kneels by a barbed wire fence and weeps with joy. On the other side of the fence, her lost child stands and stares, unknowing.

Sometimes the lost child does not wish to be found. Sometimes the lost parent becomes a burden. Sometimes the cousin is not a cousin but a cousin twenty times removed. Not all relatives are welcome. Would *you* wish to be reunited with and made financially responsible for all the relatives you ever had?

An American journalist adopts an 'orphan' and lavishes upon it all the riches of Los Angeles. She writes a book about its psychic scars. The cameras flash.

A Red Cross nurse adopts an 'orphan' and brings it up with her own brood in Sevenoaks, on a diet of shepherd's pie and Ovaltine.

A banker's wife in Geneva adopts an 'orphan' and transforms it into a mathematical prodigy.

The 'mothers' of these children meanwhile suffer from guilt, loss, anger, grief, uncertainty.

Maybe Mitra does not wish to hear from his mother. Maybe he has deliberately concealed his tracks.

*

Stephen, Konstantin and Jack Crane jolt back from the camp along the red road to Arnyaprathet in the late afternoon glare, talking of disappearances. One of the most useful UNBRO contacts in Site Ten has vanished. A trusty for eight years, he has gone, and nobody can interpret the mutterings and evasions that greet queries about his whereabouts and well-being. Has he been abducted, assaulted or killed, or has he joined the fighters? There have been stories filtering in all day about shellings and evacuations at Site Two. The situation is volatile, the tensions high. Perhaps Mr Om has decided to back another horse.

The mountains in the distance are red and a pale chalky wasted green. They are craggy and inhospitable. The light is hard. To the left there is scrub and jungle. Two kilometres away, through the scrub and jungle, is Kampuchea itself. Stephen can see it, he can see into it. Bad Time, Bad Place.

They are late leaving today. The driver puts his foot down.

Jack Crane tells a story of a mate of his who vanished in Nicaragua. A journalist. Supposed dead, but who knows, he may turn up again one day? Last seen thumbing a lift in a Contra helicopter. Stephen describes the light-hearted adventurer Simon Grunewald and his desire to eat and be eaten by his beloved. He follows in the footsteps of the vanished Michael Rockefeller, who probably was eaten some time back in 1961. Konstantin reminds them of the story of the romantic American silk merchant, Jim Thompson, who fell in love with Thailand, failed to take over the Oriental Hotel, built up a co-operative silk factory, persuaded the fashion houses of Paris and New York to buy raw silk, furnished his Bangkok home with the spoils of Ayutthaya, was visited by the rich and famous from the four corners of the earth, and then vanished, suddenly, dramatically, one Easter Sunday afternoon in 1967 while on holiday with friends in the Cameron Highlands in Pahang. His body was never found, nor any trace of him. Had he been eaten by a tiger? Had he been killed by natives and guiltily buried? Had he fallen into a cave? Had he been abducted by Thai or Chinese counter-revolutionaries? Was he a CIA agent? Was he a communist? Did he plan his own disappearance? Was he even now alive and well and living in Peking?

They speak of Raoul Wallenberg, the noble Swede who saved so many Jewish lives in the Second World War. Is he alive in some Soviet labour camp, as some of his family believe? Is Pol Pot alive? Where is Sean Flynn, journalist, photographer, and one-time actor son of actor Errol Flynn, last seen on 5 April 1970, near an abandoned Viet Cong road block just beyond Chi Pou? Is he too still alive, just over there somewhere, just over that border, in that dirty greenery? Are any of those 2,500 Americans still missing in action alive? Sightings of them continue to filter through. Shackled stoop-ing emaciated figures in airports, in labour camps, in road gangs, glimpsed in passing trucks in Vietnam, Laos, Burma. Vigils are held in Washington. Occasionally boxes of ash and bone and tooth are returned to sorrowing wives and parents, via the US Army Identifi-cation Central Laboratory in Hawaii.

Rumour has it that Pol Pot has lost a leg and been fitted with a prosthesis by Trans-Hab Care. Trans-Hab Care denies the rumour. It says it has never seen Pol Pot. It has fitted hundreds of wooden legs to the victims of the minefields, but it does not aid the Khmer Rouge. Or so it says.

Stephen speaks of Rimbaud, who tried to vanish, who undid himself and his work and disappeared from the known world into Somalia. He too lost a leg, though not through stepping on a mine. They speak for some time at cross purposes of Rimbaud, for Jack Crane thinks they are speaking of Rambo, and is eager to deny the imputation of amputation. if Rambo *did* lose a leg, it wasn't in any movie Jack had ever seen. Was there a Rambo IV or Rambo V already hitting the screens without his knowledge? You can't *do* that to a leading actor, says Crane, in a tone that reminds Stephen of his ex-agent Hattie Osborne, who had once so nearly sold his Commune novel to the agent of the then unknown film-star Depardieu. They unravel the misunderstanding, and speak of fame and the global village. Rimbaud, Rambo, myth-makers both. Which of them will live on beyond the millennium? Rambo, claims Konst-antin, is popular all over South East Asia. The Filipinos love him. The Indonesians adore him. He is the hero of Malaysia. In Korea he is king.

Stephen hopes he exaggerates. Are all the global villagers work-ing at their VDUs by day and watching Rambo movies by night? Pol Pot, where are you?

Rimbaud's leg was amputated in 1891 in Marseille in the Hôpital de la Conception.

The Land Rover judders on. To the left, Cambodia. Stephen thinks of those gunboats off the coast of Africa, firing into a continent.

Konstantin brings up the story of the legendary Jungle Actor, the vanished Number One Film Star Man, who is said to run a College of Psychiatric Theatre and Healing somewhere in the disputed territory along the border. Is he real or fantasy? He may be real. There is a real priest who runs a University of the Jungle. Jack Crane has met him.

Film is the great escape. We are extras in the great movie of history, queuing up at the food wagon for our ice-cream and maple syrup, for our bacon sandwiches and hamburgers and Coca-Cola. The stars get smoked salmon and fillet steak and champagne.

Hattie Osborne sings against the dark in gold and anguish.

Piles of skulls, emaciated living corpses, images of our time. Dirk Bogarde, the movie-actor-turned-novelist, was there at the liberation of Belsen. It did him no good. Alas, poor Yorick. It is hot.

Jack Crane sips Coca-Cola through a straw from a plastic bag. The flat brown liquor looks like some dreadful plasma, some vital drip. Stephen begins to nod. He is not as young as the others.

He jolts awake as the Land Rover comes to a sudden, bumping halt. The road is blocked. A tank is askew across it, with its snaking ribbon of cogged track spilling brokenly in the dust. A Red Cross van has collided with the entrails, and another military vehicle has come to a halt. Nobody seems to be hurt. A lot of people are standing in the road. Some look blank, some look puzzled, some look agitated. 'Shit,' says Jack Crane, ominously. Their driver sucks in air between his teeth and reverses a couple of yards, but the military wave at him to stop where he is. Konstantin reaches for his camera, then thinks better of it.

Is there about to be some action? Is this it?

Action is slow, indecisive, confused. It sticks and stands almost idly. Konstantin, Jack, Stephen and their driver sit still and try to look as though they are not really there. The driver taps his fingers anxiously, soundlessly, invisibly, against the lower rim of his wheel. There are two Europeans standing by the Red Cross van. They look towards the ICRDP van, and motion towards it, but somebody waves a gun and they shrug their shoulders and resume a posture of patience. Everybody else is either Khmer or Thai. Two officially uniformed men are having a low-key altercation. The soldiers staring at the broken snake are very young. The tank is old and rusty. Perhaps it is not a Thai tank at all? Perhaps it is a tank from over the border?

There is no way past. There would be room, just, perhaps to drive past on the right without edging into the dyke, or the paddy, but the verge is occupied by soldiers with guns.

The driver glances at his fake-Rolex watch. It is well known that it is not wise to be on the roads after dark in South East Asia. And the dark, when it comes, is very dark. Uneasiness floods and spreads from the driver. But he does nothing.

Eventually, two of the young men clamber back into their wounded monster and emerge with a tool kit. They start tinkering and unscrewing. This should be reassuring, but it is not. It is as though they were operating on a battleship with a tin opener.

The Red Cross men lean against their vehicle, and light up the inevitable cigarettes. They hand them round the knot of stranded travellers, but they do not approach the ICRDP van where Stephen sits. There is a cordon sanitaire drawn between that group and this. Why?

So this is it, thinks Stephen. Here I am, sitting here in the middle of nowhere, for no reason. Just because I wanted to see what it was like. *Tu l'as voulu*, he says to himself.

It is boring, waiting for something nasty to happen. The green light thickens towards the East, and Cambodia darkens. Stephen thinks of Malraux and Rimbaud. Men of letters playing at being men of action. There is a strange stillness in his head, and he hears a bird cry. Emerald birds, scarlet birds?

At first, nobody speaks, but gradually the tension lessens as the boredom increases. The vehicle maintenance men seem to be making some kind of progress. There is even a burst of laughter. It seems wiser to sit and wait. To avoid eye contact, as the survival manuals advise. The driver's fingers still tap nervously, out of sight.

'Where was it Rimbaud ended up?' Konstantin wanted to know.

Stephen cannot quite remember. He thinks he went off into what was then Abyssinia. The Red Sea, Somalia, the Horn of Africa. Gun-running, dealing in hides and ivory and slaves. But he died in Europe, he went home to die.

The gates of ivory, the gates of horn. Konstantin says, in desultory fashion, that he wishes he spoke better French. It would be useful. He confides that he had an odd kind of an education. His parents had quarrelled about it. His mother had had this thing about state schooling and had sent him to a crummy neighbourhood school in North London. Then his father had turned nasty and insisted on sending him to a private school. Konstantin himself had rebelled at this stage and taken himself back into the state system. 'It was kind of disrupted,' says Konstantin. 'Kind of a bit of a battleground, if you know what I mean. I see now I was siding with my mum. But it didn't seem like that at the time. And what with one thing and another, I never picked up much French. I learned the social graces instead.'

The remark is deeply ambiguous, and intended to be so. The social graces are indeed what he has acquired. Gracefully he slouches in the back seat of the Land Rover, gracefully he takes out his cigarettes, gracefully he taps the driver on the shoulder and offers one. 'Here, chief,' says Konstantin. The driver smiles, accepts, for a moment stops drumming his fingers as he lights up.

'My mother,' says Konstantin, 'is not an easy act to follow.'

'Rimbaud's mother,' Stephen hears himself say, 'was said to be a martinet. She bullied the poor boy. She made him write Latin verses. He had to hide from her in the lavatory.'

He had forgotten he knew this. It comes to him from the air.

Konstantin laughs.

'*My* mother,' he says, 'was one of those 1960s permissive mothers.'

Konstantin falls silent, at this brilliant and brutal reduction of his mother Rose, but Stephen is not listening to his treachery, he is listening to the words of Rimbaud. He can hear them approaching like flies, they buzz and settle in his brain. They murmur, they sing. They sing the 'Chanson de la plus haute tour'. This had been Stephen's silent refrain in his Paris years, but for a decade at least not a word of it had reached him. Now it forms itself, word by word.

> Oisive jeunesse
> À tout asservie,
> Par délicatesse
> J'ai perdu ma vie . . .
>
> J'ai tant fait patience
> Qu'à jamais j'oublie;
> Craintes et souffrances
> Aux cieux sont parties,
> Et la soif malsaine
> Obscurcit mes veines.

He hums to himself the tune to which he once in a former life heard these words chanted in an ill-lit cheap hotel room by a crazy Alsatian woman in a small town in Normandy. He had had to lift her in his arms to pee in the wash bowl. His past returns as to a drowning man.

Konstantin rouses himself from his mother-trance, declines a swig of Jack Crane's Coca-Cola, repeats his wish that he could speak French better. 'I mean, your life could depend on it,' he says. 'I often think that. I wonder if you forget or remember words when you really need them? I met this *Time* magazine fellow who said he'd have been shot by the Viet Cong if he hadn't suddenly remembered the word for "peace" in Vietnamese. *Hoa-binh*. That's peace. They let him off. Gave him VIP treatment. He got a great story. I learned the word off by heart myself, just in case. *Hoa-binh*. But I don't know what it is in Khmer? Do you?'

Stephen and Jack shake their heads. They say they will ask Helen that evening, over supper at the Dragon. If ever they get there. They agree that a prayer in Vietnamese might in present circumstances be worse than useless.

Stephen recalls to himself another useful emergency word of Vietnamese. *Bao-chi*, journalist. While learning it, he had thought it a pity that it began with *b*, a consonant on which his stammer has often balked. Could one be shot in the head while struggling 'B-b-b-', like a baby? But as it happens, he seems to have left his stammer at home, along with a lot of other impedimenta. He does not stammer so much abroad. He hardly ever stammers in French. That had been one of the reasons why he had liked France.

After a while, he volunteers that a poem by Rimbaud has just surfaced in his memory. As they have nothing better to do, they allow him to recite it. He offers phrases of translation. 'Delicacy has lost me my life.' What did the poet mean by *délicatesse*? Sensuality? Sensitivity? Neurasthenia? Tactfulness, surely not, in Rimbaud's case. The poem hangs around in the air. Stephen hums snatches of its *fin de siècle* musical setting. He had once chosen it as a Desert Island Disc. The words drift off, and over the border.

Stephen has an uncanny conviction that they have been uttered here before, aloud, at this very spot. Why else should they have come to him? Is Rimbaud himself perhaps there, speaking to him, as he once heard Coleridge speak on the hills behind Nether Stowey? He hears the ghostly music of a violin. He is feeling unnaturally cold as though with the beginning of a fever.

And suddenly, there is action in the little group on the road before them. One of the boy soldiers kicks the tank. Something splutters and dies. The Red Cross van's driver resumes his place, his passengers climb in, he switches on. He waves to the JCRDP Land Rover, and Jack's driver switches on too. The soldier in charge of the tank looks from one to the other, uncertainly, as he stands in the middle of the red road. His vehicle is still immobilized. There is a cry from one of the boys keeping look-out from the turret. He points to the left. All eyes turn to the left, and there, towards them, from perhaps half a mile away, emerging from the trees across the paddy, lurches a blue tin lorry. There is a moment of acute indecision, as the officer aimlessly sweeps his gun round the group and turns back to the threat from the east. The Red Cross van makes his own decision, and grumbles forward, with a punctured tyre. Jack's driver smartly salutes, and smartly takes off. 'Go, man, go,' mutters Jack. The Land Rover makes for the ditch-side, on the left, and passes the tank with inches to spare. The officer's gun veers momentarily towards them, but the other Thai soldiers are gazing in fascination at the approaching blue lorry. The ICRDP Land Rover accelerates. There is a shot, but it is not directed at them. In a couple of minutes, they are away and out of sight. Behind them, they hear another shot, and shouting. They drive on.

Jack mumbles 'Good man' to the driver, the driver grins uncontrollably as he grips the wheel. Konstantin fishes out his camera and takes a parting shot of nothing much, and Stephen feels icy cold, then burning hot. What had made the Red Cross van decide to move at that moment? Had it seen the blue lorry? Had the Thai officer wanted to keep them there as protection, as bargaining counters? Why had Jack's driver waited so submissively for the Red Cross van, when the way ahead was clear? Would the Thai officer have prevented them from passing?

Five miles further on, they come across the Red Cross van by the wayside, its driver inspecting the punctured tyre and the damage to the bonnet. Water is dripping from the radiator. They slow down and stop, although their driver would have accelerated by on the other side. The two Red Cross men agree that it had been a nasty moment. Jack offers them all a lift back to Aran, but now the immediate danger is over they are keen not to abandon their vehicle. It is still, they say, mobile, and they think they can fix the radiator with chewing gum. Jack offers them a packet of Spearmint Extra to add to their repair kit. They have already been in radio contact with their office and reported the incident, they assure Jack. There is no need to wait.

There is slapping of backs, an exchange of smiles and thanks, an agreement to have a drink and compare stories later. The ICRDP vehicle again moves onwards.

'Well, thanks, folks,' says Jack, 'for keeping cool. It only takes one move out of place in a spot like that to blow the whole thing open.'

Stephen, who has not hitherto formed a wholly favourable impression of Jack's own reliability, thinks that this is almost certainly true. On the other hand, he says to himself as night deepens, there hadn't seemed to be much option to keeping cool. Keeping cool hadn't required much effort. He wouldn't have been able to think of anything else to do.

So, not this time. Next time, perhaps, or the time after. But not this time.

He thinks of those Thai soldiers, clustered round their wounded monster, and wonders if they are keeping cool.

*

That night, after a meal spent chewing over the day's events, Stephen is wandering alone and bedwards through the busy streets and thinning night markets of Aran when he pauses by an open doorway. A whole family is sitting in its open front room, almost on the pavement, watching a movie. A candle burns on top of the television set as though on a shrine. The coloured shapes flicker. The family is divided between rapt attention and incipient boredom. A young girl looks out, sees Stephen, smiles, beckons. He shakes his head and smiles. She beckons again, the innocence and sweetness of the whole world shining from her shadowy face. He is touched. She points at the set, again beckons. She is proud of the machine, proud of the movie, she wants to share the family's riches. Stephen allows his gaze to rest for a while upon the set.

This Thai family, in this remote border town arbitrarily enriched by international air trade and money, is watching an American biblical epic about the post-Crucifixion career of Mary Magdalene. Despite himself, Stephen finds himself gripped by its gleaming blandishments. The girl beckons again. Stephen notes that the family is sleepily smiling and welcoming. He enters, and lowers himself to sit on a cushion by the girl. Surreptitiously, she passes him a boiled sweet. He sucks and watches. It tastes of harsh lemon, and has a sherbet centre.

The sound track is poor, but it is easy to make out that he has happened upon a scene in which the Magdalene is about to plead with a handsome Roman of the officer class for the life of her brother Lazarus. Mary Magdalene, played by an ageless, clear-browed, deep-lipped, deep-bosomed Sophia Loren wearing a white dress and a lot of gold jewellery, sinks to her knees in a vast marble hall before a colourful crowd of mixed WASP Romans and WASP-ish Jews. The scene, as is proper in epic, is expensive, public and spacious. There is a lot of perspective and pillarage. We see the many hostile eyes fix upon the bound gaunt handsome tormented Lazarus, we see them flicker to Mary's cleavage, we see them rest upon the blond Nordic brow of the Roman Caius Lucius. Yet, miraculously, we can also hear the intimate whisper of Mary, husky and throaty, as she speaks for the Roman's ears alone.

'Spare him!' she whispers. 'Spare him! For the sake of that night when you vowed me the moon and the stars and the gold of

Solomon, spare him! I ask not the moon and the stars and the gold of Solomon. I ask my brother's life!' Caius Lucius looks nobly embarrassed, caught in a trap of his own making.

Sophia rises majestically to her feet.

'Spare him!' she cries, to Lucius and to the crowd and to video viewers round the world. 'He died one death, and he rose from the tomb. Alone of mortal men he knows the secrets of the grave. Is it for mere man to cut short what God has twice given?'

There is a moment of passionate hesitation, as the crowd wavers and Caius Lucius wavers.

'No man may take what the Lord has given!' she declaims, and then drops her voice once more to that intimate, thrilling whisper.

'I pledge my life and my honour for him, I *give* myself for him,' she murmurs.

We know what she means. So does Caius Lucius. Indecision drops from his brow as he graciously surrenders to her, and instantly the whole rent-a-crowd begins to cry, 'Release him! Release Lazarus! Release the man who knows the secrets of the tomb!'

Stephen, watching this transition, is amused and perhaps less surprised than he should be to see, on the edge of the crowd, suddenly picked out by the camera, the well-known features of his old friend Hattie Osborne, looking a good fifteen years younger, dressed in streaked anemone tones of red and purple and black, her hair tied up in a Grecian knot. The camera lingers on her, as she too cries, 'Release Lazarus!' We see Sophia dart her a grateful, personalized glance, and, as Sophia turns to sweep from the audience chamber, it is Hattie Osborne who follows and lifts the hem of the Magdalene's trailing robe.

Stephen remains glued to the screen, hoping to see more of Hattie, but he is not rewarded. Either she does not appear again, or she has been cut from the video version – the latter seems more likely, as the narrative is full of inexplicable jerks and non sequiturs, and Stephen would have bet his bottom dollar that the look between

Sophia and Hattie had been intended as prelude to some small touching moment of probably fatal and sacrificial fealty. He finds it hard to follow the sequence of events, but is quite happy to sit there watching oriental dancing, muted sex, picturesque views of old Jerusalem, donkeys grazing in a field of flowers, and the stoning of Stephen, as his new Thai friend sucks sweeties by his side. The final sequence shows Mary Magdalene and the Roman officer sailing westwards in an anachronistic yacht towards the Riviera, arm in arm, as a light wind plays with their carelessly coiffured locks.

His friend sighs sadly when it is over. 'Is beautiful,' she murmurs. Stephen looks around him, in the semi-darkness. Most of the rest of the family, less romantic, less appreciative, are fast asleep.

'Yes, beautiful,' agrees Stephen, in a whisper. 'I think it took a few liberties with the biblical sources, but never mind.'

'Never mind,' she agrees, generously. 'Never mind.'

*

Political theorist Alan Headleand is still, in another time sequence, puzzling over his stepmother's questions about group behaviour, and about whether or not people behave worse *en masse* than as individuals. He suspects that he holds contradictory positions on this issue, and as, unlike Liz, he disapproves (professionally, as it were) of inconsistency, he is trying to work them out in order to reconcile them or to abandon them. He has already, on her implied suggestion, looked through Conrad's 'An Outpost of Progress', which turns out to be, as he had dimly remembered, a tale of two poor whites at a trading post in Africa long sustained in a belief in the superiority of their own civilization and culture by 'the crowd that believes blindly in the irresistible force of its institutions and of its morals, in the power of its police and of its opinions'. Here, alone, isolated, confronted with 'pure, unmitigated savagery, with primitive nature and primitive man' in the shape of a few indigenous

173

merchants and villagers, they fall to pieces. Things 'vague, uncontrol-lable and repulsive' take over.

Alan, an enlightened child of his enlightened, post-modern, relativist times, does not believe that primitive man is full of unmiti-gated savagery. He does not hold with descriptions of things that are vague, uncontrollable and repulsive. He does not believe that the dark-skinned races are by nature more savage than any others. He suspects Conrad of racism. Yet is it not, in a way, the cultural relativism of the poor whites that Conrad is attempting to expose? And when Conrad uses the word 'crowd', does he really mean *crowd*? He was, after all, a Pole, writing a foreign language. Maybe he means 'society'? Is the problem here partly semantic? Are *all* problems semantic?

Alan believes that man is born free and good of heart. It is society that corrupts, society that forges the manacles. Yet society itself is composed of human beings, is it not? Prime Minister Margaret Thatcher had told us that there is no such thing as society. There are only individuals.

So, the individual is progressive and flexible, while the mass is primitive and punitive? The mass throws stones, but the individual hesitates to cast the first stone? Or is the savage selfish individual socialized for the higher good of the group?

This is a complicated matter, and one over which Alan quite often ponders. How long would it take, how much social engineer-ing would be required to convert a community of pacifist American Quakers into order-obeying anti-Semitic officers of the *Schutzstaffel*? Or the SS into loyal members of the Red Cross? Would there always be a handful which would refuse to convert? And would they be heroes or villains? Why did the Germans so willingly kill the Jews? Why did the Italians refuse to kill Jews? Which is more surprising, the willingness or the refusal? Was the charismatic leader-ship of Pol Pot a socializing influence, binding the exploited peasant of Cambodia into a purposeful society? Or was it a barbaric, primitive influence, deconstructing the institutions of society and family into 'pure unmitigated savagery', into the killing fields of genocide? Is 'good' group behaviour generated and fostered by 'good' institutions, or are institutions in themselves morally neutral? Discuss.

Alan chews over these options, while continuing to nod and smile at the domestic finance controller and to munch his dinner. For I am sorry to say that Alan's reflections are not taking place in the privacy of his study, where they would not be unfitting, and where they might perhaps attain a greater clarity, but in the more confusing and sociable venue of a Founders' Feast at one of our more ancient redbrick Northern universities, where Alan has a new and pleasing post. While his memory fishes up fragments of Rousseau and Hobbes, his face expresses polite interest in the problems of portion control in the canteen. 'You don't remember the sixties,' says the controller, 'when they went on strike because they were offered chicken three times in a week. I told them they should remember the war. But of course they didn't remember the war.' Alan, who had been a baby, not a student, in the 1960s, nods sympathetically, and agrees that it is hard to believe that a whole generation has forgotten Adolf Hitler. 'Whale meat,' says the domestic finance controller, with nostalgia. 'They should have had to eat whale meat. And how do you find the claret, Mr Headleand?'

'Excellent,' says Alan, taking another non-discriminatory swig, and trying to look appreciative. If blindfolded and asked if the wine were white or red, he would have guessed correctly, but beyond that distinction could hardly have advanced. 'Excellent. And a very good' – he peers, covertly, at the commemorative menu – 'a very good piece of lamb.'

As the domestic finance controller proceeds with an account of the increase of vegetarianism amongst both staff and students, Alan has a glimpse of a lonely dark-skinned *enfant sauvage*, mute, sulky and intractable, and then another glimpse of history shaped like an hour-glass, with a primal horde at the bottom, squeezing upwards

175

through the narrow waist of the free, unchained, enlightened individual, then bulging out once more into the sublime and broad communion of the redeemed many. The shape of history, thus conceived, is not unlike the little icon that governs the many-layered brains and cells and storage systems of his new IBM-compatible computer. Now did he or did he not remember to press 'Save' before he dressed himself up in these ridiculous dusty old-fashioned borrowed robes? He ought to have a word with the domestic finance controller about the back-up generator and the electricity supply, but perhaps there is no point, for this particular controller, with his claret and his memories of the war and his Oxbridge model of college life, is on the verge of retirement, and next term will usher in a new IBM-compatible controller who will understand at once that the precious lifeblood of a university is its word processor current.

Is man a horde animal or a herd animal? Discuss.

Alan turns to his other neighbour, a visiting Canadian ethologist who might be expected to have views on this, but the ethologist is anxious to describe a new production of *Three Sisters* which he has just seen at the Royal Exchange: Alan listens with docility as his mind wanders off towards his brother Aaron, and his new deconstructed version of *Coriolanus*. Alan has so far seen only a dress rehearsal and wonders if he ought to try to see the finished product. Will Aaron be offended if he does not?

Alan looks around him, at the high Victorian gothic hall with its sombre Victorian portraits of robed and ermined chancellors and masters and Nobel Prize winners. A slant golden light falls athwart the highly polished tables, the college silver, the best college crockery, flecking them with little lozenges of blue and ruby red from round inset panels of Victorian stained glass. The panels portray Zeus visiting Danaë in a shower of gold, Danaë adrift with the infant Perseus on a perilous sea, Perseus stealing the one eye of the three Grey Sisters, Perseus severing the Gorgon's head, Perseus turning his mother's tormentors to stone, and Perseus freeing Andromeda from her rock. A gentle low hum of discourse rises from the assembled company. It is a heavily masculine gathering, black and white and crimson, but here and there a woman's dress or head of hair offers a different, dissident note of spots or flowers or ribbons or diamanté clips. An archaic gathering, Alan might well think. Does he feel he belongs to this horde, this crowd, this mob? Does his belonging elevate him? What on earth is he doing, in his father's cast-off dinner jacket, drinking claret? He looks around and wonders if he can get the ethologist off Chekhov and on to social bonding before the pudding arrives.

Soon there will be speeches, jokes and laughter. Self-congratulation, ritual expressions of mutual esteem and gratitude, applause.

Alan wonders about his own job prospects. If he sits it out here, in this uncomfortable thick suiting, in this academic robe, will he prosper? Does he *deserve* to prosper? Does he enjoy this dinner? Will it be very bad for him if he learns to enjoy this kind of dinner? Will the fusty dusty dark thick black fabric absorb and finally swallow up the light?

His brother Aaron is fortunate. Aaron can wear what he chooses. Aaron can look a freak if he wants, and wear earrings, and make himself a motley to the view. He is a free spirit, says Alan to himself, enviously, momentarily forgetting that this is the one occasion in the year that he has to get himself up like this, and that most of the time he too can slouch around looking like a rag-and-bone man if he chooses. Indeed, his students like it when he does. His oldest brother, Jonathan, thinks young Alan's clothes are a disgrace. No wonder people want to privatize higher education, when they look at tramps like you, says trendily dressed, high-earning television executive Jonathan.

Over the strawberry mousse, the Canadian ethologist is lured on to the subject of herd behaviour, and is quite informative about musk ox, elk, moose, impala, lechwe, sitatunga and wildebeest. He proffers (not too solemnly) the opinion that the more northerly the herd, the more individualistic its members tend to be. Beasts in the Arctic Circle have a much less highly developed collective unconscious than African antelopes, he suggests. Alan asks if this could be a racist remark, and if so, in favour of which geographical zone? Is a powerful collective unconscious perhaps a sign of poorly developed cultural and social organization? The Canadian mentions the allegedly racist work of the German psychologist Erich Jaensch, whose 1939 study attempted to prove the superior intelligence and efficiency of the northern European hen. Superior to what? asks Alan, entranced. Why, to the *southern* hen, the lazy southern hen, of course, says the Canadian.

Alan makes a note upon his commemorative menu.

'But it *is* true,' says the Canadian, 'that some creatures show a marked lack of interest in the fate of individual members of their own herd. I've been told that you can pick off a lechwe out of a herd of a few hundred, and the rest will hardly interrupt their grazing. I don't know whether that's true. It could be just a hunter's tale. But it *is* true that when the cat bit the head off one of my wife's lovebirds, the other lovebird just went on singing and warbling as though nothing had happened. With the headless body in the cage, and the head in the mouth of the cat.'

'Lovebirds are of African origin, I imagine?' prompts Alan.

'I never did liked *caged* birds,' the Canadian answers, obliquely.

Over the strawberry mousse, the academics in their academic uniform gossip and sip their dessert wine, a special treat from the outgoing domestic finance controller. The natural light thickens, and the candles and wall sconces take up the wondrous tale. A traditional scene of privilege, of courtesy, of ceremony, of the pure life of the mind. A colony of old rooks.

*

Alan's brother Aaron Headleand sits in the back row of the stalls, on the aisle seat, waiting to slip out when the applause begins. The show has gone well tonight: a good house, with quick responses, and now suitably silent and attentive as the end draws near. Aaron is proud of his production. His *Coriolanus* is a much more challenging, much less *frivolous* piece than his *Squeaking Cleopatra*, and he thinks it not unworthy of its place in the repertory of one of our great subsidized companies (albeit in one of their smallest auditoria). In fact, he thinks it is bloody good. Watching it, now, well into its run, he feels little tremors of invention and excitement run through him as he thinks of his new play, his very own new play, the first in which he will have cut himself free of the apron strings of the Old Master. He'd been worried, sort of, about his Shakespeare-dependence, and beyond that his Brecht, Marowitz and Stoppard dependence. It is time to find his own voice. Next time he will sing free.

His voice proves darker than he and others had expected. As clown and wit he had cast himself, as dandy and joker, but here he has unleashed something more disquieting. His *Coriolanus* is a vision of a world of arbitrary, bloody power, of power for its own sake, of power beyond ideology or justification, a world of the strong few and the weak many. Democracy, statesmanship, senates, law courts, tribunes, consuls — pfff! Thistle down. Away with them! Capitalism, communism — pfff! Words! Words! This is brute rule for brute rule's sake. The rule of the old men. He has rejected the 1930s Freudian reading, in which Volumnia appears as mother–villain, and the 1960s Brechtian reading, in which the plebs and the tribunes of the people are heroes, and the 1970s John Osborne anti-plebs pro-Coriolanean reading, and he has invented a world in which the Old Fox is King. Menenius is the villain–hero of his piece. Menenius, ex-killer, states-man, manipulator, puppet-master. They are all his puppets — vain son-and-glory-besotted Volumnia, crafty tribunes, cowardly stinking cannon-fodder populace, and above all the warrior barbarian, brain-less Coriolanus himself, the war machine, the figurehead, the idol with the dazzling jewelled eyes. In Aaron's version, Coriolanus is killed early in the plot, and only his flashing carapace is wheeled forth to terrify the Volscians and animate the Romans. It is a rendering which mirrors forth the dark gullible complicity of man, his conniving murderous stupidity, his mass cowardice, his mass obedience. *This* is how people are governed and engineered and persuaded to kill and to die – not by reason, not by self-interest, not even by threats, but by a craving for the safety of the horde. We are all slaves, we are mesmerized by the flashing eyes of power, by its fine speeches. We are ruled by the handful who set the diamonds in the sockets, who then retire behind the screen.

The nature of power is of interest to Aaron. He himself had, he had once thought, forsworn it. But now he sees he has only forsworn its more innocent and evident manifestations. He is still in pursuit.

He has had his moments. He has had a certain charisma. He has exercised power over his stepmother, Liz. He has made her flinch and tremble, first with fear, and then with desire. He has exercised power over his peer group, and over individual members of that group. He has exercised power over audiences. As an actor, at drama college, he has made others laugh and cry. He has compelled their silence. He knows the sound of applause. He has felt a whole dark auditorium gape for him, like a great maw, like a ripe cunt. Beautiful, he had been, in those early days of his youth, and popular, and admired, and fashionable. He had been a maker of fashions. He had been pursued by agents and seducers. But had forsworn the footlights and taken himself backstage.

Afraid of power, afraid of its swollen belly and its vanity? Afraid of failure? Afraid of the one-way ego-trip to nowhere?

But power is difficult to renounce. It clings to those who have once courted it. It had followed him behind the scenes. Even in the fringe theatre, as a struggling director, himself hustling for work and finance, he had found himself in possession of the disposition of favours. There were beggars and beseechers and hungry takers for scraps and leavings, for rehearsal pay far lower than the dole. He had handed out pittances, and been embraced as a god. He had learned the little games of power, and he had tried to abjure them. He had watched others playing, on the shadow stage of the theatre, on the larger stages of politics and industry and cold war, and he had taken notes, on techniques, rhetoric, manoeuvres. He had studied Scargill and Thatcher and Ronald Reagan. Ciceronian triplets, rising intonations, homespun jokes. (Who was manipulating Reagan, what mild-seeming Menenius set the sinews of his jaw smiling and twitched his vocal cords?) And now came Gorbachev, the marked man, the new darling of the ignorant plebs of the West, popular beyond all reason. How was it done?

On stage, the play is moving towards its climax. The Volscians are moving in for the kill. 'Tear him to pieces!' they cry. 'Caius killed my son! My daughter! My cousin! My father! Kill, kill, kill, kill, kill, kill!' They have not got out of hand – no, that is not part of Aaron's message. They are still in the hand of Menenius, though they do not know it and have never known it. They bay for blood. Aaron/Menenius has bullied and cajoled and terrorized this cast. They bay very convincingly. He has brought out the best of the worst in them. If he told them to kill, they would kill. And if he presented them with their own shame, they would be shamed.

Aaron's father Charles and his brother Jonathan think themselves men of power. They employ and dismiss, they control large budgets. They consider Aaron a lightweight, a dilettante. He has only shadow power, power over shadows. 'My so potent art,' he whispers to himself. He cannot renounce it. He is mesmerized by his own creation. The great shining warrior–dummy of Coriolanus topples, gushes buckets of mechanical blood, is dismantled by the hypnotized mob. The old fat fox Menenius steps forth from its belly to deliver his last speech. Aaron's mind is racing on to his next work. He scrabbles in his pocket for a bit of paper, and on the back of the envelope of an airmail letter from his old friend Eric in Hanoi he jots down in the dark:

MARGARET DRABBLE

The Man of Straw
The Wicker King
The Burning Bush
The Killing Fields
The Shadow World

The lights go out, the play is over, and there is a respectful pause before the applause begins. Aaron slips out quietly, for a quick getaway, but not before he has scanned his audience and noted the pleasing presence of Ian McKellen (himself formerly a noted Coriolanus), Ivan and Alicia Warner, and in the distance film-maker Angus Kyle with a dazzling redhead on his arm. Aaron is pleased. He is the fashion. His play is good, his next will be better. They will eat from his hand. He moves, but he does not move quickly enough to avoid hearing from a couple, who have escaped almost as precipitately as he, the words 'Well, really! What on earth was all *that* about?' The couple mutter, united in their dismissal of his masterpiece, as they move away into the foyer towards their little Italian dinner. Aaron bites the inside of his lip, smiles, rallies, and walks out into the night.

*

As Alix Bowen stands in front of the fish stall in Northam's covered market, Stephen Cox suddenly swims, for no apparent reason, into her mind. Is it because a pallid youth at a neighbouring stall is shouting half-heartedly, 'Lovely Coxes, thirty pence a pound, lovely Coxes?' She can see Stephen for an instant quite clearly, there amongst the shoppers, in his white suit, with a green scarf at his throat, smiling gently in greeting, about to speak, out of place and a little hesitant amongst the bustle and the old-fashioned smells of sawdust, oatcake, fish, blood, sugar, oranges. Then he dissolves and fades and she cannot summon him back. Where did he come from, where has he gone to? She

182

hopes this visitation is not a bad omen, and turns her attention firmly to the fish.

She likes the fleshy slabs of cod and hake, the twirls of plastic parsley, the little silver bloodshot herrings, the yellow–purple fluorescence of cheap dyed haddock. She is buying fish for a pie. Most of the things that Alix Bowen cooks turn out rather like a pie. She has long recognized this, and decided to go along with it. She buys cod, and a few pink prawns in their shells for decoration, as a compliment to her guests.

Her guests have swum towards her from the more distant past, from her own childhood schooldays in Leeds. Alix Bowen stands there, surrounded by ghosts, clutching her damp parcel. OAPs in caps and head scarfs shuffle and jostle, babes in push chairs sucking lollies and dummies are propelled over the cobbles, barrow boys shout their wares, a thin bare-legged white-faced teenage girl drags and sucks hungrily on a thin cigarette. Time stands still in the covered market. It is now, and yesterday. So little Alix stood, as a child, at her mother's side, gazing up at plaice and halibut, her nose wrinkling slightly in disgust at the strong odours, her eyes glazed with boredom, her heart yearning with pity for the dying tortoises and terrapins on the pet stall down the arcade. These fishes, these faces, these types and archetypes. Nothing changes, except for the trade in tortoises and terrapins. That now is banned. Little Alix had wanted to save them all.

The market, that relic from the Victorian past, is under threat, but it hangs on. Developers are after the site, they want to build a new air-conditioned marble-tiled superspace, they want to replace the wrought-iron curlicues picked out in garish red and gold and turquoise and to wrap up in hygienic overpriced parcels the blood puddings and the chicken's feet and the broken biscuits. They will have their way, in the end. People do not want this kind of thing any more. They want Sainsbury's, Waitrose, Tesco, Gateway, Marks & Spencer. This is shabby stuff. It smells of poverty. But the fish is good, the fish is better here than in the posher fish shops. Straight from the North Sea, it boasts.

Alix makes her way to the bus stop, thinking of her guests and of her mother and father. Both her parents have died within the last eighteen months, politely, without much fuss. Retired schoolmaster Dotty Doddridge and his vague, sharp wife Dolly have left for ever the world they tried so hard to improve, the world which mocked them and reluctantly respected them, the world which had been in so many ways such a disappointment to them. Though their last years, surprisingly, had been touchingly irradiated by a new hope. Defeated on almost every front by the swelling materialisms of the eighties and the fading of the left-wing, CND dreams, this austere and slightly ludicrous couple had found their twilight home in the Green Movement. Both had been rejectors of meat and savers of string and brown paper bags and egg boxes: both had shivered in an under-heated home and muffled themselves in extra layers of natural fibre: both had admired the culture of the bicycle and the hay box. And time had at last caught up with them. Dotty and Dolly loved Jonathan Porritt. He was the beacon for the future. He had made them happy. Chernobyl had made them happy. Things, at last, were going their way. There was a new front.

Alix and her sister and brother had agreed that they were glad their parents were too old and frail to do anything rash like strapping themselves to Japanese whaling vessels or joining the swim-in in the poisoned waters washing round Sellafield, but they were pleased by this new interest. It was rational and not undignified. It made sense of lifelong instinctively held prejudices. Alix, Jenny and John had approved and applauded. And they had recognized that they had been fortunate also in the manner of their parents' departure. Dolly had died first, one cold winter night, of nothing much. She had been sitting watching a programme about nuclear-waste disposal on BBC-1, with her feet in woolly socks and slippers, and a shawl round her shoulders, and a plaid travel rug on her knees, when, as her husband put it, 'her head just fell forward, and she was gone'. Not a moment of suffering, not a word of farewell, or so he maintained. (There were, of course, no witnesses.) He had had the satisfaction of coping gallantly by himself for six months, and then he had gone to bed one night and died in his sleep. The Home Help had found him in the morning, with his glasses open on the book he was reading. The book was lying on Dolly's deserted pillow. It was a Dick Francis. Alix, who had driven over from Northam as soon as Mrs England rang, had been much moved by the sight of the Dick Francis. Her father would never have let on to her that he was reading anything so lightweight, but there he was, caught by death *in flagrante delicto*, in one of the few misdemeanours of his innocent life.

Yes, they had been lucky, agreed Alix, Jenny and John, as they gathered at the second funeral, as they went through their parents' cherished possessions, squabbling equally over a Woolworth's glass bowl, an orange and purple thirties' geometric tea set suddenly back in fashion, a bedside table, a grandfather clock. They had all known friends with parents and ageing relatives lingering on in old people's homes at vast expense, dying painfully of protracted illnesses, losing their wits through modern tactfully relabelled forms of senile dementia. Dotty and Dolly had behaved, at the end, impeccably. One could forgive them many past embarrassments. And, after all, what was there to forgive? They had been good people. Eccentric, shaming, stubborn, dowdy, at times tedious. But good. Honest, in their fashion. God's fools.

And Alix had discovered, a little to her surprise, that others remembered them with affection too. As a child, she had been deeply self-conscious about their shortcomings, and had felt herself responsible for them. Other parents were smarter, more confident, more competent: other parents wore furs and ate meat and drank wine. Hers alone were a laughing stock, it had seemed to her, as she herself longed for wines and steaks and furs. But it seemed that others had not found them ridiculous. 'Oh, I *loved* your father,' had been one of the first things that Betty had said, on their reunion after thirty years. 'I *loved* him. Do you remember those Racine lessons? They were wonderful. I *loved* Racine. He made me *love* Racine.'

Alix Bowen, standing at the bus stop with her fish, watching the flow of traffic along the three-lane highway as it disappears down the underpass, sees the dead stream past her on the far side by the Bingo Palace windows. Her mother, her father, her first husband Sebastian, his mother Deborah, Jilly Fox. Soon the dead will outnumber the living. One may reach out one's hand, but one cannot touch them. Is that Stephen Cox? Why has he sent her his shade? Has he too crossed the river?

Tonight, Betty Sykes is coming to supper, with her friend Rho. They are very much of the living, but they bring with them echoes. Betty has returned to Yorkshire, the prodigal daughter, and Alix Bowen is making her a fish pie. Betty has been all over the world, in the thirty-three years' hiatus in their friendship, and has never sent so much as a postcard. So people can return from nowhere, from the unknown. Betty, loud, breezy, blowsy, fast-talking Betty, is proof of this. Alix had been astonished to see her at her old school's 200th anniversary, which she had attended in low spirits and piety in the wake of her father's recent death. There, surrounded by stout grey-haired matrons, by harassed embarrassed fathers, by the fading woolly retired coevals of her parents and the shrunken martinets of yesteryear and the fresh-faced dapper youngsters of today, was Betty Sykes, clad in an outrageously bright green red-buttoned jersey bedizened with knitted white lambs and yellow daffodils. The vanished Betty! Alix would have known her anywhere, across any Lethean tide of forgetting. Broad gleaming yellowy-white sebaceous brow, heavy eyebrows, sultry naturally red lips, a slight moustache: thick, greasy, heavy black hair, tied back and skewered with a wooden dagger: solid, uncompromising, shapely legs, in ribbed green tights: a broad bottom, a little broader than it had been all those years ago, encased tightly in stretched black wool. Energy, frustrated energy, flooded angrily from Betty as she stood there in the congregation clutching her hymn book in her large hand, forced into immobility for twenty minutes. Alix caught her eye, waved. Betty's face was a study. Her eyes popped theatrically, she pulled a face of mock-astonishment, she waved and gestured, she knocked her handbag noisily to the floor, and noisily regained it as the piano and the choir enjoined the Lord to dismiss them with his blessing, and once dismissed she charged her way over to Alix, open-mouthed, in mid-speech, syllables trailing behind her.

'What do you *mean*,' said Alix, when the flood ceased, 'what am *I* doing here? What are *you* doing here, more like? I *live* here, well sort of, almost.'

'Alix Doddridge!' repeated Betty, in surely excessive stupefaction. 'Well, I never. Now what *has* been happening to you? Tell all, tell all, I want to hear it *all*, from the very beginning.'

But there had not been time to fill in thirty years in five minutes, and their encounter was much intruded upon by other less assertive but more deserving claims on Alix's attention. Betty had managed to drag up her friend Rho for inspection — 'You remember Rho, don't you? Rhoda Lee?' — and to extort Alix's phone number: she had divulged that she herself was now working in the neighbourhood, running some sort of a hostel in Glydale, and that she expected to be around, rolling stone though she was, for at least a year, and they must get together soon.

Rho, during this, said nothing. Alix did not remember Rho. She would never have recognized her, if indeed she had ever known her. Rho was, or appeared to be, Chinese. Or something like that.

So, Betty Sykes and Rhoda Lee are coming round to sup on fish pie and time warp. Alix's husband Brian tactfully has absented himself: he has taken himself off to the theatre with the Bells to see a touring production of *Lysistrata*. Or so he says.

MARGARET DRABBLE

'So, now, what have you been up to in all these years?' repeats
Betty, as she sinks into her corner of the settee with a glass of
white Rioja. But she does not wait for much of an answer, interrupting herself to point out that unlike most people Rho has not yet
given up smoking and needs an ashtray, to check up that the
painting really is a Rigby, and to ask whether Brian (referred to as
Your Good Man Bowen) has gone out because he disapproves?

'Disapproves of what?' asks Alix, boldly.

'Gossip,' Betty as firmly replies.

And, over the fish pie, they gossip. Alix recounts, with many
interjections, her life story, from her brilliant career at Cambridge
(We always knew you were the Clever One, Doddridge! But why
the hell read Eng. Lit.?), her brief but glamorous first marriage
(What tough luck! Drowned? How rotten!), her lonely years as a
single parent with little Nicholas (hard times, eh?), her patchy jobs
as teacher in prisons and institutions of Adult Education (typical
part-time stuff, I know that scene), her time as Civil Servant with the
imperious Polly Piper, her marriage to Brian, the birth of her son
Sam, her work with aged provincial poet Howard Beaver, her
friendship with mass murderer Paul Whitmore, her pursuit of his
wicked dog-abusing mother, and her rescue and reluctant acquisition
of dog Bonzo, who even now loyally rests his head in ugly and
dribbling devotion against Alix's knee. Crowded into the space of
an evening, its longueurs foreshortened, it all sounds pretty exciting,
even to Alix, but not as exciting as Betty's equally fragmented
narration, which leaps from Leeds to Canada, from Canada to Hong
Kong, from Hong Kong to Sydney, from Sydney to Saigon, and
back again to Glydale.

'Rho and I thought we'd get away from rotten Little England,
didn't we Rho? And Canada wasn't half bad, back in the fifties. But
dull, you know, dull. Rho wanted to take citizenship, but I wouldn't
let her, would I? Hang on to your British passport, that's what
I said. Anyway,' says Betty, breathlessly, forcefully, 'I learned

Cantonese, and that's come in pretty useful. Well, it would, in my line, wouldn't it?'

Alix plucks up her courage before it's too late and asks what exactly Betty's line *is*?

'Refugees,' says Betty. 'I deal in refugees. Well, I don't see what's so odd about that. You were in prisons, weren't you? It's that school we went to. It got a grip of us. Good works. High thinking and plain living. Yes, thanks, I will have another glass. The toiling masses, or do I mean the tortured masses. Struggling to be free. It's a heart-breaking business. The funding game, the numbers game. Oh, I've played it all. I suppose it's partly because of Rho. Or because my mother died when I was a wee babe. Anyway, here I am, with this hostel for unaccompanied Cambodian minors. They're a wealthy lot, but they've got funny ideas. I'm there to bring them up to date. About multicultural society and assimilation.'

Alix has no idea what Betty is talking about, and it seems rude to ask too many questions. (How *can* unaccompanied Cambodian minors be wealthy? It does not make sense.) Her own life seems in contrast to unroll back into the past with a smooth simplicity, an inevitable logic. Betty's leaps and clusters and bunches and whizzes and rips. Or is it merely Betty's narrative style that is so confusing? She had always, even in her teens, been an oddball, a misfit, a hit-and-miss performer, whose school persona had teetered dangerously between popularity and derision: 'She goes *too far*,' people said, from time to time, of Betty, as she was alleged, variously, to have removed her tampon in full view in the dormitory, to have left her hair unwashed for a whole term as a challenge, to have asked Mr Bainbridge if she could have a puff of his pipe, to have jumped off the swimming-pool roof as a dare. (On this occasion she had ended up screaming in the most cowardly manner, with a broken leg: Betty was not famed for stoicism.)

'Look,' says Betty, now, to Alix, as the evening wears on and her thick hair begins to escape from its pin, 'this international thing we had at school, it's not normal, you know. All that stuff about starving babies and the Third World. Did we call it the Third World then? I don't think we did. Anyway, it wasn't *normal*. It was all a bit freakish, the way they went on about it. But the odd thing is, wherever you go, you find them.'

'Find *who*?' asks Alix.

'People brought up like us. People who don't know how to mind their own business. You'd be amazed how many there are of them about. They've spread all over the globe. It's a weird business. And here I am, back in good old South Yorks, trying to persuade the Foundation that it can't try to turn all its little Cambodian orphans into little English children overnight. They're a stubborn lot, you know. Some of them really can't see why not. Our benefactor, Lady Muck, wants them all to grow up into nice young clean-living *New Statesman* readers. She just can't see the problem. And it's her money, so we have to toe her line a bit. Even nowadays. The Save the Children Fund think she's crazy. But what can they do? She's got the dough. People think they can do *anything* to children. And that the kids will be grateful. Ooo, lovely, they'll say, when they see hot water coming out of a tap, ooo, lovely, let's all be British.'

'Now let me get this right,' says Alix, boldly. 'You're talking about a hostel for Cambodian children in Glydale? That's where you work?'

'That's the picture. Yes, me and Rhoda. We're funded by UNICEF. We're called liaison officers.'

'And how do the children get there?'

'Oh, they get flown out. Lady Muck has her ways and means. She gets them processed. And most of them *are* genuine orphans, things have tightened up on that bit. Gone are the bad old days when you could just fly out any old baby whose mother wanted to get rid of it. Or couldn't afford *not* to want to get rid of it. No, most of these are the genuine article. Poor little brats. Do you remember Operation Babylift?'

'I can't say I do,' says Alix. Betty is making her head spin, and the thought of the lost Cambodian children perplexes her imagination. She knows Glydale well: it is one of her favourite valleys. The water sings through the limestone, the little pansies scatter the short turf, violets hide in the moss, and in spring the lambs cry. It is probably not like that at all in Cambodia.

'Operation Babylift,' continues Betty relentlessly. 'Vietnam 1975, good old President Ford thinks it would be a great idea to fly a load of Vietnamese babies back to the US of A. So he puts out a lot of stories about how they'll all be eaten alive when Saigon falls, and tells everybody what great propaganda it will be when the plane flies in. Photo opportunities of President with wee babe in arms. Everyone rushing to foster and adopt. Great-hearted America. Cut the red tape, says Ford. Load 'em on, fly 'em over, get out the cameras. It will make a tremendous effect. That's what he says. I quote "A tremendous *effect*". So they stuff them on board this Galaxy. Ever seen a Galaxy? The biggest bloody – sorry, excuse-my-language – the biggest aeroplane ever built. A transport. They load it with 243 so-called orphans, flash flash, flash flash, photo photo, wave wave, smile smile, keep the weeping mothers out of the pics, smile smile and off they go, to the good life and the hot showers of the glorious West. Except they don't, they crash into the rice field a mile out of Saigon. Burned to pieces. Half of them dead. The pilot survived, poor excuse-my-language bugger.'

'How horrible,' says Alix, faintly.

'Yes, it was bloody horrible. We were there, weren't we, Rho? And you can't blame it all on the Americans. Most of it you can, fair enough, but we Brits copy them when we can. The *Daily Mail* had a go too. Flew a load to Britain. Most of those babies died as well. Of measles.'

Rho coughs quietly, and says, 'Not *most*, Betty.'

'Well, some,' says Betty, unrepentant.

'*One*, I think,' says Rho.

191

Betty laughs. Then she continues.

'Rho and I sometimes think we'll adopt an orphan, don't we, Rho? We really took to that little monster in Khao-i-Dang. Smart little brute. "Be you my mother, Mrs Betty, be you my mother, Mrs Rho." Like a bloody parrot. On and on. Tagging along. Like a bloody parrot. Clever little bastard. I don't like babies, but he was a clever little lad. He'll do fine if ever he gets out of there.'

Rho clears her throat, and speaks again, in her small voice.

'In the hostel, there are twenty young people,' she says, in her perfect, unreal, disembodied soft English. 'Twenty, between the ages of twenty and ten. And one young man who supervises. Twenty Cambodians in the Yorkshire Dales. It is a strange sight. You should come and see us, Alix.'

'Alix has got enough on her hands with her beastly murderer and that beastly dog,' says Betty. 'She can't take on orphans and refugees as well. Each to our own.'

She laughs, heartily, a deep guttural embodied laugh.

'But why?' asks Alix. 'Why Glydale?'

'Lady Muck's ancestral home,' says Betty. 'Going to rack and ruin, but still habitable. Just about. Used to be a Field Study Centre until some bright boys from Barnsley tried to burn it down. Then she decided to set up this Foundation. Thought orphans would be better behaved. Saw a programme on *Blue Peter* or something like that. Bleeding heart. The woman's mad, but then most people are. *We're* mad, aren't we, Rho?'

Alix, half listening as Betty rattles on about Pestalozzi and UNICEF and Bob Geldof, wonders if she can remember anything at all about Rhoda Lee, from that distant schoolgirl past.

There had been a few foreign children at The Heights, children of minor diplomats and travelling academics. A Nigerian, a Botswanan, an Indian Jamaican, a Lebanese. They had been tolerantly embraced by the tolerant, liberal, progressive regime, and had been tolerantly but relentlessly bullied into playing netball and cricket, into singing hymns from *Songs of Praise*, into eating up their school dinners. Differences had not been encouraged.

Had Rhoda Lee sat quietly in a corner trying to find out how to be English? To be honest, Alix simply cannot recall her. Betty she remembers vividly, Betty she would have known anywhere, but Rhoda had effaced herself from the screen. She does not even linger on as an oddity, as an anomaly. Yet here she is, sitting neatly, neutrally, listening to reminiscences, as though she had all the time been there, as though she had always been part of the weave. Had she been Betty's friend, even then? Had Betty spoken to her then as she does now?

Yes, says Betty, jumping across the decades and the hemispheres, yes, she had really enjoyed old Dotty's Racine classes. She'd never forget his rendering of *Athalie*. 'I can remember it now,' says Betty Sykes. '*Pour réparer des ans l'irréparable outrage.*' And then he'd break off and give us a little lecture on how cosmetics were bad for the skin. Funny set text to give us at that age, don't you think? I wonder what happened to Stanley Gorer? I used to fancy I really fancied him!'

Names, faces, moments. They waver and approach and dissolve. Alix has not spoken of these things for years, for there is nobody that she sees now from her schooldays. She has remade herself in a new image. 'Whatever happened to Miss Fawcett? Do you remember when she ticked you off for being a communist?' asks Betty.

'She died,' says Alix.

They play the game of Do You Remember until Brian returns from the theatre and disperses them. Betty and Rho disappear in their Ford Fiesta to their mysterious hostel full of mysterious oriental strangers, and Alix and Brian take the dog for a brief walk and then put themselves to bed.

Brian does not speak much about *Lysistrata*. Brian is not well. Alix does not speak much about Betty, but after Brian has fallen into a pill-induced slumber she lies awake, thinking about Operation Babylift, and the trade in tortoises and terrapins, and poor dog Bonzo rescued from starvation. She had never wanted a dog, had denied her son Sam a dog. He had wanted a springer spaniel.

She remembers how she had bullied her own mother over the tortoise. On and on, bravely and persistently. In the end, her mother had given in, and off Alix had gone, triumphant, to the market place, and had selected her own from the miserable expiring pile in the brutal dirty corral. She had chosen him because of the look in his eye.

He had looked at her, or so she fancied, in appeal. He had asked for sanctuary, for salvation. She had handed over her careful collection of heavy silver coins, and had carried him home in her basket. How lucky he was, to be rescued! How grateful he would be! How he would delight in the Lodge garden, with its broad lawn, its chestnut tree, its flowerbeds, its compost heap!

But Timothy had been ungrateful. He had sulked in his shell. In vain had little Alix tempted him with leaves and worms and morsels of minced meat. At first he would sometimes put out his wobbling, wrinkled old man's neck and nibble toothlessly, but increasingly he sulked. Alix took it into her head that he was lonely, and pleaded to be allowed to buy him a friend to share the green acre. Her mother put her foot down and refused. One tortoise was worry enough. Eventually he went into a perpetual sulk and emerged no more. Was he dead? How could one tell? Alix, terrified, after a few days summoned up courage to approach the immobile shell. She picked it up, and saw to her horror clinging to its base and to the stumps of decaying legs some unfamiliar, star-fish-shaped, sucking spider creatures. Timothy was dead. He had been devoured by alien monsters. Not only had he been devoured, she had herself been responsible for introducing these unknown creatures into the English landscape, where they would surely spread and maraud and multiply and destroy all native growths.

So the little Alix had feared, and, looking back, her fantasies did not now seem utterly ludicrous. Why, only the other day she had read of the new plague of New Zealand flatworms which was threatening to destroy our British earthworms. Why not an African tortoise-spider? Gnawing at the roots of our culture, our country?

Her mother had taken pity on the weeping Alix, had tried, rationally, calmly, to explain that tortoises were not really adapted to the English climate, that it was cruel to encourage the cruel tortoise trade by purchasing them. Why, if Alix were to purchase the whole pet store full of tortoises, they would only die in Alix's garden, and the pet store man would order a consignment more, and they too would die, and so it would go on for ever. But it was *nicer* for him to die in my garden than in that tin tray, sobbed Alix, duplicitous, not mentioning her fear that he had died of loneliness and grief, not daring to mention the obscene spiders on his withered armoured corpse. Patiently Dolly Doddridge had explained that this was a fallacy, it was anthropomorphism, it was imagining that tortoises saw the world as humans see it. A tortoise, said Dolly firmly, would much prefer to stay in Africa where it came from. A tortoise does not appreciate English views and English grass. Alix had allowed herself to be diverted into discussion of anthropomorphism, a new word to her. The word 'animism' was also introduced at this juncture into her vocabulary. Timothy had not died in vain.

Will the rescued Cambodian unaccompanied minors survive their multiple traumas and grow up into Wordsworthian pantheists under the soft influence of the Yorkshire hills and skies and rivers? Or is it too late for all that kind of stuff?

Brian stirs and cries out in his sleep. Brian is entering Bad Time.

Alix tries not to hear Brian. She thinks instead of her murderer also imprisoned in the Yorkshire landscape, who has recently developed a new ploy. He has taken to asking her for the means of death. He wants to commit suicide, and he expects Alix to aid him.

She has pointed out to him that he has no right to make such a demand on her. Aiding a suicide is illegal and she does not want to end up in gaol too. Anyway, she argues, somewhat weakening her position, she would not know what to get hold of for him. What does he want? Pills, a rope, a razor blade? What if he makes a hash of it?

Paul replies that it would not much matter if he did. What worse can happen to him than has happened? Has she no pity for him?

Paul can tell that Alix thinks a man has a right to his own suicide. He is quite astute about that sort of thing. You could say he has got to know her rather better than she has got to know him. She is, after all, much more knowable. And it is not difficult to work out that one of the reasons she continues to visit him is that she finds his situation both interesting and unattractive. She *ought* to want to help. Or so Paul argues.

And it is fair to say that at times Alix thinks Paul would be much better off dead. He has little pleasure in life, and no prospects. The prison food, as he never tires of telling her, is unappetizing. And although there is little evidence, Alix believes that he must be suffering from some form of guilt. How could one kill all those people and not feel bad about it? Alix knows that in his place, she would. In his place, she would certainly prefer to be dead, and would argue that she had a right to death, to her own death.

This does not mean that she intends to supply the razor blade, merely that she is forced to feel guilty for not supplying the razor blade. Cowardly, and guilty. A failure as a ministering angel.

This does not get her down very much. For, contrary to Paul's reasonable assumption, she does not feel much pity for him. A little, of course, but not much. What she feels about him is, as we have already seen, something more akin to curiosity. What will he come up with next? As a supplier of moral conundrums, he has done rather well. She had thought she had cracked him by tracking down his mother and supplying him with a tormented, psychotic childhood and a dead sibling rival, but of course the explanation was inadequate, if factually true: for there Paul continues to sit, on her monthly visits, staring at her across the little plastic-topped, cigarette-scarred table with those pale compulsive eyes, forcing eye contact upon her, making her attempt to peer into his impenetrable soul. (His wicked soul, his evil soul?)

He is as incomprehensible, as opaque as he ever was. The fact that he can conduct a rational conversation about a person's rights to terminate his own existence or about the Open University syllabus does not mean that he is any nearer to conveying to her his dark essence.

Alix is playing at being Ministering Angel, Florence Nightingale, Mother Theresa. But it is only a game. She has no belief. What is real is what goes on in that head. The eyes are the windows of the soul. Alix stares into the eyes of Paul Whitmore. One is told to avoid eye contact with terrorists, with hijackers, and Alix has come to think that Paul's victims must have become involved and sucked into death by their inability not to respond to Paul's insistent, deliberate, questioning gaze. There is some interchange, some chemical interaction. She is sure of it. She stares across from the Good Time in her own head into the Bad Time in his and feels, as lovers feel, that if she stares long and hard enough her essence will mix and mingle with his. If she had met Paul in a pub on the Harrow Road, in a café on the Mozart Estate, on a lonely walk along the towpath or a ramble round the Victorian monuments of Kensal Green Cemetery, she too might have become a part of him, an accomplice, an infused ghost-shell of dead-body-breath. Even now, as she sits safely, guarded by wardens, talking of razor blades, he may take it into his head to reach across the table and throttle her. After all, as he does not tire of pointing out, he has nothing to lose. He is already doing life.

Is it death itself that attracts her, that compels her, month after month, to sit there and gaze across the border? The notion is mystical, but death is not. There is nothing fanciful about death. Why is she drawn to this bridge, this frontier, this confrontation? Is he breathing into her, or she into him? Is she becoming a part of his plot? A flux, a sucking, a fluid transaction, through the moist films of the eyeballs. Sometimes she feels a compulsion to surrender. But the wardens are there to prevent that kind of thing. Navy-blue, buttoned, braided, stout, hung with bunches of keys. They guard the frontiers.

Paul Whitmore has heard that you can buy stuff called Fempan which, when mixed with raw alcohol, is lethal, even in small quantities. He swears it is a kind of women's pill for menstrual pains available without prescription, but points out that even if it requires a prescription, Alix would have no difficulty in getting hold of it. Alix finds this story ridiculous, and asks him where he got hold of it. He says he was told it by a bloke. It's well known to be true. Everyone inside knows it. First it gives you a high, then it kills you. Alix cannot tell whether he is having her on or not. She thinks not. Prisons are full of misinformation and disinformation, garbage mythology, legend, atrocity stories, gossip, recipes. She'd heard a few of them when working at the Garfield Centre, but she'd never heard this one before. She protests that it must be rubbish, but Paul says no, Fempan's dangerous stuff, but it's only dangerous to blokes, see? It's something to do with hormones. Women can take it, but men can't. It's said to be an easy way to go. Makes you feel high, then sleepy, then cheerio goodbye and Bob's your uncle.

Alix finds these ludicrous conversations, interwoven as they are with her more solemn reflections on entropy and the death wish, bizarrely entertaining. Perhaps after all Paul is simply *dotty*? Very stupid, and *dotty*?

Cambodian refugees, imprisoned murderers, tortoises. Alix floats lightly and fervently on the edge of sleep. Downstairs, Bonzo, sole survivor of an atrocity, sleeps and quivers and trembles in his basket. He has bad, bad dreams of mass slaughter, in this safe house.

*

There are roughly 25,000 Vietnamese refugees in Britain, and some 400 Cambodians. Home Office policy originally dispersed them in small settlements throughout the country — 20 here, 50 there, 14 to Northam, 7 to Cumbria. A lonely 2 to the Wyre Forest. But they tended to drift together again, in waves of secondary migration. They clustered in London and Birmingham, Leeds, Manchester, Bradford. The Cambodians converged on Gravesend.

Some of them learn English, some do not. Some get jobs, some do not. Some makes friends, some do not. Most of them do not like the weather. They are not wholly grateful. Many of them did not want to come to England at all, if the truth were told. Many of them would have selected, given a free choice, other destinations. But they were not given a free choice. And living in Lewisham is better than dying in a tin tray or tossing about with the dead and dying for two and a half months on an open boat. They have come into Good Time from Bad Time. Have they not?

One of the oddest things about the refugees is that they seem to want to go back to their own country. You would think they would have learned better by now, but no, many of them — most of them — continue to dream of getting out of Here and going back There. They dream of fishing boats and rice fields and lakes and blue skies. They dream of markets and temples and tea, when they ought to be dreaming of television sets and washing machines and motorcars and frozen convenience shepherd's pie. Occasionally, on a street corner, unexpectedly assailed by a familiar odour of hot oil or pungent spice or seed wafting form a Chinese or Vietnamese restaurant, they are ready to die from nostalgia.

Some of them do die. Nostalgia can be lethal. A new medical condition is discovered and named. It is called Sudden Death Syndrome. For no reason, for the sake of a smell, a perfume, a memory, a dream, the heart panics, fibrillates, then stops.

Most do not die. But they do not really like it here very much. They are polite about it, when cross-questioned, but they would really rather go home. If it were safe to go.

*

Mme Savet Akrun is plucking a chicken for the market. Her daughter Sok Sita is sitting hunched on the little platform bed in the corner of the hut, reading a comic. She is sniffing in a way that irritates her mother. Everybody sniffs. It is the dust. It gets on her nerves. In the old days, in petit bourgeois Phnom Penh, she had told the children not to sniff. It seems pointless now, to try to live nicely, in these conditions. Still, she wishes Sok Sita would not sit there sniffing.

The chicken is scraggy and very free range. Its skin is pocked and yellow. She had wrung its neck herself. In the old days, she would not have known how to kill a chicken. Now, it comes easily to her. As killing men had come easily to others. Though not everybody had become a killer.

She remembers the monkey. She often thinks of the monkey. One starry night, Mitra and his cousin had caught (illegally, of course) a monkey in a tree trap, near the first more friendly village of the Old People. They had been proud of themselves, they had brought it back tied in creeper-twine, they had intended to kill and eat it. Monkey flesh was good, it had vitamins, it sustained. But the monkey in its bondage had stared at them from terrified eyes, cowering, pleading, its teeth bared, its little child's hands clutching. She had turned away, not wanting to see its death. Willing to eat, and yet afraid to kill. And Mitra too had not wanted to kill. He and his cousin Mau had let the monkey go.

She often thinks of this. It gives her a little hope. Some kill, but some do not.

She fears that her son Kem is a killer. He looks like a bandit. He has thick dark curling hair, thick jutting eyebrows, aggressive lip-pose, and he sports a yellow metal earring and a red scarf. He is tough, loud-mouthed, quick-tempered, and at times he seems a little deranged. He reviles the United Nations Border Relief, Oxfam, the Thai Rangers, the Khmer collaborators. He despises his mother for her association with the camp officials and the relief workers. He calls her a lackey of the imperialist West. She tells him not to talk parrot talk. He yells at her that she is a slave and a servant. A great anger is bottled up in his compact body. He tells her she should never have left Cambodia, should never have led him into this prison. I carried you sick in my arms into this camp, she reminds him. You should have left me to die, he yells.

Spit out the rice, spit out the water, she says. Live without them if you can.

He spits, but he eats and drinks.

Sometimes he shouts at her, 'Mitra is dead! You think he is eating meat in a restaurant in America, but he is dead! Dead! Dead!'

He is flesh of her flesh and she has seen him suffer. She has seen his legs like twigs, she has seen his great red-rimmed eyes swim with pain and fever, she has seen his poor round skull head lose its baby hair, she has swabbed with her own saliva the ulcer on his jaw. A yellow suppurating pit, an encrusted, growing crater. She had begged for medicines, but there were no medicines. A nasty green paste they had given her, but she had not dared to use it. One night she had known he was dying in her arms. He had grown hot, then rigid, and then had gone into spasm. She had held him and rocked him and prayed for his flight. But he had cooled and recovered, and now he rages from a full UNBRO stomach.

'Mitra is dead!' he taunts her.

What will become of him? In her heart she cannot blame him for his violence. He is a child of violence, it is natural that he should rage. He has no home, no country, no language. He speaks bad Khmer, bad English, snatches of bad French. In her heart she despises the young men of the camp whose only aim is to scrounge and beg and ingratiate themselves and worm their way into a free conduct to Elsewhere. The camp breeds deviance and sycophancy, idleness and self-pity, dependence and despair, as well as violence and terror. Kem is angry, and he has not sold out. He smoulders. He is the next generation. When the fighting breaks out, as it will, Kem will be there. Where else could he be?

Sok Sita is mentally and physically retarded. Her sufferings have scattered her wits. She had once been a pretty, healthy, capricious little girl, with a passion for beads and trinkets, for finery and display. Now, while the young women of the camp breed and breed on a diet of UNBRO rice and dried fish, Sok Sita sits and sucks her thumb and sniffs and turns the pages of a much thumbed American comic dated April 1984. She is unkempt, vacant. She does not seem to be unhappy. She is twenty-two years old. She will breed no soldiers for the Resistance. She is useless. She is well adapted to life in Site Ten.

Mme Akrun plucks the last few feathers, and singes the stubs of the quills. She was taught how to do this by her friend and neighbour, the resourceful Yan, a tireless mender and fixer and contriver from Battambang, whose path has crossed hers again and again over the past years of wandering. Mme Akrun is grateful to Yan. They have both come through. The acrid, burning smell of feather is pleasant, refreshing. She ties the precious yellow soup-feet together with string. The little chickens, offspring of this trussed corpse, peck about in the dust of the hut, scavenging.

Mme Akrun sits there motionless by the flickering lamplight. She pulls up her bare heels beneath her and straightens her back and places her hands upon her knees and sets her mind free. She has practised this. She seeks images of peace. No longer are these drawn, as they had been in her childhood, from the natural world, from the family. She no longer seeks the trees, the river, the paddy fields, the water buffalo of her grandparents' village, nor the quiet comforting murmur of adult voices beyond a bamboo partition at night. These have been violated and contaminated. The village is dead. It is a place not of peace but of torture and violence. She seeks other images. A cinema, a sidewalk café, a public garden, a railway station, a schoolroom, a flower market. Urban images, social images. Step by step, stone by stone, she makes herself walk through the little suburban shopping street of Versailles, where she used to buy carrots and leeks, onions and potatoes, for the evening potage. What is time? She steps, head high, like a young girl.

*

The Turtle Lake

The turtle lake mirrors the sky. Three faceless figures stand on the little bridge, looking towards the pagoda. The willow mourns to the water and the orange flame-trees blaze. A black swan drifts. Fat carp rise for feeding, their golden spines nudging the meniscus. Darker shapes move slowly in the depths and do not rise. A stone dragon gazes for ever at a stone phoenix, esoteric symbols of power and of knowledge. The carp is patience. It waits. A fountain drips. The little house on stilts is empty now. The patient sky attends. The telephone does not ring. Dark red wood gleams. An old man in a heavy coat with a curtained helmet on his head and goggles for eyes moves madly in the distance with a long stick. His face is thin as death. He has no teeth, no nose. Uncle Ho, eviscerated, sleeps in yellow wax, in the heart of a marble palace not of his own choosing. Deaths, crimes, vengeances, oppressions, crowds, mobs and battles all slumber here, awaiting the second coming. The golden sword is drowned deep in the lake. Will it ever be restored?

Dans un vieux passage à Paris on m'a enseigné les sciences classiques. Dans une magnifique demeure cernée par l'Orient entier j'ai accompli mon immense œuvre et passé mon illustre retraite. Je suis réellement d'outre-tombe, et pas de commissions.

*

Stephen Cox and Konstantin Vassilious sit helplessly, strapped and bound, side by side, as puffs of white gas beat down towards them.

'I think this must be the end,' murmurs Stephen, politely, with the tone of amused detachment with which Konstantin has decided he would indeed meet that final thing. But it is not the end, nor even the worst. Objects begin to fall upon them, and from behind them there is a sudden thump. They are forced forward. 'Jesus,' says Konstantin, bracing his knees, rubbing his ankle, and waiting for more.

But as the aeroplane swoops upwards and levels off, things get better. The dry ice disperses, objects cease to fall, and the mountains of unattached luggage behind their seats slide back again. Konstantin pulls up his trouser leg and inspects his ankle. A roving grey metal box has gouged a hole, but it is only a small hole, and it is not even bleeding. It is skinned white and grazed. It's nothing, he assures Stephen.

It is an odd kind of flight, this flight to Vietnam. Konstantin had arranged it. After the incident with the tank on the border, both had been possessed by an urgent desire to get moving, to get out of stagnation and on to the other side of the lines. Konstantin has promised that it will be easy to get into Kampuchea from Vietnam, and he has used his contacts and his Global International credit to good effect. Stephen has been grateful for his help and his companionship. He is touched that Konstantin does not yet seem to find him an old bore. Konstantin, for his part, is touched that a proper writer like Stephen Cox seems happy to tag along with him. That is the acknowledged scenario. So far, they are getting on fine.

They are getting on better than Stephen's play and novel. A draft of his novel reposes in the safe deposit at the Trocadero. His play is still in his head.

And now he is on his way to Hanoi, to get a pass to Ho Chi Minh Ville, to get a pass to Phnom Penh, to get a pass to the end of the road. That is the way it seems to work.

The aeroplane is a Fokker carrying a mixture of soldiers and civilians. They are the only Europeans aboard.

It is not very comfortable. Stephen remembers the luxury of his last flight with Miss Porntip, eating caviare. Now he is offered a few bruised split grapes in a plastic beaker and a Ritz cracker. Don't worry, says Konstantin, the food in Vietnam is great.

Is that Kampuchea beneath them now? That mountainous impenetrable range of broccoli?

Hanoi of the Red River greets them with many forms in triplicate, with a bumpy taxi drive past flocks of geese and brick factories, with dusk and reflected lights. A Russian delegation is met with an ungainly sheaf of gladioli, but there are no flowers for Stephen and Konstantin. When they reach their hotel, the electricity supply fails, and they check in by yellow oil flickers. The hotel is vast and shabby, of ancient French grandeur. Its wide wooden corridors and staircases are shadowed in austere gloom.

Stephen's room is as large as a dormitory. He paces it restlessly. Then he rolls himself a little cigarette, and opens the windows and shutters and mosquito gauze, and leans out to watch the street scene below. There is a large unfamiliar tree outside his window, with glossy leaves and strange round fruit. Beneath, on the wide pavement at the hotel entrance, pedicabs wait for custom. There is a constant flux of people, on bicycles and walking. Most of them are hung with baskets of produce, with bags of shopping. Babies balance on handlebars or travel in slings on the backs of pedestrians. An occasional car hoots recklessly against the human tide. Stephen inhales his tobacco and watches the peaceful flow. He feels himself to be upon the verge of one of those moments of visionary sweetness, of communion with a common purpose, that sometimes comes upon him in strange places where he knows nobody. In such moments, he as observer dissolves and flows away into the daily life of others. He absents himself, and becomes what they are. The voyeur fades into the seen.

He waits, but the moment does not come to him. It comes more rarely now. He grows old.

A clock strikes seven, its amplified tones filling the city. An unhappy timbre, to his ear.

Stephen thinks of the people of Cambodia, forced to listen to hour after hour of amplified political indoctrination, night after night, at the end of a hard day's labour. Bored to death, as one survivor in Thailand had told him. Literally, bored to death. If you yawned, you were shot. Control of face, very important.

Stephen remembers his National Service days when he had met Brian Bowen. He remembers the boredom. He remembers Brian, who befriended him during those grim weeks of basic training. Stephen had been mocked for his middle-class accent, for his stammer. Brian had taken his part against his tormentors. Brian spoke, in those days, a broad South Yorkshire. Stephen had idealized Brian as a Man of the People. But Brian had been a man of the people, and, despite his progress through the educational structure, he remains one still. Brian likes people, he gets on with people. Such things cannot be taught. Brian does not need to dissolve and fade. He is at home in the Socialist Republic of South Yorkshire. Brian is a lucky man.

The people of the Socialist Republic of Vietnam move and weave beneath Stephen's window. He is shocked to see a beggar approaching hotel customers as they come and go: a teenage beggar, in ragged jeans. He knows that Vietnam is a tragically poor country, far poorer than the artificially sustained border camps. But nevertheless, a beggar, here?

He hears Miss Porntip laugh at his surprise. And in truth he is not surprised. He is sad that he is not surprised.

He could have pointed out to Miss Porntip that the streets of Washington and New York are filled with beggars. They sleep in doorways, they thrust at strangers their plastic folders of credentials.

So this is Vietnam, the legendary country. Stephen paces his room, and pauses at the old-fashioned wooden desk on which he has already placed his notebooks, his pens, his little Sony radio, his professional paraphernalia, in an attempt to legitimize his wholly gratuitous, ahistorical presence in this arbitrary place. Somebody has carved deeply into the desk an unfinished sentence, in raw splintered wounded strokes: *La Guerre n'est jamais* . . . He reads it by matchlight. What had the scribe intended to tell Stephen? And what had interrupted him? An air-raid warning, a B52, a power failure, a transfer upcountry? Boredom, fatigue, illness, sudden death?

The Americans had rained bombs upon this city. They had destroyed themselves in the process, and the aftermath of destruction continues, relentlessly. *La Guerre n'est jamais* . . . In the *Bangkok Post* that week Reuters had reported a bizarre incident from Washington. A young man from Chesapeake, visiting the Vietnam Veterans Memorial, in pious search of his dead father's name, had become incensed to find that the portion of the dark polished funereal granite that bore it was obscured by a hose, a suction pipe and a sheet of plastic. The memorial was being cleaned. He had demanded that these offending items be removed. The white guard and the two black men engaged in the cleaning operation had refused. The young man had produced a gun and had shot them dead. No dialogue was reported.

Stephen had himself visited and paid his respects to the memorial. He has noted that seventy-four Americans by the name of Cox had died in Vietnam. They had come here from the Good Time of Bedford and Pleasant Hill, from Sacramento and Pittsburgh, from Primeville and Weatherford, to die for their country.

Stephen thinks of those American airmen who had died so mysteriously during the Second World War in the Somerset Levels near the home of his childhood. How that cheap concrete cross with its cheap tin punched plaque had drawn him, again and again. He knew its inscription by heart. 'In memory of the five brave US airmen who lost their lives here on October Twenty Four, 1942'. The names themselves he had forgotten, but not that they had been followed by the words. 'And One Unknown'. Who was the

Unknown Airman? How had the authorities managed to trace *all but one*? Had he been a stowaway, a joy-rider? Had he been a spy? Had he been, like Stephen himself, a frivolous adventurer? Had his family ever known where his bones rested, or did they expect him still one day to stagger, white-haired, bowed, broken, through the kitchen door to the empty place at table? Stephen, as a child, had been haunted by the One Unknown.

Once, visiting the memorial, he had been surprised to find a floral tribute propped against the foot of the cross. A wired wreath of canvas poppies, gazing out over the flat water, the red muddy banks, the reeds and reflected willows. He had thought these dead men belonged to himself alone.

Stephen sighs, and taps his ash gently on to the window ledge outside. And suddenly, the lights in his room come on, the heavy ceiling fan begins slowly and noisily to rotate. The hotel is restored to modern life.

When he goes downstairs, he overhears two Americans arguing with the girls behind the bar about the absence of bottled water. He cannot help but overhear them, for one of them is raising his voice very loud. Fat, balding with low-slung jeans and a professional camera, he protests: 'Watchamean, lady, ya not got none? Ya get some right now. Whatcha tryin to *do*, ya tryin to poison your guests? Ya get some, ya hear me?'

The other man, a tall, thin, moustached, melancholy film-technician figure, intervenes. 'She done understand,' he mutters. 'She done understand ya.'

'Sure, she understands,' says the fat guy, loudly. 'She speaks English, sure she speaks English, when she feels like it, she speaks English. You speak English, dontcha lady?'

The girl behind the bar slightly averts her face, looking blank and bored. Again, mutely, she proffers a bottle of some kind of juice, and a can of beer. The scene has clearly been going on for some time. It is deadlock, stalemate, a little international tableau.

THE GATES OF IVORY

'I can't clean my teeth in *beer*, for Chrissake,' says the fat man.

'Aw, comeon, Packman,' says the other, keen to cut losses and get out of the impasse.

'Water. Mineral water. Bottled water. Wasser. Aqua. Voda Voda,' yells the fat man, thumping the dolorous little bar counter with his great meat fist.

The scene is grotesque, a caricature. Stephen watches with curiosity and a certain shame to see how far it will go. It does not go very far, for there is no way the American can win, and he knows it. Impassively, the woman continues to offer her juice and her beer. After a few more demands, the American is forced to quit. The two leave, with ill grace, to scour the streets of Hanoi for mineral water.

Stephen describes this incident to Konstantin over a pleasant little meal of tomato salad and curried langoustines. Konstantin shrugs. It's not easy for foreigners here, he says. They get nervous. And the Vietnamese aren't used to foreigners. They get nervous too.

After supper, Konstantin and Stephen stroll around the lake in the moonlight. They see a man pissing into the lake. They see smokers of opium and sellers of single cigarettes and a street offering nothing but painted shoes. They hear subdued laughter from behind closed doors. It is a secret city.

Konstantin leads Stephen down a long, wide, tree-lined avenue, past ornate nineteenth-century French colonial buildings of red and orange and ochre. They pass a temple and a park and a statue to Lenin. It is strange to walk in a city at night without street lighting.

They turn down a narrow street of small shuttered bookstalls, and reach what seems to be a concierge's lodge, leading to a courtyard and a larger building beyond. Konstantin taps on the door. There is whispering from within, a chain is released, the door is opened, and a small woman in a blue dress greets them both. There are introductions, kisses, cries of delight. *'Venez, venez,'* says the woman, and leads them through the lodge and out of a side door and across the corner of a courtyard to a room where brighter lights glow. She opens the door for them, pushes her way through a bead curtain, and ushers them into a larger room.

There, sitting in front of them, is a naked young woman. She is sitting on a low platform, her arms around one crooked knee.

At second glance, Stephen sees she is not quite naked. She is wearing a pair of navy-blue schoolgirl knickers, and a shell necklace.

Stephen's first thought is that Konstantin, against every probability, has brought him to a brothel. John Geddes had taken him to a brothel in Bangkok: but in Hanoi, surely not? This thought lasts but an instant, for it is at once clear that this cannot be so.

The naked young woman does not move, although she directs towards them a composed half-smile of welcome. She does not move because she is posing for a life class. Two young men and one young woman are engaged in drawing her in charcoal. The room is too small and the lighting poor, explains her mother, but it is the best they can do.

She speaks in a mixture of French and English. When Stephen replies in French, she is delighted. She sits him on a cushion, next to one of the artists, settles Konstantin in another corner, and goes off to make tea.

The artists continue to work, but are eager to converse at the same time. How is their friend Konstantin, where has he been, what news from Bangkok and the West? They chatter, exchanging news, and Stephen gazes at the woman.

She is quite an ordinary-looking young woman, with a good body and a smooth unblemished skin and a serene face. She has small girlish breasts and delicate wrists and ankles. She must be about twenty years old.

Is it the navy knickers that give her such a look of purity and innocence? Not wholly. It is more the calm, the self-containment, the everyday matter-of-factness of her willing exposure.

Stephen, who prefers corrupt and decorated women, gazes at her as though she were the clue to the history of the perversions of sex through the ages. As perhaps she is.

Tea is brought, cigarettes are smoked, but the atmosphere remains faintly studious. Hong has agreed to pose for an hour, and there are thirty-five minutes to go. These are disciplined people.

Stephen gets out his own sketch book, and tries a pencilled line or two, but gives up in despair. He cannot embrace or reproduce the human form. He has enough difficulty with simple-structured objects. The planes and angles of the body are beyond him. He notes that the sketch of his nearest neighbour-artist is not very good either, but it is far better than anything he himself could do. He decides to sit and watch.

The chatter dies away as the concentration of the artists deepens. An intent, attentive silence, as of a Quaker meeting, succeeds. The woman's necklace is made of little pearly shells, strung together on a piece of thread. They make her throat look vulnerable, defenceless. But she does not look as though she fears attack.

Why does she keep her knickers on? Is it the custom of the country?

He finds himself wondering what she will look like when she puts on her clothes. A reverse curiosity.

He has not long to wait. The mother looks at her watch, claps her hands and says 'Finish' in English. The concentration of the room breaks instantly, but Stephen watches, transfixed, as the young woman unbends her leg, stretches her arms wide, shakes her hands to restore circulation, then raises her hands high above her head and stretches. Her little breasts ride up her rib cage. She lowers her hands and wraps her arms round both raised knees, and looks around her, smiling. The others thank her, but she is still half absent, half abstracted. He watches personality flood slowly into her, as she returns in spirit to the group. She stands up, stretches again, scratches her neck, and reaches behind her for her clothes. First she pulls on a grey cotton T-shirt, then she wraps round herself a grey–blue check-printed cotton skirt. She looks smaller and thinner and a little older clothed than naked. She steps into a pair of plastic sandals. She takes the pin out of her hair and combs her hair. That is all there is to her. A pair of knickers, a T-shirt, a cotton skirt, a shell necklace, a pair of plastic sandals and a hairpin.

Now she is advancing towards him, her hand outstretched in greeting. 'Hello, Stephen,' she says, in perfect English. 'How nice to meet you, how nice of Konstantin to bring you round. I have so much enjoyed your books. For my mother and me, this is such a very pleasant surprise.'

*

Vietnam, Hong informs him over the next few days, is as fond of books as Thailand is fond of pop music and Rolex watches. Vietnam, she tells him proudly, has literary culture. Unlike the Thais and the Khmers, the Vietnamese are great readers. During the war, in the jungle, in the tunnels, in the air-raid shelters, in the field hospitals, in the cellars, the Vietnamese people read books and wrote poetry. Ho Chi Minh wrote poetry. *All* eighteen-year-old Vietnamese write poetry, she says. She herself writes poetry. She shows him the book shops of Hanoi, and her own collection of pirated editions of Western modern classics. Lady Chatterley, Graham Greene, William Golding, Bernard Shaw, Pearl Buck, Patrick White, Dr Spock, Colleen McCullough.

Hong is a conscientious guide and a patriot, and Stephen therefore takes all that she says with a pinch of salt. He thinks it is as unlikely that all Vietnamese write poetry as that all Thai mountain villagers have access to a VDU. Nevertheless, there seems to be something in what she says, and he continues to be astonished that she has read his work. It emerges that her claim to have read his books is a slight exaggeration, as she has read only one of them, the one that everyone has read, the one about the Commune, the one that won the Booker Prize: but this is to him sufficiently miraculous. He can see why the subject matter might appeal in Vietnam, and he has to acknowledge, a little late in the day, that the Booker has given him more currency than he had ever imagined possible. He is a modest man who does not rate his reputation very highly, and he is pleased to find that his works by whatever means have travelled so far. He is pleased not wholly through vanity, he hopes. He is pleased at this indication of the possibility of cross-cultural communication.

Hong had been a child during the war, and she admits that to her it is mythology. Her father had been one of the 19,000 killed in 1972 in the battle for Quang Tri on the northern border. She hardly remembers him. 'A pointless battle,' she says. 'A useless city, a very poor province. In Quang Tri, the dogs eat pebbles and the chickens eat salt, that is what they used to say. The Americans destroyed what was not worth destroying. It was,' she says, not quoting but coining, 'a famous victory.'

She shows him the streets of Hanoi, the temples, the pagodas, the gardens, the markets. They sit and drink tea in hidden cafés. They watch children whipping wooden tops beneath broad-leaved trees in avenues and squares that remind him of provincial France. She shows him the tombstones of mandarins and the remains of a B52 shot down in the Christmas bombing. She shows him a snake-charmer and introduces him to a magazine editor and a television film-maker. Yes, she says, there is censorship. Yes, there is poverty. Yes, there have been many mistakes. It is becoming the fashion, now, she tells him, as it is in the Soviet Union, to admit to mistakes. This word 'mistake' is very popular.

Her English is excellent. He congratulates her upon it. Yes, she says, her mother speaks French, but the younger generation, they learn English. It is more useful.

The tops hop and spin in the dust. These are the children of poverty, infinitely skilled.

She works as guide and interpreter by day, one night a week sh models for her comrades, two nights a week she teaches English. English is a growth industry, she assures him. Many many people want to learn. There is much money to be made in Vietnam, when and if the trade embargo is lifted. Already the Australians and the Dutch and the Indians are here. Americans and English are here. And when he goes to Saigon, as he will at the end of the week, he will find even more English.

They speak of Konstantin, whom she met through the Press Department when he was on his way through the year before to clear his visa for Kampuchea. She speaks well of Konstantin.

'Yes,' she says, 'he's a very nice-looking person. Very rich, and very nice looking. A lucky man. And you, Stephen? Are you rich? Are you best-seller?'

Stephen looks along the street, at old women crouching on the pavement chewing betel and selling single cigarettes, single eggs, single potatoes, at old men repairing bicycle tyres with rubber patches.

'Yes,' he says. 'I suppose I am.'

'You also are one of the lucky, then,' she says.

'Yes,' he repeats. 'Yes, I suppose I am.'

'I like Konstantin very much,' says Hong, thoughtfully. 'My boyfriend is quite jealous. He says Konstantin has too much luck. He says that too much luck is bad luck. *Embarras de richesse*. Is that a phrase you use in English? I think it is.'

'Tell me about your boyfriend,' says Stephen.

'I will take you to meet him,' says Hong. 'You tell me about your friend. Do you have a woman friend?'

Stephen finds himself speaking at some length of Liz Headleand, as he walks down Silk Street in Hanoi. He is not quite sure why. Does honour demand that he claim a woman friend? He describes Liz to Hong – her five children, her ex-husbands, her career. How does psychoanalysis fare in Vietnam, he asks.

Hong frowns, and says without edge that it does not fare. It is bourgeois. She herself is interested in it, but it is hard to find texts. What does Stephen think?

Stephen says that his friend Liz Headleand is deeply bourgeois. She is the apotheosis of the bourgeoisie. He is surprised and amused by the spontaneous admiration in his own voice as he speaks of her.

On the last evening, Hong takes him and Konstantin to the home where she lives with the boyfriend, whom Stephen recognizes as one of the would-be artists. In real life, he is a teacher of mathematics.

The room is tiny. It is above a store. It is about two thirds of the size of Stephen's small rented room on Primrose Hill. Books occupy an improvised shelf along the wall, with an old-fashioned Grundig radio. A stove stands on the floor, next to old enamelled tins that serve as the larder. In the corner is a bed, curtained with a faded embroidered soft green silk, a silk with a yellowy tarnished sheen and a golden thread. They sit on little bamboo chairs, and drink tea. There is a low table with a little arrangement of treasures: a whorled shell, a small family photograph framed in mother-of-pearl, a curved piece of antique tile, orange flowers in an old blue enamelled jug. A light breeze blows in through the open shutters.

'Yes,' says Hong. 'Here is where I write poems. As I told you, all Vietnamese write poems.'

She smiles, half-teasing.

'Read us a poem,' says Stephen.

And she reads them a short poem in Vietnamese. She says it is called 'Melon Flowers', and that it is about the view from her window. They listen, respectfully. She does not translate.

'I am a poor poet,' says Hong, modestly. 'But we have great Vietnamese poets, of course. I will give you a little book of translations. Here is one of my favourites. Ché Lan Viên. An uneven poet, but ideologically correct. His family came from Quang Tri, where my father died. You will like these poems, Stephen. There is a poem about Hamlet and the skull. Read this poem when you get to Phnom Penh. It is called "Hamlet in Vietnam". But it is also about Cambodia.'

Stephen accepts the gift, and puts it in his pocket.

'You will remember us, I hope,' says Hong. 'You will remember taking tea with us in this room. And in years to come, maybe it will be easier.'

Stephen does not know why he finds her so touching. He is sorry to say goodbye. He promises not to forget her kindness.

A leaf, a sparrow, a mouse, a butterfly, a shell.

*

Guess who I bumped into on Monday? Esther Breuer! We had supper together. I like Esther Breuer. Or should I call her Esther Oxenholme? Good name, isn't it? Doesn't sound quite real. Like Harriet Osborne doesn't sound quite real. But that's because it isn't. So it wouldn't, would it? Is she *The Honourable* Mrs Oxenholme? What a laugh.

Though she wasn't laughing when I caught sight of her. Quite the reverse. In fact I wondered if I should pretend not to notice her, she looked so glum. But then courage overcame me and I shouted out. I'm glad I did.

We were in the cinema. The Gate, Notting Hill. Now, *you* may think it's easy to avoid seeing somebody you know in the cinema, but I can assure you it isn't, or not at a six o'clock showing on a Monday of a bad old black and white French movie. Esther, me, and two old gentlemen were the only people in the whole auditorium. You may well wonder what I was doing there. Well, I go to the cinema quite a lot by myself in the afternoons. It's sort of work, of a kind. And it's sort of company, of a kind. I don't mind admitting that I was feeling a bit blue, on Monday. I don't know why, particularly. Stephen's flat suddenly seemed unbearably claustrophobic. I mean, it is quite *small*, you know. I'm not complaining, but it *is* small. I had to get out. I rang up one or two contacts, but everyone was out. Then I read a bit of Stephen's diary. Atrocity stories. Survivor stories. Quotes about the Vietnam war. God, how nasty and pointless. Then somebody rang me, and I perked up a bit at the bell, but it was Stephen's landlord, Mr Goodfellow, so that perked me down again. I mean, how long can we keep up this pretence that I'm only a visitor? He was only inquiring about my key to the new double door in the entrance hall, but still. Maybe he's after me. Maybe I'll be moved on. Anyway, I suddenly felt depressed like I was at the bottom of a well. So I had a look in *Time Out* to see what I could go to to shake myself up a bit, and I hit on this old movie. *La Condition humaine*. Have you ever seen it? Don't bother. I'd hoped it would be like *The Battle of Algiers*, which is one of my all-time favourites, but it was dull stuff, dull stuff. Should have been a big budget movie, with millions of revolting Chinese blowing up Shanghai, but it was done on the cheap with the same extras in all the crowd scenes. You got to know their faces quite well, even though they were orientals. I've never read any Malraux, have you? He must be out of fashion, you don't hear much of him these days. Stephen keeps referring to him, which gave me another reason for crossing London. There's some very well-thumbed Malraux paperbacks in the flat, but of course they're all in French, which is no use to me. I suppose I was wondering if there was something there that could be revived. Remade. *La Condition humaine*, Part Two, for the 1990s. But no, forget it.

Actually, that's not quite fair. It wasn't all that awful. There was a brilliant performance by this withered guy playing this ancient philosophic opium-taking Chinese Marxist. At least, I think that's what he was. Great stuff. And the subtitles were well above standard. I'm not trying to be funny, they really were good. There was a particularly good bit about sex, booze and opium, and which does the trick best. I noted it.

Anyway, this is beside the point. I was telling you about Esther, not about the movie. There she was, sitting crouched up two rows from the back, with her arms round her knees. I saw her as I walked past. She *is* tiny. I settled myself three rows in front, and then I turned round and flashed my smile and said, 'Hi!' I mean, it wouldn't have been right to sit *next* to her, would it? If a woman goes to a cinema by herself it's because she wants to be by herself, wouldn't you say? And Esther looked very much by herself. She looked in that half light as though maybe she had been crying. Well, not *crying*, perhaps, but brooding. But when she saw it was only me, she smiled back, and said across the rows of empty velvet, 'Hi, Hat, how are you?'

'I'm feeling really *morbid*,' I said, to cheer her up.

'Me too,' she said, looking better even as she said it.

And then the adverts started and we settled down to our viewing. When the lights went up on the four of us (actually six or seven others seemed to have crept in off the streets for shelter during the screening), I turned round again and renewed contact. And in no time at all we found ourselves agreeing to take ourselves out for a bite to eat at Bertorelli's.

She said she went to the movie because the Gate is her local. She says she often goes there to an early evening or even an afternoon show. By the time we settled down to our Punt e Mes she'd lost all trace of being tearful, and seemed quite lively. Nothing like a nice film about torture, bombs and death by cyanide to cheer one up, as she said. The human condition. The title's out of Pascal, according to Esther. The human condition is a room full of condemned men who watch one another being tortured to death while each waits his turn. I didn't know that, did you? They watch *avec douleur et sans espérance*, said Esther. Even I could understand that much French. We were glad to be out of that cinema and settled in the restaurant, I can tell you.

Impenetrable sort of person, Esther. I wonder what her private life is really like? Very odd, her marriage. One wouldn't dare ask, though she did let on that she'd been for her honeymoon to Scotland and eaten a few grouse while she was at it. Did she go shooting, I asked, and she said God no, Robert didn't shoot, he was far too sensitive to shoot anything. But he liked grouse. I'd never had one before, said Esther. I don't think they're kosher. But I quite took to them.

That's all she said about her honeymoon.

We both had a nice plateful of pasta. Very comforting to a lonely woman, a nice plateful of white pasta, and a bottle of Lacryma Christi. The waiter was a scholarly-looking young gentleman, bespectacled, with hair standing straight up on end in the new fashion. He was over here for a couple of months, visiting a nephew of a cousin of the owners, or something like that. He and Esther chatted along a bit in Italian. Apparently he came from Pallanza, on the shores of Lake Maggiore, and knew some old bird that Esther was in correspondence with. Quite a little to-and-fro they had, about the old girl. Esther says her palazzo is stuffed with paintings. *Stuffed*. Each one a king's ransom, a hostage's release.

When she'd stopped displaying her bilingual gifts, Esther asked me what I was up to these days, and I said not a lot (all too true) and asked if she knew of any good movie properties in French or Italian that I could buy up? She said she didn't read much fiction, but what about the life of Salvator Rosa, and had I liked the Derek Jarman movie about Caravaggio? I said I'd *liked* it, okay, but there wasn't the money for that kind of thing, with the British film industry being what it is. She told me a bit about Salvator Rosa. I must say, he was quite a lad. And a looker, she says. But he won't sell.

And then we got on to Liz and Stephen. Well, we would, I suppose. Esther was *quite* interested in the package business, but not *very*. What she was really interested in was whether Liz and Stephen had ever had an affair. She had hardly known him, she said, just to speak to at parties and that kind of thing, but she thought that Liz had really been quite close to him at one point. What did *I* think?

I said that I'd no idea. Which was true. But I certainly didn't object to a little speculation. What did *she* think? Oh, she said, she thought it was probably more of an *amitié amoureuse*, but you could never tell, could you? And then she asked me, point blank, if *I'd* ever had an affair with him, and I said certainly not. I put forward the view that Stephen was a characteristically wrecked product of our great English public-school system, and probably not very good in bed. This made Esther look quite thoughtful. Then she asked me who *was* good in bed, and we had a bit of a chat about that kind of thing — well, actually, looking back, I did all the chatting, she just sat and listened. I can't remember who I rated, I think I gave top marks to Gabriel Denham, but that's a hell of a long time ago, when I was easily impressed. I verged on telling her about that last evening with Stephen at Molly Lansdowne's, as we were in such confidential mood, but thought better of it.

Think of all the secrets. Just think of them. Secrets kept, secrets betrayed. I bet Esther has plenty. She doesn't give much. She used to be in love with an Italian Satanist. I always thought he was somehow responsible for all those Harrow Road murders. Maybe he was. We'll never know. Maybe he and Paul Whitmore were Jekyll and Hyde. If Esther knows, she wouldn't say.

But she was surprisingly forthcoming about Liz. According to Esther, Liz and Stephen used to dine there, in that very restaurant. She'd seen them going in together once, as she came out of Notting Hill tube. Esther thinks Charles and Liz will remarry. I wonder. Esther says she's never read any of Stephen's novels. She says she tried *Barricades*, but hadn't liked it. She doesn't like historical fiction. She says she couldn't think why he'd got hooked on Vietnam and Cambodia at this late stage in the game.

She's never been to the Far East. Has no wish whatsoever to go there, or so she says. I found myself telling her about my jaunt with

John Connell, in the days before Bangkok overheated and became as common as the Costa Brava. We had a good laugh. John Connell was one of the old swashbucklers of the sixties, he really knew how to live it up. She liked the story about how he tried to bribe the waiter to stick a knife through his hand. There was money all over the table, dollar bills cascading everywhere. We got kicked out of the restaurant. We moved on to a nightclub where we bumped into Rex. I remember John naked, on all fours, barking like a dog. Happy days. That was the night I lost my shoes, and they arrived at the hotel in the morning, neatly packaged, with an orchid attached.

No, we had a good gossip, Esther and me. I think she needed it. Must be odd, being married for the first time, after living so much on your own. I wanted to ask about that woman she went off to live with in Bologna, but didn't quite like to. I think she was the Satanist's sister.

Over our second double espresso, she asked me if I'd ever been married. No, I said, and she asked me why not. Nobody asked me, sir, I said, and as I was saying it I sort of thought it was true. But of course it's not. I *was* married, once. It's so long ago I'd almost forgotten all about it. It didn't mean anything. Much. He's dead now. So I can just blot him off the record. A non-event. It's as if it never happened. Two and a half years of my life, vanished. He died of a heart attack three or four years ago. Nobody even bothered to tell me. I read it in the paper. He *was* a lot older than me.

She said she was going to walk home. I said, aren't you nervous, after what happened? She said no, not at all, and set off into the night. I went down the tube. There was a row of beggars, very nice, and a not-so-young black guy with dreadlocks playing 'Daisy, Daisy' on a mouth organ. Not a very Notting Hill tune, unless it has some double meanings to which I am not privy.

There was a beggar actually *on* the tube, in my carriage. You don't often see that in London, it's more Paris style. There she was, this young woman, plodding along the aisle, trying to touch us all for a few bob. She wasn't getting much change. She was young, and very pregnant. Bare legs, thonged sandals, a skimpy flowery cotton dress, a long cardy, a dirty raincoat, a few beads and bangles. God, she looked ill. She had that sort of pale greeny-yellow washed-out religious look that comes from not being allowed to eat meat or have blood transfusions. A Vegan beggar. Anyway, I thought she looked ghastly, in every possible way, so soft-hearted Hattie gives her a sovereign. She pocketed it with hardly a murmur, and at the next station she got off to try the next carriage. But guess what? When I transferred from the Central to the Northern, she *followed* me. I didn't like that. I mean, would anyone *choose* to get on the Northern line who didn't have to? She got in the same compartment as me, and just sat there with her eyes shut. Meditating, no doubt.

Didn't Gabriel Denham's first wife turn into an Orange Person? Or have I made that up?

Begging's all the rage, these days. Who would have thought it? It's because we're so affluent, the politicians say. I don't quite get that, but maybe I'm being stupid. I think some of it *is* religious. Did you know that Buddhist monks have to beg for all their food, and that they're not allowed to beg or eat after midday, and that they have to eat up everything they are given, however nasty, like school children? The story goes that this monk is presented with this bowl by this leper, and, as he hands it over to the holy man, the leper's finger falls off into the rice. So the monk has to eat it. So the story goes. Do you think it is true?

When I got off at Camden Town, the pregnant beggar got off too. She *was* following me. I didn't like that. Maybe she was praying for me, or putting the evil eye on me. She followed me all the way to Stephen's flat. Just tagging along, a few yards behind. She didn't say anything, didn't try to approach me. When I let myself in with the new front door key, she just watched. What was she up to? What did she want? Where the hell was she going to spend the night?

Perhaps you think I ought to have asked her in. But I didn't. I shut the door.

*

In Saigon, the persistent teenage hotel beggar of Hanoi is recast in Stephen's memory as a harmless freak. Saigon is another kettle of fish altogether from Hanoi. No poetry, no pearly shells, no minnows, no little children with wooden tops. Here the sharks cruise. Saigon is trying to be the new Bangkok, and it will succeed. It has already achieved pollution and congestion. It has never got rid of corruption. Hanoi is boring, Saigon is lively. Hanoi is the past, Saigon is the future.

In Saigon, Stephen and Konstantin are gripped by visa fever. Stephen now sees that getting hold of a visa, of a *laissez-passer*, can become an end in itself. They sit in offices and hang around in embassies. They make up variant stories about their intentions. Konstantin is easier to accredit than Stephen, for the authorities know of Global International, but who is to vouch for a wandering fiction writer? Who will care if he murmurs politely that he would like to see the Death of Communism with his own eyes, or that he believes in the triumph of the proletariat? What gives him a right to a place at the ringside?

Being a novelist does not carry much weight. Shall Stephen claim to be a doctor, an engineer, an investor, an investigator? He is free to choose. He has disposed of his old passport, which had incriminated him as Writer, and has for the purpose of this trip acquired a new-style professionless passport. He can be whatever he wishes. What would be most acceptable? What would be safe? Who is he, whom shall he become?

It is his Russian that identifies him. At last this language, so laboriously acquired in the 1950s, comes in handy. It persuades a mild-mannered and helpful young Cambodian at the Kampuchean embassy that Stephen's presence as interpreter is essential for

Konstantin's enterprise (photoessay on the reconstruction of Kampuchea by heroic Kampuchean people), and they are promised a visa for the next day. They take themselves off to a nightclub to celebrate.

You will be relieved to hear that they do not there fall in with the Saigonese equivalent of Miss Porntip or of Hong. (A transvestite with a heart of gold? An air hostess-cum-double agent? Madame Butterfly?) But they do find themselves drinking bourbon in the Den of Demons with a young British medic from North London who appears to be a friend of a friend of Konstantin's. Eric has just got back from Kampuchea, where he has been working in a field hospital, and he gives them the news of the latest diplomatic rows about poisoned aid and poisoned vaccines, and some vivid impressions of various characters in the Aid World. The John Cleese of Oxfam, the Walter Matthau of the International Red Cross, the Jack Lemmon of the ICRDP. Eric is a good mimic. He can even do the Kampuchean official who insists on visiting him in his hotel room on important business every morning at eight fifteen. Yes, he tells Konstantin, Akira the mad Japanese journalist is still hanging out there. He recites anecdotes about Akira, as Stephen drifts off into an inner world of unquiet gut. All this talk about poisoned aid has made him realize he is feeling more and more off-colour. Some fever other than visa fever has grabbed him. His head swims a little. Air slops within him, and gases bubble along unimagined corridors of intestine. Membranes pulse. Is it the bourbon, is it the heavy pall of smoke, is it the soft-shelled crab they ate for lunch? He hopes he is not going to be ill, on this, the last stage of his journey. Discreetly, he swallows a couple of large chocolate-coloured pills, Diarrhoea-Aid.

The décor shimmers and wavers. Stephen tries to focus. A singer in a gold dress is crooning into a microphone. He peers through the gloom at badly painted expressionist murals depicting street scenes from Saigon's glorious history — a monk in flames, a woman drawing a revolver from her little green handbag, an exploding tank, a skeleton draped in the American flag. It is all a little military for Stephen's taste, and the singer sings not of love but of war. On each plastic-topped table stands a candle in a skull-shaped holder. Eric says they are alleged to be the skulls of American soldiers, but that they are most certainly nothing of the sort. They are not — he taps their own wax-and-nicotine embellished long-toothed grinner — really *real*. This is a thoroughly decadent dump, says Eric.

Alas, poor Yorick, says Eric, and launches into a few lines of *Hamlet*.

Stephen feels for the Vietnamese poems in his pocket. They are still there, and he has already read the piece recommended by Hong. In it, the poet looks back to the days of innocent history when one man could interrogate one skull. Nixon, the poet says, has no liking for the philosophic skull, which smiles back. He prefers the seven-ton bomb which destroys the lot. No more questions, no more hesitations, no more singularities. Big numbers. Mass destructions. Mass graves. Ash, not bone. The twentieth century.

Crouching uncomfortably the next day in the belly of the weekly plane of the International Red Cross, Stephen shuts his eyes and hangs on. It is not only the lurching of the aircraft that makes him feel rotten. He is sick. He feels like death. He notices nothing of the journey from the airport to the hotel. He scratches his name feebly in the register, surrenders his passport, observes as from a great distance Konstantin's enthusiastic greeting of the bush-telegraph-alerted Japanese Akira and crawls off to bed. He is feeling very sorry for himself. Sorry, and contemptuous. This is no way to behave. If he goes on like this, he will be in everybody's way, a useless burden. He wills himself to feel better, so that he will not waste his precious time here, so that he will be able to sup full on the horrors of Phnom Penh.

Visions of Phnom Penh animate his dreams, and vile music throbs and thumps in his heart. Ah, what will remain of Sisowath School, with its cool colonnaded verandas? Stands it still in the shadow of Wat Phnom, behind the National Museum? How fares Monivong Avenue, who studies now at the Lycée Descartes, how grow the gardens of the prince? Survives yet La Royale, where Frenchmen in the fifties, in their fifties, sipped Chablis? Where is the Roman Catholic cathedral? Where the Opium Den, where the Banque Khmer pour le Commerce? Flowers still the frangipani? Is the old railway station a deserted wreck, or is it painted and refurbished in a charming muted coral pink? Are the streets and markets silent and abandoned, or do they thrive with capitalist commerce? Who guards the grim records of Tuol Sleng Incarceration Centre? Whose skulls form those terrible pyramids? Are *they* really real?

Dreams of the tourist mausoleums of Auschwitz and Jerusalem, of film-footage from the liberation of the death camps, of the unfilmed atrocities of Tamburlaine, mingle with Cambodian images in Stephen's hot night as he tosses and turns beneath a thin sheet.

In the morning, he is purged. He has made a small recovery. He is well enough to venture out to verify some of his dream images.

The cathedral has gone, every stone of it, but the frangipani flowers.

The public gardens (could they have been created, he wonders, by the cousin of Mme Savet Akrun?) are in remarkably good nick. La Royale is now the Samaki, inhabited by the lavishly salaried international bureaucrats from the ICRC and the UN. The railway station where the First Party Congress met is, indeed, coral pink; and the sounds of thumping rhythm had been not ghostly but real. They had emanated, according to Konstantin, from Phnom Penh's top pop group, Mortal Remains. The Monorom Restaurant, which he must have glimpsed subliminally, is 1960s, Angkor Wat style. Angkor Wat T-shirts are on sale at the street corner.

Over lunch, he is introduced to Konstantin's Japanese friend Akira. Akira is an old hand, he is full of gossip.

He tells them what has been happening. Black market, food shortages, corruptions, shootings after curfew, breakdown of telex machine, vain promises of fax, romance of ICRDP boss with Vietnamese nurse, new mass burial ground dug up in eastern province, secret visit of son of Sihanouk, Romanian tour of Angkor Wat cancelled because of guerrilla movements, illicit video viewing of *The Killing Fields*, sighting of Jungle Actor Number One in Opium Den, new border trade in Chinese batteries, new barman at the White Hotel. And, above all, the regrouping of the Khmer Rouge. Arms supplied here, villagers co-opted there. Cells discovered. Retractions of confessions. Stories from the western hills. Numbers of troops estimated. Names of military leaders hazarded.

As Stephen listens, and hears Konstantin respond with news from Hanoi and the Thai border, he watches Akira the Japanese, as he sits there in the sunlight in his short sleeves with his elbows on the table, his eyes concealed behind dark shades clipped over his spectacles, a lucky charm on a gold chain round his neck. He is unlike any Japanese that Stephen has ever met. He in no way resembles the Japanese scholars of English and American literature whom Stephen had met in Japan and in the UK. He speaks a less correct, more fluent, more contemporary American English. He refers occasionally to Karl Marx and George Orwell. He laughs, he is excited, he leans forward earnestly to make a point. His ambition is to cross the lines and meet the Khmer Rouge. For months he has been learning Khmer. He has already a 500-word vocabulary, he boasts. He is a fanatic. He has been promised his *laissez-passer* thrice, and thrice been disappointed. But he will have his way. The Pulitzer is already in his pocket.

He rises to his feet, bows smartly each to each, and takes his leave. He is off to interview the Minister of Agriculture about rice subsidies. In his wake, Konstantin shakes his head and orders another coffee. Akira is a character. He is the only remaining apologist for the Khmer Rouge. He loves them. He will find them if he can.

Apologist, Stephen is to discover, is perhaps too weak a word to apply to Akira's strange position. Over the next few days, as Stephen acquaints himself with the rubble and the crumbling colonnades and the squatted mansions and the ubiquitous pigs and chickens and the ever-resilient street markets, as he fortifies himself with sugar-cane juice and seaweed and offers snacks to temple monkeys and admires an Art Deco façade, as he ponders the story of the strange exodus that emptied Phnom Penh at gunpoint and made it a ghost city, Stephen also listens to Akira. They settle down, Stephen and Akira, from time to time, over '33' Vietnamese beer, over Georgian champagne or Armenian brandy or contraband claret. For Akira, unlike the holy Konstantin, is a serious drinking man, and Stephen decides he might as well kill his fever and cauterize the aches in his gut with the traditional anaesthesia of alcohol. It works, and he begins to feel much better. He listens, enthralled, as Akira slags off the Russians and Gorbachev and Hun Sen and the puppet Vietnamese. None of them is serious. The Khmer Rouge, says Akira, are serious people.

When Stephen demurs, as he does from time to time, Akira performs a disconcerting about-turn. If, he says, Stephen thinks the Khmer Rouge such a bad lot, why is his own government and that of the US supporting them? There are Khmer Rouge weapons in a US depot in Thailand. Munitions come from US companies via Germany, Belgium, Singapore. 'You lot,' he says, 'you support for wrong reasons. You hate, and you support. That is mad. I admire, and I support. That is logic.'

Stephen listens to this in fascination. It strikes a chord in him too deep for reason. And, as he sits there late one night after a last cognac, he knows that this is what he came to find. He came to find the last believer. A breath of hope stirs like a sweet corrupt poison in his entrails. It is as though Akira were telling him that God, after all, is not dead, and salvation is still on offer. History is reprieved, the dead did not die in vain, the dry bones will live.

The immensity of this utterly impossible hope reveals to him the immensity of his depression, of his prolonged mourning for the death of the dream. So, he had, once, after all, hoped. He had, once, after all, believed that the future would be better, better *in kind*, than the past. Now, caught out in utter faithlessness, in the sin of despair, he salutes the mad Akira, who continues to defy all evidence, all reason, all history. Akira is mad, but he is divinely mad. He proclaims social hope, like a latter-day prophet. He defines Stephen as a man who has for ever lost his faith, who has come here to the graveyard of his own past. Stephen has recanted, but Akira has not. Akira believes because it is impossible. *Credo quia impossibile est.* Stephen has dwindled into reason.

Akira tells him of the battles he has had to fight to force his news agency to let him work in Kampuchea. The Kampuchean story has been costly for Japan. During the war, the Japanese lost more photographers and journalists than any other nation. Killed or missing, missing or killed. They had been reckless, excessive, expensive. Akira had been here himself, briefly in '74 and '75, he had had a gun held to his head, he had had his motorbike blown from under him, he had filed good copy. Then world interest had waned, though not his own, and other trouble spots had flared. He had made his way to Nepal, Nicaragua, Afghanistan. But Kampuchea had called him back. Kampuchea had a special place in his heart. The great experiment continued. He had pleaded, insisted, pledged cautious behaviour. And now, here he was, filing stories on reconstruction and foreign aid and the divided armies of the resistance. And working out how to get behind the lines to talk to the Khmer Rouge, how to engineer the coup to end all coups, the interview with Fate itself.

Akira's father had committed suicide at the end of the Second World War, three months after Akira's birth. Traditional death, says Akira. Akira atones.

Stephen believes no longer, but he wants Akira to believe. He wants Akira to be damned on his behalf, and on behalf of Malcolm Caldwell, and Brian Bowen and Perry Blinkhorn, and all those who were inched towards the loss of faith. He wants Akira to prove the possibility of damnation or salvation.

Akira knows all the evidence against his heroes. The deaths, the tortures, the violence, the informing, the forced confessions, the incompetence, the badly constructed irrigation projects, the ruined crops, the betrayals, the destruction. He will admit that 'mistakes' were made. He too has learned the parrot word. But he will not admit doubt of the high purpose. He will not admit wantonness, he will not admit corruption. These people, he says, are not corrupt. Little people are corrupt. Hiding money, hiding bits of food, cheating. It takes many years to weed out corruption. And remember, the Khmer Rouge were surrounded by enemies on every side. A small nation, a few million people, with nothing but their own bare hands. No rockets, no aeroplanes, no tanks. They wished to remake mankind in a new image. Who can say they did not mean well? They were poisoned by their enemies and by their friends. Americans, Russians, all guilty. They wished to be self-sufficient. They wished to detach themselves from the wheel of wickedness that is the world. Who can deny them that right? That hope?

But, murmurs Stephen, did not they behave, at best, rather like a parent who kills its own child lest it learn bad habits? Like a father who kills his daughter lest she have sex with another man?

Akira says yes, maybe, but what is so crazy about that? Death is better.

And, he unanswerably continues, if Khmer Rouge so wicked, why US and UN support?

Stephen is delighted to find somebody arguing more wildly than he has ever dared to do. The extremity of Akira's position exhilarates him. He orders another beer, and asks if Akira believes it is true

that high-ranking cadres live on pâté de foie gras and champagne?
Or are they puritan, teetotal, as others claim?

'In the socialist future, alcoholic intake will not be necessary,'
says Akira, and laughs bravely, drunkenly, glassy-eyed. A tortured
hilarity, a shivering edge of nerve vibrates through his small frame.
Stephen admires and envies this passion.

They speak of Thailand, of Vietnam, of Tokyo, of Washington,
of London. Akira seems to believe that there is a wicked ravening
Beast that runs the economies of the world, that waits like the
Whore of Babylon to drink up the red cup of monetary fornications.
'Massive slump, world slump on the way,' he gloats, foreseeing
stock-market crashes, the ruined dollar, the ruined yen, the utter
breakdown and confusion of all commerce, all trade, all financing,
all usury, all credit, all capital. Then the Khmer Rouge will come
into their own. People power, self-sufficiency, herbal remedies, the
abolition of money. Oh yes, he assures Stephen, they *had* successfully abolished money. And what choice had they but to kill those
who tried to subvert so heroic an enterprise, those peasants and
bourgeois who continued to hoard and clutch and cling to the old
ways?

Akira is a living paradox, a manifest impossibility, a composite
creature made of incompatible parts. In the humid heat, he wears
boots, because he says he is afraid of snakes. He is a devout atheist
with a lucky charm. He is a hard-drinking puritan. He is a devotee
of primal simplicity who hangs himself about with the trappings of
the most technologically advanced nation. He is bedizened with
gadgets. He has photographic equipment the like of which Stephen
has never seen. (He is not very *good* with it, says Konstantin, whose
own machinery, although fairly bulky, is more modest.) He has a
special alarm watch which will tell him the time of day in any
nation on earth, summer time or winter time, and which records the
telephone numbers of embassies and contacts worldwide. It bleeps,
says Akira, as it crosses the International Dateline. He has a radio

on which he can receive the music of the spheres and all the songbirds of opera, or, if he prefers, news from the stock-markets round the globe. (Stephen's little 2-band Sony, pointlessly purchased on impulse a lifetime ago at Heathrow, is useless here: it will emit no more than a faint crackle. He cannot afford to sneer at Akira's radio.) Akira has a word processor, which at the press of a button turns roman letters into Japanese characters. (He admits that this is not as useful as it might be, because of the absence of fax.) He has, of course, a headset and a library of tapes, and a four-inch square television set. He has a battery-operated pocket-knife can-opener. He has a silver tooth which is probably wired up to a satellite transmitter. He has a portable telephone. He lives off batteries.

Stephen feels free, as their acquaintance prospers, to comment upon this. Is there not some anomaly, perhaps, he suggests, in Akira's dependence here, in this devastated land, upon a support system of imported Japanese trickeries? Akira laughs and sparkles. Yes, of course, he agrees, of course. Of course it is paradox and anomaly. But how else can it be? Akira sees himself as a walking casualty of the second half of the twentieth century. History itself has produced this frenzy of disjunction, this violent yoke. 'I am pulled,' says Akira, 'like the man on the rack. Because I am all things and nothing. No nation, no place, all places. No thing. All things crammed into me, all contradictions of history.' He stares intently at Stephen, and he says, 'I am not *viable*. I am sacrifice. I am explosion, implosion. Wait and see.'

The rhetoric is manic and ethereal. Stephen wonders whether Akira can talk like this in his 500 words of Khmer.

Konstantin, he can see, is baffled by Akira, but proud of him. He is pleased to have brought Akira and Stephen together. He sits back and watches their flights of fancy like a stage manager, an impresario, smiling gently at his puppet children. The more sober of the aid workers give Akira a wide berth.

The talk of sacrifice and implosion becomes a little less safely theoretical, when Akira suggests that he take Stephen out to see the countryside on the back of his hired Honda bike. Can this be a good idea? But Stephen cannot resist, and off he goes, goggled and headbanded, on a morning's ride towards the north-west.

They do not get very far. The road is bad, soldiers stop them to look at their papers, the sun is hot, and the motorbike keeps stalling. The landscape is depressing. They see great dumps of rusting equipment — old refrigerators, air-conditioning plants, cannibalized and abandoned cars, tin baths, lavatory seats. Stephen thinks he sees a bit of an aeroplane and the broken curve of a dumped radar screen. Akira, understandably, is excited by all this, and tries to take artistic photographs. 'The Graveyard of the Machine,' he declares, as he plays with his lenses. 'The End of Epoch.' He is interrupted by a lorry-load of Vietnamese soldiers who tell him abruptly to pack up his cameras. Akira replies in Khmer, but the soldiers do not speak Khmer. Both Stephen and Akira say they are *bao-chi*, journalists, one of the few words that everybody can speak in Vietnamese, and Stephen haltingly tries a little Russian. He says that he is a writer from England (the Russian word for 'writer' soothingly evoking, at least to himself, another world altogether, a world of Pushkin and Tolstoy and Chekhov), and that he and his Japanese colleague would like to take a photograph to illustrate 'devastation caused in Pol Pot time'. (He is not too sure about the word for 'devastation': he tries *devestazia*, and the Vietnamese nod as though they understand.) The soldiers speak to one another, and then nod again. Yes, they can photograph. Smiles, cordiality, exchange of cigarettes.

The soldiers are impressed by Akira's cameras. Akira asks if he can photograph the soldiers, and, although they clearly long to be photographed, this makes them nervous. They ask Stephen a question in a Russian that he cannot interpret. He shakes his head. Then they ask him if he has been to Moscow. He is able to say that he has. One of them says that he spent eight years there, studying.

More smiles. A satisfactory interchange. But when it is over, the soldiers point firmly back towards Phnom Penh. On the road ahead, they indicate, things not too safe. Pol Pot men. Terrorist men. Mines, guns. They must return to the Monorom, to the bar and the swimming pool, to the safe corral.

This small excursion has a powerful effect on Stephen. He is caught by a new wave of visa fever. He too wants to travel further. He does not want to be turned back. His pride is engaged.

Konstantin, Akira and Stephen Cox hatch their plot. They will travel together, in a hired car. They will get a pass as far as the last check-point. Akira knows somebody who knows somebody who can get them a pass from the Khmer Rouge. This is dangerous, but it can be done. Akira knows somebody who went over, an Australian, and a woman to boot, whose piece in *Time* magazine describing life in the Khmer Rouge camp has filled Akira with ungovernable envy and a ferocious spirit of emulation. But the Australian woman had no photographs. Akira will outdo her, for he will provide photographs. But it would be better if Konstantin were to come too. Akira recognizes his own limitations as photographer. And as for Stephen, his new friend Stephen, his Russian is useful, and anyway, why else is he here?

Stephen demurs on the question of utility, pointing out that his Russian is useful only up to a point. With the Khmer Rouge, if they exist, it would be counter-productive. The Khmer Rouge prefer the Chinese, and Stephen cannot speak Chinese.

Nevertheless, he is hooked. If they want to go, he must go too. He cannot back out at this point.

It turns out that Akira has been hatching this plot for a long time. Why else has he been learning Khmer? So he can go without an interpreter, of course, so that he can run his own risks and ask his own questions.

Akira seems to be completely fearless. Konstantin, for his part, believes himself to have a charmed life. Since a bullet passed

234

so harmlessly, so therapeutically through his nineteen-year-old shoulder in Korea, he has believed himself immortal.

In this company, Stephen, who has never heard the noise of battle or witnessed a violent death, feels that he is on trial. It occurs to him that he is being foolish and irresponsible. But, irresponsible to whom? The only answer he receives is: yourself. As, years ago with Liz Headland in Bertorelli's restaurant he had reflected in Britain, now he reflects in the Monorom of Phnom Penh: there is nothing to keep me here.

Such a project, as all those who have embarked upon one will recognize, gathers its own potentially fatal momentum. Questions not asked become unaskable. Hesitations are swallowed up in the challenge of the plot. The satisfactions of each step taken obliterate the craziness or obscurity of the destination. A point arrives at which it is more impossible not to go than to go. The water begins to flow uphill.

The night before their planned departure, Stephen, Konstantin and Akira sit in Akira's room and assemble their baggage while listening to the taped strains of the seventh symphony of Sibelius. (My cousin, first violin in Osaka, claims Akira.) They will, of course, travel light, but plan for contingencies. Akira's version of travelling light causes some mirth. Stephen and Konstantin are more practical, though Stephen, superstitiously, has packed his diaries and papers and the poems of Rimbaud, picked up triumphantly in a second-hand bookstore in Saigon. He also takes his little Sony radio, although he could not have said why. Perhaps he envisages present-ing it in a placatory manner to a Khmer Rouge commander or a village headman? They discuss what to take for 'the natives' from the *grand luxe* of the Monorom's supplies. Would a bottle of Scotch be a passport to good will or sudden death? Perhaps the Khmer Rouge would like chewing gum, peppermints, fruit pastilles? Maybe these products are classed as the demoralizing garbage of a corrupt capitalist society? Cigarettes, they agree, are essential. Nobody in

South East Asia rejects cigarettes. They have no moral or ideological context here.

Akira will take his pistol. Pistols cannot escape a moral context. Konstantin says he has never, on principle, handled one, and will not now. Akira checks his magazines and rounds of ammunition. This makes Stephen so nervous that he asks if he can have a closer look. Akira hands him the pistol. It is a Colt Model 1911 A1, into which are incised the words 'United States Property. US Army'. Stephen is somewhat surprised that Akira has not got some new-fangled Japanese model with James Bond special triggers and catches, but Akira explains that Japanese regulations of sale and manufacture of firearms are very strict. It is much easier to buy on the black market in Vietnam or Kampuchea. He had learned to shoot in Japan, with a soft air-gun, shooting plastic bullets. 'I am no good marksman, Number Ten bad marksman,' says Akira, disarmingly. This frightens Stephen even more. The heavy metal of the gun sinks in his hand. He had forgotten the dead weight. He had been an indifferent marksman himself. His friend Brian Bowen had shown more talent on the range.

The Sibelius draws to its close, and the pistol is wrapped in a soft green cloth and returned to its holster. Akira switches on his radio, searching for news of the World Service of the BBC. He finds the World Service, but not a news bulletin. It is the Classic Serial, *Gulliver's Travels*, dramatized with strange sound effects that compel Akira to leave it on for a minute or two before he starts turning knobs in search of the price of the yen.

The yen has fallen. Akira is delighted.

Stephen, drifting into sleep, with the Yahoos still hoarding coloured stones and gambolling and yodelling hideously in his head, finds himself thinking of his friend Hattie Osborne. Some association has brought her to him, as he lies there under his mosquito netting in the flickering moonlight. Hattie, drunk in her gold dress. Hattie, playing fast and loose with time. Hattie, who as a girl threw caution to the winds. Is she still in his old flat, under the kind protection of Mr Goodfellow, or has she moved on to the protection of others? He must send her another postcard. He has been sparing with his postcards, forgetful of his old friends in the old world. They will think he is dead. He has a packet of postcards in his bag, showing in implausible orange and tinned green the inaccessible geometric splendours and tufted palms of Angkor Wat. She would like one of those. And he should send one, also, to Liz Headleand. For it is Liz Headleand's fault that he is here. Hattie is innocent. It is Liz who will be to blame if he is eaten by the tiger.

*

Liz Headleand has got round to it at last. She has been avoiding it for as long as possible, but evasion no longer seems possible. She is forcing herself to read Conrad's *Victory*.

It would not be fair to say that she is hating every word of it, but she is not deriving much pleasure from it either. She has never liked Conrad. Twice she has made herself read *Heart of Darkness*, and she still has no idea, on the simplest level, of its plot. What actually *happens* in it? Who is going where, and why? She never discovered.

Victory is easier going, but it is not easy. Her attention had been redirected to it by a spirited correspondence in *The London Review of Books* about Conrad's alleged racism, and she has decided that for Stephen's sake she must make herself look at the evidence. And there is plenty here. I mean, says Liz to herself, one simply doesn't speak, these days, of enormous buck niggers or chaps with flat noses and wide, baboon-like nostrils. It isn't done. One does not refer to the Chinese as chinks either. And it's no good arguing that Conrad's just imitating the language of simple sea-faring folk. The enormous buck nigger comes in his own revised 1920 introduction, along with a lot of (in Liz's view) pointlessly portentous and high-flowing Conradian language.

The portrait of the disgusting, fat, thick-lipped, chestnut-bearded
Teutonic hotel manager Schomberg intrigues her, but she is puzzled
to find that the hotel in question, from which Heyst abducts the
lady from the ladies' orchestra, is not in Bangkok, as she had
supposed, but in Surabaya, Java. She had been sure that Stephen's
notes had referred to a hotel in Bangkok.

But Alan had been right, *Victory* is the one with the Caliban
figure, the hairy ape from the Amazon, he of the baboon-like
nostrils. Liz reads on with revulsion, as Conrad mocks and torments
his poor savage diamond-hunting Yahoo. She thinks with tenderness
of sweet Simon Grunewald and his head-hunters. She winces as she
reads the scene in which the pock-marked green-eyed Martin
Ricardo hits the ape-man on the head with a heavy piece of wood.
The violence both of the language and the action is extreme. How
can the gentle Stephen have admired this sort of stuff?

And she finds the chronology confusing. What is the point of all
this skipping about from one time scale to another? Is it incompetence or ingenuity? And if it is ingenuity, what is Conrad being
ingenious about? Liz likes to know where she is in a novel. She likes
a novel that begins at the beginning and moves inexorably to its
end. She does not like confusion for its own sake. There is plenty of
confusion in real life, without inventing more of it.

*

Stephen Cox, Konstantin Vassiliou and Akira Tanaka put up for
the night at the Hôtel de la Paix. Gutted by war and apparently
deserted, it still stands by the verge of Highway Six. Once it had
received tourists on their way to the ruins. Now it is empty, its
door ajar, its windows broken, its veranda invaded by creepers.
They knock on the open door, and call. Nobody answers, so they
penetrate to find a reception desk, a few old ledgers, a dusty glass
jug, a cracked vase and the remnants of a bar and a restaurant. In
the courtyard a fig-tree breaks the paving stones. There is, of

course, no electricity to operate the 1930s wall brackets, the large ceiling fan. A 1950s advertisement for Pernod is still attached to a flaking wall next to a photograph of the Bayon and a faded list of Prices for Tours and Guides. They explore the bedrooms, and find that some have been recently occupied; some are newly swept, with mattresses on low wooden beds. On a bedside table stands an ash tray with a few butts, a candle end, a saucer. A spotted mirror reflects a calendar for 1979 with a picture of a Peugeot car. A half-burned stick of incense leans in a jam jar in front of a carved stone and a Buddha head.

They return to the courtyard, squat on chunks of masonry, light cigarettes. It is half an hour before the sudden dusk that will overwhelm them. The road had been difficult, at times almost impassable. They have had to get out and push. They will stay here. As they sit and chat, to the relentless chirruping of the cicadas and to strange cries from unknown birds, they find that it is, after all, peaceful. Mournful, but peaceful. It is better here than in the false garden of the Monorom, better than in the dark halls of Hanoi. The noisy silence is soothing. It has its own life. It is not human. They listen to it.

And, as they listen, from it emerge, quite silently, two human figures. An old man, and a small boy. The three intruders jump nervously when they find they are being watched from the door-way, and Akira reaches for his gun, but the newcomers are not bearing guns or spades or axes. They smile and bow and nod to indicate their good intentions. They inform them that they are the only remaining staff of the Hôtel de la Paix, and would the guests like some dinner?

The meal is very simple. A bowl of rice, bamboo shoots, a salad, a watery soup, a plate of bananas. The old man cooks over a fire in the derelict courtyard, in a cooking pot resting on three stones. They eat outdoors. The old man is wrinkled, very dark of skin, wizened, bent. His gestures have a timeless gentleness. The small child watches, open-eyed, open-mouthed, as the old man stirs and scoops with a ladle made from a coconut shell.

The three guests offer their chef a beer from their own provisions. His labours over, he comes to join them, and sits cross-legged with his head propped back against a peeling column. The child plays a mysterious game in a far corner with some sticks in the gathering gloom. There is no light but the light of the fire and one flickering candle. The old man says he has no more oil for the lamp.

He tells them his story, softly, with many pauses. It is the usual story. Akira interprets. Most of his family are dead in the wars and troubles. He had once worked here, in this hotel, as porter. In the old days, he had seen many Europeans come this way. Now, nobody comes. Last year, one white woman, with guide. Since then, nobody. How does he live? He lives off the forest. This child is his great-grandson. For me, he says, the night is near, but for him the day begins. The child will be a monk. He will be a holy man of the forest.

They can almost believe this as they sit there in the vibrant mystic dark beneath a crowded sky.

He asks where they are going, but shows little interest in their replies. Yes, he says, the Khmer Rouge, the black-coated men, they are near, they are not far along the trail. They do not bother him. He is too old. Yes, they will find them in the next day's journey.

'You look for them, but many people run away,' he says, equably, as a fact, not as a warning. 'They have many friends,' he adds.

Akira smiles.

The child has curled up in his corner and fallen asleep. The old man nods over his pipe.

How can they pay him, they wonder? What use would Kampuchean riel or dollar bills or yen be to this survivor? What would he want from their stores?

They sleep in the same room, the three of them, Akira, Stephen, Konstantin, sleeping-bagged, beneath tattered mosquito nets, bitten by a myriad insects, to the sounds of the forest. Such a croaking, quaking, singing, twanging, rustling! The forest invades the fragile hotel. It moves into their room. Stephen, lying awake, thinks of the little boy, the Lost Mowgli Child with the old man. He thinks of Mme Savet Akrun, who had hated the forest and its *saletés*. He wakes at dawn to what he takes to be the sound of rain, but there is no rain. It is the rustling of dry leaves. The little boy is standing in the open doorway, watching. He has brought them a bucket of water for washing. Leaves and seeds float in it. It is soft, like brown silk. The boy stares, as they wash and shave, these two big white people, this un-Khmer brown man. Unlike his great-grandfather, he is curious about them, he is interested in these strange people and their strange possessions. Akira takes his photograph with one of his instamatic cameras and he smiles with delight as the picture develops and peels off before his eyes.

The child hovers and circles round their breakfast of banana and plantain and Monorom-supplied coffee. His short dark hair grows in a perfect circle, in a neat whorl from the very centre of the back of his head. His neck is fragile, like the stem of a flower. His feet are bare, his toenails jagged.

Akira, who happens to have two small children at home in Tokyo, takes seriously the task of entertaining him. He finds him music on his cassettes and plugs him in to his Sony Walkman. He shows him his torch, which has a beam so powerful that it shines right through the child's little brown paw, through pink irradiated flesh, revealing within the wonder of a small skeletal hand. Finally, he gets out his telephone, and tries to show how it works. Stephen is as entranced as the child by this example of high technology, and hopes that Akira will get an answer as he dials random numbers wildly into the jungle, but Konstantin (a little piqued by Akira's success with the child?) turns suddenly serious and tells him to stop: the Khmer Rouge have field telephones, better not to interfere with their circuits, they do not want Pol Pot or Ta Mok hissing at them down the line.

Konstantin wants to photograph the old man with the child. It is easy to see why. They pose for him, on the hotel veranda, side by side, staring gravely. Konstantin sucks out their souls through their eyes.

The old man offers them fruits for their journey. They accept. They ask what he would like for payment? He shakes his head, uncertainly. He does not know what he wants. The old customs no longer pertain. The cash nexus is broken. He consents to pocket a ten-dollar bill, the equivalent of several months' wages, but it is clear that its fate is doubtful. A spill to light a cooking fire, perhaps? He says he is pleased with the photographs of the boy, because the boy is pleased. Stephen and Konstantin feel ungracious, inadequate. Konstantin takes one of the gold chains from his neck, and offers it. The old man smiles, showing his hard brown gums, and shakes his head. Konstantin makes gestures of insistence. The old man softens, accepts, puts his hands together in acceptance. Konstantin returns the courtesy. The old man gives the chain to the boy.

As they prepare for departure, the old man brings them one of the hotel ledgers, and presents it to them for their inspection. Stephen the historian looks with interest at the faded spidery handwritten columns of accounts and names, at the bundle of old menus. A predominance of French visitors, but a scattering of Germans, Scandinavians, British, Americans. What had this old man made of them? Does he regret the passing of the old days, when money worked? His attitude is ambiguous. It is polite, but not deferential. Bisque d'Écrevisses, Pointes d'Asperges au Gratin, Poulet au Riz, Salade de Dalat. Fruits du Pays, Coupe Khemarin, Coupe de Candiole. Monsieur le Professeur Gillet de L'École Française d'Extrême-Orient, Monsieur Benoît, Nicholas Hastings Esq and Mrs Hastings. If he takes time enough, will he discover here the names of Somerset Maugham, of André and Clara Malraux, of Gore Vidal and Pett Petrie? He is sure that he will, and half of him wishes to stay here in peaceful scholarly seclusion. He is safe here, as he is safe with the Russian of Pushkin, of Lermontov.

But the others will not wait. With some regret he surrenders the ledger to the old man, who lays it carefully upon the reception desk. A small lizard scuttles away. The old man suggests that they add their names. He is sorry, the more recent volumes have been destroyed, but they can insert their names here, on the last page of the 1950s. Here too the white woman signed last year.

The sight of the white woman's signature arrests Akira. He stares at it in fascination. Yes, it is the Australian woman, the journalist of the *Time* magazine coup. There is her name, Jacqueline Lowe, and there the signature of her guide, Mr Chet Samon. They have been here first. Is this good news, or bad? It is good news, Stephen reasons, for she got home to tell her story. They sign their names with a flourish, below that of Jacqueline Lowe. The old man watches with a half smile. He is the keeper of the books.

As they get into their car, after carefully checking air, water, oil, reserve petrol cans (what if the KR had syphoned them off during the night, what if the old man is a double agent, a porter at hell's gate?), they say their farewells. The child looks grave, attentive. The old man raises a thin hand on a bony wrist, as Akira jerks the car into motion. The expression on his face is deeply complicit and compassionate. He seems to pity them, with their heavy equipment, their dollars, their clinking armoury of cameras, their cans of Coca-Cola, their warm beer. He pities them, perhaps, because they have *so long, so long* still to endure?

Or again, perhaps not. Perhaps the reverse?

Stephen tries out the phrase *Moriturus te saluto* on the air, but wishes he had not, as he then has to try to explain it to his companions. Neither of them grasps it very quickly. Latin is not their lingo.

Akira, in retaliation, embarks on a description of how four-wheel-drive really means two-wheel-drive. Two-wheel-drive means one-wheel-drive, according to Akira. It is a semantic nicety. Stephen is slow to get it.

The road fills up with bullock carts and bicycles. They are approaching a new centre of activity. These are the peasants who support and feed the guerrillas. Willingly, unwillingly? Who can tell?

Their progress is arrested, briefly, by an excursion off the road, down a track, through neglected fields, to inspect a temple glimpsed through the trees at the foothill of an encroaching forest. There is a clearing, much overgrown, and a small stream flows past, musically, attracting insects and some large, black-and-white, long-tailed butterflies. It is not exactly Angkor Wat or Angkor Thom, for the single stupa is only about twenty feet high, square, crudely carved, heavily eroded. But it is picturesque and private. They can just make out the shapes of beast-figures crouching at the four corners of the square base. Konstantin and Akira take photographs, Stephen sits in the shade and sketches. A few yards away, cut into the hillside beyond the stream, is an opening into what Konstantin says must be a meditation cave. Akira will not go near it for fear of snakes, but Stephen and Konstantin scramble over the stream and push their way along the once-trodden ledge of the hill. The cave's opening is hung with creepers. It is utterly desolate, utterly abandoned. Konstantin bends low and crawls in, carrying Akira's torch. He calls to Stephen to follow him.

Once inside, they do not need the torch, for the cave is open to the sky through a hole in its natural roof. Bats hang upside down and hardly stir at the intrusion. A leaf drifts and spirals downwards. In the cave stands a stone Buddha image, some four foot high. It is covered with bird and bat droppings. Wisps of rotting gold cloth, like tattered baby garments, hang from it. It smiles.

Konstantin stares at the stone face. He wants to tidy him up. But what is the point? They will leave the image to its lonely, pointless, eternal vigil, in the semi-gloom of the cavern.

Stephen no longer wants to find the Khmer Rouge. The old man, the child and the Buddha image have disarmed him. Already they compose themselves into new phrases, new sentences. He wants to stay here. He wishes he had thought to give his worthless 2-band radio to the child.

Akira is hopping with impatience when they return to him. He is already sitting in the car, alert in the driver's seat. He does not say so, would never admit it, but he had not liked being left alone in this deserted rustic spot. Abruptly, he bundles them in, and back they go, along the track eagerly, to the old road, to the road block, that awaits them.

*

The moon is full again. It is pale swimming gold, and it rises. I can see it rising as I watch. My belly is swollen. It feels as though there were a fish hook inside me pulling and pulling. An ache at the base of my spine, a swelling in my soft parts. I need to bleed. I am a day late.

As a matter of fact, there *is* a fish hook inside me. It's called an IUD. An intra-uterine device. It looks just like a fish hook. It is a fisher of men.

Do you know what that big-head loud-mouth small prick said to me once? He said, I'm going to screw you until it comes out of your left ear. And *I* said, thank you very much, get on with it. But could he? Could he hell. Promises, promises.

I keep thinking about what Polly Piper said to me last month in Sainsbury's. About having a baby. I'm only forty.

A few years ago, my IUD came out accidentally. While I was removing a tampon, to be precise. Out it came. I was surprised. I put it in an envelope. I've still got it somewhere. I think. I went off and had another fitted, although they say they give you all kinds of pelvic diseases and probably make you sterile. I wonder what I'm playing at.

I *do* wonder what I'm playing at. The most extraordinary thing has happened. Well, several extraordinary things. But the most extraordinary is that I seem to have been fallen-in-love-with. Let me tell you that this is a damn sight odder, at my age, than falling in love. I don't know what to do about it. It's all Stephen's fault. This narrow little monastic bed reproaches me. I am drinking the last bottle of his Château de la Plus Haute Tour 1981 as I write. Eleven years early. Sorry, Stephen. It is delicious. It is too good for me.

You may think that Elizabeth Headleand and I have been a little dilatory in our response to Stephen's SOS, and you would be right. Don't worry, things will speed up. The truth is that at this point neither of us could think of what the fuck to do next. If anything. I've made the point that we don't much like each other, haven't I?

Anyway, a week or so ago I had this bright light of inspiration. It came to me in the middle of the night, but it still seemed good in the morning. I decided to BUY AN OPTION ON STEPHEN'S LIFE!

Several things put the idea in my head. First of all, I bumped into Pett Petrie in the churchyard of St James's, Piccadilly. (I was on my way to Fortnum's, he to the London Library, if you want to know.) We stopped to chat of this and that. He's going through a bit of a down phase, poor old Pett, his last book got shocking notices and there had been a Godalmighty balls-up about the filming of *Ziggurat*. Law suits and all. He's beginning to wish he'd never emerged from obscurity, he says, what with the Inland Revenue and Meryl Streep and his ex-wife and his ex-mistress all on to him at once. Oh for the quiet days of penury, he said, as I treated him to a coffee and a piece of carrot cake in the Wren. So I tried to cheer him up by teasing him about having drinks named after him in the Oriental Hotel in Bangkok, and he did begin to perk up a bit, and said how did I know, and I said I'd seen a copy of the Cocktails of the Month menu in Stephen Cox's effects. What, is Stephen *dead*, he said, with a look of mixed horror and hope on his big round mug, and I said no, well, probably not, and had to explain myself. And in short I found myself taking Pett back to my pad and showing him some of the photocopied stuff, and do you know what Pett said? *He* said, this is never all there is of what he's been writing out there, this is just rough *notes* for a novel, I bet you my bottom dollar — well, no, I don't bet you a *penny*, on second thoughts, he said quickly, I just *assure* you on my *lost honour* — that this is the *surrounding rubbish* of a real text. That text exists, elsewhere, said Pett. This is just the dross! I know old Stephen. I know writers. This is the kind of package people sell to American universities. First drafts, bosh shots, that kind of stuff. The real thing is *elsewhere*. Safely tucked away in a suitcase, or a left luggage locker, or a hotel safe, or with his American publishers.

Well, I must say I found this a pretty attractive notion. It really would be rather interesting if this novel did exist. But how to get hold of it and Stephen?

And this was when the idea of Stephen as *subject* first came into my mind. I think I went a bit quiet as Pett rambled on about the iniquities of movie-makers over his ink-stewed octopus. (We'd got to Ruby in the Dust on Camden High Street by this stage: ever been there? I don't know why, but I just love its name.) Yes, I fell silent. I was already plotting my next move.

Frankly, I've always thought Stephen a bit of a romantic hero. Old-fashioned, but romantic. And now I began to see real possibilities. English writer disappears into jungle. English writer captured by Pol Pot. English writer turns native in Killing Fields. English leftie forced to eat his own ideology. It had potential, this idea. And if it turned out that Stephen really had written the Great Cambodian Novel, well, all to the good. But meanwhile, I ought to get the rights. Just in case.

I'm in a strong position, as Stephen's agent. I decided to sell them to myself.

The night Stephen left — you remember, that night we spent chatting after that ghastly appalling *wake* of a party at Marjorie

Kinsman's seventieth – he said I could be his executor. He was joking, of course, but he actually wrote on the flyleaf of my bedtime book (a paperback copy of *Gulliver's Travels*, if you want to know): 'I hereby appoint Harriet Osborne as my literary executor and leave her in charge of my estate.' It *was* three in the morning, and he did write it in red biro, but who knows, it may be legal. Why not? They say you can write a cheque on the hide of a cow or the skin of an orange, so why not your will in a paperback book? And it was a Penguin Classic.

I was further spurred on the next morning by yet another dawn phone call from Marlon. I knew who it was this time and didn't tell him to piss off. I chatted him along quite nicely. He was still interested in Stephen's French novel, believe it or not, but I sort of insinuated to him that there was an even bigger better Cox novel in the pipeline, and that he ought to keep an eye on it. He asked for its title, and quick as a flash I said *The Leper King*. He liked that. I said it was about Pol Pot and an adventurer from the West, hoping he wouldn't think it sounded too like *Apocalypse Now*, but he didn't seem to spot the connection. I promised to keep in touch.

I wonder if Marlon could play Pol Pot? They're about the same age. And they're both quite fat. It doesn't seem to matter so much about nationality these days. Look at Peter Brook's stuff with Japanese playing Indians and Indians playing Swedes and Jews playing African Ik. And Mark Antony wasn't an American, after all, was he?

Look, I'm sorry I called Marlon a fool, or an idiot, or whatever it was I said. The man's a hero. The man's a genius. I love him to death and the last tango on the day of revelation when the seventh seal and all the waters break. And I was tickled pink to get a phone call from him, even at seven in the morning. Sorry, Marlon. I wonder if it really was him? I suppose it *could* have been a hoax?

Anyway, enough of this frivolity. I'd convinced myself by now that I was on to something, and that at the very least I ought to register an interest. I'd kick myself if suddenly the news came buzzing through the wires that Stephen had been found dead in the Gulf of Siam or in a Penang gaol in dramatic and mysterious circumstances. Everyone would be on to him. Like vultures. Look what happened when that ex-opium-dealer forest monk died in Chiang Mai. There were three major film companies on to his remains within days. People who wouldn't have coughed up a penny to support his mission when he was alive were hustling for his story. I suppose filming is cheap in Thailand. Well, I know it is. They made *The Princess and the Talisman* for only a couple of million, I'm told. Amazing. Hawaii's quite cheap too.

So I drew up an agreement selling myself an option in both life and book for a thousand pounds, and paid the money into a special new bank account called *The Leper King Account*. Efficient, wasn't it? I had it witnessed by Mr Patel in the chemist's on the corner. I like Mr Patel. Some days I think he is my only friend.

(As a matter of fact, I've discovered there *is* a book called *The Leper King*, by a French writer called Pierre Benoît, but I don't think it's ever been translated and I'm sure nobody's ever heard of it. I'm told it's a 1920s job, sort of Buchanesque, about the Princess of Burma and peaceful fun-loving Cambodians and a plot to blow up Angkor Wat. Come to think of it, it sounds quite interesting. Perhaps I ought to buy that one up too while I'm about it?)

Anyway, then I got cold feet and thought I ought to consult Liz Headleand. After all, she was technically and actually in possession of the originals of these papers and had a better right to them than I. She might take a dim view of my entrepreneurial activities. So I gave her a buzz and invited myself around for another drink. I've got this thing now about not letting her into Stephen's pad. I do not want her here.

I could tell she felt a bit shifty about having done fuck-all about the package. She did mutter something about research into the postage stamps, but it didn't sound very convincing to me.

So off I set again to St John's Wood by taxi on a cold dark night. I must say her house looks very welcoming. I like her little leaded coloured window panes. And there's a tree by the front portico that smells wonderful, even at this time of year. It smells of honey. Her drawing room is nice too. I'm not really much of a home bird myself, more of a bird of passage and a percher on hopeless twigs, but I can tell a good new yellow wallpaper when I see one. She's been redecorating, must have spent a fortune. And I appreciate a jug of flowers. Red and yellow dahlias, and those tiny little deep bronze pom-pom chrysanths. And there was Liz, sitting in her rocking chair with her feet up on a tapestry footstool and one ankle in bandage. She hadn't got up to open the door. The door was opened by another largish woman who introduced herself as Marcia and said she was on her way out. And Liz said she was sorry, she'd sprained her foot, would I mind helping myself to a drink, and to make sure it was a proper one, not just a half-hearted little visitor's drink. Now, was that rude or polite? I don't know. Meanwhile the Marcia person sort of disappeared. She put her head back through the door, with a rather smart floppy green felt hat on top of it, and said, 'Bye bye Lizzie, bye bye Harriet,' as though she knew me, and I had a feeling I knew her, which it turned out I sort of did, as when she'd gone (I heard the door bang) Liz said she was her half-sister Marcia Campbell who's always on the radio. (I heard her only last night, in a Radio 4 adaptation of *Tom Jones*, giving us her Jenny Waters.)

So I got myself a drink while Liz explained to me that she'd done her ankle in by falling off a stepladder while trying to adjust the new curtain track. 'It's my weak ankle,' she said. 'I broke it years ago tobogganing on Parliament Hill. It's never been right since. Is it the beginning of the end, I ask myself. Frail bones. Old age. Osteoporosis.'

I told her that she looked pretty robust to me, which she did. There's nothing very frail about Liz Headland. But it is true that I rather despise people who break their bones. I think they're clumsy. I've never broken anything in my life. So, I said, in a businesslike way, to cut through all this woman-to-woman small talk, what about the postage stamps?

They're definitely Kampuchean, she says. She's had them officially identified by a man at Stanley Gibbons, who said they were a rather unusual selection. . said that would figure, because Stephen had once confided in me that he used to collect stamps when he was a little boy. For some reason this made us both feel rather sad. In softened mood I told her about Marlon, which she had the grace to find quite exciting. My stock rose when she found I was on telephone terms with Marlon.

I didn't mention my option. It suddenly seemed rather a tasteless notion.

As we skirted about and rabbited on, it became obvious that we were both paralysed in this Stephen business because of our *lack of status*. I mean, who were we to poke our noses in, and if noses were to be poked, why should it be hers or mine? Odd how deep womanly diffidence can go, even with hard cases like Liz Headleand and me. Now if we'd been wives or sisters or even fiancées, we wouldn't have been so backward. But I was only an ex-agent and an illegal sublet, and she was only a friend. We hardly qualified as next of kin, we agreed. We'd never be allowed to the hospital bedside.

The idea of next of kin did prod us into thinking we ought to try to contact Stephen's brothers. To get the go-ahead for whatever we decided to do next. I said I'd try to track them down. I was just about to bring up the name of Mrs Vassiliou, when the door bell rang, and someone or some persons, without pausing for a response, let themselves in with a key.

I could tell both that Liz wasn't really expecting anybody, and also that she wasn't particularly surprised. 'Who's that?' she called, to the person who was noisily trying in the hallway to sound as unlike a burglar or a murderer as possible, and received the answer 'It's me', which satisfied her and indeed brought a better smile to her face than I'd so far summoned forth. Naturally the words 'It's me' didn't mean much to me, and I had to wait until the door opened to see that the intruder was Aaron Headleand.

I'd never met Aaron. I've been in the same room as him, but I'd never *met* him.

'Darling,' said Liz, comfortably, from her rocking chair, in a way that made me feel the loneliest woman on earth.

'You silly silly old thing,' said Aaron, as he crossed the room to plant a kiss upon her cheek.

Well, I *am* lonely, and that's the truth. But I suppose I'm not the only one.

'I just thought I'd pop in and see how you were getting on,' said Aaron. 'I feel sort of responsible for it, you know. What *were* you doing clambering around on stepladders at midnight? This décor fever will be the death of you!'

It was as though I didn't exist. Liz was positively smirking with pleasure. Like a cat.

I think they exchanged a few more sentences about Liz's ankle (I mean, God knows, you'd think she'd had a major operation, the amount of solicitude and sympathy that was cluttering up the room), and then they both seemed to remember I was there, and Liz got round to seeing fit to introduce me.

'Aaron,' she says, 'this is Harriet Osborne. Do you know Harriet? She's a friend of Stephen Cox's. We were just having a talk about Stephen. Harriet, this is my stepson Aaron.'

Aaron, who was standing by Liz's chair with his hand on her shoulder, sort of looked round towards me and gave me the full benefit. At least, that's what he meant to do, but I could see *at that instant* that something had gone slightly wrong, and that *he* was getting the full benefit instead. It was a really odd moment. I mean, all the times I've tried to pull it on people, and failed. Whereas there I was, this time, just sitting there, looking I imagine slightly irritable, and feeling very left out, and Aaron looked at me, and I suddenly knew he'd seen the Hattie Osborne that had once been intended. Before the world was made.

He's a very good-looking guy, is Aaron. In a casual, sloppy, rather sultry sort of way. Dark, big-eyed. You know the kind of thing. Mean but sensitive.

'Hello, Harriet,' he said, and I could see he couldn't wait to get hold of my hand. Which he did. Unnecessarily, in my view. He had to walk five paces to get it.

We shook hands. I began to wonder if my bra was showing. Or if I'd left a diamond tiara on by mistake. But no, it was just me he was looking at. I was wearing my old black Warehouse dress and an even older Liberty shawl.

'I think I've met you before,' he said. An old ploy, but fair enough, in front of your stepmother.

'I don't think so,' I said. 'But of course I know your *work*. In fact, I went to see your play only the other night. So I *feel* as though I know you.' There was a little dangerous pause, and I said into it, quickly (because theatre people are *so* sensitive), 'I *loved* the show.'

'Thank you,' he said, bewildered, without much interest. (Still, it was just as well I said it.)

By now, Liz was probably feeling a little *de trop*, so rapidly and devastatingly had the room rearranged itself. She suggested that Aaron should have a drink. He said he couldn't stay long, he was on his way to see a rude movie at the Screen on the Hill, but he would have a quick one, and would we like a refill? We both accepted.

Aaron sat down. I can't really remember what we talked about. Liz's ankle, to begin with, and how it all was his fault because he had been in charge of the sledge when she'd first broken it. All those years ago. Then he and Liz had a quick canter about his father Charles, who had been suffering from a fit of hypochondria about what had turned out to be a benign lump of fatty tissue. They both relished that phrase. Then Aaron asked me what I'd *really* thought about his play, and I said I thought it was brilliant, and a highly original interpretation, and had he by any chance been influenced in his reading of the text by Julian Jaynes's *The Origin of Consciousness in the Breakdown of the Bicameral Mind*?'

Well, that was a winner. I'd won anyway, but that was a winner. The title was enough. He didn't cross-question me, he just took it. Instant rapport, instant understanding.

'Yes,' he said.

Like a man. I admired him for that.

Half an hour later, we found ourselves walking up Belsize Park together to see the rude movie.

It was an inspired choice. I mean, he can't have planned it, can he? Fate must have planned it. It was a special Club Showing, and he had special tickets proving we were both over the age of eighteen and fully consenting adults. And wow, were we over the age of eighteen. In my case, well over. But Aaron is only thirty. A baby.

It was a German homosexual movie about sex in public lavatories. And bondage, and flagellation. The lot. It was remarkably frank and visual. I've never seen so many erect penises. I didn't think it was allowed. It could have been a turn-off but it wasn't. Oh, not at all, not at all. But, old as I am, I think I did hear myself say 'Dear *God*' at one particularly uninhibited moment, and Aaron reached for my hand, and that was that.

We had supper in that little Turkish café down Chalk Farm. I have to tell you that the whole of this affair is deeply, deeply local. Aaron lives in my patch, and I live in his. Half a square mile contains us both. No frontiers. Over supper, Aaron did bring up the subject of Julian Jaynes, and I had to explain that I'd never actually read the book myself, I'd had it described to me in somewhat excessive detail after the show in La Barca by this friend of Ian

McKellen who was the person who really spotted the Intellectual Debt. But by that stage it didn't matter, we were getting on swingingly, and, as he said, it took an IQ of 2,000 simply to memorize the title, let alone read the book. He saluted me. He kissed my hand.

You know those evenings on which one can't say a wrong thing or give a wrong look? It's a long time since I had one. God in his mercy gave me grace, as the poet said.

'Hattie,' he said, and touched my arm. A little pulse jumped up at him like a small frog. I was burning.

'I know I've met you before,' he said, staring at me and into me. 'I just *know* it. It sounds corny, I know it does, but I've even dreamed about you. No, don't say anything, let me tell you. I had this dream in which you were standing in this huge room by a great open hearth with flames and logs and firedogs and stag's antlers and all that kind of thing. A baronial hall. And you were wearing a long white dress, and your hair was all piled on top and done up with gold string, and you had a gold-leaf necklace on. I can see you now. As you were then. You looked like some kind of priestess. There may even have been oak leaves and mistletoe and that kind of stuff. Now, how could I have made all that up? If I hadn't met you before?'

'In another life?' I said. As a tease, because it was suddenly, blindingly clear where his dream came from and why he thought he'd known me for ever. And, although it was pretty odd, it wasn't exactly mystic. Not, even, very nice.

'In this life, another life, I don't know where. But somewhere. Or else you're not real at all. You're just a product of my imagination. And if that's what you are, you are mine.'

He encircled my wrist with his hand. I have a slim wrist (nay, *bony*), and he has long fingers. He held me like a manacle.

'I'm yours anyway,' I risked, smiling at the handcuff to show I might be joking.

He kissed me, over the remains of the kebab.

'In a way,' he pursued, when we'd finished with that bit, 'it's rather a vulgar dream. A sort of Hollywood dream. A B movie. Historical romance and witchcraft, that sort of thing. With the difference that it's real. If a B movie were real, it would be an A movie, wouldn't it?'

I thought I'd better come clean. 'It *was* a B movie,' I said. Modestly. 'A *very* B movie. A C or D or E movie, to be honest. And not Hollywood, either. Shepherd's Bush. Well, East Acton 1970 vintage. My finest role. I remember that white dress very well. They let me keep it and I wore it to parties for years. My career was downhill all the way from then on. It was a ghastly movie.'

Aaron was staring at me, his eyes glittering. His breath was coming quite fast and shallow. He'd gone very pale, and drops of moisture stood up on his white brow. Perhaps he looks just a teeny bit like Cornel Wilde? Playing Chopin?

'Are you serious?' he said, in a husky tone.

'Quite serious,' I said. 'Would I lie to you at an hour like this? That film was released in 1970. It was directed by Philip Eager. Ever met Phil? Lucky you. I played the lady of the manor who'd got mixed up in some black magic. The lord got annoyed because he thought I was two-timing him with the devil. Does any more of it come back to you?'

He looked as though he were straining hard into the dark backward and abysm of time, with much result.

'God,' he muttered, 'how old can I have been when I saw it? 1970, you say? You realize I could have been dreaming about you for *seventeen years*? Since I was *fifteen years old*? God, you were beautiful. God, you *are* beautiful.'

'It's much more likely,' I said, 'that you saw a repeat on TV late one night and switched off quick. Or a video. Though come to think of it, if you *did* see it within living memory, I'd be obliged if you'd try to remember because I could try pursuing a repeat fee.'

THE GATES OF IVORY

He smiled at this attempt to lighten the atmosphere, but he obviously hadn't done with the intense brooding phase. He kept on staring at me, and mumbling about his dream life, as though he could read the whole of his past history in my face — and who knows, perhaps he could? Stranger things have happened, though nothing quite like this has ever happened to me. I never expected my ill-starred and brief acting career to have results as interesting as this. Whoever could have guessed that I'd infiltrate the dream time of a fifteen-year-old boy? I used to be in love with the Wicked Queen in Snow White, myself. Along with a million others. But I bet Aaron Headleand was the only young lad to fall in love with Hattie Osborne camping it up in the Barbara-Cartland-Middle-Ages of East Acton.

I felt a bit responsible for him, to tell the truth. I mean, I am ten years older than him, and I ought to be ten years wiser. I didn't want to wreck his childish fantasies. I didn't want to disillusion and disabuse. And anyway, maybe he'd never seen the whole movie, maybe he really had just caught a snatch of it? I myself, sitting there, both hands by now firmly clasped in his, undergoing a session of deep impromptu mutual memory-dredging psycho-analysis, was acutely conscious of the fact that the most notorious scene in that movie, the only sequence that showed any glimmering of life, had been a rather daring flagellation tableau that probably owed a stylistic something to one of those sado-masochistic 1960s Italians. Myself tied all but naked to a post, and 101 serfs and vassals wreaking their lord's vengeance. I wasn't *actually* naked, I was wearing an obscene little pink silk cache-sexe, on my agent's insistence. Fat lot of difference it made to the impact. Well, no, I take that back, compared with the German extravaganza we'd just witnessed, I suppose my film was pretty discreet. But its intentions were impure. No mistake about that. (The German movie was actually, in contrast, quite wholesome.)

So I was wondering, you see, if these impure intentions had

reached young Aaron, and whether they'd lingered all this while in his psyche. And if they had, was it to my advantage or not? Or to his, come to that? I don't need to tell *you* what I thought the implications might be.

Anyway, I judged it wiser to try to shift ground for the time being, and I managed to divert him to a harmless chat about why I'd given up my screen career or vice versa, and who was about to take over what at the National, and whether or not *The Beast with Many Heads* was going to transfer or be recorded on video. I was congratulating myself on having cooled things down, when he suddenly pulled a fistful of fivers out of his pockets, shoved it under his plate with the bill, and said, 'Come on, let's go.'

And we went.

Aaron lives in a flat over an antique shop. It's a disgrace. I told him, for a rising young power-man of the theatre, this place is a disgrace. He didn't seem to care. He didn't even listen to me. He just went for me. The bed is one of those futon things, very low and hard, and God knows when the sheets were last changed. I tried to keep things on a light-hearted level, asking him if he'd got AIDS and all that, but all he said was, 'I know I haven't, and I don't care if you have, I don't care where you've been, I don't mind dying on the job,' which wasn't much of an answer but I knew what he meant, and after that I gave up trying to be responsible, and we agreed to die together.

And now Aaron is in love with me, and I suppose I might as well be in love with him.

I've never had an affair with a younger man. It's always been a bit the other way, for me. He's ten years younger than me. And I'm ten years younger than his mother. More or less.

It's had an odd effect on me. I think it really *has* made me more responsible. I've run some wild risks in my time, but most of them have been at my own expense. This time it's different. I feel protective about him. He's a dreamer. He's not a practical man. In the corner of his bedroom he's got a sort of shanty town of beer cans and bottles and bottle tops. He's built it into a little city. A mini stage set. I really must do something about it.

I've changed the sheets. He didn't seem to take offence.

He can't leave me alone. I find it very moving. He rings me from work (he's rehearsing a takeover for Volumnia) and wants to know if I'm all right.

We eat together, shop together, sleep together. You should see us in Sainsbury's pushing our trolley together, buying soap and beer and lettuces. I did hope we'd bump into Polly Piper, to be honest, after that humiliating episode with the box of eggs. Saudi Arabian diplomats, forsooth! I'm proud of Aaron. I love to be seen out and about with Aaron. I don't care who knows that. I am shameless, and at the moment I've got something to be shameless about. Aaron is the best-looking man in Camden Town, by a long chalk. He shines out like a hero amidst the knee-deep garbage and the old boys dossing on doorsteps and the pretty pasty-faced sulky little louts with earrings.

I don't care about my wrinkles and my ankles and my belly. Who cares? Aaron doesn't care.

This is the first night I've spent alone since we fell in with one another. I told him I had to have a night to myself to bay at the moon and to make a few phone calls. I've been good, I've washed my hair and shaved my legs and I've rung Stephen's brother Francis in Taunton. Quel *bore*. Quel *drag*. Not much joy *there*. But there's a lot of joy here, right here, in me. Please God let me keep it just a little longer.

We're going to the movies again tomorrow. We like going to the movies. Aaron's good at winkling out the odd ones. So far we've seen a Chinese shepherd epic set in the uplands of Mongolia, a French provincial murder mystery set in the Auvergne, an arty Portuguese meditation on life in Lisbon, and a heavy Japanese tragedy about a young man obliged by honour and tradition to kill his mother. (During this last, he wept. I noticed, but I pretended not to.)

I wonder what Liz Headleand will make of all this, if ever she finds out. At the moment I'm not all that keen on bumping into *her* in Sainsbury's. I draw the line somewhere. But I don't think she shops in Camden Town. Rumour has it that she favours Waitrose on the Finchley Road.

*

Liz Headleand's daughter Sally is on the phone to her half-brother Alan. She is complaining about sexual harassment and discrimination at work, but her real complaints are grounded elsewhere.

'I mean, fuck it,' says Sally, 'why the fuck should I put up with it? And they call themselves Equal Opportunity Employers. Opportunity to make the fucking tea and go out and get them a round of fucking tuna-fish sandwiches. And then they call me Poppet. I mean, I ask you. Poppet.'

Alan, tilting back his chair and putting his feet up on the table by his humming word processor, unobligingly laughs.

'Don't you laugh, buster,' says Sally, irritably. 'It may be a joke to you, up there in your cushy little sinecure, but down here it's seriously threatening my life chances.'

'Your what?' says Alan, intrigued by this unexpectedly sociological turn of phrase. But Sally is not to be deflected from her purpose.

'Yes, it's always been a joke to you,' she continues, with an exaggerated bitterness which is not wholly assumed. 'Didn't you boys have it easy. Who was it that was always expected to lay the table? Who was it that had to empty the dishwasher? Who was it that had to put away the laundry?'

'I always thought it was me,' says Alan, leaning forward to delete a tautologous adjective from his luminous prose.

'Don't try to be funny. You know it was always me. Well, me and Stella. Calls herself a modern woman, she was as sexist as

Queen Victoria. It was always us girls. You three never had to lift a finger. All you had to do was to pretend to be reading a book, and she'd shout upstairs for one of us. She'd even do things herself rather than disturb you lot. And that's saying something.'

'I don't remember any of that,' says Alan, pressing a mouse button to split his screen.

'Oh yes you do,' says Sally. 'Look, it was Stella who really lost out. I didn't do so badly, I agree. But poor old Stell, I mean, was it fair?'

'Life isn't fair,' says Alan, pressing Escape.

'She doted on you all,' says Sally. 'I mean, she just wasn't up to date. Nobody seems to have told her that mother–daughter relationships are all the rage. Mothers and sons are out. I hope my children are all girls. I bet she never *thinks* of Stella.'

Alan reflects. He is of the opinion that Liz's maternal energy had over the years through descending offspring run a little thin and that not only Sally and Stella but also, to a degree, he himself had suffered from this watering down of attention, but he does not wish to concede this to Sally. And he does not think it is anything to do with sexism. Sally's eagerness to ascribe everything unpleasant in life to sexism annoys him. It oversimplifies.

'I think it was always Aaron that had the easy ride,' he offers, as he playfully adjusts some punctuation. 'She adored Aaron.'

Sally is silent for a moment, and then responds, thoughtfully, 'Yes, that's true. He was the blue-eyed boy. Hasn't done him much good, has it?'

'Oh, I dunno. Aaron's doing okay. I thought his play was okay, didn't you?'

'I haven't seen it yet.'

'Disloyal Little Sis. Isn't it coming off soon?'

'No, it's transferring or so he says. I hate *Coriolanus*. Military crap. Death and glory. That's the sort of stuff that makes the world the mess it is.'

'No, it's not. You haven't seen it. It's not a pro-war play. Well, I mean, knowing Aaron, would it be? Give him a chance.'

Sally softens, her voice lightens, she giggles.

'I say, do you remember that time he got lost on the Channel ferry, and she got in such a panic because she thought he'd fallen overboard?'

'And that time when you and he disappeared into the gents and made us miss the flight back from Paris? What on earth did you think you were playing at? Charles was furious.'

They reminisce, affectionately, as Alan continues to correct his chapter, as Sally stirs a Bolognese sauce. They have reached an age where they find it amusing and surprising to be old enough to have a shared past. They are too young to find time a threat, for the future is still illimitable, and they know they will never die. But they already have a history, and they can afford to smile at its idiocies, its embarrassments, its errors. Sally's sense of grievance abates.

Absorbed in their evocation of some of the high points of their infancy, Sally almost forgets to tell Alan the latest gossip about Aaron. He has been sighted, according to her friend Brodie, with a new woman. Holding hands over a plateful of mussels in the Camden Brasserie. What kind of woman, Alan wants to know? Oh, the usual, says Sally. Theatrical type, according to Brodie. Long red hair. Oh, one of those, says Alan, worldly-wise.

As Sally's sauce and Alan's text now need two-handed attention, they wind up their chat, and ring off, with mutual expressions of goodwill. Sally, slicing mushrooms, continues to summon up the many manifestations of Aaron. He'd always been a lad of the theatre. Aaron, at primary school, taking the part of Joseph in the end-of-term biblical epic: Behold, this dreamer cometh! Aaron, taking his coat of many colours to bed with him, and pillowing his cheek against it. Aaron trying to organize his brothers and sisters into a Christmas pantomime for the amusement of Liz, Charles and Granny

Headland. Aaron, in his conjurer phase, endlessly practising Magic Circle tricks that never worked, though they sometimes deceived baby Stella. Aaron, in the school play at the City of London, camping it up with his friend Eric in a Joe Orton black farce. Aaron, playing Miss Julie at drama school in that cross-dressed Strindberg production, with Marie-Louise Baxter playing what's-his-name, the valet. Bloody good, he'd been, in that one. Did he ever regret not being an actor, these days?

Sally tips the mushrooms into the murky red sauce, sniffs, stirs, tastes. Aaron is quite a card. She really ought to go and see his play.

*

Is this a committee meeting, or is it a social occasion? Notebooks and neatly knotted ties and upright postures suggest the former; an intimate glow of yellow lamplight, golden and red flowers, fresh coffee in white and gold porcelain cups suggest the latter. If it is a social occasion, the hostess is the large woman with a bandaged ankle who pours the coffee and hands round a plate of austere but sugar-gritted oblong biscuits. She is in command of the deployment of chairs and sofas, and it is she that has given this room its unaccustomed air of slight formality. She presides over the polished wood, the woven fabrics, the sea-green curtains that exclude the night. The odours of the Blue Mountain and sweet faint sugar crumbs and distant linseed and beeswax and Eau de l'Herbe Bleue are hers, and hers is the portrait of the voluptuous false white-breasted ancestor in crimson velvet and badly painted pearls. Hers is the chipped eagle mirror, and hers the cut-glass vase. She is at home here, she sits firmly and heavily, her foot resting upon a little tapestry-covered stool. The distress of the lamp brackets is hers, and hers too is the drag of the cream paint.

If, on the other hand, it is a committee meeting, who is in the chair? It is not Liz Headland, for by her manipulation of the apparatus of coffee she dissociates herself from that role. There is nothing delicate about her renunciation, nothing shy or womanly. She has decided, positively, to sit back, and now, her own last cup poured, she sits back precisely: she balances her cup and saucer in deliberate hands, and sits firmly in her familiar chair, squaring her shoulders, in a manner that confirms that it is now the time for the business of the evening to begin.

Who will take up her challenge? It will not be that little woman curled up with her feet beneath her in the corner of the settee. She has placed her small shoes neatly, side by side, beneath her on the carpet, as though she has removed them for ritual reasons rather than for comfort. Nevertheless, comfort is what she has withdrawn to, and Liz Headleand's tabby cat has settled itself warmly on her lap. Esther Breuer strokes the cat, and the cat purrs deeply. No, it does not seem that Esther intends to take an active part.

Nor, at this stage, will the red-headed woman in the Windsor chair. Her bright insubordinate hair is tied firmly back in an efficient black scroll of scarf, and she is wearing a long plain matt-black dress that buttons down the front and reaches demurely down to her little laced boots. Her blacks have a hint of greenness and decay, a touch of academic mould. She is making an effort to look sober and serious, but cannot conceal the fact that she is feeling quite unusually well. A distracted radiance glows from her, betraying her dull widow's weeds. From time to time she smiles, inappropriately, at some private joke. Is it hormone replacement therapy, wonders Liz Headleand, achronologically and autobiographically, that makes Hattie Osborne look so radiant?

No, it will be one of the men who takes command, despite the fact that it is the women who convened this gathering. It will not be Robert Oxenholme, for he rightly considers himself marginal in this company, of limited use and with limited grasp of the proceedings. Robert, who makes a habit of considering himself marginal, adds colour and tone, with his shimmering kingfisher tie and his flashing malachite socks and his heavy-framed square mauve-tinted spectacles. But he does not add weight. He will not speak until spoken to.

It will not be Hattie Osborne's contact, John Geddes, as he has not yet turned up. He may never turn up. It has already been agreed that anyone who has anything to do with the film industry is more than likely not to turn up. It has already been decided that there is no point at all in waiting for John Geddes, however helpful he might prove to be (and doubt is expressed about his possible utility anywhere, in any circumstances). Even if he were here, he could not take the chair. His credibility is too much in doubt.

Melvyn Stacey is a possible candidate. Pink of face and silver of hair and smooth grey of suiting, he looks around him over his half-rims with the air of one accustomed to commanding rather dull battalions. He has sat in many a long-tabled room, he has dozed through many a long afternoon behind his place name, he has endured many a point of order and kept his equanimity through much Other Business. He is emollient, experienced. But he also is, like Robert, out of place. This is not his territory, he is slightly ill at ease amongst the flowers and china. Fluorescent lighting becomes his manner better than this more sumptuous glow. He will step in if needed, as he has been obliged to do on so many occasions, but he will wait to be asked. He surveys his colleagues, hesitates, and, as he begins to clear his throat, Charles Headleand speaks.

'We are here,' says Charles, with a magnificent combination of pomposity and informality, 'to work out what it would be sensible to do about the disappearance of Stephen Cox. If we decide to do anything. I think we all know the outlines of the situation, but shall we just run through it, so we all have it clear in our minds?'

Everybody looks sage, everybody nods. Everybody listens, attentively, as Charles Headleand marshals the facts and lays them before the meeting. Some doodle in notebooks, some play with biscuit crumbs, and Esther strokes the cat, but all listen.

Charles establishes: Date of departure: confirmed by H.O.

Sightings abroad: by Simon Grunewald, John Geddes, Peter Bloch, members of the ICRC and the ICRDP

Stephen's known intentions: as evidenced by his advice to accountants, etc., and verbal communications with L.H. and H.O. (Some slight discrepancies here?)

Presumed locations: Bangkok confirmed, Vietnam recorded in diaries and confirmed by hotel receipts and currency exchange forms

Presumed destination: Kampuchea

Charles lays before them: Stephen's long silence, followed by the arrival of the package which now lies as evidence on the coffee table.

'I think we are all agreed,' says Charles, 'that the dispatching of the package, whether by Stephen or Another, seems to invite some kind of action on our part? Or rather, on Liz's part?'

It seems that we are agreed. Some of us seem to think that there may already have been significant delay in taking action, but we do not like to sound censorious. After all, it is a delicate, an unusual situation.

Charles lists lines of inquiry already explored and found unhelpful.

1. The Cox family. H.O. reports that she has spoken to Francis Cox in Taunton and received the information that none of the Coxes has heard from Stephen since he left the country, and that they have not been either surprised by or interested in his absence. Stephen's mother, in her nineties, is in a nursing home in the Quantocks and would not know if she had heard from

him or not, as she is senile and does not know anybody or anything. Stephen has not been an attentive son, H.O. had gathered.

2. Stephen's various publishers. Here too both H.O. and L.H. have drawn a blank. L.H. reports that, according to Stephen's friend and fellow-novelist Brian Bowen, Stephen had fallen out with the most recent of several publishers of his 'serious' work over the sacking of a copy editor, and had been talking of returning to his first editor, newly divorced from a newly merged conglomerate.

3. The Foreign Office and the Home Office. C.H. has made inquiries here, as he once in his television days had made a programme about a proposal to establish a Missing Persons Register and therefore knows the people who are interested in such matters, but he has not come up with anything. R.O. says that he also has made discreet inquiries and got nowhere. He and C.H. agree that more could be done in this direction if deemed advisable by the group.

Charles then asks the meeting to suggest any other obvious contacts. Melvyn Stacey asks if Stephen had an American Express card, because it is easy to track down people's movements abroad through their Amex transactions. It is unethical, he agrees, but easy. This notion is not considered very helpful because it is felt that (a) American Express probably does not operate in Vietnam, and certainly not in Kampuchea, and (b) Stephen might not have been the kind of chap to have had an American Express card anyway. A fruitless and digressional discussion on Stephen's political and financial attitudes and the inconsistencies thereof is cut short by Charles, who is not interested in personalities.

Liz Headleand asks if anyone wants some more coffee.

Harriet Osborne brings up the question of Konstantin Vassiliou, whose presence is conspicuous in the diaries and notebooks, and whose absence is now almost as conspicuous as Stephen's. His own mother does not know where he is, claims Hattie.

There is a delay while H.O. and L.H. try to explain about Konstantin Vassiliou. Charles, to their surprise, knows who he is without explanation: Yes, he says, of course, he knows Vassiliou's work well, surely everybody does, in fact he had himself been trying to contact him over the last few weeks to commission a photoessay for the Royal Geographic on the subject of logging and oil drilling in Irian Jaya. But had failed, for Vassiliou had, indeed, vanished. This had not surprised Charles at all, for Vassiliou is notorious for his disappearances. If Stephen is with Vassiliou, says Charles, then both of them are alive and well and holed up in a hut in the rain forest or lying low in a penthouse luxury suite in Hong Kong. Charles is surprised that the name of Vassiliou is not current in the worlds of M. S., L. H., H. O., E. O. and R. O. Hadn't the Red Cross itself used one of his photographs on a Christmas appeal?

Melvyn Stacey, a little nettled, decides that however talented as a photographer, Konstantin Vassiliou is a red herring. He points out that he is no use as a contact if he cannot be found.

Liz Headleand thinks that perhaps she should offer people a drink soon. Whisky and soda? Brandy? Wine does not seem correct for such a meeting. Wine is too womanly.

The direction of the agenda wavers. There is a tendency towards disintegration. Liz and Hattie embark on a private chat about other names encoded in the diaries, and Hattie mentions the possibility of speaking to Marianne Sanderson, who had worked as a doctor in a field hospital in Kampuchea before being invalided home with malaria. Marianne, she tells the meeting at large, had certainly known Konstantin in Kampuchea, for he had photographed her patients. They had appeared in a colour magazine. Charles notes her name efficiently upon his pad.

On his pad there is a diagram, with names and arrows, pointing in a pincer movement towards an empty space, which is Kampuchea. Space Zero. In the space, he writes, 'Marianne Sanderson?'

Stephen is absence. Kampuchea is vacuum. One has engulfed the other.

Stephen's friends, gathered to discuss him, feel that in some strange way he is disintegrating rather than assembling as a result of their attention.

It occurs to Esther, who had known Stephen hardly at all, who had met him once at Heathrow on her way to Bologna, who sits there quietly stroking the cat, that the only people who really knew Stephen were Alix and Brian Bowen and they have not been summoned to this meeting. Stephen has fallen into the hands of strangers.

She now wonders if this is her fault for not inviting Alix Bowen to her wedding. During the past months, she and Liz have been seeing more of one another, and Alix has been exiled. The balance of power has shifted. During Esther's self-imposed exile in Bologna, Alix and Liz had become close, had excluded her from their friendship. Now it is Alix's turn to retreat to the circumference. Esther and Liz are Londoners now, married to Londoners. The Headlands and the Oxenholmes move in circles that the Bowens never enter. Robert and Charles even show signs of liking one another, in so far as men ever know one another well enough to like one another.

Esther is amused but a little discomfited by these reflections. She does not much care for them. She is sorry now that she did not ask Alix to her wedding, and cannot think why she did not. Did she think Alix would disapprove? Has she wanted to favour Liz? To curry favour *with* Liz? Had she tried to alienate Alix *from* Liz?

Little jealousies flutter in the air. Esther does not like them.

Stephen Cox is not there to speak for himself. He falls to pieces, as others claim his parts. He floats downriver.

Hattie Osborne introduces a character called Miss Porntip. They all laugh merrily at the notion of Miss Porntip, and decide that with a name like that she cannot but be a figment of the imagination. A fiction, a bad joke. Had Stephen not realized that foreigners were no longer funny, that racial stereotypes were out? If Stephen's novel features a Miss Porntip, then perhaps it is just as well that it has been mislaid.

At the introduction of Miss Porntip, the evening disintegrates further, concentration dissipates, frivolity prevails. Liz offers tumblers of spirits, and all but Hattie Osborne accept. (Hattie takes a glass of soda.) The committee is dissolved. Jokes are made about Stephen which are not wholly in good taste. Miss Porntip's name releases other anecdotes about impossible names that cause problems of taste and tact in the media: The Reverend Canaan Banana and the brothers Aircraft and Danger Darker represent Africa, and the palindromic Lon Nol's military spokesman Am Rong speaks up for South East Asia. To provide ethnic balance Esther murmurs the names of the Lords Killbracken and Clashfern. Charles reminds them of the bomb blast at the Martyrs Mausoleum in Rangoon in which died, among some twenty others, the Korean Foreign Minister Lee Bum Suk. How they had laughed, the foreign correspondents! C.H., L.H., H.O., E.O., R.O. and M.S. do not laugh, for they know they should not, but there is an unpleasant laughter somewhere in the room with them that they cannot entirely disown or dispel. It is caught in the folds of the heavily lined curtains, it sticks to the varnish. Stephen Cox is dead! The vacuum yawns and sucks. Thus one will vanish, leaving a faint trail of receipts and jottings and junk mail and postcards and credit cards and little bones and sniggering laughter. Nothingness triumphs. The suck of nothingness fills the room and almost overpowers the valiant lights and odours.

Liz Headleand cannot bear it. Suddenly, she cannot bear it. Something clicks in her head and she hears herself speaking loudly and clearly, into the twittering, as though she were addressing a public meeting.

'I shall go and look for him,' she says. 'There's no way we can get anything done by sitting around here chattering. I shall go and look for him. It is the least that I can do.'

She means what she says, and a silence follows her speech.

Everything in the rooms shifts. Liz has dared to lay claim to Stephen. She has salvaged him. She has become the betrothed and the widow in an instant.

An explosion of meanings follows her speech, like a silent distant burst of fireworks on the night. Flames burst from the smouldering wood.

Charles Headleand loses his second wife a second time, and a second time is defeated in his search for Dirk Davis. (*So she and Stephen Cox were lovers, after all.*) And Liz is not his ally but his rival. Charles stares into his glass and sees the spider.

Esther knows at that instant that her husband Robert sees constantly his first wife Lydia. The knowledge fills her with dread. Little sparks flash and glitter on and on from the fuse, noiselessly, into the obscurity.

Hattie Osborne at that instant relinquishes all rights save the contractual in Stephen: Liz Headleand can have his bones, though Hattie has bought his story. She lays her hands demurely on her soft belly, and she feels within her the gathering clots of blood that are to be Liz Headleand's grandchild. She will risk it. She quickens, she feels herself quicken, as the small cells cluster.

Robert Oxenholme sees before him the smiling features of the Leper King, and thinks that perhaps he will quit the thankless sponsorship game and go back into the art business and Serious Money. He has a friend who is an orientalist, who is looking for backing for a gallery. The Orient, which has never much appealed to him, has of late exerted a strange attraction. A strange attractor has found him wandering round obscure collections in St James's, and lingering by small statues in back rooms of the British Museum and the dusty Musée Guimet. He has found himself dreaming of Sihanouk and the Bayon. Shall he abandon the Renaissance of the

West, and look eastwards to the Temples of the Eternal Dawn? There the sun rises: shall he follow Liz Headleand towards its rising? Shall he invest in the Orient?

Melvyn Stacey, more prosaically, is thinking that things would have gone better had he been in the chair. He recognizes that now is the time to be practical, to welcome Liz Headleand's initiative, to proceed to dates and details. He clears his throat and is about to speak, when there is a knock at the door.

It is not Stephen back from the dead to claim his bride, nor Aaron from Chalk Farm to claim his. It is only John Geddes, dinner-jacketed and a little drunk. He is sorry he is late, he says, as he settles into the suddenly reconvened meeting: he has just been to the West End Gala Theatre Awards Ceremony and couldn't get away earlier, but here he is at last, and can he be of service?

John Geddes does not look as though he could be of service anywhere to anyone ever. He is grotesque. He is small and round and fat and polished like a black button. The frills of his shirt flounce, his scarlet bow tie looks as though it is about to light up and flash and wink like a Christmas tree decoration, and his paunch swells proudly through straining canvas beneath a scarlet cummerbund. His face gleams white with excitement and fluster, his bright eyes dart, his hair glistens, his voice is high-pitched and sibilant. He accepts a glass of weak Scotch, and sits forward intently from his Victorian button chair, his thighs roundly alert, his black shoes glistening, his whole body expectant. He is a figure from music hall. Can this be the man who braves the Amazonian jungle and the guerrillas of Peru in search of dangerous and exotic film locations? He looks as though he can never have left the West End. He has found it hard enough to make his way to St John's Wood. What possible use can he be?

His apparition threatens to plunge the gathering into farce, but they rally and confront him, they reinforce their own high seriousness of purpose. (Hattie Osborne, who knows John well, hides a

smile.) Introductions are made, and Dr Elizabeth Headleand is
presented almost unambiguously as the proprietor of Stephen Cox,
about to set forth to claim her own. John nods and puffs and gulps
a little, as he accepts this newly minted version of events. It is
romantic. Liz's departure has become a fact. Minute by minute it
grows more imminent. John listens eagerly as Charles gallops
through the draft Minutes of the Meeting, and nods approval as Liz
says she could make herself free to leave in a couple of weeks. Yes,
he agrees, Bangkok is the proper starting point. Bangkok is abuzz
with contacts and cross-currents, it is a hive and a port and a
melting pot and a trading station and a source of visas real and
false. He produces from a bulging pocket a little bulging address
book, and proceeds to copy out names and addresses and telephone
numbers. 'Some of these people are *crooks*,' he breathes, with manifest admiration, 'but they're useful crooks, and hardly at all dangerous, no, hardly at all.'

A serious attempt is made by the meeting to pool its contacts.
Melvyn offers the services of the Red Cross Tracing Agency,
Charles knows various journalists and stringers and a chap negotiating a deal over shellac in Saigon, and Robert admits to a second
cousin working at the Thai Marine Institute on the conservation of
krill. Liz listens to this networking with a look of brave amusement.
What had she undertaken? She herself knows nobody in the whole
of the Orient, although she has once been to Japan to a psycho-
analytic conference. Is there psychoanalysis in Thailand, or do they
have Buddhism instead? She turns to Esther, for comfort, and says,
'Now, Est, don't you know any Old Boys out there?'

'Not a one,' says Esther modestly. 'But Robert does know Sihanouk. Robert, why don't you get in touch with Sihanouk? Robert
knows *everybody*,' says Esther, proudly but not wholly amiably.

Robert disengages himself from this remark, but says that, although out of touch with Sihanouk, he may have an ex-girlfriend
who is married to a property dealer and hotelier in Chiang Mai.

Once more, the conversation falls apart. It is agreed that the official business is over. John Geddes, on invitation, tries to recall his last encounter with Stephen in the Hotel Nirvana, but his heart is not in it. His heart, it emerges, is still with the more recent, the more vivid Gala Awards and the crazy apparition of the Princess and the drunkenness of the Star and the graciousness of the Grande Dame and the inedibility of the Bœuf Wellington. He is bursting with his stories: they spill out of him, popping from him in all directions like festive corks, like bubbles, like burst buttons. My dears, the *limpness* of the Handshake! My dears, the velvet tights of the hostess! The corruption of the judges! The odiousness of the Starlettina! The serenity of Dame Peggy! The vanity of Queen William (I *swear* he was rouged!) And the ineffable, intolerable, incomprehensible, unprecedented small-mindedness of not giving the Best Play Award to *Taboo*, when everybody knows it was the only play of the year worth crossing the Charing Cross Road to see! I mean, Jeffrey *Archer*, groans John Geddes, the Entrepreneur of the Year, I ask you!

Despite themselves they laugh. They cannot help but laugh. There is no harm in John Geddes, no danger, no threat to anybody. He brings to them a splutter of fantasia. He has *enjoyed* his evening. His description of the hostess's outfit (scarlet velvet tight-*bootees*, one thigh length, one knee length, balloon skirt and sleeves, velvet *décolleté*, emerald bows in her hair, bows on her lips, bows on her bosom and bows on her bum, oh bows my darlings everywhere!) is rivalled only by his account of the munching of the beef (the *tooth* picking, the contortions, the misery, the broken dentures, the lost fillings, the impacted bridgework, the abandoned *tranches*, you can't *do* that to old folk on a public occasion!) His loyalty to the brilliance of Steve Stone's *Taboo* shines touchingly forth from this outpouring of bacchanalian excess, and is only slightly tarnished when Hattie Osborne asks him point-blank whether or not he is a backer of the show. (She knows he is.) Unperturbed, he admits it, and says he has a slice of the film interests too, and is off shortly to Zaïre or Zimbabwe or Zambia to look for suitable locations. And yes, since they want to know, he *did* come back from Peru sort-of-sharpish. There were too many beans in Peru. Too many *what*? Too many beans. Horrid things, beans. He'd never gone much for that sort of cuisine. Beans with bread, beans with rice, beans with chilli, beans with beans. No, Thailand's the place, he tells Liz. Great food in Thailand. Would she permit him to take her out one evening to the Thai restaurant on the Fulham Broadway to introduce her to the pleasures of dining Thai style?

John Geddes does not say so, but he had been *shot at* in Peru. He does not say, My darlings, they *shot at* me in Peru! He cannot think of a way to make the story amusing. He may, in time. But not yet, not yet.

Some stories really are not very funny. Some teeter nervously on the brink of a kind of laughter. Stephen Cox hangs between two worlds. He is a go-between. Fragments of him drift on the river, surface from the mud.

Stephen would have enjoyed this conversation, Liz thinks, as she admires her new yellow wallpaper and experimentally wiggles her sprained ankle. Stephen would have been amused by its idiosyncrasies, its heterogeneity, its switchback tone. Stephen, despite his primal hopes and interests, because of his primal hopes and interests, was a slave to irony. He would never escape it, not even on his deathbed. Thus reflected Liz Headleand, uncertainly, as she joined in the fun.

*

The sun is high. They break their journey, eat a banana, smoke a cigarette, drink a beer and doze beneath a mango-tree. Stephen's eyes begin to close. Akira and Konstantin will keep guard. They are young, alert. He grows old.

Stephen drifts. He sees the smiling abandoned Buddha image in the cave, he sees Konstantin's look of concern at its neglect. His mind wanders back to their journey to the north of Thailand, to visit the forest monk. They had sat with him on a wooden platform overlooking the valley, as the evening sky darkened. Ajahn had told them of the twenty years he had spent alone in the forest, speaking never a word, as he had travelled the Eightfold Path to salvation. He had lived on fruits and seeds and gifts from the villagers. He had been befriended by a bear, and he had shared his drinking water with a python. He had watched the leaves uncurl, and he had watched the seeds fall. He had watched the copulation of insects and the laying of eggs and the migrations of caterpillars and the hatching of chrysalides and the slow unfolding and drying of damp wings. He had seen flights, he had seen devourings, he had seen decay and rebirth and transmigration. He had learned the slow cycle of the seasons in his own body, and now he had returned to the land of speech and of men, to sit there, cross-legged, stout, saffron-robed, bald, tattooed, affable, eloquent, to warn them of the death of the rain forest and the threat of the cabbage.

In his former life, he told them, he had been a boxer. He had muscles. He was a fighting man. He was fighting against the loggers and the cultivators and the Highland Development Project and the ignorant benefactors of the West to save his forest.

Politician or Holy Man? How could one tell?

Stephen knows nothing of Buddhism, of the Eightfold Path, of the wanderings of the Sangha, of the harmony known as Silah-damma. Konstantin had tried to explain, but Stephen had not listened. And yet the messages of the forest had reached him then, as they reach him now, as they had reached him in the quiet shell of the Hôtel de la Paix.

Perhaps, it occurs to him, it was not the Fighting Men, nor the tanks and trucks of the Fighting Men, nor the Death of Communism, nor even the colonnades of Angkor or Angkar that he had come to find, but the forest itself.

He nods and dreams, as images cross the lowered threshold. He sees shifting colours. He smiles at the python, the bear and the bat. He is loosening his hold. He is detaching himself from the wheel of being, from the wheel of ignorance and illusion. The Lords of Death gather benignly. They are waiting for him.

One of them taps him on his wounded ankle. He starts, opens his eyes. It is Konstantin, offering him a cigarette. He jerks himself awake, accepts, leans forward for the light.

*

Liz tried to do some homework before she set off to the East. As Charles had studied the Koran before flying off to Gatwick and Baldai in search of the dead Dirk Davis, so Liz studied books on the history of Cambodia and the Vietnam war and the rise of Pol Pot. She distressed herself with Shawcross and Becker and Kiernan (see bibliography), then she calmed herself with photographs of temples and Buddhist monks. But, as Charles had been baffled by the Koran, so she remained baffled by much of what she read. She could not concentrate as she would have wished. She had her practice to wind down, her patients to redeploy, her bills to pay, her body to take for its jabbing. She was a fast, impressionistic, careless reader, and monstrous gobbets of information bobbed and bucketed and eddied in the turbulence of her mind. Crocodiles, white elephants and tigers! Sihanouk's mother with a tarnished sword! One million, two million, three million dead! GRUNK, FUNK, FANK and FUNCIN-PEC! Starvation, genocide, torture! Tuol Sleng Incarceration Centre! Do not trust the Vietophile Oxfam! Do not trust the Vietophobe ICRDP! Do not eat the soft-shelled crab!

The mess of Stephen's papers she could no longer bear. A panic stumbled through her fingers as she turned the folders. What should she take with her? Was she doomed to leave behind the vital clue, the saving talisman? Should she take, for example, those terrible little bones?

Two days before her departure she forced herself to go to see Marianne Sanderson, Quaker, linguist and doctor. She did not look forward to the encounter. What would this Mother Teresa of the Killing Fields make of the fashionable overpaid psychotherapist of St John's Wood? Liz felt guilty even before she set off to Marianne's garden flat in Islington.

But it was not quite like that. Perhaps it never is.

Malaria had subdued Marianne, and her first concern was a generous if limited wish to spare Liz her own misadventures. They spent the first quarter of an hour discussing mosquitoes. *Plasmodium vivax* and *Plasmodium falciparum* were given an airing, and dengue fever made its entrance, as it had, three years earlier, into Marianne's bloodstream. 'Dengue was *weird*,' said Marianne. 'All my hair fell out, and I hallucinated. There I was lying on the bed in the Trocadero, with sweat dripping *through* the mattress and *on to* the floor, and I thought I was in the sickbay at school! Can you imagine? Apparently I kept calling for Sister. And all sorts of faces came back from the past, faces I thought I'd completely forgotten. Freckles, plaits, spots, braces, the lot. Berets and hockey shorts. It's a sort of yellow fever, you know.'

Liz, who did know, was both disturbed and reassured by these anecdotes. Kampuchea did not sound a very safe place, but then, on the other hand, Marianne had survived it, and she seemed to have done so with good spirits. She did not look as though she came from *outre-tombe*. Over Earl Grey and Marks & Spencer's lemon cake Marianne even fell to uncharitable abuse of her patrons, the Cambaid Action Group, run by a completely *mad* Englishwoman, a Third World Groupie, as Marianne described her, a Jungle Fever Freak, whose incompetence was matched only by her insistence. 'Strong men fall down before her like *ninepins*,' said Marianne, 'because they can't bear to argue with her. It's easier to donate ten thousand quid than to have another lunch with The Hon. Mrs P. I'm never getting mixed up with anything sponsored by *her* again, I can tell you.'

Marianne was small and animated, in her faded baggy cotton turquoise trousers and her patterned green batik shirt. Her black bubble curls bounced as she reviled Mrs P. A thoroughly modern missionary, a Florence Nightingale for the eighties. It was hard to believe she'd really been out there.

But she had. After a while, she got down to business, and produced a map labelled Democratic Kampuchea, November 1973, Destroy When No Longer Needed, which she spread upon the floor, on the cheap jazzy red and brown and blue kilim. They knelt over it together, comrades, explorers.

'Now, *this*,' said Marianne, jabbing at the south-west, 'is where I was stationed. Near Pailin. In the foothills. Those are the Cardamom Mountains. Those are the ruby and sapphire mines. A lot of guerrilla activity, a lot of Khmer Rouge. That's where Konstantin Vassiliou came to see me on his motorbike. How far from Phnom Penh? Oh, no distance, really, less than a hundred miles. A bad road, but not far. Konstantin just arrived out of the heat one afternoon, with his bags and his bike and his camera. Easy rider. He fancies himself. But then so does everyone else. *Everyone* fancies Konstantin!'

Marianne laughed.

'And what kind of hospital, what size?' Liz wanted to know.

'Well, when I say *hospital*, don't imagine a *hospital*,' said Marianne. 'I mean, forget the Charing Cross and the Royal Free. It's more like a kind of camp. Bamboo huts, wooden beds, wooden legs. What we call "appropriate technology". Not much white tile and shining metal. Not much medicine either. They're trying to develop herbal remedies, but it's all a bit desperate. The KR wouldn't accept foreign aid and medicaments, and of course, the Vietnamese don't get much, so it's all a bit dodgy and shoestring. I suppose that's why people like Mrs P. flourish, God bless them.'

'The work must have been quite – grim?' said Liz.

'Well, yes. But the hospital wasn't all *that* bad. I once saw a hut in Africa with the word "Hospital" written on it. It was just a hut.

Inside, a bed. Well, a bed*stead*. On the wall, a chart. Not even filled in. Nothing else at all at all. No, Kampuchea's bit more sophisticated than that. It's all relative. They used to have doctors in Kampuchea, you know, it's just that they killed them off. The official figures, the ones we were always quoted, parrot fashion, were these: *"Out of 6,000 doctors, 57 remained alive in 1979. 57 doctors, 15 pharmacists, 500 nurses."* That's what was left. Did you ever see Konstantin's pics?'

Marianne Sanderson spread the pictures all over the map of the Cardamom Mountains and the Mekong and the Tonle Sap.

Young men lay on camp beds, smiling at the camera. Children played in the dust. Women carried buckets of water. (There were portraits of Marianne herself, her hair tied back in a head square, or face-masked, in various ministering poses, but these she modestly shuffled out of sight.) There was a whole sequence portraying one young man, handsome, fine-featured, vain, brown-bodied, in the prime of grace and beauty. A curled darling. Both his legs were missing. He wore a kind of baggy nappy, and from this garment protruded two stumps, and two articulated, home-made-looking structures of wood and crude metal pins and bits of canvas. A harness attached them to his shoulders. In the last frame, he propped himself upright, free-standing, on two wooden crutches. He gazed at the camera with a brave generosity. Defiant, angry, despairing, wistful, he stared forth at the world. He was a very good-looking young man.

Liz stared and stared.

'And what will happen to *him*?'

Marianne shrugged.

'Who knows? He learned to walk a bit. By the time I left he could stagger about. At least he doesn't have to fight for the army or the resistance any more. There's an awful lot of young men without legs in Kampuchea. An awful lot of mines.'

Marianne began to shuffle the photographs back into their envelope.

'Konstantin was very good to me,' she said. 'He was a nice boy, and good company. I hope you find him. I hope you find your friend.' She paused, hesitated, then said, '*My* friend was killed out there. Oh, nothing to do with the hostilities. Just an air crash. A routine flight, Hanoi–Saigon–Phnom Penh. He'd been back to the head office in Hanoi. He was one of the reasons why I went out there in the first place. Now, there doesn't seem so much point.'

'Tell me more,' said Liz.

'Oh, there's nothing much to tell,' said Marianne, and then told.

They'd been medical students together at St Stephen's, she and Eric, they'd had a lot of fun together. Laugh? With Eric, you never stopped laughing. He was a mad guy. Very small, about my size, curly hair like me, they used to call us the Terrible Twins. He was a joker. Mad keen on the theatre. Used to break into blank verse or Woody Allen or Noël Coward at the drop of a hat. Brilliant entertainer. Kept everybody's spirits up. They'd been together in various tight spots – Glasgow, the West Bank, and finally Kampuchea. Why? Well, why does one do anything? Eric was Jewish, North-London Jewish, *you* know the type. Motivated. Muswell Hill. Yes, it was a tragedy. He was only thirty-one. But we were lucky to be able to stick together for so long. It was a laugh at Phnom Penh! And even when we were out in the sticks, he used to get people going with a bit of theatre, a bit of mime, a dance routine, a sing-song. Eric loved a sing-song. He was a great mimic. Do you want to see some pics?

How could Liz say no? She was presented with out-of-focus ill-tinted Snappy Snaps of a fuzzy-haired, bespectacled young man pulling faces, fooling, holding a skull and doing his Hamlet. Marianne and Eric appeared arm-in-arm in a hotel foyer, in a hut, by a noodle stall, in a cyclopousse. The contrast with Konstantin's work was striking, but the snaps, though less universal, were in their own way as touching.

Liz, turning them over, said suddenly, 'Was Eric's second name Rosenberg?'

Marianne nodded.

'And did he go to the City of London? Yes? I remember Eric. He was a friend of my stepson Aaron. He used to come to tea. I remember seeing Eric in the school play. It was hilarious. Something quite unsuitable. What was it – Osborne, Pinter, Orton, something like that?'

'Well, there you go,' said Marianne, suddenly subdued and far away. 'Small world.' And she stared at the pattern in the carpet.

When Liz moved towards departure, Marianne produced for her a package of envelopes and messages. This for Sally in Bangkok, that for Dick in Phnom Penh, this for Bophana, that for Dr Chhi Beng Sam. Here, a list of the good eating places.

'And here,' she said, taking a ring from her finger, 'is my lucky jewel. It's a Pailin ruby. Or so they told us. Actually, *I* think it's just a bit of glass. Go on, you wear it. And if you ever get to the field station, you can give it to Chhi Beng Sam. She'll remember it. Give it to her with my love.'

Liz protested, but could not refuse. How could she say that death of lover, dengue fever and malaria did not seem to her to constitute good luck? She slipped the ring on to her little finger. It sat there comfortably.

'Actually,' said Marianne, pausing at her own threshold, 'sometimes I think Eric isn't really dead. I mean, all we were told was that the plane had crashed in Ratanakiri. They never produced any bodies. So if you bump into Eric, give him my love and tell him to come home soon!'

She smiled, to show that she was joking.

Liz, twisting the amulet upon her finger, walked out into the night.

*

On the following morning, Liz received a letter addressed in what looked like Alan Headleand's writing. She opened it and was

282

momentarily puzzled to find only a word-processed list of titles. When she got the point, she said 'Good boy' aloud. She did not think she would find many of these texts in Bangkok and Hanoi, but who knows? Marrakesh market had been full of French deconstructionists. Why not Canetti in Phnom Penh?

Here is Alan's list:

Barrows, Susanne   *Distorting Mirrors*, 1981
Canetti, Elias   *Crowds and Power*, 1960
Hobson, J. A.   *The Psychology of Jingoism*, 1901
Le Bon, Gustave   *Psychologie des foules*, 1895
Lombroso, Cesare   *Innumerable titles on criminal man, anarchists, anti-Semites, etc. (all in Italian, sorry)*
Moscovici, Serge   *The Age of the Crowd* (pub? trans. 1985)
Nye, Robert A.   *The Origins of Crowd Psychology*, 1975
Rudé, G. F. E.   *The Crowd in History*, 1964
Sighele, Scipio   *La Folla deliquenta*, 1895
Tarde, J. G.   *L'Opinion et la foule*, 1901

That should do to be going on with, Love Alan.

Liz folded the list neatly and put it in her bag with her passport and air ticket and other important documents. Maybe the list itself would infuse her with the necessary information.

Bypass reading: cut out the text: inject the title. A technique for the year 2000.

Three hours and two aggrieved patients later, she set off to meet Alix for lunch.

Alix was in London for the day, and had agreed to meet Liz at one p.m. at the Mandala Indian Vegetarian Self-Service just behind Camden Town Hall.

Alix had not come to London on purpose to see Liz, as she had made perhaps unnecessarily clear: she had come to see the new tenants of her Wandsworth house, but she did not mind fitting Liz in, if Liz could spare a convenient hour.

Something was up with Alix, Liz suspected, as she hung her bag and coat on the back of an ornate, uncomfortable high-backed wooden chair and prepared to wait. This choice of venue was indicative — a dark, clanging, cheap, underground, oppressive, gloomy, ethnic dump, new to Liz, but clearly much frequented by solitary *Guardian*-reading Alix-types from Camden Social Services and semi-down-and-outs from local bed-and-breakfast joints. True, it was near King's Cross, which was why Alix had selected it, but surely she could have thought of somewhere more salubrious? Liz would have preferred to have had her farewell lunch in a more up-market ambience. And where *was* Alix? Was her train late? Liz did not like being kept waiting. She was a busy woman herself.

The waiting gave her time to reflect that she had not seen Alix for months, whereas she had been seeing a lot of Esther, one way and another. She pondered this, while lighting a cigarette. (Was it her imagination, or did the *Guardian* readers stare at her crossly as she lit up? Yes, it was her imagination: this lot was far too tolerant of the poverty-inspired, Thatcher-created need for opium to sneer at a smoker.)

So, why was Alix sulking in her Northern tent? Had she felt left out of things?

Liz recalled that Alix had been the first person she had spoken to about Stephen's effects. (Good word, that, she noted; *effects*.) But — and had this been the source of the drifting? — Alix had *never rung back*. Or not very promptly. *Why not?*

Was it, perhaps, could it be, *jealousy?*

Liz bristled and bridled a little in her new striped Jean Muir sweater, as she confronted the prickly misunderstanding that would inevitably flow from her pursuit of Stephen Cox. What would Alix think she was up to? Surely Alix would not think she was in any way going *after* Stephen? Trying to take *possession* of Stephen?

Why, she was only doing her duty, and doing that rather late in the day! It wasn't as though she was looking forward to her trip, it wasn't as though she expected to get anything *out* of it! And why shouldn't she go to the opera with Robert and Esther? The box was free, a government box, as Esther had explained: she and Robert had to fill it up every now and then, or Robert would get the sack. It wasn't as though Liz *enjoyed* the opera. Mozart she could stomach, just about, but the atonal life of Father Damien and the lepers — well, no, not really.

And dammit, where was Alix? It was already ten past. Liz looked at her watch ostentatiously. The spicy odorous cavern with its advertisements for bucket-shop flights to Bangalore and AC Hire-cars in Delhi, with its ill-painted tantric symbols and its peeling white-washed walls, was filling up fast and Liz had already twice had to defend the chair she was keeping for her faithless friend. Annoying music twanged incomprehensibly, mockingly. Her dignity was at risk. Had Alix arranged all this on purpose? And who *was* that extraordinary gross woman sitting further down the bench, in layers of fur and beads and shawls, with cupid-bow lips and streaked henna hair, reading of all things, the *Spectator*? Was she the new-style neo-Tory ex-wife?

Liz was seriously thinking of leaving when Alix arrived, hurried, a little flustered, apologizing. Yes, the train had been late, it had broken down at Newark, sorry, should they go and get themselves something to eat at once?

The beans and the rice, the spinach and the vegetable stew, the lentils and diced potatoes, were doled out in ladles from unpromising metal troughs on to oval tin platters. A choice of nan, poori or paratha was laid upon the side. Liz looked at hers suspiciously, but to her surprise it tasted excellent. Mollified, she munched, as Alix explained that this was one of her old haunts, well known for its good value and fine food. The Moong Daal was famous. Quite the In-Place, said Alix, as you see; and she was only slightly teasing.

But there remained an obscure shadow, a veil over Alix, even as she joked about the dead Beaver and gossiped about Esther and Robert and asked Liz about her sister Shirley in Alberta. She did not re-engage with Liz. Something was wrong. Gone was the old ease, the old intimacy, gone the short cuts of thirty years. Alix was keeping something back. Discreetly, but firmly.

Liz inspected her expertly as she wiped up the traces of her daal and licked her fingers. The problem did not seem to be Esther, for Alix had come out on that, had indulged freely in aspersions on the recently wed Oxenholmes and their eccentric union, had even demanded a reprise on the story of the wedding breakfast and the cannibals, and had sympathized with the ordeal of the post-modern opera about sanctity. Nor did there seem to be any trouble with the boys – on the contrary, Alix was delighted to report that Nicholas's wife Ilse was at last, and happily, pregnant, and that Sam was enjoying his first year at Sussex. About Brian, Alix was more reticent. Was he about to get the sack or some unwelcome promotion? Liz (respecting the marriage bond) did not pry, but she took note. She thought she might have stumbled on a menopausal explanation for Alix's abstraction when Alix, out of the blue, suddenly said, 'Do you know anything about the toxic properties of some stuff called Fempan?' and then was sidetracked by Alix's flippant account of Paul Whitmore's death wish. They had a good laugh over Paul Whitmore, then moved on to hormone replacement therapy (Alix, predictably, gazing out of her robustly blooming mop of witch-white-steel-grey hair, disapproved, whereas Liz wavered) and thence to the nature of spirit and matter.

Alix had of late been more and more persuaded that all is matter. She had read a philosophical book about matter and neurons and quantum particles, and it had persuaded her that there was after all no ghost in the machine. Rather late in the day, said Alix, I have come round to the view that not only is there no God, there is no Spirit either.

'Is this to do with Paul Whitmore?' asked Liz.

'Partly, I suppose. I think he and I interchange *particles*. Not spirit, but *particles*. Through the eyeball.'

'If you were one of my patients,' said Liz, 'I'd have you certified.'

Again, they both laughed, and Alix continued, 'But the odd thing is, the more I convince myself there is no Spirit, the more apparitions I see. Like Burne-Jones and his angels.'

'What do you mean, apparitions?'

'Oh, you know, appearances. Images of dead people. Waking images. You know how when you're in love, you see the person everywhere in other people, in total strangers?' Liz shook her head, having forgotten what it was like to be in love, but Alix went on, 'You know what I mean, the set of a pair of shoulders, the turn of a cheek, the way a person walks? Ghosts of the real person? After Sebastian died, I saw him everywhere. Well, I'm getting more and more like that. I see my parents — I've started to see Sebastian again. I see Jilly Fox. I see Deborah. And I see a lot of old Beaver, which isn't surprising. Is it?'

'What do you mean, *see* them?'

'I mean I *think* I see them. Really *see* them. I think I've seen them just turning a corner, just walking down the steps, just leaving the room. Out of the corner of my eye. And it happens more and more, the more I tell myself there is no Spirit. As though they've been released. It's weird.'

Alix smiled, comfortably. She did not look at all mad. She was almost her old, friendly, communicable self.

'It's quite nice, really,' she said. 'It's better than bad dreams, where people are all decayed and deformed. And it sort of means that it doesn't matter whether you're alive or dead. Which is just as well, really, isn't it? Would you like some pudding? I don't really recommend it. It's too syrupy and sticky. They don't understand pudding here.'

'No, thanks,' said Liz.

'As a matter of fact,' said Alix, 'I thought I saw Stephen the other day.'

'Where?'

'In Northam's covered market, by the fish stall. *Not* a very likely place. But he looked quite real. He was wearing a green scarf. A sort of greenish cravat. I didn't know he wore cravats, did you? And then I began to worry that because I'd seen him, he was dead. Because most of the other people I see are. What do you think?'

'I think you're *crazy*, Alix. I think you'd much better go back to being a half-baked agnostic with pantheistic yearnings and Christian hangovers.'

'So, you're going to look for Stephen Cox,' said Alix, after a certain pause. 'Don't you think *that's* a bit crazy?'

Liz shrugged her shoulders. The bits of naked Velcro from which she had ripped away Jean Muir's excessive and expensive shoulder pads scratched and itched, ominously.

'Yes, I suppose it is,' she conceded. 'But I began to feel I had to know. It's so unsatisfactory, his having just disappeared. Don't you think? Doesn't Brian think? Doesn't Brian think we should do something?'

Liz's attempt to pass the buck failed. Alix stared blankly, then said, 'I suppose there's no reason why Stephen shouldn't have been in Northam market. I mean, it's a free country, isn't it?'

Liz gave up, sighed in mock exasperation. Perhaps Alix was, temporarily, mad. Mid-life madness, a well-known, a well-documented phenomenon. Well, if Alix could not be sensible, she could at least be sensible herself.

'I just wanted to see you before I went,' she said, in a tone of attempted seriousness. 'Just in case I never come back either. To say goodbye.'

And she undid what she had said by smiling, as Marianne had done when speaking of her lost lover.

'Well, goodbye then,' said Alix, with infuriating calm, also smiling, but in a different mode.

Liz, teased beyond endurance, started rummaging in her over-loaded bag, and flung on to the table her contact book, her passport, her air ticket, Alan's reading list, a dossier of letters of introduction, John Geddes's Thai-restaurant-inscribed mix of menus and vital fax numbers, a vaccination certificate, a strip of Prontoprints of herself, and one of Stephen's diaries.

'I just thought you might have some useful suggestions,' said Liz. 'About where to start.'

'Oh no, I don't think so,' said Alix, idly picking up Liz's passport and inspecting the grim-faced pop-eyed Euston-station-snapped features of her friend. 'So you still call yourself Dr Elizabeth Head-leand, do you?'

'Of course I do. That's my name.'

'I suppose Charles will come and rescue you, if you get lost. But he'd better try a bit harder than he did with that hostage telly chap. Have you any addresses you can leave with me?'

Liz, a little mollified, wrote down the addresses and phone numbers of the Trocadero and the Oriental in Bangkok, the number of Peter Bloch at the embassy, and the number of Robert's second cousin in krill.

Alix folded them and placed them absent-mindedly in her bag. Then she picked up Stephen's diary and opened it. Clipped into it, on opposing pages, were photographs of Stephen Cox and Mme Savet Akrun. Mme Akrun was asking, as usual, 'Where is my son?' Stephen was leaning back upon what looked like a balcony balus-trade, next to a potted geranium and a smirking tabby cat, against a cloudy sky, and smiling enigmatically in his white suit at the camera and behind the camera at an unseen Lord Snowdon. Alix gazed at these two images. The photograph of Stephen she knew well: it was cut out from his Booker book jacket. The other image also looked familiar, though she could not think why. She read the accompanying piece of reportage. Liz, watching her, reflected that she ought also to try to get hold of a photo of Konstantin Vassiliou, for identification purposes, before she left. She should have thought of this earlier.

'Amazing pic,' said Alix, pointing at Mme Akrun. 'Haven't I seen it somewhere before.'

'I think it was used as a poster,' said Liz. 'She's a real person. Stephen met her. According to his diary. I'll go and look for her, perhaps.'

As she spoke, the impossibility, the needle-in-a-haystack nightmare-nature of her pursuit struck her forcibly, and she suddenly said with a moment's wild hope, 'I say, Alix, why don't you come with me? I'm not cut out for this kind of thing. Why don't you come with me, Alix?'

'How can I, at a moment's notice?'

'How can I? But I'm going!'

'Well, you'll have to go without me. Don't look so glum, Liz. It might be *fun*. You might find Stephen and have a lot of fun.'

This did not sound very likely.

Alix continued to stare at the features of Mme Savet Akrun. Both English women stared at the Khmer woman. Liz twisted the red glass Pailin ruby upon her finger and sighed heavily. Alix sighed too, for many reasons. She thought of mentioning her new-found friend, Betty, and the mysterious Cambodian hostel in Glydale, but she did not bother. It could not be relevant to anything.

'Well, lost, found, dead, alive, it all comes to the same thing,' said Alix finally, in her new, disconcerting, mystic-materialistic manner, and then added, even more disconcertingly, as Liz began to collect her scattered items from the table, 'I say, Liz, your handbag. Look at it. It really isn't worthy of a top Harley Street psychotherapist. Is it?'

Liz looked at her handbag, surprised. It was not like Alix to pass comment on one's personal appearance. She was hardly a fashion-plate herself. And at first sight, Liz could see nothing wrong with her bag. True, she had had it a long time, and various biros and felt-tip pens had leaked into its battered leather and canvas, but it didn't look all that scruffy, surely? Liz was fond of it, as she used to be fond of her old school satchels. In fact, it looked rather like an old school satchel. But the more she looked at it, the more she realized that Alix was right, it *was* a disgrace. She peered at Alix's bag, and noted with relief that hers was not all that much better. It too had done good service, it too bulged. Liz pointed. Alix laughed.

As they took their leave of one another, on the shabby rubbish-strewn pavement, they indulged in a rare embrace.

They held their arms around one another, a little awkwardly, and squeezed, through layers of coat and cardigan. The odours of fenugreek and garlic mingled with the odours of face powder and Eau de l'Herbe Bleue, and dry-cleaning spirit and garbage.

'I'd better go,' said Liz. 'My meter will be over the limit.'

Alix stood, on the street corner, and watched, as Liz began to walk out of frame. On the corner Liz paused, looked back, and waved. Alix saluted, hesitated, then also turned to go.

Liz marched towards where she hoped she had left her car, quickly, head down, past ageing red brick *fin de siècle* Camden tenements with rustic names — Dovedale, Goredale, Ryedale, Nidderdale. A cry from an upper storey caught her ear, and she looked up to find herself walking past a gloomy mansion entitled Glydale. From the upper window descended an object, aimed at Liz Headleand's head. It fell slowly, in a light curve, missed her, and splattered dully on the pavement: a plastic box of polyunsaturated Flora. From it bloomed a dull oily yellow daffodil stain-flower. Liz sidestepped, looked up more in curiosity than in anger. A high grimy tattered old-world net curtain twitched, but whether in satisfaction or disappointment she could not see. Liz feared the worst for her car, but nothing very bad had happened to it: a scribble of hieroglyph in thin beige plastic foam-spaghetti, already hardened, adorned its shiny blue Japanese flank, but the aerial, which she had forgotten to

retract was still erect. She switched on the engine and switched on
the radio: *Woman's Hour*. What a comfort. She set off, soothed by a
speech on salmonella, towards her nest in St John's Wood, leaving
dangerous Alix-territory firmly behind her.

*

Alix Bowen stands on the bridge and stares at the Thames. The
slate-grey ruffled water flows beneath her, the slate-grey sky dully
swoons above her. An ancient flaking barge called *Perseverance*
travels slowly upstream. A bald huge-bellied man on a wharf shifts
sacks, apparently aimlessly, from one corner to another, beneath a
damaged sign that reads BRIGGS BRICK AND TILES. He is watched
by a one-eared black and white tomcat, and, from above, by Alix
Bowen. A damp sheer concrete cliff of dark green moss drips into
the low ebb. Rusty hoops and bosses and fragments of old chain
dangle from the embankment wall. Plastic bottles and containers
bob and dip in the scum. Alix gazes downstream, towards Chelsea,
towards the distant Post Office Tower and the high rise of the
City, towards the Buddhists of Battersea, towards the upturned
stiff-legged dead sow of Battersea Power Station, and then she turns
and leans on the low metal-studded parapet and gazes up towards
Putney, Richmond, Kew and the mild light of the west. The river
skyline is changing. Everywhere there are new developments: dinky,
red-brick, paint-bright, triangle-and-porthole apartments, soaring
superior icy glass-and-metal mansions, supermarkets, river walks,
plazas, alpine towers, floating bubbles and insubstantial domes of
paradise. Soon there will be river buses, the glossy brochures promise. Wandsworth by water! No more waiting at Waterloo! No
more commuter chaos! No more queues at Clapham Junction!

Alix stares at the shifting surface of the water, and wonders how
she fared in her encounter with Liz. It would have been easy to
have made all well with Liz by telling her that Brian seems to be
dying. Liz would have understood, sympathized, comforted. Liz

dislikes marriage, but does not dislike Brian. But Alix had been unable to speak. Alix feels that if she speaks of Brian's illness she will make it real. If she does not mention, it, it may go away.

She knows that Liz is wary, suspicious, obscurely disappointed in her. But she has put Brian first, as a wife should. She has protected him and will continue to do so. She does not want Liz to enter the circle of grief. Or not yet, not yet, not yet.

She sighs, and wonders what will happen to her if Brian dies. She has already been widowed once. If she is widowed twice, will that make her a killer of men? A widow-maker? The thought is ignoble, but it recurs. She is depressed by her own selfishness.

She thinks of Brian, and Paul Whitmore, and the old poet Beaver, and the Celts and the Romans, and the Battersea Shield. Somewhere beneath this bridge, in the mid nineteenth century, in that muddy silt, the shield had been found, after lying unseen for two millennia. Some Victorian scavenger-entrepreneur of the river had salvaged it and sold it to the British Museum for forty pounds. Nobody knows how it got into the river – in battle, from a boat, or as a trophy to a Celtic god? London had then been No City, Zero City, none of this had been here.

Alix never crosses this bridge without thinking of that shield. It is part of her memory, part of her London. It is the Shield of Albion. From its dull drowned bronze, from its curves and roundels and prophetic swastikas, it reflects past, present, future. The pale multitudes gather and cluster, thin ghosts summoned from remotest antiquity, from the dimmest reaches of mortal unrecorded time: from the ages of stone and iron and bronze, from the ages of steel and gunpowder, from the ages of brick and steam and gas and railway: the No-people, the Celts, the Belgae, the Romans, the Angles, the Saxons, the Normans, the Huguenots, the Dutch potters, the refugees from the pogroms of Russia and Poland, the survivors of the Final Solution, the Hungarians, the Turks, the Indians, the Pakistanis, the West Indians, the Africans, the Cypriots, the

Vietnamese, the Cambodians. The Child of Albion peers into the darkening glittering dance of light, into the bleeping, blinking, winking echo-located future.

The afternoon thickens, buses burst into cheerful and colourful illumination like cruising fun-steamers, cars confidently unlid their hooded metallic eyes, the city braids itself with moving jewels. The oily skin of the river reflects garlands and spotlights and soft blue blooms and harsh yellow neon alarums, and red warnings and green invitations. The sky fills with the complex coded messages of aeroplanes descending westwards to the Gates of Empire at Heathrow. A helicopter descends, inquisitively, circling lower towards Alix Bowen as she stands conspicuous upon the bridge, staring across the frontier into Bad Time, but it dismisses her and moves on towards its heliport.

The flood of history pours helplessly downstream against the struggling tide. The tide is on the turn: the water stands, eddies, shifts. The water and the bronze beat back images. Do they foresee the fatwa of the Ayatollah, do they foretell rivers of blood? Will they flow uphill?

A strong smell of powdery, indestructible, acrid detergent suddenly, with a change of breeze, rises, the sweet clean seductive preservative smell of pollution. The fat bald man sits down on a bollard and fishes in his bulging back jeans pocket for a fag. He is out of date. There will be no more in his mould. He has made himself extinct.

Alix looks at her watch, and sighs. She has a train to catch. She must get home to Brian.

As she begins to walk back across the bridge towards Wandsworth Town Station, she sees a cormorant. A neat, smart, sleek, snake-necked historic bird, its head held high above the shimmering effluent and bobbing polystyrene, it rides the flood, then dives, and then resurfaces. It knows the river. It risks the river. It knew Caractacus, it knew Captain Cook, it knew Conrad, it knew Stephen

Cox, it knows Alix Bowen. It is a river-wise London bird. It cheers her. Her step quickens.

The fat bald man sees her depart with relief. He hadn't half begun to think she was a jumper.

*

Esther Breuer, having said her farewell the following day to Liz Headleand, finds herself wandering apparently aimlessly through Mayfair, pausing every now and then to gaze in a shop window. Like Alix, she is worrying about her husband, though for different reasons. On one level of her mind, she is engaged in composing a lecture for the Gallery Osiris on the disputed iconographies of the Neapolitan still lives of Paolo Porpora (she plans a flight of eloquence on his use of frogs and flamingos, and is even now, as she stares at some diamond bracelets, putting together scholarly allusions and innuendoes); on another, intrusive, invasive, insistent level, she is thinking about Robert.

It is a curious fact, she acknowledges, as she moves on from jeweller to shoe shop, that since marrying Robert Oxenholme she has found herself suffering from jealousy and suspicion. She cannot account for this. She had throughout her adult life prided herself on her lack of possessiveness and jealousy, and indeed it was the jealousy of Elena Volpe that had driven her from Bologna. She had herself felt no jealousy either of Claudio Volpe's relationship with his wife Roberta Volpe or of his sister Elena's relations with the world at large. When Elena began to manifest jealousy about Esther's own connections, she had at first felt flattered. She had been amused by Elena's irritation at the mention of the harmless names of Liz and Alix, and by her random accusations of interest in Other Women. As Esther had never had any developed physical relationship with a member of her own sex until she had found herself charmed and seduced by the confident Elena, she was surprised to find herself suddenly suspected of jumping into bed with

295

every attractive woman in Bologna. In vain did she protest that none of them interested her at all, or not 'in that way'. Elena was convinced that converts must be both passionate and promiscuous, and would not believe Esther's protestations. There had been comedy in this, but also, increasingly, discomfort. Esther did not like murky disputes over possession. She did not care to be accused of lying. She had turned, increasingly, to the calmer suit of Robert Oxenholme, who had wooed her in a pleasantly half-hearted, polite British way. No scenes, no shouting, no cross-questioning. She had preferred Robert's style. And she had married him.

Now she finds herself in the ludicrous position of being forced to recognize in herself the emotions that she had so despised in others. They are not very violent, but they have a disturbing undercurrent of violence. In dreams, fears, starts of surprise, hesitations, she finds herself encountering little fits and spasms of jealousy. She does not like to ask Robert where he has lunched, with whom he has spent an evening. Their marriage had never been intended to knit them closely, and it offers both a good deal of freedom of movement. Before it, she had never thought of wondering where he was when he was not with her. Now she jumps slightly when she sees from the corner of an eye a car number-plate that resembles his, when she catches sight of a familiar vanishing shadow in a crowd. She is afraid to surprise him. How can this be? Legitimacy has engendered suspicion. Is this in itself a retrospective justification for her long delay in marrying, for her earlier scorn of the conventions of the married state? Was it possible that a simple marriage ceremony in a register office and a snack of trout and champagne in a garden with Liz Headleand and Simon Grunewald could have added this new colour to her emotional spectrum?

Esther has never met Robert's ex-wife Lydia, and as far as she can tell has no desire to do so. But Lydia Wittering is anywhere and everywhere. She may be there, in that shoe shop, trying on a pair of maroon bootees. She may be purchasing a ruby ring, or sitting in a taxi at the traffic lights, or walking up the front steps of Sotheby's to a preview of Victorian sporting oils. Why is Esther convinced that Robert is seeing Lydia? Why, come to that, should he *not* see Lydia? If he *is* seeing Lydia, why is he concealing the information from Esther? Why had Esther disliked the very mention of an ex-girlfriend married to a hotelier in Chiang Mai? Did she not expect Robert, at his age, to have ex-girlfriends all over the world? Would she not think less of him had he not?

Esther wanders on, mingling flamingos and little green toads with her image of Lydia, the first Mrs Oxenholme. Christmas is approaching, and the shops already twinkle with extravagant little white and gold and silver trees and plump velvety fleshy packagings. Precious stones repose in red wells and clefts.

Lydia and Robert had spent their honeymoon in Sicily, in the decaying borrowed grandeur of the Casa Maladetta on the lower slopes of Mount Etna, waited upon by a retinue of aged eccentrics from another epoch. Robert has never confessed to Esther that Lydia, too, is something of an Italian scholar. He has never told Esther that Lydia had spent much of that honeymoon, bizarrely, traipsing around in the unfashionable footsteps of Giovanni Verga, master of *verismo*, exclaiming with delight whenever she came across an identifiable location. She knew his novels almost by heart. Vibrating with emotion, she had caressed the perverse yellow blooms of the prickly pears in the cactus grove at Canziria, swearing that this was the very spot where Alfio and Turiddu had fought to death over the farmer's daughter. Robert, shamefully, had been afraid of kidnappers, for Lydia had money, and so did he, and they would have been worth a few bob to the heirs of the gallant Gramigna or the poor Malavoglia. He had tried to keep her to the beaten track, but she would wander off, amidst dry stones and old donkeys and olive-trees.

Robert quite correctly supposes that Esther would perceive such interest on Lydia's part as unsuitable, as threatening. He prefers, when required, to foster the notion (also correct) that she is interested in horses. Horses, forsooth! She had been a devious one, had Lydia. But nevertheless, despite Robert's own deviousness, an approximation of the real Lydia is assembling slowly in Esther's imagination. She has picked up clues, she has overheard references at gatherings, she has come upon old books, old photographs.

Lydia Oxenholme, in a red dress and a broad-rimmed black straw hat with trailing red ribbons, sitting on a terrace beneath the lofty snows and flowery fields of Etna, reading a battered copy of *Cavalleria rusticana* and sipping a deep green drink through a straw from an iridescent glass with a long thin stem: captioned, in Robert's own hand, 'Herself a fairer flower.' Lydia Oxenholme, carving Robert's initials into the fleshy flank of a giant cactus-tree; Lydia Oxenholme, dancing on a Roman mosaic pavement; Lydia Oxenholme, in the back of a fishing boat beneath a yellow parasol; Lydia, parading the Corso of Taormina robed in white.

Lydia's maiden name, inscribed in a copy of Cavalcanti. Lydia's school annotations, in a bilingual text of Dante's *Inferno*.

Marriage, thinks Esther Oxenholme as she mingles unnoticed amongst the early Christmas shoppers, is a rum business. It has a special poison brewed in its very name. Once I knew who I was, and now I no longer know. Is it good for me, this uncertainty?

The traffic shakes and judders slowly onwards, the lights change and change again. Esther crosses the road, and stares through the windows of the Goetz Gallery, which is showing new paintings by Hanna Stapledon. Large, rich, thick, dripping oils. Webs and nets and ruches of colour: dark reds, ochres, oranges, sandstones, flames. Lifeblood, deathblood. Anger red, womb red.

Esther thinks of her new red room. Something has gone wrong with her decorations. She had tried to re-create the mood, the colours of her old room at the end of Ladbroke Grove, but she had not succeeded. The reds no longer warm and enclose and glow, they oppress and stifle. Is it something in the mix of the paint, the angle of the light, the pigment of the paper? A hard dark dried colour, an old-blood, ox-blood, cruel slaughterhouse tint has invaded her sanctuary. Is it the memory of those dismembered bodies, of the Black & Decker at work above her, that now poisons her dwelling? Or is it some other, fresher crime?

Esther had, one evening, on impulse bought herself a selection of watercolours and oils, and had taken them home to try to find colours and shades that would liberate her from the dried blood. She had dipped and daubed. Pale greens, turquoises, lichen-green: yellow of sunflower, daffodil, mustard. She had not held a paint-brush in her hand since her early school days, and a strange feeling of fear and danger overcame her as she played in secrecy. Such power, such incompetence, such a gulf between the known and the unknown! Her hand trembled. How dare she speak of the paintings of others, when her own hand would not obey her? How timid her life had been, how unadventurous! She boldly swept an arc of emerald across the acid-free paper. Perhaps she would get rid of the red?

She wanders on, thinking of Robert's apartment, of his tapestries and his high ceilings and his four-poster bed and his bonsai-trees. She thinks of his Pugin wallpapers where vast red eagles pluck at dusky bunches of golden grapes. She thinks of the Brancusi bronze and the Urbino bowl and the Veronese, of the wax fruit and flowers in glass cases, of the arum lily growing in a green art nouveau jardinière, of the Venetian glass chandelier. She is still not at ease amongst these things, she is still a guest, a visitor. Her own home repels her, but his does not receive her. She thinks of his fish and his lizard, stolen from the ruins of Angkor Wat, in days when he had never heard her name. Had he known Lydia, in his Angkor days? Had she too pranced along the terrace trousered in silk? She knows nothing of the chronology of his past, of the layers and sediments of his history. She does not wish to know.

Idly she drifts, past windows full of Lalique glass, windows full of Zoffany wallpapers, past pale pink composition façades, past a photographer displaying the vast more-than-lifesize plump pampered features of an Arabian infant princeling in a silver frame, past a blue plaque to a Russian ballerina, past Chinese vases and rugs from Afghanistan. She pauses before the display in Purdey's Gun & Riflemakers, admiring the gold lettering on the deep rich solid royal blue of the glass pane, admiring the little gilt coronets on the ornamental iron railings, remembering her honeymoon on the grouse moor, wondering if Lydia had been a shooting woman. Towards the park she loiters, and sees a little turning she has never noticed before, beneath an archway. She turns down it and there is a little gallery, tucked modestly away, in an enclave of early nineteenth-century cobbles and hanging baskets.

In its bay window stands a small Buddha image, before a large stone-rubbing of a bas-relief from Angkor Wat. A great winged garuda carries a supple god beneath three pretty parasols. On side-panels, maidens dance and seven-headed snakes coil. Esther gazes, hesitates. She does not understand this kind of art. Toads and flamingos she comprehends, but crocodiles and elephants are not in her frame of reference. Why has she never seen this gallery, this courtyard before? If she steps over the threshold, will she vanish for ever?

Shall she go in?

She hesitates. She pushes the door, but it is closed, although it proclaims itself open. A little silvery bell tinkles at her pressure, and a young woman approaches, from an inner room: a young woman with a solid cloud of straight-edged fair hair spun out like floss round her cheekbone, dressed in a white tunic over a plain white skirt. She smiles at Esther, and opens the door. Esther is obliged to enter. The young woman continues to smile, indicates the catalogue, backs away discreetly to her desk. No words are exchanged, but the small rooms are vibrant. The gallery is empty, save for these two.

Esther makes her way round the snakes and maidens, trying to puzzle out the story. As well as the rubbings, there are photographs of Angkor Wat, the Bayon, Takeo and Banteay Srei, dating from the innocent 1950s.

Great fig-trees reach for the sky. Stones crack and splinter. Rocky faces stare forth. The Leper King smiles. The young woman is extraordinarily beautiful. Her skin is smooth and and fair, her lips are carved from something more durable than flesh. A page-boy angel, a nurse in white uniform. She watches Esther. Her features are precise, firm, chiselled. She sits there in her cell, alone, behind her desk. Esther dares not look her way. Shall she ask a question? What question shall she dare to ask? The silence deepens and rustles.

It is broken by the tinkling of the bell. Another visitor is seeking admittance to the sanctum, is taking refuge from the street. The young woman rises and softly crosses the tiny gallery on her delicate soft-slippered feet. She opens the door, but hunted Esther does not look to see who enters. She gazes with fixed intent at the celestial dancing girls in their flame-towered head-dresses, at the battle of the Devas and the Asuras. The room crackles, the woman returns to her desk again, no words are spoken. Esther bravely stares straight ahead. The visitor approaches her, stands behind her, touches her gently on the shoulder.

'So *there* you are, Esther,' says Robert Oxenholme. 'So *there* you are!'

Esther turns, and there indeed is Robert, smiling at her and reaching out to take her into his arms. She leans against him briefly, and he kisses her brow. The woman in white watches.

'I didn't think this was your kind of thing?' says Robert, politely, as both bend their attention upon the dancing girls.

'It isn't,' says Esther. 'I don't know why I came in. I was thinking of your little lizard and your fish.'

Robert squeezes her arm. Suddenly a great lightness of heart fills Esther, a white wave of happiness.

'*I* came in because I saw you,' says Robert. 'I saw you standing there, puzzling. I like that look on your face, when you're puzzling.'

'Look at the little parasols,' says Esther, pointing.

Anything and nothing can be said. She is saved, she is rescued.

'And the crocodile,' says Robert.

Slowly they pace the gallery together.

'I was on my way home, when I saw you,' says Robert.

'I too was on my way home,' says Esther.

'We could go home together?' says Robert, politely, tentatively. 'We could take a cab?'

Esther nods her agreement. They purchase a catalogue, they sign the visitors' book. They nod and smile to the woman in white. She opens the door for them, and closes it behind them. A light drizzle is falling upon London. It rests in rounded beads on the smooth impermeable shoulders of Robert's raincoat, on the hooked and wiry wool of Esther's black jacket. Robert waves at a taxi with his umbrella. Obediently it glides to their service. There is a moment of hesitation as Robert glances at Esther, but then, without words spoken, by mutual consent, he gives his own address.

They settle, comfortably, into the back of the cab. Robert takes Esther's small hand and holds it in his, nursing it as though it were a little ill. The hand is cold, for Esther does not wear gloves. Robert warms it. The taxi enters Hyde Park, and Esther gazes out at the dark sky and the dripping trees.

When they get to Holland Park, Robert pours Esther a glass of red wine from an open bottle. He asks her if she would like to stay to supper. Boldly, she consents. He says that he will prepare it, if she is willing to accept a simple modest meal. She smiles, nods. Then she wanders round the apartment, interrogating the paintings, the mirrors, the walls. She pauses, balanced, in front of the lizard and the fish. She moves on, to the bedroom, to the Renaissance bowl presented on their wedding day by Simon Grunewald, and gazes at Romulus and Remus and the god of the Tiber. The bowl stands upon a little mahogany table, a table inlaid with brown and cream shapes of whorled pointed shells. She touches it. She sits for a moment, perched on the edge of the high double bed, on the embroidered coverlet. Robert's maroon slippers are lined up neatly beneath the dressing table. His dressing gown hangs on the back of the door. She sips her wine.

Over a salad of hard-boiled eggs and tinned artichoke hearts and tinned fagioli and tinned anchovies and fresh goat's cheese, they speak of Angkor Wat and Prince Sihanouk and Cambodian dance. Robert describes to her the moat at Angkor, with its pale mauve water-lilies, its flashing kingfishers. He describes the storm dance of Thunder and Lightning, Mekhala and Riemso, soberly performed by the prince's professional dancers, tipsily travestied by his guests. Sihanouk had wept with delight. Who will remember it now? Are they all dead now, those courtly dancers? Are all those songs, all those mythical stories of the imperial past forgotten, slaughtered, rooted out of the memory? Has Pol Pot destroyed them all, and would it matter if he had?

Robert is uncertain. Esther would not have liked the dance, he suggests. It was too ceremonial, too folkloric for her taste. There is a Cambodian dance company seeking to regroup itself in Paris, trying to raise sponsorship. But, realistically, what is the future for such an enterprise? How can it interest the sated audiences of the West? It can survive only as travelogue, as airport posters and hotel entertainment. Or on a passing sympathy vote.

Robert suddenly leaps to his feet, and makes off towards his bookshelves, as is sometimes his way. Esther sits and tidies up the crumbs of her cheese while he searches. He returns to the table, triumphant, and leafs his way through a volume bound in reddish brown cloth with silver lettering.

'Here we are,' he says. 'Geoffrey Gorer, *Bali and Angkor: Or, Looking at Life and Death*. 1936. May I?'

Esther nods. He reads.

'"And the Cambodians? An ugly, dull-looking people, diseased and undernourished, cowed and frightened, drably dressed in dingy black; with Buddha as their god, and opium as their way to Him. When I saw the Cambodian dancers at the Colonial Exhibition in Paris, I was very impressed with them; I still think their 'lifting' movement on one bent leg so that the whole body seems to be raised into the air very impressive; but their whole performance . . . de da de . . . is far pleasanter when seen in a European theatre. And they gain nothing by repetition."'

'Hmm,' says Esther. 'Remember that Frenchwoman, at that dinner? Didn't they bump off her father? Not surprising, really, is it?'

Robert is riffling through the pages. 'Yes,' he says, 'they would have agreed with one another about the ruins too. "Dead . . . badly put together . . . no signs of any architectural ability whatsoever . . . incompetent . . . unskilled . . . lethargic . . ." I'd forgotten all this. He seems to think the whole thing was the product of an opium binge. What do *you* think? Do you think *he* was on an opium binge? The photos are a bit –?'

'I quite liked the parasols, and the dancing girls,' says Esther, cautiously.

'Yes,' says Robert, his eyes still on the text. 'He admits the dancing girls. He thinks they are quite lively.'

'Well, I don't think one can tell. From a rubbing,' says Esther. And she gets up to make the coffee.

They both fall silent, as they settle themselves to watch *Newsnight* on television. The programme is an investigation of nuclear energy, Chernobyl, Sellafield, and the privatization of electricity. Robert and Esther appear to be paying attention, but are they? Perhaps they are thinking about the Dark Ages and the Renaissance, about Morris dancers and Bakst and Russian ballet and Marcel Proust. What is certain is that their attitudes alter when the item alters, and a picture of Van Gogh's *Sunflowers*, accompanied by a great deal of money-talk, fills the small screen. They both sit upright, and Robert reaches for the remote control, but he is too late, for there he is, sitting in his ministerial office, talking about the Art Market and inflated prices and the Japanese and Paul Getty. Esther does not let him switch off or over. She watches, proud, amused, as Robert speaks of the dangers of treating art as investment and the need to sponsor living artists. The venue changes from Robert's office to a studio in Brixton, and action shots of handsome Hanna Stapledon working on a large oil: these give way to film of a blue-eyed bearded young man sitting by a brook beneath a rowan-tree stitching a sculpture of leaves. 'Permanence or transience, immortality or ecology? And which is which?' demands the soundtrack, as the millions of dollars' worth of Van Gogh sunflowers return to the screen.

'*Very* nice,' murmurs Esther.

'Thank *you*,' says Robert.

And a scandal in the Church of England sees them safely to their bed.

*

The Leper King

Jungle Actor Number One Film Star Man sits on a straw mat at the entrance of a cave and meditates. In front of him is a soft black cloth bag containing a skull. Alas, poor Yorick! The roots of the sacred fig rise and clutch at the air. The bats hang upside down. The water flows uphill. A necrophiliac sweetness pervades the hot air. The Leper King, the Judge of the Dead, smiles with contempt. One skull is chosen from so many. Boum boum, a thin giggling, a bang and a whimper. The red flags of victory and the black flags of death fly from the ruins. The cameras whirr and click. The vultures circle. Words crack and buckle. The tiger waits. Jungle Actor Number One Film Star Man does not move. The diplomats of Democratic Kampuchea dine at the United Nations. This is the Death of Pity, this is the Death of Meaning. A small child watches from the edge of the clearing. Laissez passer! Laissez passer!

*

Well, yes, I am! Preggers, up the spout, in the club, knocked up, *fertilized*! Jesus! *I* blame Polly Piper. I mean, *what* a question to pop at me in Sainsbury's! What joy, what fears, what expectations! I *thank* Polly Piper! Polly will *die* of envy. How *can* it have happened? Well, I'll tell you how, I'll tell you what they say happened, *they* say that the fish hook got dislodged and crept somewhere up into the wrong soft parts where it wasn't doing its job at all and I'm bloody lucky not to be dying of fallopian gangrene, that's what *they* say, but they've tweaked it out and thrown it away and tidied me up and now I'm right as rain and two months gone. Amazing.

I suppose you want to know what Aaron thinks about all this. Well, he is DELIGHTED. Do I detect a cynical look in your eye? Of course I do. But believe me you're wrong. Oh, I'm not going to marry him, or anything tiresome like that. All these years on my tod aren't to be thrown away lightly even for the likes of Aaron Headleand. But I've told him he can help push the mobylette. If he's a good lad.

I suppose you want to know whether I *asked* him to marry me, or vice versa. Well, no, as a matter of fact, it didn't come up. These are modern times. But he did ask me about my pa and ma. Genetic inheritance, you know. After all, his mother is a doctor. Of sorts. Well, I told him pa was killed in Malaya, and he nodded, and said, That figures. I told him ma had remarried and was living in Amsterdam which is sort of true, after a fashion. I mean, would I lie? (If you talk like what I talk, you don't *need* to lie.)

And what about Liz Headleand, you will want to know. Well, yes, this time spot on. It has to be said that a certain queasiness overcomes Aaron Darling and myself when we think of telling Liz. But luckily Liz has just flown off to the Shining Orient so we don't have to confront the confrontation yet. But I can hazard that she will not be pleased. I mean, would *you* be?

Maybe she'll get captured by the Khmer Rouge. Maybe she'll die of malaria. Maybe she'll marry a monk.

I haven't thought of my father for years. I hardly knew him. Aaron doesn't remember his mother at all.

Aaron's mother was killed in a head-on collision on her way back from Glyndebourne when he was a wee toddler. Or so he says. (He says she was alone in the car. Does anyone *ever* drive back from Glyndebourne alone? I smell scandal.) She was as rich as a Rockefeller. Or a Rothschild. In fact I think she *was* a Rothschild. Aaron is half-Jewish. Well, he would be, wouldn't he, with a Christian name like that?

My dad was killed in Malaya in the fifties, fighting the commies. I was at an impressionable age but I don't remember being much impressed. Sometimes I say he died in combat, sometimes I say he died of malaria, sometimes I say he was a colonel, sometimes I say he was a sergeant major. It depends on my mood and my company. I don't suppose you care which he was, but as a matter of fact he was a sergeant major. Surprised? Wonder where I picked up my fancy accent? Want to know about my childhood dreams and traumas in Colchester, Kettering and Caterham? No, I don't suppose you do. I'm an actress, remember. Well, I was an actress. Three months in rep, and then B movies and TV commercials. That was me. I was also a great beauty. In my genre. Got it?

I don't think there was anything *physically* wrong with my dad, and so I've told Aaron. He was just a sadistic bastard, that's all. He hadn't got syphilis, or Huntington's chorea, or haemophilia, or anything hereditary like that. He was just a bastard. He died in the jungle. They sent his body back, or so they said, but how would you know? We buried something in St Stephen's churchyard, but we sure as hell didn't want to have to look at it. Could have been a barrow-load of monkeys for all we knew.

My dad had this thing about monkeys. Monkey's brains. He used to tell this ghastly story about what the natives did to monkeys.

The clamp, the basin and the spoon. Eating their living brains. I expect you've heard it, and anyway I couldn't bear to write it down. Even thinking about it makes me feel sick. Human beings, how could they? It's probably not *true*, but if it's not true, why would people want to *make up* such a story? My dad loved it. He liked to rub it in. He'd make me cry. He'd make me cry, and then he'd laugh and laugh.

He was as racist as they come. You should have heard him, on about the commie chinks and the nignogs and the savages and the wild women of Borneo. Old stuff, but he *meant* it. I suppose you've forgotten the war in Malaya, it wasn't much of a war to write home about. I was only a kid. I'd no idea what it was all about. My mum used to try to explain, but it didn't make much sense.

Yes, my dad didn't have much to say for the black and brown and yellow nations, for the tinted folk. He used to go on about their nasty habits until the eyes popped out of my little head. A savage lot, the Malaysians, the Filipinos, the Javanese, according to my da. The Chinese were the worst because they were the smartest, but anyone east of Suez was into torture and mutilation. My da loved talking about torture and mutilation and bloodthirsty natives. He'd have loved Stephen's Atrocity Section. But I don't think that kind of stuff *is* hereditary, do you? I mean, I don't think I'm a sadist, do you? I think the worst I got from him was a mild dose of ladylike masochism, a taste for a bit of harmless fladge and bondage. S & M, the young folk call it, these days. I can remember exactly how and when I got that. I know you're not supposed to be able to remember this kind of thing so easily, but I do. It was that day he spanked me with the hairbrush when I'd refused to go to bed. I can't think what got into me, but I just wouldn't go, and when ma started to scream at me I started to scream back. All the words I'd heard off them, of course. *Rude* words. And he started to bawl at me, and there we were, all three yelling at one another, and then he dragged me up to my room and sat on my bed and put me across his knee and pulled up my dress and spanked me with the hairbrush. I really enjoyed it. Sorry about that, but I did. Well, no big deal there, everyday stuff, and ma was furious with him, she didn't approve of corporal punishment (or of orgasms or of the bloody army, come to that, no wonder they didn't get on too well), and he never did it again, no matter how hard I tried to provoke him. And Jesus did I try. I must have been a right little tart. Well, I suppose I still am. (Or *was*. Sorry, Aaron.) But I didn't get much chance because off he went overseas to a hero's death in the service of Her (or was it His) Majesty. Saved from seduction by his own little Kathleen. Rescued from incest by the Queen. (No, Harriet is not my name. I'm Kathleen, if you want to know. God knows why. We weren't Irish.)

Poor old da. Not much of a life. Not much of a death.

I must have been about eight or nine when that incident occurred. I was thirteen when I seduced the headmaster. Well, when I say *seduced*, don't take me too literally. But it was all my fault. I take full responsibility. It happened like this. It was the end of mid-morning break and I was loitering around in the cloakroom, pretending to look for a hankie in my mac pocket, when I spotted him up by the washbowls combing his hair. I knew he shouldn't of been there really, it was the girls' side, and anyway why wasn't he in the staff lav? So I sort of sidled towards him and caught him from behind. Caught his eye in the mirror, got quite close before he turned. Sort of Grandmother's Footsteps. I had him at a disadvantage. He started breathing all funny. 'Hello, Kathleen,' he said, and I said, 'Hello, Mr Everard,' in a suggestive sort of way. And then I just stood there. I may have moved forward an inch or two, I can't remember, but I kept on looking and smiling, and then he sort of moved towards me and kissed me. No, he didn't grab, or do anything *louche* or nasty. He just leant forward, inclined sort of from the waist, rather stiffly, and kissed me on the lips. He did it rather well. It was all rather slow motion. I think I moved in half an inch further, and he kissed me again. He sort of slightly opened my mouth and delicately tongued me. But he didn't *touch* me. Didn't lay a finger on me. He knew he ought not to. He knew he'd gone too far. I could have done anything with him. You know that feeling? Power. Sheer power. Destruction and power.

But I didn't. I let him off.

'Thank you, Mr Everard,' I said, and backed off. Kind of me, wasn't it? And back I went to my biology lesson.

I never mentioned it to anyone. I went a lot further, two years later, with Mr Potter Maths. (Mr Potter Art I *didn't* fancy.) But then Mr Potter Maths had a reputation for that kind of thing. Mr Everard didn't. He was my secret.

I suppose I was a disturbed kiddie, what with my da dying like that, and all those removals, and then my ma taking off. But I didn't feel disturbed. I felt I was totally in control. Even when I was eight.

It is true that da died in Malaya. I've never been to Malaya, or Malaysia, or whatever they call it these days. I hardly even know where it is. Thailand, yes, Singapore, yes, but not Malaya. Though I did appear once in a movie set in Malaya. Filmed mostly in Ireland. That's what gave me my Conrad thing, that movie. You may have noticed I have a bit of a thing about Conrad. Not that I *read* him, you understand. I never read anything much, except to get ideas for screenplays. But I was in this movie. I had a bit part. Half a dozen lines. A sweetheart waving from the shore, that was me. It was the year after O'Toole's *Lord Jim*, mid sixties I think, there was a bit of a Conrad boom. *Lord Jim* was filmed in Angkor Wat, did you know that? You couldn't do that now, could you? Our movie was made just south of Dingle. It never did anything. Didn't deserve to.

I wore a sort of flouncy Spanish-style skirt and an off-the-shoulder almost-off-the-boobs blouse. I don't suppose the get-up was very authentic. Gypsy earrings featured, I think. They usually do. *Freya of the Seven Isles*, that was the title. A sort of cross between *Blue*

Lagoon and what was that Somerset Maugham play about planters and adultery and a piano? There was a lot about a piano in the movie. Violins and pianos. I digress. Look, I just sort of assume that you *know* all about Conrad, that you know a damn sight more about him than I do, because I can't bear to spell it all out, right? Short cuts, right? You with me so far?

That was my first movie. I was in love with the movies. When I was a child, I used to wait to be talent-spotted. You know, the handsome stranger walking past would suddenly say, 'Now, young lady, what a wonderful face you have, what fine bone structure, *quel profil*, come and be in my film/sit for your portrait/model for my collection.' Or whatever. And as a matter of fact that's exactly what happened. Shall I tell you the story? Yes, I think I will. I don't know why my mind is roving back like this, it must be something to do with being pregnant and in love and happy, somehow all my squalid past seems redeemed, and I can even look back on the happy times without wanting to scratch my own eyes out and tear my cheeks and howl like a bitch at the moon.

And that was a happy time, that summer at Butlin's. I was just eighteen, I had this summer job at the Pwllheli Butlin's, I thought it was the smartest place out although I sort of knew it wasn't. But it was fun. Awful, but fun. Anyway, it was a damn sight smarter than the job I'd been doing shelf-stacking at a supermarket in Ilford. I ran off to Butlin's with wings on my heels, I can tell you. The hours were hell, and the accommodation rough, and the pay was lousy, but so what, everyone was having a Good Time, that's what they were there for, it was laughs all the way, and a good summer too, lots of sunshine. I started off as a chambermaid but I got talent-spotted pretty soon by Terry O'Flynn and promoted to barmaid. I loved that bar. The Merry Mermaid. You should have seen the mosaics! Enormous, stinking of beer and fags, pools of doubtful liquor on every surface you can think of. And you should have seen what some people drank. Yellow egg stuff, white fluff egg stuff, green syrup, rum and peppermint, orange soda with whisky, gin and It. You name it, they mixed it. I learned a lot that summer. Snowballs, crinolines, sidecars, pigeon's blood, a three-piece suite. I lapped it up. I used to finish off what got left in the glasses. I was tight as a kite by the time each evening was over, but nobody gave a damn, nobody even noticed. I've always been good at holding my liquor. Well, up to a point. Oh, I was the star turn, better than the dancing girls or the lady wrestlers or Bud and Bartle Busby. We laughed and laughed. And though I say it myself, I was a pretty good barmaid. Quick with the drinks, quick with the change and the mental arithmetic, quick with a laugh and a joke and an innuendo, that was me. And I had this adorable little uniform, really dinky, black and white with a bit of bosom-and-thigh-lace, sort of nippy-rape-fantasy style. Terry was a raver, an Irish raver, a moustached con man and a charmer and a dream. A really nice brogue, and a sweet hairstyle. Curly ringlets. Every night we'd bounce around in the little concrete bunker I shared with Audrey. Audrey had to pretend not to hear. She used to turn her radio up real loud, and turn her face to the wall. Oh, I was happy, and going places! You see what an innocent I was. Tawdry Audrey, Tatty Hattie. The Good Time Girls.

And then along came Mr Big, and whisked me away from my concrete bunker into a world of unknown sophistication and corruption. I suppose Mr Big was pretty innocent himself then, come to think of it, but he didn't seem like that to us. He was younger than Terry, he was only in his twenties, but it wasn't a fair match. He was a television director, and in those days to a girl like me that was big news. He was making a documentary about the camp. We all thought he was the cat's whiskers and so did he. I saw at once he was taking the piss, trying to make us and the campers look like knees-up-Mother-Brown yokels and slaves and peasants, but I don't think everybody spotted it. Some of them really *were* innocents. But not me. I noticed that Mr Gabriel Denham couldn't keep his camera off of me, and I also noticed (and this was smart of me) that I wasn't really what he wanted on film. He really wanted Irene, twelve stone Irene, with her carved canary yellow perm and her cupid lips and her bulgings-out of her lacies and her Lancashire accent, or Tawdry Audrey with her rickety skinny knees. They were what he'd come to find and make fun of, not a Slim, Sexy, Glorious Eighteen-Year-Old Redhead. But the camera kept coming my way just the same, he couldn't help himself. Days he hung around, we were amazed, I hadn't realized in those days that filming took so long, and this was arty filming, early BBC-2 filming, not just get-it-in-the-can-and-run stuff. Our Gabriel was *nouvelle vague*. An up-and-comer.

Anyways, he says to me, one evening, handsome Mr Denham, what about a drink out of bounds, you know, somewhere civilized? And I simpers and giggles and says, Don't insult my Merry Mermaid. And off we whizz in his white Vauxhall to this roadhouse motel called the Grapes and Vine on the A497 to Criccieth. And we down a few, and then he says what about dinner, and I munch my way through a prawn cocktail and a steak. I must say he was a good-looker in those days, our Gabriel. Sort of square-jawed, chunky type. Casual but smart. Check shirt, open throat, low-slung jeans. Hairy chest. A bit pock-marked, but I've always liked that kind of thing. You don't want a man to be *too* smooth do you? (Unless he's Aaron Headland. But that's another matter.)

We got on famously, Gabriel and me. I made up bits of my life story for him, and he made up bits of his for me. A wife who didn't understand him, kids, a mistress, the usual. I goggled and gulped it all down. Then I began to get a bit frisky and suggested bed. He was off to reception like a light, and back with a key in three minutes flat. We lingered over coffee gazing into one another's eyes, and then he said a very nice thing. He raised his brandy glass and said, 'Well, I knew as soon as I saw you that this would have to be done, but I didn't dare hope we'd get around to it so soon. Cheers, and congratulations!'

I thought that was very sweet and very civil. And he remained very sweet and very civil, while he was doing it *and* after, I must say. And he did it very nicely too. He was a good chap, Gabriel. Destroyed by his own good looks, or that's what Aaron and I think. I mean, what can a man do, if he looks *that* good? It's exhausting. As a *man*, you just can't be a serious person, if you look like that.

But he was very good to me. There was a bit of a nasty scene the next day with Terry, who caught us red-handed and knickers-round-the-knees on our return and wanted to know how I could let him and Irene down like that, and we spun him some rigmarole about a flat tyre, and he said Pull the Other One, and that sort of thing. But Terry wasn't the type to stand in a woman's way. He really *did* have a wife and kids. Well, so did Gabriel, as it turned out, but he had a bit more leeway, finance-wise, than poor Terry, who had to save up for the girls in Galway.

Gabriel and I had our fling, and he got me into the theatre and the movies. Introduced me around here and there. Found me an agent. The swinging sixties. I served three months in rep, but it was easy pickings, money for old rope. Look, I wasn't really ambitious. I didn't want to play star parts. Acting wasn't really my thing. Looking was my thing. Looking and fucking.

That film that seduced Aaron, that was my largest part, my finest hour, my swan song. I decided to retire after that and earn my living from other people's options. I'm quite shrewd, in my own way. Or I could have been, if I'd tried harder.

Aaron and I went shopping yesterday. He wanted to buy me a white dress. For old times' sake. To re-create the kinky memory. What he really wants is a video, but so far he's drawn a blank on that, and with any luck he won't find one. Though I suppose I did *look* quite good, back in 1970. Perhaps it would be a *good* thing to find the video? Then again, perhaps not. Beauty vanishes, beauty passes, however rare, rare it be. It really is an odd thing about looks. I suppose it was always obvious to me that if I played my cards right I could cash in on mine. Even as a child I knew it. Poor da.

So we went to Liberty's, and Selfridges, and a few boutiques in South Molton Street. At first we couldn't find anything I liked. I'd thought it might be a bit embarrassing, shopping with Aaron, but it was fun. He understands clothes, and the shop ladies like him. He even knows the names of fabrics. I began to have a hunch that we'd only get what we were looking for in somewhere quite mass-market, like Dickens and Jones, and I was right. I was feeling a bit tired and footsore by this stage, having taken my clothes off and on several times already, so I was relieved to see this whole row of long white dresses, dangling for our approval. They were pretty vulgar, some of them, but then so in its day was the archetype. Shoulder pads, dove-grey and bluey silver sequins, bits of white fake fluffy feather stuck on, beaded butterflies, that kind of junk. But there was one Aaron liked straight off. 'This,' he said. 'Feel this.' It was a lovely slinky falsey, a sort of acetate. I've always loved acetate.

(May I digress for a moment? I think I may. I just wanted to tell you that I've always *hated* natural fibres. Wool, silk, linen, cotton. I mean, I just hate the *feel* of them. They make me prickle and sweat. I don't know how people can say they breathe naturally. They don't. And who wants to be dressed in the hair of sheep and the spit of worms? Cotton's not so bad, it's just that it doesn't iron properly. No, give me the false stuff every time. Acetate, nylon, rayon. Acrylic, polyester. Coal tar, water, ammonia. Delicious.)

The dress fitted. Aaron insisted on coming into the fitting room with me, and he sat there on the little stool in the corner, nursing my bag and my old black Warehouse dress. (God knows what that's made of — a sort of wadding, I think.)

It fitted. Floor length, low cut, sub-Grecian. One bare shoulder, draped bust, nice folds, no shoulder pads. What's a chiton? I think this could be a chiton. Aaron carefully put my dress and bag on the floor, and then he knelt and put his head on my belly and his big nose into my cunt. I could see him from all angles, the back of his head, his curly black hair, his dark suit jacket, all buried against me, again and again and again, in those refracting mirrors. I stroked his hair. The dress was so thin I could feel him and his breath through it as though I were naked. He nuzzled and rested, with his arms around my bum. I could hear shop talk in the next cubicle, two women on about how small a size fourteen can be these days. I could hear neon and smell carpet and powder and old perfume and old sweat. Aaron knelt and the tears leaped into my eyes. We were in another time. I love Aaron. I love Aaron for loving me. Everything vanishes, everything passes, but that person made by Aaron, that dream image, that devil's bride, that B movie star, that shop's dummy in a white dress, *that* person is not made of flesh and blood, that person was made before the world was made, out of vanity, out of time, out of beauty.

I don't know how long we stayed in our little classical tableau. Ten seconds, thirty seconds, an hour. I looked at myself, I looked at him, and there we stayed. I could see his hands with the bloodstone ring, I could see the nape of his neck, I could see my naked back, I could see us all in 3D like a hologram, like a group of statuary, like a frozen moment in a ballet. In our little cubicle, our Eros box. And then the tasteful pale-blue-and-pink-and-ivory cloud-pattern curtain twitched, and I found myself looking straight into the mirrored eyes of one of those middle-aged old-fashioned black-robed pin-and-sewing-cushion dress-shielded sales-ladies. She did a sort of double-take but stood her ground. Aaron couldn't see her, of course, he was too busy emoting into my private place. I was well on the way, myself. Classical tableau, French farce. I didn't know what to do, so I stared her out. Dignity won the day. She looked at me, into me, very intently, and then she backed off. As she pulled the curtain rather noisily back again, I called out to her, 'Thank you, I think we'll be taking this one.' And she colluded. 'Oh, thank you, madam,' she called, as though she'd never put her nose in at all, and reappeared, politely, once we'd sorted ourselves out in there.

And take it we did, wrapped up in tissue paper and coffined in a nice big rigid-sided, cord-carrying cardboard carrier box.

I think that was the most erotic experience of my life. And all Aaron did was breathe into me. His hot sweet breath into my thighs.

We did a bit of re-enactment last night, involving the white dress and a gold belt. It was most satisfactory. Aaron directed it all very well. He's not at all embarrassed about that kind of thing, like what most men are. But after all, he *is* a man of the theatre isn't he? And I am compliant. That's the very word he used. 'My lovely compliant darling,' that's what he said. He can't believe I'm willing to play along. But I am. Oh yes, I am.

I suppose we'll both have to grow up a bit when the baby begins to grow. This white dress stuff is a bit of regression, I realize that. But we've a lot to get in, we've left things a bit late, we've got to get on with it *now* while things are good.

I suppose we have Stephen Cox to thank for this whole affair. If Liz brings him back to the land of the living, he can be godfather to our child.

It's my view, between you and me, that Aaron had quite a serious thing about Liz. Phèdre and Hippolyte. Well, there aren't all that many plots in the world, and that's certainly a classic. Better than Jocasta and Oedipus, if you ask me. More plausible. And it's not really incest, with your stepmother, is it? I mean, there's no blood tie. Liz must have been a pretty young stepmother. I don't think I'd quite realized what she'd taken on. Three stepsons, and herself only in her twenties, and then those two girls of her own. She must have had her hands full. No wonder she looks a bit solid and smug these days. Just staying alive must have seemed quite an achievement.

And you could say Aaron is a credit to her. If you want to look at it that way. And I think I do.

Aaron has a *divine* nature. He is divinely forgiving. I know I am tat, I know I am tinsel, I know I am safety pins and loose threads and frayed edges, I know I am wrinkles, I know I look better from a distance. And he forgives all. And to think I used to think he was gay. You never can tell, can you?

He's writing a play about the Wicker King. It's something to do with Old Albion and Human Sacrifice and Paul Whitmore and the Scapegoat. Or so he says. The white dress features. The white dress inspires. *La Muse inspiratrice*. He asked me if I'd still got a script for that old movie. I told him he must be joking, how could anyone who'd moved their bags as often as me be expected to hang on to old scripts?

He's got a lot of Satanic videos. A weirdo genre. I don't quite get it, myself. I mean, what are people playing at, in the 1980s, trying to frighten themselves with goats and crucifixes and the Black Mass, when they don't believe in God, let alone the Devil? I don't expect you to answer, but it *is* a question. Aaron has this theory that it's something to do with the Legacy of the Enlightenment, and the disaster of the Restoration, but I wouldn't know about that.

I'm off the booze. I don't think it would be right to give birth to a baby addict, do you? I didn't think I could do it, but I can. It's been hard going, but I'm surviving. It's not too bad, with Aaron to hold my hand. When I get edgy, we play pontoon or Scrabble. He's tried to teach me chess, but I think I've already rotted too far for that. Not enough brain cells. I have the odd Guinness, but I don't count that as booze. It's good for you.

I don't like to think how I'd get on if Aaron ditched me at this stage. Look, I know what you're thinking. I know you think it won't last. And it won't. Things don't. That's the way it is. But at the moment, I don't believe that, although I know it is so. At the moment, I think that love can last for ever. Although I know it won't. It will die, as it always has and always must. But things will be different this time. When Aaron turns to dust and ashes in my sight, and I in his, there'll be a baby. Mystic, isn't it?

*

So far, so good. Liz Headleand is enjoying her Air France flight to Bangkok. She has done her best to follow Stephen's itinerary to the letter, hoping that, as in a police reconstruction, her pursuit may throw up witnesses and clues. Like Stephen, she has taken a glass or two of champagne. Like Stephen, she has savoured a little glass pot of caviare. Her seat is not as privileged as his, nor is she sitting next to the male equivalent of Miss Porntip: no Playboy Prince is enticing her into personal conversation. But then, Liz Headleand does not believe that Miss Porntip is a real person, and she is perfectly satisfied with the silent and dignified presence of the Indian gentleman at her elbow, reading his *Economist*, and with her own copy of *Cosmopolitan*, thrust upon her at parting by her daughter Sally, who had driven her to the airport. Liz does not often read women's magazines, and is momentarily seduced by an article on the chic lesbian, an informative photoessay on Dr E. C. Haas of Colorado and the history of the tampon (yes, of course, the Egyptians must have used moss, *of course*) and – good lord, yes, an interview with her very own stepson Aaron! So *that* was why Sally had presented her with *Cosmo*! Dare she read it? Yes, she must.

The photograph of Aaron does him credit, or does she mean justice? There he is, the mean angel, the dangerous joker, thin and lean and delicate, wearing a 1980s sharp-cut jacket, with wicked lapels. His hair is very slick and trim. 'Aaron Headleand, the Darling of the Gods' runs the caption, and the text informs her that he is the Man of the Moment, that his play is a critical hit, that he lives in Chalk Farm and plays the piano at parties. All this she knows, but she does not know that he is writing a new play about Old Albion and Paul Whitmore (Does Alix know? Surely she would have mentioned it over the curry? Has he paid for the rights?); nor does she know that he is living with ex-film-star Hattie Osborne. This last bit of information astonishes and enrages her. Really, magazines will make up *anything*! Have they no conscience? Have they no sense of plausibility? Could they not have chosen a more fashionable name to fill up their gossip-bite? Hattie Osborne? Ex-film-star? Why, Hattie is old enough to be Aaron's mother! Try again, pull the other one!

Why, she knows for a fact that there is not *room* in his Chalk Farm flat for Hattie Osborne. She knows for a fact that Hattie Osborne lives in Stephen Cox's old flat on Primrose Hill. So she tells herself as she toys with a little pink fish, aware even as she prevaricates that the phrase 'living with' has nothing to do with living accommodation, and that there is something sinister and suggestive both in the nearness and the smallness of their residences. Maybe they have taken to 'living together' because their flats are indeed so small? And how old *is* Hattie Osborne, anyway? She had looked unrealistically young at their last encounter, she recalls. Liz forces herself to reread the text, and notes that Aaron had said nothing about his alleged relationship, either to confirm or contradict the information which is offered by the interviewer, as it were, as an afterthought. Does this mean that the interviewer made it up? Or that Aaron would not speak about it? Or that the news was so 'hot' that it came to the knowledge of *Cosmopolitan* too late in the day to check?

These trivial thoughts and unseemly doubts pursue her for the rest of the flight, nibbling at her like midges, detracting from the high seriousness of her role as Stephen's saviour. By the time she disembarks with an aching swollen ankle and a low cramped back ache into the heat of Bangkok Airport she has managed to brush them aside, by admitting that there may be something in the story after all, and that if there is, it is not the end of the world. Had not Aaron and Hattie met and been introduced by her own self, in her own house, with her blessing, and gone off together like good children to the cinema on Belsize Park? So what, if they have a little fling? It will not last for long. So reasons Liz with herself, as she tries to stifle the mounting apprehension that fills her at the thought of this unknown city, this unpleasant task.

The airport is easy to negotiate, and she follows without difficulty John Geddes's advice about obtaining an air-conditioned taxi for 300 baht. The taxi driver tries to persuade her that the Trocadero is not a good place for her, offering her the rival delights of various other establishments, but she rightly assumes that he is trying to earn a small commission from a brother-in-law, and sticks with increasing obstinacy to her original destination. It is night, and she is too tired upon arrival to play detective: she takes the room she is given and follows her suitcase and the small boy carrying it meekly upstairs to bed.

She is luckier than Stephen had been: instead of the view of the filter dripping on to the gravel roof, she looks over the street, and she has a small balcony. Her shower curtain is not torn, and her bedside light and her television set work. She does not appreciate these comforts, as Stephen had not thought fit to describe their absence. Instead, she forms the same view as Stephen: that the Troc is a gloomy dump. The noise from the street and from the air conditioning is very loud and the décor is unappealing. She takes a swig of duty-free Cognac to cheer herself up, and addresses herself to the unpacking of her bags. She does not get very far with this, as she discovers that she has mislaid the key to her suitcase. Uncharacteristically, she had tried to behave like a serious traveller and taken the trouble to lock it, and now she realizes, as she sits on the end of her bed with the contents of her handbag strewn around her, that she has left the keys both to her house and her suitcase on the mantelpiece in the bedroom in St John's Wood.

Furious with herself, she sips her Cognac, and wonders whether to go to bed and leave the problem until the morning. She has her sponge bag and nightdress in her hand baggage: she could chicken out. But this, she knows, would be the coward's way, and on this trip she must not permit herself cowardice. She approaches the telephone, which is curiously lacking in dial or instructions. She searches the room for guidance and finds none. What shall she do? Shall she go down and explain her plight? She has already started to undress, and she is damned if she will go down. She lifts the telephone receiver, and explains to whoever is on the other end that she needs somebody to come and cut open her case. Yes, in room 412. Now.

She has no idea whether she has been understood. What if they refuse to help her? What if they refuse to believe that the case is, indeed, her own? Can she prove it? She lights a cigarette, and tries the door on to the balcony. It opens, and a breath of hot night air charged with the scent of chicken and squid and oil and noodle and pineapple greets her. She ventures out, to a roofscape of little balconies, to strings of washing and aerials and pot plants. Across the road from her, directly opposite, a young woman discreetly wrapped in a length of blue cloth sits in a large yellow plastic bowl of water, taking a bath. She scoops the water over her shining shoulders. Behind her a little spirit house dances with fairy lights. Further off, a Japanese lantern flickers. Liz Headleand's spirits rise. Towers and palaces shimmer in the distance. The traffic roars. Little coloured taxis bedizened with coloured bulbs and blinkers weave and rush and bleep beneath her. The street is thronged, although it is after midnight. So this is where Stephen Cox stayed. Her courage is up.

It is further fortified by the appearance of a Thai night porter, a capable middle-aged man who takes in her suitcase problem in a glance. First of all he produces a large bunch of keys — 'My house, my sister house,' he explains, as she tries them all. Then he fiddles with a penknife, also to no avail. By mime, she conveys that she does not mind if he breaks the lock. 'Wait a minute,' he says, and returns with a large pair of heavy-duty pliers. He is reluctant to commit assault upon her property, but she eggs him on, and he manages to slice his way through the fancy little metal loops on the lock-tethered zip. They are both very pleased. He smiles, she smiles, they shake hands on this cutting of the Gordian knot. She gives him a note. She has no idea whether it is twenty pence or twenty pounds that she gives him, but he smiles politely and conspiratorially as he pockets it, and wishes her goodnight.

May everything, she prays as she falls asleep, be so simple.

In the morning, she discovers that the telephone at the Trocadero is not at all simple. Her failure the night before had not been induced by fury or fatigue. There is no dial. Every call must go through the operator. She can hardly believe this. She has a hundred calls to make, and each one must be channelled through that light vague little girlish voice that chirps unconcerned like a parrot at the end of each number 'Caw you back'. She reminds herself that this is, after all, a developing country, but still she feels outraged. Do all hotels have such a primitive system? She contacts the embassy, a chap at the *Bangkok Post*, a chap at the ICRDP, Marianne's friend Sally at UNICEF, makes a few appointments, and gives up. That is enough for the morning. She cannot face any more dictation, and more false connections. She goes down to explore.

Ah, the heat, the fumes, the smell, the exhaustion! She battles her way for a few hundred yards up Silom, then retreats to the air-conditioned foyer of the Trocadero to take stock.

Shall she, she wonders, approach the management about Stephen, about Konstantin Vassiliou? There is no doubt at all that they stayed here; she has documents to prove it. But what if her inquiries cast her own status as guest into doubt? What if the management looks askance at the name of Cox? What if she and her mutilated suitcase are put out upon the street?

She decides that the solution is to put herself out on the street first, by reserving herself a room at the Oriental, where surely the phone must work. Then, with her retreat covered, she will investigate. It is beyond the call of duty to expect herself to stay longer in this place. She has not committed herself to rivalling Stephen's stamina. She will move.

The Oriental sounds pleased to receive her. It asks her on what plane she will arrive. She says she has arrived already and is staying at the Trocadero. She will be along that afternoon.

Yes, madam, they say, with sympathy.

Her escape confirmed, her heart warms towards the Trocadero. The boy in the Café Maxime who serves her an omelette and fresh fruits and coffee is very sweet. The fresh fruits are very sweet. Mango, papayas, pineapple. Pinks and oranges and yellows. Refreshed by a short nap, emboldened by another roof-top vision, she makes her way down to the cashier who guards the heavy metal safe by the registration desk, and nervously produces Stephen's docket. Is there any chance, she murmurs, that this — this document of her friend Mr Cox is still on deposit?

The prettily lipsticked high-coiffed cashier stares and puzzles over the paper. Understandably, she does not like the date. She shakes her head. Is very very old-ticket, we only keep three months, she says. But still, you could look, says Liz. Who is this Mr Cox? asks the young woman.

'He is my friend,' says Liz, firmly. Even to herself, the claim sounds fraudulent.

The cashier swings open the thick armoured door of the safe, and pretends to look, but Liz can tell she is not trying very hard. She is very neat and dapper. Liz feels large and red and hot.

The cashier shakes her head again, returns the ticket to Liz. 'Sorry,' she murmurs, unconvincingly.

Liz is about to give up, but tells herself she must not be so feeble. She dives in her bag, and produces the diary, and the photograph of Stephen. 'Mr Stephen Cox,' she says, pointing at it. 'English writer. Do you remember him?' The woman looks blank, incurious. Liz fumbles, and finds the photograph of Konstantin which Charles had prised out of the files of Global International for her at the last moment. Although she herself has never set eyes on Konstantin, she feels it must be an eloquent likeness; a sunny young man with an open face, smiling at the camera.

'Do you know this person?' she asks the cashier. The cashier, on the verge of turning away and dismissing Liz as a nuisance, deigns a glance. And is transfixed.

'Ah!' she cries softly. 'Is him. Is Konstantin!' She grabs the picture from Liz, and stares at it eagerly, smiling to herself, shaking her head, muttering, moved. It is a moment of emotion. Liz knows she is on the trail.

'He your friend? Your friend also?' she asks Liz, touching the photograph with soft fingers, reaching again for Stephen and looking at him with a different, an awakened curiosity.

'Do you know him?' asks Liz.

'Mr Konstantin, yes, we know him.' She calls to her friend in reception who approaches, exclaims, expresses astonishment. They converse with one another rapidly in Thai, then turn back to Liz.

'You have see Mr Konstantin?' they ask her. No, she says, she has not, have they? No, they have not either. He has vanished, Mr Konstantin. A long long time no see.

Liz asks them how long. Again, they confer in Thai. They are very excited. They ask Liz why she is here, and she tries to explain. They tell her she needs to speak to Mr Phaiboon. Will she come back in one hour, please? What is her room number?

Guiltily, Liz explains that she is moving to the Oriental. They do not seem to find this surprising. They are eager to help. Come back in one hour, they say. One hour, two hours. They will find Mr Phaiboon.

She wonders, as she transfers herself by taxi to the Oriental down the road, whether this will be it. Will Mr Phaiboon tell her all she needs to know? She thinks not all. There is a mystery. She could tell, from the faces of those girls, that there is a mystery.

And Mr Phaiboon does not tell her all. He leads her into a little office, gives her tea, asks her questions. She tries to explain herself, thinking as she does so that things would have been much simpler had she in truth been Stephen's wife or fiancée. They will assume he was her lover anyway, so why worry? She shows him Stephen's effects, she shows him the receipt from the safe deposit and the diary and the photographs. She tells him they came in a package from Kampuchea. He shakes his head. This is not good news. As he listens, an inescapable image of Stephen's last days begins to form in Liz's mind. Yes, that was how it must have been. Why had she not seen it before?

Konstantin's disappearance is a separate, though related matter. Phaiboon strokes his small silky moustache anxiously as he tells her that Konstantin had not been back to the Trocadero for more than a year. Yes, he had been away for long periods before without a word, but never for so long. His rooms have been kept on, but they are beginning to give up hope of seeing their friend Konstantin again. There have been no messages. The bank pays for the rooms, the bank will not say where he is. Konstantin is very very rich man, says Phaiboon, with admiration and love. Money no problem. But money is not everything. They would like to see their friend.

He thinks he remembers Stephen. The English gentleman in the white suit. Two years ago, was it? He stayed for some weeks, months. Very nice, very polite gentleman.

Liz begins to feel a real shit for deserting to the Oriental.

'What can I do to help?' asks Phaiboon.

Liz is at a loss. What can he do? He could give her the names of Konstantin's Bangkok friends, she suggests. Phaiboon offers Jack Crane (gone back to Boston) and Piet Dieper, who is still around. He will try to think of others.

Meanwhile, would she perhaps like to see Konstantin's rooms?

Yes, she most certainly would.

She follows the light-footed Phaiboon along corridors and round corners and along more corridors. 'It is not the hotel proper, it is the annexe,' he explains, as he produces keys from a bunch and unlocks a door.

And there is Konstantin's room, lovingly preserved, dusted and polished, his pot plants watered by devoted attendants, waiting for his return. Liz stands there and gulps. Phaiboon too is visibly affected. His brown melancholy eyes soften and mist.

A guitar, an embroidered elephant, a pile of records, a poster stuck up with Blu-Tack, some extraneous blobs of Blu-Tack, a half-full bottle of whisky, a tray of neatly arranged glasses, a row of well-thumbed paperback books. Where is their owner, where is the spirit of the house? Konstantin's effects are far more vivid, far more evocative, far more three-dimensional than Stephen's. They suggest a young man with his life before him. How can he have risked all this and vanished? What will his mother do if he is truly dead and gone?

Liz wanders around, touching the objects, while Phaiboon delicately adjusts the curtains against the evening sun. On the bookshelf, there is a photograph of Stephen. It is a photograph she has never seen before. It shows Stephen sitting cross-legged on the ground, on dry leaves and grasses, by a corner stone of crumbling statuary at the base of a vast religious tree. His hands are on his knees. His posture is contemplative. He looks calm. It is immediately identifiable, even to Liz, as the work of Konstantin Vassiliou. She points it out to Phaiboon, who nods, and says, 'Wat Nam Tok. They went to see forest monks in northern forests.'

Liz feels she is very near Stephen, in this undisturbed room. But he does not speak to her.

She thanks Phaiboon, as they retreat along the corridors. He says that he will do all he can to help her in her quest. He repeats that Konstantin was good friend and good man.

Liz returns to the Oriental, sits by the pool, orders an iced coffee, and thinks. She thinks of the unknown Konstantin, and of his

mother Rose Vassiliou. She had spoken to Rose, back in England.
Hattie Osborne had given her the number. She had been reluctant
to telephone, and had not enjoyed the conversation. Rose Vassiliou
had sounded distinctly frosty. Not at all pleased to hear from a
random stranger inquiring about the whereabouts of her son. Her
voice had been tight, closed, guarded. Liz had explained the nature
of her mission, and asked whether Mrs Vassiliou knew anything of
her son's friend Stephen Cox. Mrs Vassiliou denied all knowledge
of him. Did Mrs Vassiliou know how Liz could contact Konstantin?
No, she did not. She had not herself heard from him for some time.
He was still out East, she believed.

Liz, on her end of the telephone, nervously drawing noughts and
crosses in red felt tip on her desk pad, had not known what to say
into the small ominous silence. How could she say that Global
International seemed to have lost contact with Konstantin? She was
ringing to sound out Mrs Vassiliou, not to offer her bad news.

Into the silence, Mrs Vassiliou said, in a tone of willed, stone-
walling normality, 'I'm sure Konstantin's quite okay. He always is.
I'm sorry I can't help.'

'Not at all,' Liz had said, 'I'm sorry to have troubled you.'

And the other woman had put her receiver down first. And that
had been that.

The interchange ended in rebuff. It had made Liz feel intrusive
and gross. She had been hurt, though she would never have
admitted it, by Rose's tone. Unlike Hattie Osborne, she had taken
the trouble to do a little (well, a *very* little) research into the
Vassiliou scandal, and had discovered through the *Times* index in
the London Library and her old lawyer friend Roy Strangeways
that Rose had enjoyed a brief notoriety in the sixties for having
married a penniless Greek Cypriot against her parents' wishes, for
having given her money away to Africa, and for having made her
children wards of court to prevent their being kidnapped by their
father. Rose had espoused simplicity and poverty, and had not

wanted any part in her family fortune. She and the Greek Cypriot were now reconciled, Roy thought, but both of them had vanished from the scene. He did not know what had happened to the grand house in Norfolk. The National Trust, perhaps?

Liz, reading old newspaper stories and piecing together bits of gossip, had been rather taken with the notion of Rose. Rose, however, had clearly not been at all taken with the notion of Liz Headleand.

When she got back to England, should she report to Rose Vassiliou on the empty, deserted room? Or should she mind her own business? She had been given no commissions. Maybe Rose knows more than she wishes to say.

Over the next two days, which seemed to extend for weeks, Liz pursues the ghostly footprints, but she never gets as near as she had felt on that first evening. There are distant traces in the Press Club, where the secretary allows her to leaf through the members' register and the visitors' book: she finds the name of Simon Grunewald, but Stephen's she does not find. She speaks on the phone (an instant Oriental connection, as clear as a bell) to Piet Dieper in Aranyaprathet, who tells her he would be pleased to see her at the border, but that he too has heard no news for many months. She is received at the embassy by a most unsatisfactory person who seems actively suspicious about her inquiries: the amiable and helpful Peter Bloch is on leave, and the white-faced, white-fingered black-bearded tallow-mannered Grimswade has taken his place. Grimswade makes it clear that he has never heard of Stephen Cox, does not read fiction, and distrusts Liz's credentials. He is at once icy and lubricious. Liz is reduced to producing a British Council leaflet on Stephen's work, and pointing out that he had, after all, won the Booker Prize. Grimswade is not impressed. He claims not to have heard of the Booker Prize. Lost writers, even when alleged to be eminent, are not the responsibility of the embassy, his manner proclaims. The British Council itself makes a black mark in his book. Liz leaves, discouraged.

After Grimswade, her researches falter and drag. He has put the kiss of death upon her. She meets with stone-walling, with coldness, with obstruction everywhere. Even Konstantin is disowned by some of those who surely knew him. She gets the sense that she is an intruder. Those who know will not tell. This is their patch, they do not want to hand over their hard-won connections to an outsider. She begins to think she had been lucky to be so well received on the phone by Piet Dieper. Maybe she should go to the border to see him? At least he had been civil. She could go to the border and the camps and try to speak, as she had long ago but dreamily intended, to Mme Savet Akrun.

But it is not so easy to go to the camps and the border. She is informed that she needs a pass from the military. She has to go through the British Embassy and Grimswade. She will need a car and a driver. It will cost much money, many dollars.

Grimswade does his best to put her off. She momentarily gives up, and turns to her second list of contacts, her frivolous list. She rings Robert Oxenholme's second cousin in krill. He is of no practical use, but he offers her a tour of the Marine Institute or a pre-Christmas cocktail party. Neither appeals, but his voice cheers, and it is nice to be asked. She rings up a couple of friends of John Geddes. The gynaecologist is out ('A *charmer*, darling, and you never know when he might come in handy: he was an *angel* with Vanessa, he really saved the show'); the critic of restaurants is very much in, delighted to hear from her, and obliges her to accept an invitation to dine with him that night at the New French Grill at the Nirvana. He has to review it, do please come. Doubtfully, she accepts. This is not what she is here for, but there may be a lead in the Nirvana, who knows?

She cannot think of anything more to do. Time seems to have stuck, here in Bangkok. She has been busy but has got nowhere. It is too hot. Five minutes of walking along the street is too much. Perhaps, as the advertisement suggests, she needs her character radically improved by Skull Expansion? In an hour, she will leave for the Nirvana and while away the evening. In the morning, she will approach once more the problem of visas and passes and border camps. She sits in her hotel room and fiddles with the television news (an American network clearly aimed at small children) and gazes at her brown-and-orange spotted orchids with their fleshy velvet odourless leafless drama of display. She drinks some mineral water and wonders whether she remembered to take her malaria tablet the night before. She wonders whether there is an aeroplane to Aranyaprathet. Why not? She rings Thai Airways, but all she gets is a Hold Tune: a heartless, tinkling, mechanical, improbable reproduction of 'Greensleeves'. 'Alas, my love, you do me wrong, to cast me off discourteously . . .' I am a rotten sleuth, says Liz to herself crossly, as she puts down her receiver. She pushes a button and the TV Jolly News turns into Michael Hordern soundlessly fishing in a trout stream on Exmoor. She begins to change for dinner.

Bob Berry at the Nirvana is something of a surprise. She had expected a round and portly figure from his voice, name and provenance, but he is tall, thin and freckled, with a domed forehead and sandy wisps of hair clinging gamely to his shining skull. He is full of nervous energy. The Nirvana too is surprising. Liz had thought herself in the heart of luxury at the Oriental, but here is nouveau opulence, architectural extravaganza, Hollywood megaluxe. And it is not paste and cardboard, it is, in a sense, real. Real marble, real waterfalls and fountains, real ponds heaving and swelling with real carp, all-too-real descending forests of liana and creeper and Gargantuan floral displays eight feet high. Trees full of fairy lights twinkle, lackeys dressed in pink and white silk with tall head-dresses worthy of the court of Genghis Khan bow and wai and back away before them. Liz, marching briskly through carpeted foyers and tiled arcades towards a deeply carpeted lift, wonders, Alix-Bowen-style, what the lackeys are paid, and where they sleep at night.

The French Grill is on the twentieth floor, with a view of glittering acres. Liz and Bob Berry chatter and gossip about John Geddes and his Indian lover Indra. They nibble lightly at salad and grilled fish. Bob tells her about the tourist boom and the opium trade. He loves Bangkok. It is paradise, he says. Over coffee, he asks her what he can do to help. She says he can tell her how to get to Aranyaprathet. That is easy, he says, just ask Grimswade. Liz says that she has already asked Grimswade. She ventures that she had not been well received. 'But Grimswade's a *lovely* man,' cries Bob Berry, in astonishment. 'A lovely man! Delightful. Of course he will help. Leave it to me. I'll give him a buzz. I'll give him a buzz right now.'

Liz protests, demurs. She cannot think of anything less likely to advance her cause than a surprise phone call to Grimswade from a highly strung foodie in a French restaurant. But she is wrong. Bob Berry calls for a phone, and when one is brought to the table he dials at once, and is at once received. An animated, rapid interchange ensues, full of laughter, gay innuendo and arcane references. Liz can make nothing of it. Can that be Grimswade on the end of the line? Yes, apparently it can. Bob Berry puts down the phone, and waves for its removal. 'Consider it done,' he says. 'Call round in the morning, you'll find a letter to the ministry waiting for you. Nice chap, Grimswade. Says he's very glad to help.'

Liz gives up. She understands nothing. She understands nothing the next day as she does her round of various government offices, collecting pieces of paper covered in a script that means nothing. And, as she sits in the back of a hired car, travelling along the Red Road, she fears that when she finds what she is looking for, she will not understand that either. She may not even recognize it.

Piet Dieper is in the realm of the known. Grave, courteous, conscientious. Yes, he remembers Stephen Cox well. Yes, he remembers Stephen saying that he wanted to go to Cambodia. He had gone off with Konstantin Vassiliou. So both have vanished? Piet shakes his head.

He is afraid he cannot be of much assistance. He will alert his network, but that is all he can do. Who else did Stephen hang out with? Well, there was Jack Crane, but he has gone back to Boston. He can find her the address. And Helen Anstey, but she is now in Hong Kong, working with another agency, or so he has heard.

He tells her there is no point in going to the camp. She will find nothing there to help her in her search. But, as she has the papers, well, perhaps she should go. Why not, she agrees.

Liz Headleand shows him the crumpled photograph of Mme Savet Akrun and says she would like to speak to her. Again, Piet tells her there is no point. People come, people go, she will not remember. But Liz has set her heart on finding this woman. She does not know why. How shall she find her?

Piet tells her where to ask, how to make her way about the camp. Then he says, you know, things are not too good on the border. There was shelling yesterday. We could hear it from here.

'Who is shelling whom?' asks Liz, before the possibility of so crude a question passes. But it has already passed. It passed long ago. Piet shrugs his shoulders. Who knows? Who cares? The Vietnamese-backed Kampuchean army? The Khmer Rouge? Sihanouk's men? The KPNLF?

It had not really occurred to Liz that her mission might be foolhardy. It does not really occur to her now. As she is driven the next morning towards Site Ten, she knows that she is far more apprehensive about other things than about being killed by a Vietnamese or Pol-Potist shell. The chances of her being blown up by a shell on a day trip are, she calculates, somewhat lower than those of being blown up by the IRA in Selfridges' food department. No, she has other fears. She is afraid of finding Mme Akrun, and of not finding her. She is afraid of her own irrelevance, her own intrusion. She is afraid that she comes bearing the wrong gifts to ease her passage. She is afraid that her reluctant driver will mutiny and ditch her. She is afraid that she will not find a lavatory all day. Her ankle aches, and she has a permanent low ache in her back. She feels unnaturally hot. Is it malaria, or is it a hormonal flush? Or is it, simply, the heat? In short, she is afraid.

She finds Mme Savet Akrun exactly where she had hoped to find her, in the Khmer Women's Association Centre for Adult Education. There she is, sitting at a desk in a bamboo hut. Red canna lilies and French marigolds bloom in a little garden. There are pink chalk words on a blackboard.

Liz introduces herself. She is invited to sit down. She sits. She explains herself. She shows her photographs.

Mme Akrun smiles, and says that yes, of course she remembers Konstantin, because of the photographs he took. She looks more puzzled by Stephen, but then seems to recall. Yes, she remembers the English writer. He spoke good French.

She regrets the news that both are missing.

Mme Akrun looks older than she looked in Konstantin's portrait, as indeed she is, but she looks less sad. Liz had half expected her to recite her sad story, but she does not. Time has moved on, even here. She has other things on her mind. She has a new grandchild, she is very pleased, she tells Liz. Liz too declares a grandchild, and produces a photograph of young Cornelia. Cornelia is only a step-grandchild, but she serves as a passport, and Liz loves her. Mme Akrun smiles, is pleased for Liz. Then she speaks a little about her work. Adult Education, an important job, but then the women here are not interested, she says. They do not see the point. They want to go home to their farms, or they want to go to America. It is hard to motivate them to learn here.

Liz finds herself, incongruously, remembering Alix Bowen's struggles to interest young female prisoners in English Literature.

Liz volunteers the information that she is a doctor. That too, Mme Akrun says, is important work. There are English doctors here, much respected, she says, politely.

Far off, a distant rumbling can be heard. Is it gunfire, shelling, thunder? Neither of them pays it any attention.

Liz, embarrassed, hands over her appeasing gifts, chosen according to the advice of Marianne Sanderson. Perfumed soap, and copies of *Time*, *Newsweek*, the *Bangkok Post*, *Asia Weekly*. She even hands over her copy of *Cosmopolitan*. Mme Akrun seems pleased. Her students, she says, turning the pages of *Cosmo*, will like this. They like Western fashions. Mme Akrun says she thinks it is a good thing for the women to learn English. Her friend and neighbour thinks it not so good. Her friend and neighbour Mme Yan thinks that the Khmer language will die. Already the young people speak very badly. The nation dies, says Mme Akrun. It is sad, but what can one do? One must learn to begin again.

There is a resignation in Mme Akrun, a stoicism. Liz recognizes them. But there is something missing, something she does not find. Where is the obsessional, grieving mother, whose image she had constructed from the photograph, from Stephen's jottings, from her own instincts? She does not feel the presence of the absent Mitra. She does not sense the hollow pit. She looks at Mme Akrun, smiling, insisting on a little eye contact (remembering Alix and the molecules of her murderer), but still she sees no shadow, no funnel into the backward dark. Instead, Mme Akrun smiles back, and turns the pages of *Cosmo*, lighting briefly and without particular interest on the image of Aaron Headleand, and moving on to the tampon. Shall Liz speak, shall she claim her stepson, shall she inquire after Mitra?

No, she shall not. The moment passes. The shelling sounds a little nearer, and Mme Akrun is obliged to notice it. She coughs, drily, and listens, then shrugs her thin shoulders in her thin cotton robe. It is an irritant, her gesture indicates, a customary irritant.

Liz's driver is less phlegmatic. He appears and hovers in the doorway, looking pointedly at his watch. It is nearly curfew time, it is a seven-hour drive back to Bangkok, it is not safe on the roads after dark.

Liz feels there is something that might be said, at this far end of the world, but she does not know what it is. Perhaps it is enough that she sits here.

Mme Akrun speaks a little more of her grandson, and of her other daughter, her sick daughter Sok Sita. Poor girl, she says, she is simple, she will never be well, she remembers nothing. Better not to remember some things, says Mme Akrun.

Something has snapped in Mme Akrun, or time has healed her. How can Liz know which? Is it the same thing? She cannot read this woman.

Her driver has got back into the hot driver's seat and switched on the engine. Liz knows she must leave. There is no more to be done here.

*

Mme Akrun watches the dust of the departing car, and then she goes back into her hut and rubs the pink words off the blackboard. Liz is right to guess that she has changed. She has relinquished Mitra. His shadow no longer haunts her. She has let him go. He must take his own chance, wherever he may be. Los Angeles, Toronto, Siem Reap, Hong Kong, Gravesend. He is on his own now. She returns no more to the clearing in the forest. She has other preoccupations now.

It is not time alone that has accomplished this. She had begun to believe that time would never heal her, for she had not wished to be healed. She had hoped that her own hope would keep Mitra alive, and with the dirty needle of hope she had picked at her memories, had infected them and kept them as a running sore. She had watched others around her deal with their memories in this way, and in others. Some, like her daughter Sok Sita, had lost their wits. Some had cauterized the past with rage, and lived off anger and hatred. Some had been arrested as by a flow of burning lava in postures of bowed submission, of cowed despair: and now crawled around, bent and deformed. Some of the young fed off film-star dreams of escape. Playing ping-pong, they chattered of visas and papers that would never come. Some plotted revenge. Some went back across the border to join the resistance. Some lived for the moment, learning camp ways, learning to wheedle and exploit and profit, to scavenge and trade. Even here, there were objects to sell and recycle, there were unexplained arrivals of snakeskin and pig meat and musical instruments. Of late, a new supply of small carvings had begun to appear on the market. A lizard, a fish, a flower, a crocodile: antique or fake, who cared? They fetched a price.

Some despair and some cultivate their gardens. Mme Akrun and her colleagues water the red lilies and the marigolds with water provided by the United Nations and recycled from washtubs and cooking pots. There are no crops here, for this is bad land. Life here is neither urban nor rural. It is a parody of the town, a parody of the village.

Time has passed, but it is not the passing of time or the birth of a grandchild that has closed the wound of Mitra.

Mme Akrun tidies up her meagre worn text books, shuts and locks the drawer of her desk, hangs the key on its string round her neck, collects the placatory offerings of the large white woman from London, and sets off towards her home down the dusty red path, nodding and smiling to friends and colleagues as she goes, a respectable matron, honoured amongst her fellows.

She had not thought it would turn out this way. She had not thought that it would be her youngest son, Kem, who would rescue her from the lingering death-grip of the ghost of Mitra.

This place is neither town nor country. This time is neither peace nor war.

When Kem had gone missing, at first she had refused to respond. In her heart she felt nothing, to her community she said nothing. So many go missing. Now the photographer and his friend from England have gone missing. One more, one less, who cares? After

Mitra's loss, how could she care? Kem had gone over the border with the bandit called Lek Let, with the men with guns. She said to herself that she would never see him, would never hear from him again. He was well lost, the bad boy, the delinquent, the drug-addict, the bitter child of No Man's Land. Let him call himself a resistance fighter. What did it matter? He was lost.

So she told herself, as day succeeded day. She would send no messages after him, as she had sent after Mitra. She would not alert the Red Cross, the United Nations Border Relief, the camp commanders. She would wait for her heart to turn to stone. And hour by hour, it petrified.

Mme Akrun smiles, waves. There is Chin Sokha on his bicycle, there is Mme Yan's youngest grandchild, there is the mad monk, there is one-armed Proap Am beating tin cans into cooking vessels, there is the secretary of the Khmer Women's Association with his new Panama hat.

She had waited for the triumph of nothing, for the victory of indifference. And when the news came that Kem had been found, that he was lying in the camp hospital, she had gasped with distress to feel that she could still feel distress.

She had not wanted to go near him. She was told he was mortally ill. He had been blown up by a mine, he was in pieces, he would surely die, rumour had told her with vindictive relish. If only she could stay away until it was all over!

But she was drawn, she was pulled. A hook had entered her guts, and she was pulled. She could not force herself to stay away. The hook was lodged in some soft nerveless hidden tissue, and, although she could not feel it, she could not resist it. It tugged her, towards the bamboo shack that called itself a hospital, towards the camp beds with their rows of injured and their buzzing flies. Resentment and foreboding dragged her back and made her as heavy as lead as she approached. Her feet slurred and stumbled. She did not want this confrontation. But on she went.

She could not at first identify her son amongst the maimed and the sick. Where was he, which was he, was he dead and buried already, was he that hunched shape with the bandaged skull, was he that heap of rags? And then she saw him. He was sitting, propped up, in the middle of the row, awaiting her visit, his face hot with pain, his brow damp, his eyes and nostrils distended, his breath short and quick. His eyes were searching for her, and when they caught her, he in hope reached out a hand, and then in despair, in submission, let it drop. She paused, frozen, the blood drumming in her ears. The moment lasted for ever. He continued to look towards her. It was his pain that filled her. It flowed from him to her until she was drowned in it, flooded by it. She could see that his face was full of doubt, he expected chastisement, rejection. She could not move. She tried to move towards him, but she staggered as though under a great burden, as she had staggered through the undergrowth with his feverish seven-year-old body in her arms. She was suffocating, she would die. His eyes had dropped from hers, but he made one last effort, and cried out. 'Mother!' he called. 'Mother!'

And she made it to his bedside, and collapsed there against his mattress in the dust.

They had taken off his leg. The stump, brutally bandaged, struck at her and her own flesh bled. She shut her eyes, and moaned, and shook her head. All of her past and of his seemed to be gathered up here in retribution, in reproach. She had abandoned and betrayed him, and now he would die, her little one, her baby, he would die in terrible pain.

'Mother,' he whispered. 'Little mother.' He dared to touch her hair.

And so they had been reunited. She had wept and wept. He had comforted her. He too had wept. He had become her son. He had been returned to her, and she had forgiven him.

He did not die. She watched over him, tended him, endured with him each pang and each spasm. The pain persisted, and stubbornly she partook of it. She was driven away by hospital orderlies, and she returned with offerings. Hour by hour, inch by inch, she regained him, as she tried to make amends.

As she sat by Kem's bedside, the plaintive ghost of his brother Mitra slipped quietly away into the shades of the jungle. Mitra was forgotten. Kem was her salvation.

Gradually, the pain diminished. She wept bitter tears of joy when he was fitted with a wooden leg tipped with old rubber from a blown tyre. She smiled and wept as he practised staggering round the hospital compound, to the cheers and jeers of his fellow-amputees. And when he was allowed home, she killed the fatted chicken and bought pig meat and cooked a feast for the prodigal son. Ah, such an evening, such happiness! Sok Sita giggling nervously, and Am Nara at last vastly pregnant, and her son-in-law Chut Pek, and her friend Mme Yan and Yan's family, a whole reception committee for Kem's return. There was rejoicing and hope and excitement. Now they were reunited, now their luck would change!

And the good luck is still with her, thinks Mme Akrun, as she walks homewards through the throng of bicycles. Kem remains sweet of nature. He is transformed, he is humble, he is grateful. He is safe, he is good, she knows where he can be found at any time of night or day. He occupies himself, he has even started to study a little, he is learning English. He will be pleased with the magazines that the Englishwoman brought, with their news of the outside world, with their advertisements for aftershave and car telephones and tennis rackets and Wedgwood china. He can no longer wander off in bad company. He is no use to the guerrillas or to the bandits now. He cannot play at soldiers any more. He is her darling, her favourite, her little one. She is reborn as Mother. Her family is complete once more. She is happy. She walks towards him as he sits waiting in his bamboo prison, with her head held high, with the step of a young girl. It has been hard, but Kem is her reward.

*

Site Two South
PO Box 67
Aranyaprathet 25120
Prachin Buri
Thailand

Dearest Mrs Betty, Dearest Mrs Ro, Dearest Mothers,

Today I have received your one letter. I thank so much for you.
How are you and yours? I do hope you are all keeping well than I
am here. Now I would like to tell you about my leaving here that I
was telling you before to my homeland. Now I cannot leaving here
to Cambodia because my friend told me that it is very difficult to
across the landmines and the line of [illegible] troops along the
Khmer–Thai border. On the other hand in Cambodia have a lot of
problems. So I decide that I cannot leave here although here is very
badly for me. So now I make up to live here until mine have
freedom. I know it is very late for Cambodia people. I do hope you
will help me soon. I'm sure you have a very good kindness to me.
Oh! I'm so sorry.

Now at the end of this letter I'm goodbye from you. May God
bless you and yours everytimes. Don't forget reply to me. Please. I
wait to get yours every times.

Your affectionately son

*

Mitra Akrun is a para-social worker in a resettlement centre in
Montreal.
Mitra deals in crack in Washington.
Mitra is writing his life story in little red notebooks.
Mitra is a born-again Christian.

Mitra has murdered a fellow-refugee in a hostel in New Zealand.

Mitra sits in front of a prison psychiatrist in New Zealand and confesses to multiple trauma.

Mitra is working as a garden maintenance man in Kent.

*

Edith Cox, mother of Stephen Cox, mother of sons, lies on her bed in her private nursing home in West Somerset staring with near-blind red-rimmed rheumy filmed eyes vaguely in the direction of her television set, on which dazzling young men in white with sweatbands on their foreheads are playing tennis on green grass. She does not see them and is not conscious that they are there. The television is on for the benefit of the nursing staff whose dreary daily round is a little lightened by the hope that some of these incarcerated senile wasting creatures may occasionally get a little pleasure, a little distraction from elsewhere. And the plock, plock of the balls and the commentator's droning voice help to stifle the occasional cry, the occasional moan, the general low-pitched tenor of despair in this place that is neither life nor death. Edith Cox, some cell of memory activated by the plock, plock, drifts back into the days of her former glory when her boys won trophies at the tennis tournaments of Taunton. How proudly she had grumbled as she drove them from fixture to fixture, as she washed their sports-wear, their shirts, their trousers, their socks! Francis, Jeremy and Andrew. They had all been good at tennis. Of course they were good at tennis. They were Coxes!

Edith Cox, in this time that is no time, does not know whether her son Stephen is alive or dead. He does not enter into her ramblings at all. No cell of recollection ever illuminates him. It is as though he had never been. She has forgotten that she had four sons. Three only she records. He had been a mistake, an after-thought, and he had dropped from the tally.

Love–fifteen, love–thirty, love–forty. Now she is herself a child again, a wetness leaking from her into her thick pad. Naughty Edie, naughty girl! She starts to cry, but the nurses do not hear, the young men playing tennis do not hear, her sons do not hear. The long unchanging afternoon wears on.

*

Ruby Fox, mother of murdered Jilly Fox, is at the tennis club, knocking up with Betsy Yarmolinsky. Plock, plock, laugh, whoops, sorry! Her dyed strawberry hair is tied back with a green ribbon. She is tanned and freckled. The Californian climate suits her. Her sunglasses are framed in white plastic. She keeps herself trim. She braves the tennis club, she has weathered out the social disgrace of a murdered daughter. Back in England, people had been very sniffy, but here they are much more sympathetic, much more chummy. Ruby Fox is beginning to see herself as something of a heroine. She has vanquished disgrace by pluck! 'Shall we have a game, Betsy?' she calls, confidently, across the net. Betsy Yarmolinsky is putting on weight, her shoulders in that sleeveless top look quite puffy. Ruby jogs a lot now, up and down the raw newly terraced hillside with its view of the Pacific, past the plate glass windows and the lawn sprinklers and the notices with portraits of guns that promise Armed Response. She likes this expensive urban landscape. She does not enjoy tennis as much as she used to when she was a girl, but she still likes to win.

She serves. 'Fifteen–love,' she calls, brightly, across the net, under the unchanging blue of the Californian sky.

*

Rose Vassiliou, mother of Konstantin, sits in a shabby little fourth-floor campaign office in Bloomsbury drinking a cup of tea. The walls are lined with posters, many of them portraying Nelson

Mandela. The desk is piled high with papers. Rose is examining a postcard showing a coconut palm. Yes, that is from him, that brief, that woefully inadequate, that cruel little message. But when had it been posted, in what time scale? She looks up from it to her walls. There is Mme Savet Akrun, Konstantin's handiwork, asking, 'Where is my son?' Rose gives Mme Akrun a somewhat bitter little smile. Then she returns the postcard to her bag, and gets on with her afternoon's work.

*

Angela Whitmore Malkin, mother of murderer Paul Whitmore, is walking with her favoured dog along a cart track in Upper Hartdale. She is in a vile mood, and she cuts at the heads of teasels irritably with her stick. Things look worse than they have ever looked. The Doctor and the Colonel are out on bail, but she fears that they have gone too far this time. They will get put away, and then what will become of her? She blames that interfering Bowen woman. Nothing has gone right since she came poking her nose into Angela's affairs. The Doctor and the Colonel have turned on Angela. They have turned very nasty. They blame her for attracting the attention of the police. She blames Alix Bowen. Shall she pen her another poisoned letter? What is the point? Now, if she could get at that pig son of hers, that would be worth doing. But there is no way. He is locked up, the pig boy.

Her stout shoes tramp on across the frozen mud. The bull mastiff scents a rabbit, and lunges for freedom. She shortens his studded leash. 'To heel, Trojan,' she commands, and the dog cringes and sulks.

*

Liz Headleand hated her journey back from Mme Akrun and Site Ten to Bangkok. Darkness fell, and the road went on for ever, monotonous hour after hour. The nervousness which should have accompanied the sound of shelling now, belatedly, possessed her. She hated the dark, she longed to be back in the land of marble and fairy lights, she longed for a proper lavatory. The road was full of sinister traffic, trucks without headlights, army vehicles, tanks. Terrorists, rapists, bandits. When she shut her eyes, the despair of the camp filled her, and the long red intersecting roads glimmered in repetition through her mind. Roads of limbo, roads peopled with wanderers who would never rest. The hopelessness of the life of Mme Akrun, the pointlessness of her own mission pervaded her. It seemed clear at last that Stephen Cox and Konstantin Vassiliou were as dead as Mitra Akrun. They had left no trace.

She tried to sleep, but she could not. So that had been the sound of shelling? Liz Headleand did not even know what a shell was. She would not know one if she saw one. She would not know one if one hit her on the head.

She tried to think of pleasant things, of Bob Berry and grilled fish, of her bedroom in the Oriental, of her garden and her fishpond in St John's Wood, of walking in Regent's Park, of the Italian lakes, even of eating curry with Alix in Camden. But none of these seemed very real or possible.

She could sense that the driver was not enjoying himself either, and this made her even more nervous. He kept making little hissing noises through his teeth, and when he was obliged to overtake his tension palpably mounted. What was he afraid of, and should she fear it too? After a while, he switched on the car radio to comfort himself. An American child's voice was singing 'Silent Night, Holy Night' in a sickly-sweet treble. Liz thought she could not take much of this, but luckily he could not either, for he changed bands to find some more local rhythm.

Liz rubbed at her aching ankle.

Liz had broken her ankle while tobogganing with her stepson Aaron on Parliament Hill on a Boxing Day in the early 1980s. She tried to think of Aaron, of the steep descending swoop in the dusk, of the feel of his jacket as she clung to his back, of the crash and crunch when the sledge turned over. But Hattie Osborne got in the way. She tried to think of her St John's Wood drawing room and her new curtains. But Mme Akrun got in the way.

When she finally got to bed, she was too tired to sleep. She lay there, her ankle throbbing round its metal pin. Dozing, she heard a faint hot thunder, and saw the red roads.

Aaron had lugged her back up the hill on the sledge to the parked car, and he had sat with her for hours in the Casualty Department of the Royal Free amongst Christmas hangovers and festive mutilations in penitent intimacy. It had, he said, been all his fault.

Liz groaned and swallowed a sleeping pill. She fell asleep, and dreamed of Mme Akrun.

In the morning, she tried to take stock. Her trip to the border had taught her nothing at all. The best that could be said of it was that she had accomplished it. A negative gain. She knew now that there was nothing of Stephen left there. For all her trouble, she has acquired the address of one Jack Crane on Fennel Street, Boston, Mass., which she could probably have discovered from England by ringing up the ICRDP.

Well, what had she expected? A tombstone, with dates and an inscription?

She supposes she should try to go to Vietnam and Kampuchea. And what does she expect to find there? A white-bearded skeletal Stephen in a wicker cage?

She spends the day hassling embassies and airlines. It seems that all flights to Hanoi and Saigon are booked, though how any of the putative passengers managed to acquire a visa defeats her. There are no commercial flights to Phnom Penh, though travel agents still vainly advertise trips to Angkor Wat. She sits in offices and jumps into tuk-tuk taxis and makes telephone calls. Grimswade has reverted to type and will not speak to her. She is too proud to appeal once more to Bob Berry.

In the evening, as she paces restlessly and unevenly up and down the terrace at the Oriental, watching the lanterns and the lights and the river traffic, she begins to see why Charles had given up so quickly on his mission to rescue Dirk Davis from Baldai. The temptation to do nothing, to stay here doing nothing for the rest of the ten days she has allotted herself, is almost overwhelming. No one will know how quickly she has given up. No one will know that she did not expend every effort. She has a sudden insight into the lives of the less ambitious foreign correspondents: of course, so this is what they do. They pace up and down terraces, or drink in bars, or lie by the pool at the Oriental, making up stories, recycling stories about the shelling on the border.

Liz limps back up to her room and drinks some mineral water. She is at a low ebb. Her whole hard working life seems a frivolous waste of time. She rings Charles, but he is not in. She tries to force herself to ring Charles's friend in shellac to ask him how the hell to get a seat on a plane to Saigon and where to get a forged visa, but she simply cannot make herself do it. Her nerve fails her. She hates cold calling total strangers. She rings her own number in St John's Wood, knowing that nobody will be there, simply for the comfort of the thought of the sound moving amongst her own yellow curtains. Perhaps her cat can hear it? She lets the tone ring and ring across the world, finding just enough curiosity as she does so to wonder if this noise is costing the Oriental, or the Thai post office, or the GPO, and if it is appreciably diminishing the earth's resources. Can it be good for Gaia, to have all this bleeping and trilling circling around her? She decides it cannot, and puts down the receiver. Instantly, as though waiting, it responds. Startled, she picks it up.

It is Phaiboon from the Trocadero. He has remembered a name which may be of use to her. Has she got a pen? It is a difficult name. He coughs discreetly, and begins to spell it out. He dictates to her the name of Miss Porntip Pramualratana, with her telephone number and her address.

Liz conceals her astonishment and thanks him profusely. He, ever courteous, says he is glad to be of service, and assures her that Miss Porntip Pramualratana is very useful contact, very powerful person, and a good friend of Mr Cox. There is nothing at all suggestive or unpleasant in his tone. Liz loves Phaiboon and all Thai people.

She does not allow the moment to cool. She rings Miss Porntip at once. Miss Porntip is not in, but she has a long and animated Thai message on her answerphone. Liz waits for the bleep and then says, 'I am Elizabeth Headleand, a friend of Stephen Cox, and I am staying at the Oriental Hotel in Room 159.' Then she puts the phone down and nervously eats a rather unpleasant Thai fruit from her fruit bowl. She follows it with a gulp of Cognac. Then she goes down and orders a bowl of soup in the Veranda.

As she sits there, watching a row of slow heavy sand barges moving upstream, she hears the gentle tinkling of a bell approach. It is attached to a liveried boy with an oblong white message, carried aloft. 'Dr Elizabeth Headleand,' it requests, in perfect spelling. Liz leaps to her feet, abandoning her soup, and pursues the boy. He leads her to the Authors' Lounge, where, upon a chintz-covered rattan couch by the white and ivory grand piano, perches like a bright small bird Miss Porntip.

*

'Yes,' says Miss Porntip, or 'O', as Liz has already learned to call her, 'yes, this was his dream. To have Named Cocktail. On this seat, Liz, he say it to me. Named Cocktail.'

'I don't think much of this candiola juice stuff,' says Liz, who is on her second Pett Petrie. 'You've done better.'

Miss Porntip thoughtfully sips at her second Gore Vidal.

348

'So, Liz,' says Miss Porntip. 'Is sad. Is very sad.'

Both women sigh. It is hard to feel very sad in this charming setting and in this flattering conjunction. Yet it would be wrong to think that there is not a sadness, that both do not feel a sadness. It is connected with the names of the cocktails, with the nature of fame, with the nature of ambition. So, one wanders off into Bad Time, into a nightmare of Blood and Sweat and Tears, into Year Zero, clutching a talisman, hoping to be allowed back across the dark river to the immortality of a Named Cocktail. They have all been out there – Conrad, Somerset Maugham, Paul Theroux, William Golding. They have ventured into the dark spaces of the globe and the white tracts of the heart, and returned to this triumph. So it goes.

Miss Porntip is dismayed to hear of Stephen's disappearance. She has not seen him for more than a year. She has not heard from him for many months. She tells Liz of his departure, his itinerary. Aranya-prathet, Hanoi, Saigon. She had received postcards from all these places, and then, silence. She had tried to warn him against these nasty journeys, these bad regimes, but he would not listen. He would go. 'From Hanoi,' she says, 'even postcards no good. Bad printing. Bad colour. Stamps not stick. No damn good.' She explains to Liz that she had assumed that he had got bored with her and had stopped writing. 'We good friends, but so many good friends everywhere,' she says. She had not grieved over Stephen. She had written him off, had assumed him safely returned to London, safely engaged on writing his best-seller Bad Time Book. She was not a one, she told Liz, to shed false tears. She has new friend, in business. Tourist developer. Big hotel and property man. New airline man. One-time Air Force Pilot man.

But Liz's news alters things. She becomes, increasingly, distressed. 'Not good, not good,' she repeats, as she anxiously frets at a little salted almond with her even white teeth. Liz was quite right to pursue, she says.

Being a woman, she grasps Liz's relationship to Stephen in an instant. 'You close friends, maybe, maybe not love, nothing happen, so nothing end?' she hazards. Liz nods assent. Miss Porntip pats Liz's knee in sympathy.

'Is bad news,' she echoes, again. 'We must make plan.'

They adjourn to Liz's room, where they sit together on the settee to inspect Stephen's papers. They have been there only three minutes when the phone rings, asking if Dr Headleand would like her soup sent up, and would Miss Pramualratana care for some too? Truly, this is the all-seeing, god-like hotel. They accept soup. They make a plan. The next day they will go together to the embassy. O will organize. She has friends in military, friends in airlines. She will pull strings.

Liz thinks she believes her. She has faith in O. She is immensely relieved to have a comrade. If Stephen or his remains are ever to be found, O will help her to find them.

Miss Porntip is touched by the references to herself in Stephen's diary, but disappointed to learn that no photographs seemed to have been preserved. 'I give him nice nice picture,' she says, mournfully. 'Nice nice PR picture as memento. Why he no keep my picture?'

'Maybe he was buried with it next to his heart,' says Liz, to her own astonishment. Miss Porntip hovers on the edge of bursting into tears, but thinks better of it.

She gazes at the picture of Konstantin with some animosity. 'Is no good, this young man,' she says, firmly. She tells Liz that Konstantin was a dangerous person, a bad influence, a destroying angel. 'He bad person, he attract bad things,' she says. No, she never trusted Konstantin. 'Everyone say, he so nice, he so good. But not so. He danger person.'

As the evening's strange conversation draws to a close and Miss Porntip begins to make noises of imminent withdrawal, she suddenly leans forward across the little table and the soup bowls, and grabs

Liz's hand. Liz at first takes this for an emotional gesture, but it is not. Miss Porntip is trying to inspect the red stone in the unlucky ring of Marianne Sanderson. Liz allows her to focus upon it. Miss Porntip moves Liz's huge veined freckled buckled hand about in the light, making the reds flicker and dart. 'Hmm,' says Miss Porntip, eventually. 'Is Cambodian ruby? Is Pailin ruby?'

Liz concedes that this is probably what it is. Present from Stephen, asks Miss Porntip, present from Stephen in Cambodia? Liz shakes her head, and tells the story of the jewel. Once it is freed of Stephen-sentiment, Miss Porntip condemns it. 'Is not good stone,' she says, confidently. 'Is real, but is not good. Tomorrow we go shopping, buy good ruby.'

Liz protests that she has not come to Bangkok to go shopping, but her new friend will not hear of this sacrilege. Of course she must go shopping. Everyone who comes to Bangkok goes shopping. She will show Liz all the best places. There is plenty plenty time. Good ruby, good luck. American Express fine. Great bargain. Great opportunity. Tomorrow, she and Liz go shopping, then to Visa Office. Special prices, good stones, instant visas.

Liz begins to feel exhausted. She is quite glad to get to bed, and forgets, again, to take her malaria pill. She dreams of Stephen Cox's mother.

*

After visiting the Old Man, the Child and the Cave, Stephen Cox, Konstantin Vassiliou and Akira Tanaka stumbled into Bad Time. They had been looking for it, they had been travelling towards it, but so far it had eluded them, it had folded itself away into the trees and the hills at their approach. But now, at last, it was there before them, on the road. They had reached the frontier. This was it, the many-times rehearsed moment.

The car was travelling slowly, picking its way through craters and potholes. The men with guns, alerted to their approach, were waiting for them. Akira stopped the car. Should he have tried to drive on, should he have drawn his pistol? What would have been the point? This was their appointment. They could not fail it now.

Akira, smiling broadly, speaking in Khmer, empty hands extended, was the first to get out of the car. The others followed.

The Khmer Rouge did not like the look of Akira, his car, his friends, his equipment. They did not like the 500 words of Khmer. His *laissez-passer*, passed from hand to hand, did him no good either. They did not like his smile. They made him put his hands in the air, and they searched him, and stripped him of his pistol. Akira continued to smile, as one of the men put a gun in the middle of his back and marched him off into the trees. How many others accompanied them? Afterwards, Stephen and Konstantin could not remember. Two, three? They listened for a shot, but there was no shot.

Stephen and Konstantin were left waiting by the roadside. When Stephen tried to speak to Konstantin, the guns were raised threateningly. So they said nothing. The men muttered amongst themselves. Stephen tried to observe them, but he could not read them. So much he had heard of the iron discipline of the Khmer Rouge, of their terrorizing of the villages and the countryside, but this bunch was ill-assorted, oddly dressed. Their Chinese rifles were too big for them, and they wore a strange insouciant mixture of denim jackets, camouflage shirts, black trousers, tracksuits, rubber sandals, flat caps, berets, checked scarves. One sported a T-shirt emblazoned with a red image of Angkor, like the one Stephen himself had purchased in Phnom Penh. Another wore a lady's paisley print blouse. A rag-tag and bobtail army, but their weapons were real.

Stephen found himself wondering, quite calmly, if he was about to be killed. One part of him was frozen with terror, another more interesting and unexpected part of him was watching to see what would happen next. He watched as Konstantin, in dumb show, requested permission to get out a cigarette. Permission was granted.

Konstantin offered round the pack. Two young men accepted. Was this good news? The Khmer Rouge are pure and do not accept bribes. But you do not light a match for a man you are about to shoot.

After an immeasurable period of inaction, one of the soldiers who had marched off with Akira returned. He proceeded to inspect the vehicle, removing photographic equipment, radio, petrol cans, tins of food, and dumping them by the side of the road. Konstantin winced as he saw his cameras hit the dust.

They were obliged to leave everything behind, except for one bag each. Stephen interpreted the permission to take a bag as a sign of favour. Rightly, as it turned out.

They were made to walk for some hours, off the road, uphill, along a rough track, through trees. Stephen's ankle began to give him trouble, but he thought it unwise to protest. Where were they off to? A military camp, a secret training school for guerrillas, a killing field? Were they about to find themselves at last face to face with the elusive Pol Pot, or with Ta Mok, or Son Sen, or Nuon Chea, or Som Keng, or any other of those legendary leaders? Had Akira's random telephoning into the air waves prepared them a welcome, had it procured for them the Pulitzer-winning interview of all time, and if so, would they live to file it? Stephen, as he stumped and stumbled uphill, wondered what questions he would ask Pol Pot if he were to find him. He tried to prepare questions, in French.

'Combien d'hommes avez-vous sous votre commandant? Où est le quartier 87? Est-ce que vous bénéficiez de l'appui militaire ou de l'entraînement des SAS ou des Américains? Quels sont vos contacts avec Sihanouk? Votre femme a-t-elle oui ou non étudié Macbeth à la Sorbonne? Êtes-vous mort ou vivant, un ou plusieurs? Est-ce que vous aimiez votre mère, est-ce qu'elle vous aimait? Est-ce que la fin justifie les moyens?'

He counted his footsteps, in French, to measure out the forced march. He recited Rimbaud to himself. He wondered what had happened to Akira. He tried to remember if he and Konstantin had registered any protest about Akira's disappearance, or whether they had simply, silently, like cowards, relinquished him. Should he demand an explanation from Pol Pot?

But when they reached their destination, no military commander was waiting for them. They found themselves in a small, almost deserted hill village. They were greeted by two old women, one young woman, an old man with one leg, an old man with two legs, a few children and some dogs. It was a long way from the rue St André des Arts. It was a long way even from the railway station of Phnom Penh. It was about as far as you could go. There did not seem to be much prospect of an interview about the strategy of guerrilla warfare or the future of Marxist-Leninism here.

And there, their captors abandoned them. And there they were obliged to stay.

In theory, they could perhaps have escaped from their village guards and made off into the landscape, they could have tried to retrace their route to the Hôtel de la Paix. But in practice, they could not move, for the first night, Stephen fell ill. The sickness which had flirted with him in Ho Chi Minh City and sneered at him in the Monorom had taken advantage of a few hours of weakness and fear and exhaustion and had moved back in to possess his entire body. By the morning, he had a high fever, and was moving in and out of delirium.

Over the next three days, most of his hair fell out. He could feel tufts, wisps, still clinging to his cranium.

He lay on a little wooden platform, under a roof of leaves, amidst buzzing flies. From time to time the young woman came to stare at him. She offered him water, which he was afraid to drink. He drank. She offered him green pellets, which he resisted, remembering the oft-repeated advice: Beware the Medicine of the Khmer Rouge.

Konstantin sat cross-legged under the thatch. He stuck with Stephen.

'You must go,' whispered Stephen, from a dry throat. 'You must get out of here. You can send for me later. Go, while you can, before they get back.'

But Konstantin shook his head.

'You will get better soon,' he said, stubbornly. He pointed out that the villagers did not seem hostile. They were doing their best. He and Stephen were both safer here. They did not want dead white men in their hut.

Akira was not mentioned.

Stephen could not eat, but the woman brought small dishes of food to Konstantin. There was not much. The menu at the Hôtel de la Paix had been rich in comparison. Now they were offered shoots, roots, very little rice. Stephen stared at the scanty offerings with dismay. Too late, he realized that he and Konstantin were mouths to feed, they were trouble. They were taking food from the poorest of the poor. They were parasites. This was not what they had intended.

Stephen believed that this was the end of the road, that he was dying. He felt like death. Was it dengue, was it malaria? What did it matter? It was a killer. Would Konstantin catch it, or had his years of travel rendered him immune? His ankle seemed to be infected. Pus gathered round the metal pin. He was puzzled by his own calmness. It was not so bad after all, the end of the road. He was a little depressed by his own acceptance. Had life so little charm for him that leaving it should come so easily? Had he given up? Or was it the illness itself that gave him this lightness, this weightless indifference?

But even as he lay there, he felt a small pride in having got to the other side. It was an end in itself. It was not very interesting, there would be no revelation, no confrontation, no lights from heaven would flash, neither God nor Pol Pot would speak from the burning bush. There would be no message to take back to the shores of the living. There was simply this place. Why trouble oneself with messages? He had got here. Enough books, enough writings, enough reports. Why try to describe the real thing? It was not even very real. It was a shadow of a shadow on the wall of a cave. There was nothing in the locked cabinet. *Laissez passer, laissez passer.*

As he lay there, tuning his breathing laboriously to the incessant monotonous slow rhythmic chirp of a small insect in the dry thatch, as once, an infant, he had tuned it sleepless to the rise and fall of his mother's sleeping breast, those French writers of his youth rose before him from beyond the grave. He recognized them. They had brought him to this pass. They had inspired him, and now they withdrew their breath. They filed past him, and stared at their dying comrade with curiosity. Did they admit him to their company? Or did they turn a cold indifferent eye? There was Rimbaud, the dirty child, tattered and drunk and sodden, his hands in his torn pockets: Rimbaud, who had walked on foot to Charleville, through the lines of Prussians as they marched into Paris; Rimbaud, who had celebrated the Commune by writing his own communist constitution, now lost for ever. There was Edmond Goncourt, the last of the Goncourts, reading night after night from Chateaubriand's *Mémoires d'outre-tombe* to his dying brother Jules (and reading reluctantly, irritably, at times): Edmond Goncourt, dining fastidiously on larks and horse meat as he charted the rise and fall of the Commune, as he noted the bodies of the dead, the marked faces of the condemned, as he worried about the safety of his old books and his *objets de vertu*. There was Malraux, setting off with his wealthy young bride to this very Cambodian jungle where Stephen Cox now lies wasting. There was Gide, embarking for the Congo in middle age for no reason, because he had once said he would, simply to see what he would find there. Leaping, as he had put it, like Curtius into the void.

Beware what you read when young. Beware what you feed upon. It may bring you to this shore, this brink, this bridge.

Stephen asked himself, now, too late, why he had been so obsessed by the Commune, by the Khmer Rouge. The woman stared at him with brown, opaque, impenetrable, expressionless eyes, as silently she set before him another warm shell of water. Was it because he did not love the people? Was it because he feared and hated the people?

He had cashed in on the Commune, he had turned it into fiction and sold it. The Commune had done him proud on the market. Gide had sold the Congo. Malraux had sold the spoils of Angkor. This was what writers did. They seemed to purvey messages, but in truth they sold commodities. Art was nothing but a trading speculation. Rimbaud had sold poetry and skins and gold and ivory and guns and slaves. Rimbaud dreamed up a new communist constitution, and then he had become a seller of men.

Stephen wondered what would happen to the unfinished novel he had left behind in the safe in the Trocadero in Bangkok. How many weeks, months, years would it languish there before it was thrown away or shredded or fell to dust? He did not care what happened to it. It had been thin, bad, tricksy, broken-backed. There had been no way of writing of the preoccupations of this last year.

And Konstantin, sitting over there, patiently, cross-legged, immobile, was he grieving over the loss of his camera, his photographs, his life? Maybe Miss Porntip had been right. Maybe Konstantin was the Angel of Death.

Beyond Konstantin rose the green flanks of forest. The little clearing in the valley was deep, small, lost: a fold, a cleft, a private place. A bald dog with hanging teats scratched its own pink leprous skin. A red eagle circled above. A chicken squawked. A child wailed. Seeds drifted and twirled and descended through the hot air. Insects sang, flies buzzed. Burned tree stumps surrounded the clearing. Where were the men who had slashed them? Had they all gone off with their guns to fight? Had they been killed, purged? This was the death of the village.

Stephen watched the sky, and he watched Konstantin. Konstantin watched Stephen. He too thought that Stephen was dying. He knew he should stay until the end. Hours passed. The sun moved through the sky. Days passed. Konstantin sat it out.

Konstantin knew himself to be neither magician nor hero nor Angel of Death. He was young, dirty, hungry and frightened, and he had a hunch that his luck had run out. He fingered the bullet scar in his shoulder. Would they get him this time? He felt clouds of an old familiar blackness building up, far out, on the rim of the horizon. He was guilty. He had done this thing to Stephen. He had been irresponsible, he had played games, and he had lost. He should never have brought Stephen and Akira together.

He could not make himself meditate, he no longer sat still. Why was Stephen so bloody calm? Konstantin got up, walked around the village, watched silently by the women, the old men, the children. He paced from the tall bamboo grove to the dry paddy. He trod the dry footpaths. He gazed at the tempting green poison globes of the strychnine-tree. He gazed at a buffalo skull, hanging from a branch. He watched the butterflies. He thought he remembered the way back to the road. He was probably only eighty miles, a hundred miles from Phnom Penh, from the Monorom, from the airport. A hundred miles of mass graves.

The blackness bunched and bellied into great storm clouds. Was he condemned to return into that night? He remembered the pain, the horror, far beyond any pain and horror of the body. He had survived once. How many lives were left? He had lost his masterpieces, his photographs of the Old Man and the Boy. They had been taken from him. They would have justified this crazy expedition, these deaths. They would have brought him immortality. But they had gone.

Konstantin did not know what to do. Stephen was getting worse. He had lucid intervals, in which he would embark on long but muddled anecdotes about his brother Jeremy, the jailbird drug-pusher, about his friend Brian Bowen, about an Irish woman who cooked at the Carlton, about American airmen lost in the war. Konstantin could not follow the narrative, the connections. Was Stephen in much pain? It was hard to tell. On the fourth night, he started to speak in French and what Konstantin thought must be Russian. Was it poetry that he droned and mumbled? *'J'ai tant fait patience, qu'à jamais j'oublie . . .'* He looked ghastly, skeletal. He had aged ten years in four days. He had turned a strange deadly yellow colour, the luminous yellow–white of parchment, of old bone. He shone like a corpse candle, like the ghastly Fever Tree of the East with its pale glimmering shredding bark. Had he already entered the death journey, would Konstantin be called upon to read to him from *The Book of the Dead*? Konstantin found himself wishing he had never met him. Why had he spent so much time trying to impress this man?

Stephen moaned and tossed. He said he could no longer see very well. He said there was an espionage balloon ship hovering above them in the sky, a Khmer Rouge balloon made in China. He called out, 'Le radio! Le radio!' and pointed to his bag. Konstantin made a pretence of looking for it, but he knew that the little 2-band Sony was not there, it had been commandeered at the road block, along with anything else of value. Only useless objects had been left, with a few rags of clothing – poems, papers, postcards, a shell necklace, an amulet of finger bones tied with ribbon. Zipped into an inner pocket, a passport, an old Air France boarding card, a few hotel bills.

Stephen thought he could hear the radio. 'Shh,' he said. 'Listen!' He thought he could hear the Book of Revelations. 'Listen, it is the Seventh Seal!' he murmured.

Then he fell into what appeared to be a coma. Konstantin could not bear this any longer. He felt himself about to crack. He would have to leave. He would kid himself that he was not out to save himself, that he was going to get help. Without medical help, Stephen would die. It was his duty to go.

Konstantin left in the first light of dawn, picking his way back down the track with careful footsteps. Stephen lay unconscious, breathing dangerously, noisily, from his thin chest. He was quite bald.

*

Konstantin stumbles through undergrowth, his legs scraped and bleeding, leeches attached to his ankles.

Konstantin hangs himself in a Meditation Cave.

Konstantin steps on a mine.

Konstantin sits on the back of a bullock cart, smiling stupidly as he hitches his way towards the capital.

Konstantin sits in a roadside bar drinking a Trente-trois and smoking a Liberation cigarette with Mitra Akrun.

Konstantin is bitten by a snake. Konstantin is eaten by a tiger. Konstantin sends a postcard home.

*

Stephen dreams again of the man with the skull. The man keeps the skull in a little black bag. He gets it out to show it to Stephen. He makes its jaws move with his fingers, and laughs. Alas, poor Yorick, says the skull. Alas, poor Akira. The skull is one of many. Three million, two million, one million, eight hundred thousand. Who is counting? Are not five sparrows sold for two farthings, and not one of them is forgotten before God? Stephen sees his mother across a widening flood. She sits in silence, vast, obese, beside the blood. He runs towards her, stumbling, to be gathered to her great breasts, her warm lap, but she turns towards him and tells him she is a phantom, he may not touch. Her face dissolves in fire, her flesh sweats away, the skull glows incandescent like the bald egg of a phoenix. The hairs of our head may be numbered, but she is skull, she is bald.

'Mummy, mummy,' he calls (as the condemned child cried for his

360

mother on the scaffold). 'Mummy, mummy,' cries the fat mound of clothes, the glowing skull. Stephen struggles against the grave clothes. He is strapped and bound, wound like a mummy, already bandaged for burial. The leper king smiles.

*

The woman comes and stares at Stephen. Then she goes away again. She thinks he will open his eyes soon, and find he is alone.

She is right. Stephen, the crisis over, begins to recover. The woman brings him a little watery soup. He sips it, and, feebly out of politeness, tries to smile. She stares. He cannot read her expression. She has no expression.

When she comes back the next time, or perhaps the next, she brings him a handful of green leaves in a coconut shell. She gestures that he should eat them. He shakes his head. She takes them away.

In the evening, she returns with a fresh selection of the same green leaves. Again, she offers them. Again, he declines.

In the morning, she is there again, with the leaves. She squats before him and speaks to him, gently. She urges him to eat. She has a new insistence, a new urgency, a confidence. And Stephen, gathering courage, takes one and crumples it in his fingers. It is a sharp, small, crisp, pinnate leaf, like a tiny fern. It smells pungent, bitter, not unpleasant. It smells medicinal.

The woman picks one up herself, and chews it. She gestures once more to Stephen. Obediently, he begins to nibble at her offering. It tastes strong, but good.

She nods. She is pleased. She smiles. Her smile comes from far, far away and long ago, and it gathers slowly and breaks in the foreground of her face. She leans forward and pats Stephen's arm.

Days pass, and Stephen continues to recover. He can stand, he can take a few steps, though he is still very weak. The swelling of his ankle has subsided. The hours pass evenly, rhythmically. The woman is pleased with his progress. She brings him little gleanings from the forest. He trusts her and he eats.

With returning strength comes returning clarity. He looks back on his past life, on his many failures. He had failed in love, and now he has failed also in fear. This test too has found him wanting.

He marvels, now, not that he has failed, but that he had ever been viable. Could it be that he had written all those books, had turned out those crude pseudonymous action-packed thrillers, those fastidious teasing tableaux of historical pastiche? He cannot do it any more. The gods have left him. He lies here, on a platform in a bamboo hut, and admits it. He can even remember moments at which he thought he heard them depart from him, with a twang as of a broken string, with a diminishing cry as of a bird flying south, with a stiff creak as of the quills of passing wings over the salt marsh. A moment on Westminster Bridge at high tide, a moment at low tide walking on a shingle beach in autumn, a moment sitting on a bench in Regent's Park, a moment over grilled sardines in Bertorelli's. A sigh, a creak, a moan, and the spirits had passed on.

Had he betrayed his gifts? It all seems very small and faraway, that world of books and ambition. Who cared? He himself does not care. But what else is there that is of importance?

There is this place. The woman brings him a handful of seeds, and sits by him as he eats. She brings him an egg. It is a prize, a treasure. He eats it with reverence. She smiles. She brings him a boiled frog. He eats. It is delicious.

Stephen reads and rereads his volume of Rimbaud, and wonders who he would now have been if, at the age of sixteen, he had been seduced by Mozart, or Titian, or Tolstoy. He remembers his choices for *Desert Island Discs*, and tries to replay them in his head. Monteverdi, Lotte Lenya, Sibelius, Vinteuil, the Grateful Dead. Roy Plomley had thought them a little highbrow, but the musical technician in the recording box had enjoyed them and complimented him on his selection. What had he chosen for his book? It had not been the poems of Rimbaud. Proust, perhaps. And for his luxury? Claret, he thinks he recalls. A case of claret. Oh yes, relentlessly highbrow. Relentlessly elitist.

Rimbaud had capitulated at the last, poor bugger. No man of the people he. Dying of gangrene, writing back to Martinet Mother for cash. In comparison, Stephen has not done that badly. He is still solvent, in theory. Though his funds are not much use to him here. One thing at least he had achieved: a world without money. It is a small triumph.

He thinks of his own mother, and wonders if she is dead yet, or if she lingers mindlessly on. The vision of her old, witless, incontinent, had pained him, despite his shield of indifference. He had visited her only twice. What would have been the point? She had not recognized him. She had altogether forgotten him. He hopes she is dead.

He thinks of Hattie Osborne, and the wife of the French minister, and Deirdre Kavanagh, and Porntip Pramualratana, and all the other mad bad women he has known. Are they perhaps all one and the same woman? All leaves of one green tree? They swim together in memory, they merge, they echo and recede. Perhaps there are no individuals, no singularities. There is only the tree, the river, the forest. Which woman was it who lay below him in that lofty hotel room in Milan? Who was it that licked and sucked him in a four-poster bed in a mews behind Harrods? Who was that woman who sang so plaintively in that doss house in Normandy? Whose hand wore that signet ring, whose throat that locket? Whose stained torn violet lace mesh knickers had hung upon the brass doorknob all through the night?

He should have deafened himself to these sirens. He should have strapped himself to the post. He should have spoken openly to Liz Headleand. She could have saved him from the flux, from the shadowy vanishings and from the dim arcades of repetition. She would have forced particularity upon him. She would have organized him, and given him credence, and kept him alive.

His mind roved back to his first meeting with Liz, at supper, with Brian and Alix Bowen. Oh yes, he had liked Liz. He had taken to her. A clever woman, confident, full of her own opinions. An adult woman, an embodied woman. There had been nothing insubstantial about her. Solid, fleshly, she had eaten her food and licked her fingers. She had husbands, children, a large house. She had bank accounts, investments, employees, employment. She was plugged into Reality and Property. He had enjoyed her company. He had enjoyed watching her eat. He sees her dip a macaroon into her coffee, and lift it to her lips.

The woman brings him a brown tea with floating twigs that makes him feel high. She crouches by him, watching with interest to see if it will go to his head. Then she smiles. She tells him that it is very, very good for him. She persuades him to let her dab at his bad ankle with a grey paste and moss. He lets her do what she wants. He has abandoned all hopes of hygiene. The paste is cooling, comforting. Her hands are firm and gentle. The throbbing in his ankle abates. She is very kind. He cannot be an attractive spectacle – thin, lank, pink, burned, bald. She must find him gross. Yet she is kind.

In dumb show, he asks her name. She says she is called Chan Tu. He repeats the name until he has it by heart. She has become a person. She tries out the word 'Stee-ven' until she has captured it.

Why is she being so gentle with him? Is it her nature? Is Chan Tu, he wonders, the Alix Bowen type? If she had been born in England, would she have gone around in winter in a woolly hat, and taken in stray dogs?

He smiles to himself, at this somewhat reductive recollection of Alix. He remembers his last visit to the Bowens, who had been his only good friends. He had been to see them in their new rented home in Yorkshire. It had been bitterly cold. He tries to remember the sensation of cold, but it is not easy. He had been giving a lecture at the university on the use of fact in historical fiction, and at the reception afterwards – suddenly it returns to him – he had been tackled by an extraordinary woman clad in bottle-green sequins, who had simultaneously invited him home to bed down with her that very night and proposed to him that he might like to use her husband's studies of Celtic Britain as the basis for his next novel. He had declined both offers, but had been impressed by her panache. She had been in the Hattie Osborne mould. Perhaps she *was* Hattie Osborne? Perhaps she was Hattie Osborne's sister?

Alix, interrogated later that evening over a reddish-coloured stew, had identified this temptress as the Madame Bovary of Northam, the wife of a television archaeologist called Kettle. Alix had spoken up for Fanny Kettle. She said she was really very nice, and anyway what was wrong with propositioning visiting lecturers? Some of them are glad of a free bed for the night, she says. She must, she says, in parenthesis, remember to find him a hot-water bottle. It is bloody arctic up there in the spare room. Stephen may be used to spartan conditions, she says, but she can assure him it's appreciably colder up here than down on Primrose Hill.

The conversation had then moved on to Pol Pot, and whether one could use monsters in fiction. Alix mentioned Heathcliff, and Charlotte Brontë's apologia on behalf of Emily. Brian spoke of George Steiner's play about Hitler. A Good Time conversation. It was during this evening that they had spoken of the concept of Good Time and Bad Time. Brian attributed it to Steiner. Stephen thought it came from William Shawcross. (Both were right.)

So, is he any the wiser now than he had been then, in that suburban drawing room? Has he learned anything about the lost years of this country? Has he been able to step into Bad Time? Is *this* Bad Time, this quiet, dying village? Has he stepped through the permeable membrane without even noticing the frontier?

Chan Tu brings him a delicate little snack of grilled white grub. He eats.

Stephen Cox replays to himself the moments when one time had seemed to fold into another, when he had seemed about to step across. As Mme Savet Akrun for years replayed the sound of spade on skull, the moment by the fire in the clearing; as Charles Head-leand replayed in his memory the sudden news of the car crash that had killed his first wife, and replayed on video the death of Dirk Davis.

Stephen sees the tank on the road near the border, the approach of the blue tin truck. He sees Akira's face as he brakes at the road block, as he takes in the motley armed assembly confronting the hired car. Had Akira stepped through the veil at that confrontation? Had he walked away into Bad Time with a gun in the small of his back? Or had the shield of faith defended him from pain and doubt as it had defended martyrs at the stake or on the rack? Had Akira marched off into the certainty of immortality?

Stephen knows he does not know the answers. They are not available to him.

One night, he thinks he hears the sound of gunfire, of explosives. But as the commotion moves nearer, he realizes it is not shelling. It is a storm. Lightning splits the sky, and deafening cracks of thunder bounce and ricochet from steep hillside to steep hillside. Great swathes of electric silver-blue pick out the tall bamboo grove, the abandoned terraces, the mango-tree, the strychnine apples, as by a searchlight. Looking across the compound Stephen sees Chan Tu crouching at the entrance of her hut. She has made herself very small, and her hands and arms are wrapped around her head. She rocks a little, backwards and forwards. Is she afraid? Should he call out to her to comfort her? The light comes and goes, picking her out, losing her. A child shrieks in the distance, a dog or a wolf howls. And as Stephen watches, he sees Chan Tu rise to her feet. There, in the violent magnetic brilliance, she begins to dance. It is a simple dance. She bends, sways, raises her arms. Her ankles are sturdy and supple, her body compact. Her face is expressionless. And as she dances, there is a sudden rattle, and hailstones begin to clatter down out of the hot air. They fall like hard white pellets of celestial ammunition. Then, as suddenly, they stop, leaving a thin icing over the hard dry red earth. The atmosphere chills for an instant, then heats again, but the pellets do not dissolve. They carry with them the diamond hardness of the perpetual cold five miles above. Chan Tu dances. Is she entranced? It is a strange sight. The swaying woman, the hut, the flailing trees, the dark sky, the tropical hailstones, the white glitter. Stephen feels an intense happiness. It is a vision, and he has seen it. It is the heart of darkness, it is the heart of light. It is beyond irony and beyond parody. It is doomed, but he has seen it. And then the rains come.

In the morning, when Chan Tu brings him his food, she sits down by him for a while. She tells him by gestures that the storm was a freak, a miracle. Never, at such a time of year, such weather. It is good. The rain was good. The seasons alter, says Stephen. It is caused by global warming. He mimes global warming — spray cans, refrigerators, motorcars. They both laugh. They are innocents.

They are friends now. She hangs around, and he shows her his stamp collection and his postcards. She expresses particular approval of Prince Charles and Princess Di, but she may be being polite. Does she know who they are? It seems she does, but perhaps she mistakes them for Sihanouk and his wife, for one of Sihanouk's sons and his bride, for Ronald and Nancy Reagan. He presents her with a Vietnamese stamp portraying oyster mushrooms and three rather dull views of an oil rig, and assures her she may keep them. He is too mean to part with the Kampuchean stamps. They are interesting, some of them he suspects are very rare, and he has gone to much trouble to collect them. They may even have cost him his life. He conceals from her attention the variant portraits of Ho Chi Minh, in case she should share the Khmer hatred of the Vietnamese. He wishes he could have found out whether there had ever been a philatelic rendering of Pol Pot.

That evening, the men come back. They arrive on foot, still

carrying their battered AK47s, and stand around, smoking, talking, glancing towards Stephen on his platform from time to time as they cross-question Chan Tu and the old men. The boy in the paisley shirt offers Stephen a Liberation cigarette. He accepts, gratefully. How will Chan Tu explain the disappearance of Konstantin? Have they already rediscovered Konstantin? Chan Tu becomes animated, he suspects in his own defence. She is his champion. The whole population of the hamlet turns out to watch. The bald dog scratches, the children squat, the old men and old women chew with hard red gums and stare. They are deciding his fate.

That evening, with his bowl and with a couple of cigarettes, she brings a message. She is not pleased by it. She frowns, anxiously. The message is one word, which she repeats again and again until he has got it. 'Klee-neek,' she says. 'Klee-neek.' In the end, he gets it. They are going to take him to the clinic.

So he packs his bag, and the next morning he submits to removal. He has no option. How long has he been here? He has no idea. He is still very weak, and does not know how far he will be able to walk. It is hardly likely that these men will bother to carry him if he collapses. It would be much less effort to kill him, and they may prefer the spade on the head. Why waste a bullet? But having got this far, maybe they will persevere. He remembers Konstantin's optimistic view that a dead white man is trouble. The Khmer Rouge are not looking for white enemies now, they are looking for white friends. Surely they have kept him alive too long to want to kill him. To Chan Tu he has become almost a pet. He is bald and old and sick and harmless. These people are simple people, country people. Surely there is nothing in him to psyche them up into violence?

One million, two million dead. Corpses, skulls, killing fields. How can it all have happened? How could a French infection from the Sorbonne drive this quiet, faraway peasant people mad?

As he packs his few possessions, he thinks of fellow-traveller

Malcolm Caldwell, shot in the official guest house on Monivong Avenue in Phnom Penh after his final friendly interview with Pol Pot. Who had shot him, and why? The Khmer Rouge, the Vietnamese? It is still disputed. His body had been returned via Peking to London and given a martyr's burial. In 1966, Malcolm Caldwell had given a fund-raising garden party in Blackheath for the Viet Cong. It had raised £26 7s. 8d. It had been a long journey, from that Blackheath garden to death in 1978 in Phnom Penh. Had he had time to recognize his killers? Nobody knows. Nobody will ever know.

Who shot Malcolm Caldwell, and who will give the *coup de grâce* to Stephen Cox? Will it be one of these young men? Their rusty rifles are too big for them, but they look as though they have seen good service, and the cartridge belts they sport are not for show.

Stephen thanks Chan Tu for her good care of him. He says he is sorry he cannot express his gratitude. He ventures the view that no nurse in any clinic can be as kind as she. He says he is sorry he distrusted her medicines. He says she has given him a lasting happiness. She has given food she could ill spare. He will not forget this either.

She smiles in reply, but she is anxious. She is proud of her ministry of bitter herbs, she is proud of her patient's recovery, she does not trust the clinic. In her view the clinic is a no-good place, a death trap. People die there. But what can she do? The men say he must go. They say he is Russian adviser, important hostage, in Vietnamese employ. She does not believe this, but who will listen to her?

She speaks to him in her own language, wishing him well. She tells him he has been a welcome guest, she apologizes for the poverty of her hospitality. They bow, gravely, to one another, and she gazes after him as he sets off with uncertain steps down the hillside track. She is not happy about his ankle. He turns, and waves. She lifts one hand in salute. She wonders if he will make it as far as the clinic. She feels sorry for the old Englishman.

*

It must be admitted that Liz Headleand embarked on her morning's shopping expedition with Miss Porntip with extreme reluctance. She felt both nervous and irritable at the prospect of the waste of time. Her money she had no intention of wasting. But she knew she had to placate Miss Porntip, or she would never get her visa. So off she went.

It must also be admitted that by the time she tried on her seventh jewel, she was hooked.

The first ring rode with difficulty over her knuckle, and its oval red stone sat on her finger bone uncomfortably, glaring at her from its ugly golden claws like an angry carbuncle. Her skin wrinkled and puckered unbecomingly around it. Liz looked at it with puritanical disapproval. Miss Porntip shook her head. The Chinese gentleman shook his head as she dragged it off, and opened another little red velvet bag. Liz wanted to leave. She felt frightened and foolish. Shopping for personal items always made her feel foolish and impatient, and this kind of shopping seemed the apotheosis of all shopping folly.

The second ring she disliked as much, although Miss Porntip liked it more. The central ruby was surrounded by a perky little frill of diamonds. 'Cushion ruby, millegrain-set,' murmured Miss Porntip. At the sound of these words, Liz began to take slightly more interest. Scholarship always interested her, and Miss Porntip was clearly a scholar of rubies. Liz stared at the gem. She had never really looked at a gem in her life. Its deep claret flame glowed back at her from its silly border. She remembered the little Victorian ring of seed pearls and sapphires with which Edgar Lintot all those decades ago had pledged his troth. A modest, pretty little ring, prelude to an immodestly brief and acrimonious marriage. Where was it now? In a little blue ruffled plush box somewhere, in the back of a drawer? Lost? Stolen? On Sally Headleand's finger?

The third ring was a ruby and diamond cluster: a central diamond was surrounded by a border of seven little golden hearts, each heart set with three tiny rubies. Liz liked the ring. It had a story to it. It had charm. But it looked ridiculous, on the finger of a woman of her age. It was a romantic ring. Liz shook her head, sadly. Back it went into its little velvet ribbon-noosed sack. Liz touched the silver locket at her throat, the twin to the locket on her sister Shirley's throat, her only inheritance from her unknown father. Charles had bought his third wife Lady Henrietta a splendid ring, a fancy yellow-brown diamond. He had never bought Liz a ring at all. He had wedded her with Edgar's old wedding ring. They had been above such things, Charles and Liz, in the freestyle sixties.

The fourth ring, another cushion-shaped ruby ('Collet-set,' murmured Miss Porntip) began to arouse prickles of desire in Liz Headleand. Little spiny injections of longing and greed and female indignation penetrated through her finger and into her bones. Why had none of the men in her life thought her worthy of ornament? They had got good use out of her, and all for nothing. What had Roy Strangeways given her? A cameo, and probably not even an antique. And the pin had come off after its second outing. Still, he had been more generous than Jules, who had thought he could get away with a painted Indian bangle.

'Burmese ruby,' insinuates Miss Porntip, 'Burmese, pigeon-blood.'

And as for that bounder Philip, he had never given her anything at all, except for a black eye. In fact, come to think of it, he still owed her £1,500. An expensive diversion, Philip had been. But (Liz Headleand smiled to herself, as she twisted the ring and watched its deep flames glow and sparkle in its cavernous depths) – but he had been worth it. She didn't regret it. No, one wouldn't expect to get jewels out of Philip. One was lucky to get offered a cup of tea. He had had other functions.

The fifth was a delicate spray, the sixth a heavy Duchess of Windsor 1930s Boucheron buckle design with, as she was informed, calibré-cut rubies and pavé-set diamonds. Neither of them pleased or suited, though both interested. Liz was beginning to see the point of jewels. Little prickles of desire entered her fingers. She was infected. No longer did the stones frighten and repel. They cast their spell, they enchanted.

The seventh ring was a solid, octagonal, step-cut ruby with a plain border of baguette diamonds. Liz repeated the magic words, and memorized them, as she inspected the stone. It sat firmly upon her finger, as though it had always been there, at once plain and opulent, severe and dignified.

'Very good price, also,' said Miss Porntip, as Liz twisted reluctantly at the ring. 'Is very good, very good on hand. Strong hand, strong jewel. Ruby is antidote to evil thoughts and all excess of luxury and poisons.'

Liz thought she would buy the ruby. She would buy it, and make Charles pay up. He could afford it. Well, she assumed he could afford it. Dared she ask the price? She knew that once she asked the price, she was sunk.

She asked the price, and sank. It cost less than her air fare, she reasoned, and unlike her airfare it was redeemable and would last for ever.

'Is very good price,' repeated Miss Porntip. 'In London, in Paris, in New York, four to five times more. He give you certificate.'

Liz succumbed. The ring, now hers, remained upon her finger, the certificate was tucked into her bulging bag.

Shopping fever overtook her. By the time she and Miss Porntip sat down to their little light lunch in the Hotel Nirvana she had purchased not only a ruby ring, but also a necklace of lapis lazuli for Sally, a cornelian pendant for her step-granddaughter Cornelia, and an assortment of silk ties for various stepsons and ex-husbands. She had also ordered a jacket of saffron silk for herself, to be made up and delivered to the Oriental that evening.

Overcome with emotion and exhaustion, she sat in the coffee

shop of the Hotel Nirvana and sipped a long fruit punch in a
frosted glass stuck about with orchids. Miss Porntip was proud of
her. She had done well. She had done so well that she was allowed
to move on to the next phase, of serious discussion of visa for
Vietnam and Kampuchea. Miss Porntip, it seemed, had already been
making inquiry. She had set things in motion. She would like to see
Liz's passport, please.

Liz took out her passport and laid it upon the turquoise table
cloth. Miss Porntip picked it up, as Alix Bowen had done, and
inspected it.

'Hmm,' she said, 'is pity you not wife, Liz. Is easier with wife of
person. This Elizabeth Headleand person, why is she seeking Mr
Cox?'

'I could be his sister?' volunteered Liz, who had been brooding
on this issue herself.

Miss Porntip considered. It was not a bad idea, she agreed.
Sisters are okay people. But see here, maiden name, Ablewhite.
Why not Cox?

'Oh, surely the Kampucheans won't spot that,' said Liz, whose
shopping euphoria had clothed her with confidence. 'We can tell
them the customs are different in England. They won't even know
which name is which. I don't understand their name system, why
should they understand ours?'

'Okay, okay,' said Miss Porntip, as she tucked heartily into her
hamburger and salad. But Liz continued to stare at her passport
with suspicion. A memory was returning to her, a recollection of
the first time she had acquired a passport in the name of Headleand.

It had all been most unsatisfactory. She had taken in to Petty
France the document which briefly recognized her first marriage to
Edgar Lintot, Edgar of the sapphires and seed pearls, and had
requested a new one to certify her the wife of Charles Headleand of
the borrowed bond. There had been some urgency, as there was a
question of a trip to Paris, and Liz, deeply in love with Charles, had

wished to legitimize, to celebrate the journey. She had gone as instructed, armed with birth certificate, old marriage certificate, divorce certificate and new marriage certificate: she had queued patiently, as instructed. She had childishly looked forward to receiving a brand-new dark blue leathery gold-embossed imperial British passport, which would declare her with ceremony to be Charles's wife, which would banish for ever the pale mistaken shade of angry Dr Elizabeth Lintot. A new name, a new life, a new authorization. But to her dismay, instead of cancelling the old and presenting her with the new, the woman at the counter had simply written in blue ball-point, beneath the words 'Dr E. Lintot', in the white oval space, 'Now Dr Headleand'. Not even a Dr C. Headleand. And inside, in the same hand, she had scribbled, in an unsatisfactory mixture of upper and lower case script, the same rubric.

Liz had not liked this at all, but had not known how to complain, so petty were her objections. She had objected not merely to being condemned to travel as an appendage of her first husband for another nine years after only nine months of marriage, but also to the inelegance of the script. The ill-born Liz was a snob about many things and she had not liked this ill-formed writing that had announced her change of marital title. It had seemed an ill omen. Her dignity had suffered. She had been glad when that old passport had expired.

Her current one (also, as Alix had remarked, a little misleading) had only another two years to run. She stared at it, and ate a mouthful of chicken and lemon grass. Then she took a ball-point pen from her bag, and beneath Dr E. Headleand she wrote firmly and elegantly 'Now Mrs S. Cox'. She felt quite cheered up by tampering with this piece of property belonging to Her Majesty's Government in the United Kingdom. She felt sure that her act of bravado would lead her to Stephen. And if she ran into any trouble trying to leave the country, that two-faced slug Grimswade could get himself off his backside and get her out of it.

Miss Porntip was impressed by this decisive move. Yes, they would tell the embassies that Liz was in search of her husband. Why not? But had not Liz been a little too precipitate? In her wish to claim wifely status, she had denied herself doctorly status. Why not *Dr* S. Cox? 'Doctor is good, doctor is useful,' Miss Porntip pointed out.

Liz agreed. She could not explain why she had thus impulsively struck herself off the medical register. But, she said, it would not be wise to deface the document twice. Once, yes: twice would raise eyebrows.

As they made their way through the shopping arcades to Miss Porntip's air-conditioned limo, Liz looked around her with a small renewal of astonishment. Had it looked like this when Stephen and John Geddes had met here for a drink? And was it true that they had then proceeded to a brothel?

*

Miss Porntip works wonders. Doors open for her, men in uniform leap to attention, documents write themselves for her in magic ink. From thin air she conjures a ticket to Hanoi on Thai Airways. She gives names of contacts in Hanoi who will obtain tickets from Hanoi to Saigon. Pronto-pronto. From Saigon, Liz must telephone her, Miss Porntip, and she will come with lover in executive jet to collect. Executive jet cannot go to Hanoi. Miss Porntip cannot go to Hanoi. But Saigon, yes. Saigon different kettle. They will meet again in Saigon. Two days', three days' time.

Liz Headleand thinks of Miss Porntip with longing as she leans on her bedroom window sill in Hanoi and gazes at the street scene beneath. She really does not like Hanoi. It is a dump. She hates her hotel room, with its bleak furniture. She has a huge, claw-footed bath and bathroom to herself, but she cannot find a proper lavatory. Her only consolation is the knowledge that Stephen stayed here, in this very room. She has his hotel bill, and she has also located the source of one of Stephen's jottings. Chiselled into the desk, she finds the unfinished phrase, *La Guerre n'est jamais* . . . It justifies her journey.

Well, n'est jamais *quoi*, she wonders, as she sucks hungrily at her cigarette. 'All that it's cracked up to be?' 'As bad as you think it is?' 'Much fun?' 'An answer to your problem?'

So this is socialism. Liz hates it. It is the past, and does not work. She can tell that this had once been a good, prosperous French hotel. It is finished. Or almost finished. It has reduced her. It has even made her lose her temper. Anxious about the tap water and the iced water in the bedroom Thermos (how can she tell if it has been boiled properly?), she had tried to purchase mineral water at the bar downstairs. The young woman had shaken her head in obstinate bewilderment, had proffered beer and various juices. Liz had refused them, had insisted on water, without success. She had heard herself shouting, 'Water! Water! I want some water!' like an angry old blimp, like a Home Counties bully, like an outraged upper-class matron from a sitcom. She had shocked herself, though she had produced no effect at all upon the impassive woman. And now she sips, disconsolately, at neat brandy, and wonders whether the sterilization tablets she has sunk into the Thermos can be trusted.

She has appointments for the morning, with various officials, to discuss the disappearance of her so-called husband. For more than twenty years now Americans have been trying to trace missing prisoners of war. Why should she have any better luck?

She feels rotten. She puts herself to bed.

In the morning, as she visits the nearest lavatory she can find, armed with a box of tissues, she is appalled to discover that she seems to be starting a menstrual period. Now this cannot be. She has not menstruated for nearly five months, and for three years before that only intermittently. She is well into her fifties. She had assumed all that was over and done with. Why now? She sits there, in the clean tiled white cubicle, in disbelief. It is shock, she supposes, or the heat. She should have heeded the warning backache.

Returning to her room, she contemplates the problem. She is of course unprovided with sanitary protection. It is likely that the flow will be light, but by no means certain. The last period she can remember, which had caught her out in a conference in York, had been unexpectedly heavy. Her brief acquaintance with Hanoi as shopping centre had not suggested that tampons or even sanitary towels would be readily available. A few months' research might of course reveal a supply, but she has not got a few months. She has got an hour before she goes out to see the Minister for the Press, or whatever he is called.

She wonders if there might be any tampons lingering in the secret pockets of her suitcase, then remembers that her suitcase is in Bangkok. She has brought only her overnight bag. She rummages in that, without hope and without success. So the ancient Egyptians used moss? She wishes she had not parted with her copy of *Cosmopolitan*.

Her last hope is her handbag. It is a large, old, voluminous handbag, with several zipped sections. Who knows what may linger on in its manifold and complex interiors?

Imagine the handbag of Liz Headleand, the handbag described by Alix Bowen as unworthy.

It is made of a slightly pocked and dubious pale brown leather with canvas insertions. It was once rectangular, but has settled into a shapeless lumpy sagging organic droop. It has an adjustable shoulder strap attached by two worn yellow metal loops. It has two zips to two separate compartments, and a flap secured by a buckled fastener adorned with a metal logo which its owner has never paused to examine. Its yellowish stitching is in some way suggestive of horses. It is stained with leakage from felt-tip pens. It is scratched and weathered. Some of it gleams dully from rubbing against its owner's flank. It is very heavy.

When opened, as Liz now opens it, it reveals a jumble of objects. A defaced passport, a pink-and-purple orchid-featuring Thai Air ticket, a silver-walleted Executive Class Air France ticket, a booklet of travellers cheques, a frayed leather purse with coins of many realms caught in its bared metal teeth, an envelope of paper currencies, an address book adorned with a Gainsborough duchess, a notebook bearing a Union Jack, and various other loose-floating pieces of card and paper, some lined, some yellow, some blue, some dog-eared, some neat and some scribbled, all containing potentially useful information. Two torn-out Yellow Pages with the telephone numbers of the curtain makers and soft furnishers of North London. A plastic tub of aspirins, advertised by a sweetly smiling nurse. Two lipsticks, one in a newish gilt-edged smart dark blue hexagonal Christian Dior container, one an aged cheapo nameless brand with a transparent sheath revealing a gritty orange shade that Liz has never liked. A yellow metal powder compact and a blunt blue eyeliner which has lost its cap. Several tissues, in various stages of crumpled decomposition, and a strawberry-spotted Liberty print handkerchief, presented to Liz by Xanthe Headland two Christmases ago. Three pairs of glasses, one for reading, one for surveying the world, and one for protection from the sun. A bunch of keys, comprising car key and ex-car key and the key to Charles's flat, but not, alas, a suitcase key. A book of postage stamps and a flattened empty cardboard packet which had once enclosed some mentholated throat sweets. A red plastic comb and a blue plastic comb. A Hyatt Regency ball-point pen, a red felt-tip, and a green Glowpen. Some safety pins, a paperclip, some wooden toothpicks. A cheque book and a seashell. An unidentifiable white pill and a rubber band. Some bits of fluff.

There is nothing very helpful here, but Liz has hopes of the important back pocket. She unzips it, discovering her driving licence, plastic credit cards, a map of the car parks of Westminster, visiting cards from people from many lands, a paying-in slip, a British Library reader's card, a blue button, some diarrhoea pellets in silver foil, and Charles Headleand's proposal of marriage, written on the back of a menu offering Chicken Chow Mein at five shillings and sixpence. And there, also, she finds two Tampax and one little pink-packed plastic-backed Sanipad.

Thank God, thinks Liz, that I did not throw away my bag and buy a new one when Alix insulted it.

Her relief is, however, tempered by closer inspection of the tampons. They do not look very hygienic, although they are, luckily, super-absorbent. The paper wrappings are more or less intact, but they are not exactly clean, and they may be *punctured*. They have been in that back pocket for a long long time. The tampons themselves are squashed, but that is no problem.

Oh well, says Liz to herself, I'll just have to take the risk.

Imagine Liz Headleand, sitting listening to the speeches of some minister or other, as she sips a cup of bitter tea. She is not really listening very hard, as he explains that there is no record of a Mr Stephen Cox, but that he will note the name in his files. She is worrying not about death but about leakage. She continues to worry about it, as she is passed from department to department. It is unreal, it is ridiculous. She cannot take in what is said to her, she cannot follow her interpreter. She is bleeding. She is treated with courtesy, with delicacy, but this she does not even notice. The entire male world of communism, Marxist-Leninism, inflation, American imperialism, rice production, exchange mechanisms, statistics, hostages, the CIA, the SAS and the KGB, the Chinese, the KPNLF, Sihanouk, and Hun Sen, war, death, and Ho's marble mausoleum dissolve and fade before the bleeding root of her body, impaled on its grey-white stump. Woman-being, woman-life, possess her entirely. Shames and humiliations, triumphs and glories, birth and blood. Let armies fight and die, let peoples starve. She hopes that the seat of her skirt will not be stained when she rises.

MARGARET DRABBLE

The day is a nightmare. Why is she doing this, for a man she hardly knew?

When she returns to the hotel, she finds two envelopes waiting for her. One contains an air ticket for the next day to Saigon. An evening flight. She gazes at it with rapture and blesses Miss Porntip. She knows there will be tampons in Saigon. There are nightclubs and sunglasses and drugs and corruptions in Saigon, so there must also be sanitation and civilization. She can last until the next evening.

The other contains a letter.

Dear Mrs Cox,

I hear you are inquiring for Stephen. I wish I could meet you to say hello, but they tell me you leave tomorrow and tonight I am working. I am so sorry, but maybe we will meet another time. I met Stephen when he was here with Konstantin. I so much enjoyed his company and so much admired his books. I showed him Hanoi and we had a very pleasant time. I thought it might be of interest to you to know that I had a postcard from Stephen, from Ho Chi Minh Ville, and another one from the Monorom Hotel in Phnom Penh. They came some weeks after he left here. Also (and this is maybe of more significance) I had a postcard quite recently from Konstantin, about four months ago, from Borneo. I was worried because we had not heard from him for so long, but he said he was well. I hope this was true. Perhaps he is still in Borneo. Where Stephen is I do not know. I wish I could be of more assistance. One day perhaps I will be able to invite you to my home. I am guessing that Mrs Cox is not your correct name, but your *nom de guerre* or perhaps I should say *nom de voyage*? Are you perhaps his friend Liz of whom he spoke to me? Forgive my curiosity! I do hope we may meet one day in happier circumstances.

Yours most sincerely, Hong.

This letter greatly impresses Liz. She is impressed by its impeccable grammar, by its luminous intelligence, by its astute recognition of her own veiled identity, and by its relatively hot news of Konstantin. Four months ago is but yesterday. But does it mean she will have to trail on to Borneo?

On reflection, she realizes that somebody has been inspecting her passport (which has been impounded by the ministry) and that the somebody has passed its details on to Hong, whoever Hong may be. Hong has not seen fit to give her address. Liz assumes that Hong is a woman, and never stops to ask herself why. She is so sure that Hong is a woman that she even wonders if she can get hold of her to ask about tampons, but Hong clearly does not judge a meeting at this juncture to be well advised.

Squatting over the huge stained ancient bath, mopping herself in the thin trickle of water from the great green–blue lichenous tarnished brass tap, she feels that a whole hidden world speaks to her through Hong. In this secret city, real lives are led. A buzzing fills her ears, and when she rises to her feet little white veins explode silently. If only she could know what *real* is!

Real is this dark gout of blood. Am I mad, thinks Liz, but could it be that despite the inconvenience, despite the potential embarrassment, despite the mess, despite the fact that my youngest child is well into her twenties: could it be that I am *pleased* that I am bleeding? Pleased that I can do this without hormone replacements?

She thinks of Mme Savet Akrun, and her daughter Sok Sita, and the stories of premature menopause from the camps. And now the birth rate rises. To what end? To its own end. A strange elation fills Liz, as she squats in a bath in Hanoi.

The elation accompanies her on her morning's round, it reunites her with her defaced passport, it sees her off to the airport past the bicycles and bullocks and brick factories and flocks of geese. She is wearing her last tampon, and has lined and padded two pairs of Marks & Spencer's size 16 knickers with a pinned and folded white handkerchief and some paper tissues. The folded handkerchief reminds her of her childhood, but she cannot place the memory. A holiday? But they never went on holidays. Perhaps it is her mother's childhood that she recalls? An ancestral memory?

So Konstantin has been in Borneo. Liz, sitting on the aeroplane, settling down to indulge in a paperback novel, wonders if Rose Vassiliou knew this. And if she did, why didn't she *say*?

She has no idea what she is going to do in Saigon, and she does not care. She fights her way into a taxi, and demands the hotel recommended by Miss Porntip: 'New hotel, modern hotel, American-style hotel, I send message for you book room.'

And lo, the room has been booked. In the name of Cox. Liz, signing the register in her *nom de voyage*, wonders what would have happened if on that evening long ago, in the Italian restaurant, she had said to Stephen Cox, 'You could stay for me.' Would she now indeed be Mrs Cox? She wonders how her friend Esther is coping with married life. She wonders if Charles will ask her to remarry him. Vaguely erotic speculations chafe against the uncomfortable thickness of her padded pants. The ambience of the hotel is sexy and suggestive. She walks through the foyer towards the lift with her bag and her key, and feels a certain electricity. A broad dark-suited businessman stares at her openly over his newspaper. A couple of girls in shining dresses whisper at a small table. A boy in uniform smiles and bows deeply as he pushes a button for her.

As she stands there waiting, she notices a woman reading a book. A white woman, in a weathered cream safari suit, with her hair tied back by a brown scarf. She is wearing flat leather thonged sandals. She too is on the look-out, although she is reading with some attention. Liz peers for the author and title of the book, as she always does. She is not wearing her glasses, but nevertheless she manages to make out that the book is by Stephen Cox. It is not a jacket she knows – an American edition, perhaps? It is *Barricades*, his Commune novel, and it portrays (she peers more openly, risking a

THE GATES OF IVORY

conspicuous angle of the head and neck) a bare-breasted woman with a red flag. Marianne, no less.

And then the lift arrives.

Liz, in her modern anonymous hotel room, as she unpacks, and rearranges her underwear, wonders if this is much of a coincidence. She wonders if it is a coincidence with or without meaning. She wonders if the woman is enjoying the book. (She herself is very much enjoying her Barbara Vine.) She wonders if she should try to strike up a conversation with her over a drink, to while away the rest of the evening? It is a comfort to her, to have seen Stephen's novel. It is also exciting. Tired though she is, she thinks she will go downstairs in search of adventure. The terrain is known and unknown. She will not simply put herself to bed.

When the smartened, refreshed, pink-lipsticked blue-eyelined Liz returns to the foyer, the woman reading Stephen Cox has vanished. Liz is not much put out. Other eyes are willing to meet hers. She wanders around, noting that there is a little shop which sells newspapers, magazines and toiletries. It is shut, but it says it will open at nine in the morning, and she believes it. Nine will do. The flow, so far, is not heavy.

She is offered a choice of bars, a coffee shop, a restaurant. The hotel is not as glitzy as the Nirvana nor as gracious as the Oriental, but it is a damned sight better than the Thong Nhat. She does not feel unpleasantly conspicuous, as she felt in Hanoi. In her new yellow silk jacket with her crimson Jean Muir skirt, she thinks she looks quite chic. She does not mind if people stare.

She settles down in the brighter of the bars, orders herself a brandy and soda, and applies herself to her paperback. From time to time she glances admiringly at her new ruby. She wonders if Miss Porntip will turn up in the morning, as she had promised. She is in that acute state of semi-conscious alertness that often grips one in a public place: she feels she can take in conversations without hearing them, can see without looking, can communicate without words or movement. Her eyes rest on the page, as she registers the configurations and the solitary figures around her. Sombrely dressed Asian executives are plotting over beer, leaning forward into their glass-topped table as they negotiate. Japanese tourists are writing postcards, an American photographer is reading *Newsweek* while trying to pick up a Vietnamese woman, a stout large-featured pale-skinned, pale-haired woman (Russian? German?) stares into space and moves her aching toes in her flat canvas shoes, a young European couple dressed in jeans and Angkor Wat T-shirts hold hands and sip soft drink, and yawn. Other negotiations, other contracts, other conspiracies rustle and breed at the far end of the room, beyond Liz's book-centred vision. Oil, shellac, drugs, cheap labour, tourism. A Frenchman is wondering about the possibility of a Club Med at Pineapple Bay. His Saigonese chum nods and concedes and recedes behind his concealing shades. In the far distance, Liz dimly senses an English presence, but it is too far away for her to distinguish it clearly, and anyway she is approaching the climax of her Barbara Vine. Her attention withdraws its feelers from the room, attaches itself more closely to the page.

But even as she follows the novel to its expert unravelling, she continues to be aware of disturbances and movements around her, and begins to sense that she is herself in some way the object of attention. She does not wish to raise her eyes and risk contact, but she knows that somebody is watching her. Is it the broad business-man seen earlier in the foyer? Is it the American photographer? And is the attention flattering, impertinent, ominous, ignorant, informed? She turns the pages as her suspicion intensifies, and at length cannot resist looking up. She finds herself in sudden, close communion with a Japanese engaged in carrying three drinks from the bar to the far end of the room. His eyes swivel abruptly away, but she has caught him in the act of staring. She knows that he came to the bar in order to stare at her. She watches his receding figure, watches as he joins and merges with a conspiratorially animated group. He is not a tourist, although he carries cameras. His are serious cameras, not holiday cameras. He is a man of work.

Puzzled, she returns to her mystery, and sips her brandy and soda. He had looked at her as though he recognized her, but she knows that she does not know him. She does not know any Japanese photographers. Can he be a Japanese psychiatrist in disguise, an acquaintance from her visit to Japan a hundred years ago?

She knows now that she is being watched, discussed. Her reading is a pretence, although she keeps her eyes down.

She keeps them down even when she senses the deliberate approach of another figure towards her. This is a measured, direct approach, not an oblique one. Somebody from the distant group has risen, and is crossing the room, is standing above her. Somebody says to her, 'Liz Headleand, is that really you?'

Liz looks up and finds herself looking up at the familiar features of her old friend, television documentary man Gabriel Denham.

She allows herself to be surprised, as indeed she is. She had not known what she had expected, but Gabriel had certainly not been it.

'Good God, Gabriel,' she says. 'Whatever are you doing here?'

'It's a long story,' says Gabriel. 'And you?'

'Even longer, I bet,' says Liz.

They gaze at one another silently for a few moments, in multiple appreciation. Liz is glad that she had bothered to change into her yellow silk and her best skirt, that she had taken the trouble to paint her face and comb her hair, for Gabriel is a handsome man and she has fancied him for well on thirty years. He is an old rival of Charles, a friendly enemy, and although his looks are not quite what they were, they have worn well. He is an ostentatiously sexual person, the kind of man who draws the eyes of men and women alike, and he stands there now, a little closer than most would stand, his hands on his hips, his hips thrust slightly forward, his shirt as ever open at the throat, his trousers tight, his whole body declaring, here I am. He smiles with a pleasure and an amusement that are both worldly and fresh. Old intimacies lurk in the wrinkled corners of his eyes. 'Well, Liz my dear,' he presently says, 'this *is* a nice surprise. I couldn't believe it when I saw it was really you. Are you waiting for someone, or will you come and join us?' Oddly, he does not look surprised, but then, perhaps he never does. He plays things cool, does Gabriel.

Liz, at a seated disadvantage, her face slightly too close to Gabriel's crotch, cannot see round him to discover who is comprised in the 'us' that he offers at the far end of the room, but she is in an adventurous mood, a gambling mood, and she thinks it would be folly to decline. She smiles assent, closes her book, reaches for her bag. Gabriel offers his hand to help her from her seat. She takes it, and he heaves her towards him and puts his arms around her and kisses her on the mouth. This has always been his way. He links his arm in hers and starts to walk her towards his table.

'It's the crew, as usual,' he says. 'Well, as usual with variations. We're filming. Or trying to film.'

And, as they approach across the marbled floor, a group comes into focus – the Japanese with cameras, a young Cambodian in jeans, a grey-haired technician, a young woman with short cropped silvery-gold hair and dark glasses, and the safari-suited woman who had been reading Stephen's book. Liz had expected her to be of this party, and she is. They look towards Liz with what she interprets as more than common curiosity. Is it so strange to find an Englishwoman alone in a hotel foyer in Saigon? Surely not. This well-travelled company must have seen odder sights than Liz Headleand drinking brandy and reading Barbara Vine.

But, as she comes within hand-shaking range, she sees there is some strangeness here.

For the table is covered not only with drinks and overflowing ashtrays, as one might expect, but also with copies of the novels of Stephen Cox, and with photographs of Stephen. There is his enigmatic smile, there his white-suited figure, there a Penguin copy and a hardback copy of *Barricades*, there a paperback of his pseudonymous thriller *Mr G*. There are reviews and newspaper cuttings and French translations. And there, most bizarrely, is a London Library book about the Paris Métro with Stephen's name attached. A Stephen dossier lies here, in the Victory Hotel. Liz takes it in, as Gabriel offers introductions.

'My old friend Liz Headleand,' says Gabriel, with that warm, husky proprietary note that suggests more than it reveals. 'This is Oko, this is Bill, this is Chet and this is Jacqueline Lowe.'

Liz can tell that she is meant to respond with admiring recognition to the name of Jacqueline Lowe, the woman she had seen earlier; and although she does not, she manages to shake hands with her in a manner that implies a suitable deference. She is in a state of slight shock over the Stephen display before her. She cannot take in so many new people at once. A chair is pulled up for her, a new round of drinks is ordered by the person called Bill, and explanations begin.

'So, Liz, what brings you to Saigon?' asks Gabriel, again with that slight shadow of precognition in his voice, as though he knows already what the answer will be.

Liz gestures towards the books and papers, and goes straight in.

'I'm looking for Stephen Cox,' she declares, laying all her cards upon the table.

Gabriel, Oko, Chet, Bill, Cathy and Jacqueline Lowe glance at one another. Their group reaction is intense, emotional, confused. She can tell that Gabriel is worried, but that he does not wish to declare his own hand yet.

'But Liz,' he says, playing for time, patting her arm, then suddenly, hotly, squeezing her fingers. 'I didn't know that you and Stephen ever . . . I mean, I didn't know . . .?'

He seems to be uncharacteristically at a loss, but his message, his unfinished question, is clear. Liz realizes that she has hidden cards, but she does not know how to play them.

'No,' she says. 'I never.' Her tone is bright but ambiguous, and can be taken either way. 'But I came to look for him just the same. Somebody had to, we thought.'

Again, that quick, uneasy group reaction.

Liz begins at the beginning. She tells of the parcel, of Hattie Osborne, of the committee meeting, of her journeys. She keeps her tone breezy, and as she proceeds, the group begins to relax, although it continues to listen with unnatural interest. One could not wish for a more attentive audience.

She is in the middle of describing Piet Dieper and the border camps when Gabriel leans forward, takes hold of her hand once more, and interrupts her.

'Stephen's dead, you know,' says Gabriel.

Liz stops her narration, and takes a gulp of her refreshed drink.

'Yes,' she says. 'I know.'

She stares at Gabriel, who forces himself to stare back, with an expression delicately adjusted to cover the range between sympathy to a bereaved lover or sympathy to a good friend. Liz herself is not quite sure which she is. Either way, the news, if it is news, is no shock, and tears, if tears there will be, are not required yet.

Jacqueline, who turns out to be Australian, takes up the other side of the story. As she speaks, her name begins to register, and Liz's memory slowly, as from a dissolving capsule, releases the information that she is the journalist who, some years earlier, had crossed the lines and returned with a coup interview with Khmer Rouge leaders. *Time* magazine had bought it, and Liz had read it at the dentist's. Now Jacqueline reports that she and Gabriel had been filming in Cambodia. She had used her contacts and got over again. They had film of resistance fighters, they had an interview with Som Keng, they had film of a Khmer Rouge clinic. And as they filmed, they kept hearing stories about a white man, a tall white man who had been found in a village and who had died in the clinic. Their friend here, Chet, is their interpreter. Chet, tell Liz what we found.

Chet takes over. Yes, they had heard these stories. They had been looking not for a white man but for a crazy Japanese, Akira Tanaka, who had disappeared, but they had found instead the trail of Stephen Cox. The Khmers had taken him at first for a Russian, but then had decided he was British. They did not know what to make of him. He had been very ill for quite a long time. Then he had died. They handed over some identification. A passport.

'Conclusive, I'm afraid,' says Gabriel. 'I've got it upstairs. I'll show you. His passport, and a paperback book. I'm sorry, Liz.'

Liz shrugs her shoulders. She had expected nothing better.

'They said they'd sent stuff back to England. There was a doctor there who spoke a little English. He said he'd arranged to have it sent. Oh, ages ago. It must have hung around for months in Phnom Penh.'

'But why did he send it to *me*?' asked Liz.

'But that's obvious. Stephen had put you down as next of kin. In the bit at the back of the passport. Your name and address. I'll show you. Yours, and Brian Bowen's.'

Liz stares at the table. Stephen smiles enigmatically back. Next of kin.

'Well,' she says. 'He was a good friend. I suppose.'

A silence falls. Bill waves for another round.

'Was there — was there a grave?' Liz now plucks up courage to ask.

Jacqueline shakes her head. No, there was nothing. Just the passport, and the paperback. If there had been other effects, they had been snapped up. It was good of them to release the passport. Passports are worth money. Not that we didn't pay for it, says Jacqueline. We did.

The mild-spoken Chet leans forward once more. He affects more sympathy than the hard-boiled Jacqueline.

'Identification question,' he murmurs. 'There was a metal plate in the ankle. Did Stephen have a metal plate?'

'Yes, he did,' says Liz. She and Stephen had often in happier days compared news of their bad ankles, she volunteers.

'Conclusive,' repeats Chet.

'And what happened to the metal plate, then?' Liz suddenly wants to know.

'Recycled,' says Chet, with a gesture of apology. 'Very great shortages. Recycled.'

Liz begins to laugh. Chet smiles in complicity.

'Oh God, poor Stephen,' she says. 'Recycled! Well, I suppose that's okay. And you've got his passport, his very passport, upstairs?'

Gabriel nods.

'And we've got rushes of the clinic. The so-called clinic. We'll show you, if you like.'

'I suppose I *do* like, after all this trouble,' says Liz. 'Well, well, what a surprise. And what's all *this* stuff' (gesturing towards the books and papers) 'doing here?'

Gabriel looks just slightly embarrassed.

'I know,' says Liz. 'You're making a movie. The disappearance of Stephen Cox. Death of author in Cambodia.'

'Well, we were sort of thinking of it,' says Gabriel. 'I sent one of the girls back to send the books and cuttings. I told her to contact you, but she says you weren't there. Gone East, she was told by your secretary.'

'But why me?' says Liz.

'Because of your name, in the passport.'

'Oh, I see,' says Liz.

'So I wasn't wholly surprised to see you,' says Gabriel. 'We are on the same trail.'

'So it seems. But you got to the end of it.'

'Only with Jacqueline's help.'

Liz stares at Jacqueline. She is just beginning to take her in. There is so much going on, she is confused, but now she begins to register Jacqueline, from whom she senses faint hostility. Jacqueline is in her thirties, and she has a clear brow and a thin, pointed chin. She is triangular and sinewy. She has long hands and long feet with tendons. She is cat and cobra and diamond, and her grey eyes have a curious intensity, a fanatic glimmer. Her skin is pocked and greasy and her hair is lank. She is tough and butch, and she is in mid-affair with Gabriel. All this Liz now sees, as the dust settles. Jacqueline is hard and possessive and jealous. She has marked her man. Liz Headleand can have the corpse.

This is okay by Liz. Gradually, she feels her way through the story. The disappeared Japanese journalist is being sought by his agency. Oko knew him well, was a colleague. Sightings of Akira, Stephen and Konstantin Vassiliou together have been traced. Gabriel and Jacqueline have no news of Konstantin. The clinic denied all knowledge of him. Only one Englishman, they had insisted. One dead Englishman.

'Konstantin is in Borneo,' says Liz, flatly. She does not give her source. She does not want to give too much away. She does not trust these vultures, these pickers of bones, these recycling machines, these devouring camerafolk.

Nevertheless, two hours and several platters of spring rolls, curried shrimps and soft-shelled crabs later, she finds herself lying full length on Gabriel Denham's large emperor-sized double bed, staring at the ceiling.

Gabriel and Jacqueline Lowe are also lying on the bed. Gabriel is in the middle.

They are staring at the rushes of the documentary, projected on to the ceiling by Bill. Chet sits on his haunches in a corner, interpreting the speech of the Khmers. Oko too sits on the floor in deep withdrawal. Cathy, exhausted and excluded, has gone to bed. She is good only for fetching and carrying, she has irritably implied, and anyway there is no more room on the bed.

On the ceiling, a black and white Jacqueline is staring boldly into the camera. 'This,' she says, 'is the hidden headquarters of Som Keng, just south of the Great Lake.' She gestures rather woodenly, as the camera takes in a few huts on stilts and some trees. 'Here, we talked to elite Khmer Rouge cadres trained by Pol Pot himself at the villa called Zone 87 in Thailand's Tat province. We are four hours' drive from . . .' The film splutters and sticks, and Bill says, 'Damn.' He reloads, while Gabriel lights a cigarette. The ashtray is balanced on Liz's belly.

In jumbled sequence, Liz sees an earnest interview about military strategy and peasant support with a bespectacled middle-aged guerrilla leader, who is interpreted as saying that the Khmer Rouge are no longer terrorists or communists, they have rejected revolution and embrace the possibility of a market economy. She sees a group of resistance fighters eating noodles and watching a video of what looks suspiciously like an American thriller. She sees some women in limpet hats and baggy trousers working in a field, and a soldier supervising distribution of rice. She sees a mewing baby born without arms, and, more horribly, more unexpectedly, a baby without eyes. The upper part of its head is blank, a smooth blank sightless brow. (Agent Orange, murmurs Gabriel, as Liz cannot repress an indrawn breath of distress). She sees Gabriel and Jacqueline laughing as they swing in a hammock under a mango-tree, and she sees a Khmer Rouge cadre pointing at a half-exhumed mass grave. Chet explains that the cadre pointing at the bones and rags of cloth is blaming the atrocity on the Vietnamese.

How can one believe anything anyone says? How can one even believe the evidence of one's own eyes? How can she tell if these characters *are* Khmer Rouge? They could be actors dressed for the part and fed their lines by Jacqueline and Gabriel. That guerrilla leader could be a fake. He could be a cooker of noodles, or a film extra, or a spy. He could be Chet's brother-in-law.

The bones are bones, it is true. One could be sure of them. It would be too expensive to fake so many. There is footage of them in the Atrocity Museum in Phnom Penh, familiar footage. Piled pyramids of skulls, assorted thigh bones. Liz knows where she is with those. But what of the deformed babies? Could they have been got up by a special effects film team?

Bill cannot immediately find the film of the field hospital, and begins to grow irritable, reviling the incompetence of the absent Cathy. By mistake he replays the mass grave and the noodle eaters. But here, at last, is the clinic. Young men on crutches, similar to those photographed by Konstantin at Marianne Sanderson's field hospital. Rows of beds. A close up of flies buzzing round a bandaged head, a blood-oozing stump. And then, an interview with a young doctor, Chut Pek, who speaks of Stephen Cox. Chet translates, and Bill plays and replays the sequence slowly.

Chut Pek says that an Englishman was brought to the clinic some time ago, from a hill village. He cannot remember how long ago. A year, two years. He was very, very ill. He had malaria, and an infected ankle. What did he look like? He was tall, thin, bald. He spoke no Khmer, but he spoke French and Russian. 'I speak little English, very bad English,' says the young doctor, smiling shyly at the camera. 'Very sorry, for so many mistakes.' Yes, he had tried to look after the Englishman, but he had died. Many, many deaths. Much sickness, no medicines. Much infection.

He is asked what the Englishman was doing in Kampuchea. The young doctor, hesitating over words, said, 'He journalist. He English journalist. He very nice, very nice man. But very ill. He die.' The doctor said he had done his best. He repeated, forlornly, 'Very nice man. Good discussions. History, politics, democracy. Very sad.'

Bill replays this sentence several times. Liz feels a slight prickling behind her nose.

Jacqueline, on film, asked where his body was.

'Buried,' says doctor. 'Hospital burial. Proper burial.' He lowers his head, with a heartbreaking deference to fact.

Then there is film of him handing over the passport and the

paperback of Rimbaud to Jacqueline Lowe. The camera identifies the items, as in a police record. At this point Chut Pek's smile becomes uneasy, prevaricating. He reports that he sent the rest of the Englishman's things home, to a friend in Phnom Penh, to send to Englishman's family in England. He hopes they arrived. The post is very bad.

The film splutters and ends. There is a small silence.

'Did you ask,' says Liz, 'whether he was *asked* to send the stuff home? By Stephen?'

'He said it was something he wanted to do,' says Gabriel. 'At least I think that's what he meant. He was very unhappy about that package business. I think it could have got him into trouble. It was his own initiative. My hunch is that the rest of them were happy for Stephen just to disappear, and no questions asked, but this guy had struck up some kind of relationship with him and wanted to do the proper thing. I don't think we could have got much more out of him. He was nervous. They wouldn't let us film the graves. Bad luck, they said, ancestor trouble, but I think they were just ashamed of the state of the dump. A hell of a place to die. Sorry, but it was.'

'Still,' says Liz, looking on the bright side. 'He found a friend. Of sorts. And you say you never heard anything about that Japanese who was said to be with him?'

'Akira Tanaka? Fuck all. Guilty silence. We asked old moon face at the camp, but he just smiled. Never heard of a Japanese. Never heard of Japan.'

Oko, from his corner of the floor, nods agreement.

'And Konstantin?'

'Same story. Nothing. Disappeared into thin air.'

'But how the hell did Stephen find his way by himself to a hill village? It doesn't make sense.'

'That young chap didn't know. He just stuck to his story, that Stephen had been brought in from a village for treatment.'

Liz sighs, and the ashtray heaves.

THE GATES OF IVORY

'I'm sorry, Liz,' says Gabriel. 'It's not much fun for you, coming all this way for news like this. But at least we know what happened to him. I mean, that was what I call evidence.'

Even Liz, who does not share Gabriel's estimate of the veracity of film, has to agree. And she is, in a way, relieved. She had been comforted to see her name and address, written firmly and clearly on the back page of Stephen's passport. It had validated her quest, and it had spared her further inquiry. It was over.

She heaves herself up, and props herself against the bedhead, and lights another cigarette. In this bad company, she is smoking far too much.

'So you're sure,' she says, 'that there's no point in my trying to get to Phnom Penh?'

'None at all. There's nothing there. We asked at the hotel, for the stuff the three of them had left, but it had all been nicked or sold off long ago. The management could no longer accept responsibility. Hardly surprising. I'll tell you what we did pick up, and you're welcome to it. The tab for the car that disappeared. They wanted us to settle it. I told the bastards they must be joking. If they see a television camera, they think you're made of money.'

'I suppose,' says Liz, 'that I might see some Cambodian, wearing Stephen's cutdown white suit. But it's hardly worth going all that way, just for that.'

She says this as a poor joke, but Gabriel picks it up. 'Make a good end to the movie,' he says.

'You're not *really* going to turn Stephen into a movie?' asks Liz, against her judgement allowing a suddenly revived Oko to pour her another slug of brandy. Her surprise is feigned, for nothing would startle her now.

'Well, a documentary portrait. A biofilm,' says Gabriel.

He describes his ideas for the project. Liz listens with interest, although she is beginning to feel slightly unwell. Is it tiredness, belated shock, smoke, drink, malaria? She shivers, and pulls herself a little higher on the sagging pillows. As Gabriel speaks of lyrical portrayal of Somerset Levels of childhood, satiric treatment of formative public-school ethos, romantic Orwellian days with Stephen down and out in Paris, dramatized extracts from *Barricades*, and the last doomed journey to the East, she find herself recalling Alan's conundrum: can a man buy back his life by another's death? Is life, unlike an air ticket or an invitation to lunch with the Prime Minister, transferable? And if not, why not? She had never found an answer to this one, she concedes, and she stops listening to Gabriel as she tries to puzzle it out.

She fails: and when she comes round, Gabriel is saying, 'Do you think there'd be any family objections? Would they talk to us, do you think?'

Liz shrugs. 'Why should you need to ask them? He doesn't belong to them. He never had much to do with them.'

'Did he have an agent? Do you happen to know if he sold the film rights in any of the novels?'

'Maybe. Maybe not. I've no idea. You'd have to ask Hattie Osborne. She's his literary executor. Or so she says.'

Gabriel responds oddly to the name of Hattie Osborne.

He cross-questions Liz about her. Liz hears herself saying that Hattie Osborne is having an affair with her stepson Aaron. Gabriel confesses that he himself had once long ago had an affair with Hattie Osborne. Indeed, he takes upon himself the credit for having launched her on her career. She is an old chum. He hasn't seen her in years, but she is an old chum.

Jacqueline has fallen asleep in a boredom protest. She begins to snore. Oko, Bill and Chet take their cue, bow out and take themselves off to bed. Gabriel and Liz, holding hands, reminisce. They speak of old times and loves of long ago. The pillow talk of thirty unconsummated years softly unrolls. They speak of Stephen and his lonely death. Will they ever know more of his last days? Will they ever find Konstantin? Had Konstantin deserted Stephen? Had

Stephen found his heart's desire? Should Liz have asked Stephen to marry her? Should Gabriel divorce his third wife?

They speak of Charles and his surprising constancy. They recall a dinner of yesteryear in a Chinese restaurant in Wardour Street, when Gabriel had made a pass at Liz under Charles's angry nose. How young they had been, how glorious their hopes and prospects, how certain Gabriel had been that one day he would sleep with Liz Ablewhite Lintot Headleand!

'In my dreams, I have slept with you,' he says.

'And I with you,' confesses Liz.

But it is too late now. She begins to shiver again, and this time she cannot control it. Her teeth chatter, and she turns very cold, then very hot.

'I'd better go to my bed,' she says. 'I think I've got malaria.'

Gabriel kisses her on the mouth. Jacqueline stirs angrily.

It is Stephen who should receive this kiss, but he is dead and gone.

*

The Fever Hospital

The lords of death gather. A heavy dull grey light beats. It is the light of the last days, the last hours, the last things. The Yellowish-White Vulture-Headed One approaches, holding a skeleton by the hand, with a corpse upon his shoulder. The Dark-Red Cemetery-Bird-Headed One also heaves upon her back a sagging corpse. The Black Crown-Headed One holds a severed head dripping blood, and the Dark Blue Owl-Headed One a severed leg. The Red Lion-Headed Iron-Chain-Holding Goddess rides in from the West, and from the North descends the Goddess with a Green Serpent Head.

The bear and the python wait in the shadow.

Fear them not! Fear not the Horse-Headed Delight Goddess, nor yet the Yellow Bat-Headed Goddess! Fear not the Fever Demon! Fear not the drinkers of blood!

The maimed stagger, the unsighted children present blind fronts to the blind sky. The Orange Bird-Beaked Lion-Maned One howls and roars.

Fear them not!

The six lights shine. The smoke-coloured light of the Hell World shines. It is time for the crossing. And beyond the lights, beyond the wailings, beyond the buzzing of the flies, shines the clear and infinite blue!

*

The newly widowed Liz wakes in the morning with worse than a hangover. Something is really wrong. As she takes a bath, she remembers that she is still wearing the last of the two tampons, and she has been wearing it now for twenty-four hours. She extracts it and throws it away, pausing to note that the flow seems to have stopped.

She continues to shiver and shake. She swallows aspirins, and rings Gabriel. Gabriel says he had been trying to contact her, but the hotel disowns her. The Victory says it has never heard of a Dr Elizabeth Headleand.

That's because I'm checked in as Mrs Stephen Cox, says Liz. I see, says Gabriel, with increased interest and bewilderment.

Liz says she feels ill and will stay in bed. Her quest over, her body and her will have collapsed, she tells Gabriel.

At noon, arrives in Saigon Miss Porntip.

At the Happy Hour, Liz Headleand, Gabriel Denham, Jacqueline Lowe, Cathy, Oko and Bill find themselves high over the Gulf of Siam on their way back to Bangkok in an executive jet. Bill helps Miss Porntip's lover to read the map, while pointing out features of interest below, and Miss Porntip messes around with the drinks cabinet. Liz has never been in an executive jet before, and is determined to get the best out of the experience. If she dies now, she will not care. She accepts some salted almonds and a gin and tonic with ice and a slice of lemon. If it is malaria, the quinine will help, she reasons. She is high and excited. She watches in a trance as the pips from her lemon descend through the frosted liquid of her glass, and then ascend again, and then again descend, like divers clustered with haloes of tiny little silver bubbles. 'Look, Gabriel, look at the lemon pips!' she says. Gabriel glances at Miss Porntip, Miss Porntip minimally nods. A doctor for Dr Headleand, they agree, is required.

A doctor is summoned to the bedside of room 159 at the Oriental. Liz now has a sore throat, a high temperature, diarrhoea, and her hands and feet are peeling as though from sunburn. The doctor looks nonplussed and prescribes some pills. Liz nods and dozes and dreams of the baby born without arms. It lies in a nest of rifles, and it speaks to her. It says, 'Mummy, mummy, be my mother!' Liz wakes, in a start of horror, and reaches for her phone, and rings her stepson Alan in his Northern university. He answers, and she hears herself tell him that Stephen is dead. 'Dead,' she repeats, mournfully. 'Dead, dead, dead!'

'Are you all right, ma?' asks Alan, anxiously.

'No, I'm ill,' Liz hears herself saying.

'What with?' asks Alan.

'I don't know,' says Liz. But even as she speaks, diagnosis bursts upon her. 'I think,' she hears herself saying, 'that I may have got toxic shock.'

*

So the gynaecologist of John Geddes comes in useful after all. He approves Liz's theory of TSS with almost excessive enthusiasm. She cannot blame him for being unable to conceal his delight at meeting first-hand for the first time an example of this very rare condition, but is slightly less charmed by his insistence on the fact that she may be making medical history as the oldest known sufferer. He orders immediate hospitalization. Liz is glad she had followed Charles's advice and taken out medical insurance. She is whisked through the traffic jams of Bangkok, gynaecologist at her side, siren wailing, and soon finds herself installed in a private room, with the inevitable displays of orchids already arranged around her bed. Doctors come and peer at her and cross-examine her. She owns up to everything – the unexpected period, the ancient tampons (when she confesses to super-absorbency, they disapprovingly shake their heads), the twenty-four hours of uninterrupted insertion. Yes, she says, it is all her own fault, she has deserved this. They mutter to one another and take notes.

When she is left alone for a few minutes to contemplate, she finds herself able to appreciate the ironies of her situation. Here she is, afflicted with one of the most new-fangled of feminist disorders, while Stephen Cox has died in a field hospital of old-fashioned malaria or dengue.

To whom had Stephen spoken on his deathbed? Had it been that anxious, conscientious young Khmer, who had risked perhaps his life to send across the lines the package that had brought her to this room, these orchids? Had he sat by Stephen as Stephen died? And if so, why? Had he wished for other things? Why had he kept back the Rimbaud? To save on the postage? Had he been able to read the Rimbaud? Was he a doctor–poet? Well, why not? And where, come to that, is the Rimbaud now?

Perhaps the young man was Mitra Akrun, student of medicine, protector of his family, ripped from his family, willing or unwilling convert to the Khmer Rouge.

She summons up the face of the young doctor. She summons up the face of Mme Savet Akrun. She summons up Stephen Cox. The ghosts drink by the blood. She dozes.

Stephen's deathbed had been ill attended, but Liz Headleand's sickbed is well visited. Miss Porntip arrives, bearing gifts of fruits and flowers and colourful books from her library. Gabriel Denham arrives, on a breather from Jacqueline, bearing Stephen's passport, which he urges Liz to keep. (Liz is not wholly pleased by this generosity: does it mean she is dying?) Bob Berry arrives, with a delicious little snackette of reconstituted krill-oysterette to tempt her, and is very pleasant, although Liz suspects he has really come to see the gynaecologist. Grimshawe arrives, with a bunch of marigolds. (This *must* mean she is dying: or is she perhaps already dead?)

Oko arrives, and sits himself down by her side for a serious conversation about Akira Tanaka.

This convinces her that she is still alive. She listens.

So, Akira had a wife and family back in Tokyo. So, Oko sees the wife. So, Oko is in love with the wife, and therefore wishes to establish that his old friend and colleague Akira is safely dead. A sub-plot.

Oko shows Liz photographs of the characters in this new story. Akira himself, wearing a baseball cap, with a gold medallion round his neck. Two small children, neatly ranged side by side. And the wife, Yukio. Oko has dozens of pictures of Yukio. There she is, in restaurants, in temple gardens, in departmental stores, on beaches, in cemeteries, in airports, in railway stations. She is ubiquitous. A thin, waif-like creature, with a pale thin peaky pointed elfin face, and short hair cut like a neat black cap. She too is a journalist, Oko says, she writes largely on feminist matters. She is New Japanese Woman.

'You must tell her about my interesting illness,' suggests Liz. 'You should speak to the gynaecologist.'

Oko takes this seriously, and makes a note.

So, what is he to do, he asks Liz. Without a body, it is difficult to establish death. The likelihood of Akira's survival is remote, but by no means impossible. Akira had been a man of parts, he had escaped from many tight corners. Will Yukio remain a grass widow for ever? There had been no trace of Akira. If Akira had been dead, would not there have been some signs to read, somewhere? A trail of ash and bone and abandoned equipment? A lingering aftermath of anecdote?

'If he's not dead, and if he pops up again and finds you are carrying on with his wife, how will he take it?' asks Liz. The question is a little brutal, but the intimacy of the sickroom renders tact irrelevant. It is like a confessional in here. Truths can be told between strangers.

Oko sighs, and gazes at a photograph of black-trousered Yukio standing smiling in an eerie garden of red-draped statues to dead babies. Little windmills turn above their heads.

'He does not care for Yukio,' he says. 'He does not love Yukio. He neglects her, he is always away at the war and the fighting. Akira loves war.'

'Well, I don't know what to say,' says Liz. 'Perhaps you'd better go to Borneo and try to track down Konstantin Vassiliou. He could be a useful witness.'

She shows Oko the letter from Hong, but they agree there is not much to go on there. Borneo is a big place, and tricky for travellers.

'Why don't you just go back to Tokyo and forget about Akira?' suggests Liz. 'Just carry on as though he had deserted? Which, in a sense, he has. Alive or dead, he's not putting in much time on the home front, is he?'

Oko acknowledges the sense of this. But, he murmurs, it is his duty to do his best. Honour depends.

Liz suddenly feels very tired and dizzy, and says she must rest. Oko apologizes for tiring her, and bows his way out.

An hour later, Chet arrives. He too sits himself down by her side for a serious conversation. He too tells Liz his story. Liz begins to think she is back at home, in her own consulting room, at work. Is her professional identity so powerful that people will struggle to tell her their secrets even as she lies dying? Do they wish to transmit their messages through her to the other world?

Chet's story is terrible and ordinary. Here it is.

He was born in 1952, the son of a Lon Nol supporter, an anti-Sihanouk banker. He had been studying chemistry in Phnom Penh when the men in black marched in on 17 April 1975. ('I was keen student. Good teachers. French teachers.') Fourteen members of Chet's family had set off on a two-week walk to his father's birth village east of the Mekong. They had been put to work by the Old People. His mother looked after the infants in the nursery, his father was yard guardian, the children minded the buffaloes and cows, and all the able-bodied worked to make new fields and build dams. No trucks, no tractors, no bulldozers. They worked long, long hours, late into the night, sometimes by the light of petrol lamps. ('We hated sun and moon. We loved dark nights and stars.')

His brother-in-law went first. He had been a high-school teacher in Phnom Penh. He was called away for further study. He never returned. Study was death.

The family was forcibly moved, from village to village. The harder they worked, the shorter the rice ration. His brother was imprisoned for speaking a few words of English to a friend. Chet was sent away from his family to work in a potato yard.

After a year, Chet received a message from his father, telling him two brothers had died, his mother was ill. Chet got permission to visit. His yard leader lent him his bicycle, and he went home for three days. ('He was a good and gentle leader.') Chet never saw any of his relatives again.

They had been taken from the village in ox carts with all their baggage. The baggage had returned, but not the people. The next day, more families. In all, about 500 New People had been killed in the wood with sticks and knives. This was the news that reached the potato yard.

As the regime disintegrated, he and a friend hid in the yard until the Vietnamese Army arrived. He never went back to Phnom Penh. He lived as a farmer for a year before escaping on foot across the border to Khao-i-Dang Refugee Holding Centre. A seven-day walk.

That is Chet's story. He has written it down. He had been forced to write his biography by the Khmer Rouge. Now he writes it for anyone who will read. He writes it for history. He has also drawn a chart. It is called 'Death List in My Family'. It records the deaths of those thirteen who set out with him from Phnom Penh. Brother-in-law, killed June 1975. Brothers, Map Be Huch and Map Be Nay, born 1953 and 1954, died of sickness, June 1977. All the rest were killed in the wood in July 1977. His youngest brother had been five years old.

Liz gazes at the list, and looks up from it to Chet. He sits there, patiently, waiting for her comment. As she continues to say nothing, he adds, as though to make this appalling tale more convincing, 'My older brother next to me, he was art student. Very good painter.'

Liz still has nothing to say. Chet says, gently, to encourage her, 'Very sorry about your friend Stephen.'

Liz has nothing to say to this either.

Chet tells her that he was lucky to be processed as a genuine refugee. Now he has Australian citizenship. Those in the border camps are not so lucky, they are displaced people, not refugees.

'Some luck,' says Liz.

Liz describes her visit to the border camps. She describes her conversation with Mme Savet Akrun. Chet says that his medical-student brother Saem was a friend of Mitra Akrun. He says this quite casually, as though it were the most natural connection in the world. Oh yes, he remembers Mitra quite well. He had a motorbike, and Saem and he would roar round the streets of an evening. So Mme Akrun is still alive. He does not remember her so well. But he remembers Mitra.

Liz looks at Chet, as though she herself were now seeking a message from the dead. Has he not almost crossed to the other side? But he remains opaque, despite the length and compulsive detail of his narration. She will never be able to understand his ordeals. Is it enough, to listen and to believe? He has come back from Bad Time, and now he lives off the fat of the land, in the expense-account, brandy-and-soda, chatter-giggle, all-chums-together world of a television crew. Yes, he has been one of the lucky ones. Luckier than Mme Akrun, luckier than his own brothers. Luckier than Eric Rosenberg.

She does not know why Eric Rosenberg has suddenly jumped into her mind, but as suddenly she remembers her Pailin ruby. She has failed in her mission to give it to Dr Chhi Beng Sam in Kampot. Now she tries to give it to Chet, half expecting that Chhi Beng Sam will turn out to be his cousin or his aunt, but he will not take it. But you are far more likely than me to be able to find someone who will give it to her, she protests. She, Liz, will never get to Cambodia now. She will never come back to this part of the world again. But Chet will return, surely. Why, Gabriel says they will be back next month, filming.

Chet shakes his head. He cannot be responsible. She must take it home to England, to Dr Marianne. Yes, he has heard much of Dr Marianne. And of Dr Eric. A very sad thing, the death of Dr Eric. The Vietnamese planes are no good, says Chet, a look of contemptuous rage fleetingly possessing his mild features. He hates the Vietnamese and all things Vietnamese.

And now, says Chet, I must let you rest. Thank you for listening to my sad history.

Politely, he withdraws.

Liz wonders who next will call on her with a catalogue of grief or with little Good Time gifts. She lies in state here, receiving. The hospital is ultra-modern, futuristically equipped. It hums and sings quietly. How can it exist in the same century, the same decade as the potato yard, as the wood where the New People were killed with sticks and knives? So much machinery, to keep one woman alive. Is one life worth so much more than another?

Her next visitor is film editor and dogsbody Cathy Upwood, and the story that she brings is not very pleasant either, although it does not make Liz feel quite so irrelevant. At least it occupies home ground.

Cathy Upwood sits by Liz's bedside, peeling a candiola fruit. She has exchanged her dark glasses for large purple-framed mauve-tinted ones, through which she peers at Liz with what seems to be a mixture of apprehension and anger. At first Liz thinks she has come to complain about the *de haut en bas* behaviour of Jacqueline Lowe and the neglect of Gabriel (is she in love with Gabriel, perhaps?), but this is well wide of the mark. After a few preliminary and routine reflections upon the status and pay of junior editors, and innuendoes about Becky Aldridge who'd been sent back to England early because she couldn't stand the heat, Cathy, presenting Liz with a juicy segment, and eating another herself, suddenly says, 'Was it you I saw on TV a year or two ago, talking about child sex abuse?'

Liz, who has received a lot of flak over this programme, replies cautiously.

'Well, yes, it might have been,' she admits.

'And was it you that was saying it didn't do any harm?'

Liz, cornered, thinks hard.

'Well, that wasn't *quite* what I was saying,' she says.

Cathy wipes her sticky fingers on her trousers, then runs them through her short white hair.

'That *is* what you were saying,' she says, quite aggressively.

'Was it? I can't remember,' Liz prevaricates. Was this pale child about to tell her that she had been abused since infancy? Yes, God help her, she was.

But, mercifully, she does not seem to blame Liz for this.

'I mean,' she pursues, 'it was quite a *relief*, in a way, to hear you speak out like that. Because, after all, one of the worst things was that I went along with it. So what did that make me? I hated it and I liked it. There. I've said it now.'

'Say more,' says Liz. 'Say it all.'

And Cathy says it all, in a slightly monotonous monologue, in a strangely affected young person's classless London drawl familiar to

Liz from the speech patterns of her own daughters: had she perhaps been educated at the same school?

It is, even by Liz's standards, a startling story. Father, good-looking, a Don Juan, quite successful, quite well-known musician. Two wives, two families. Three daughters, Cathy the eldest of the first-in-time, second-in-status family. Four sons. Mistresses all over the place. All over the world, as far as I know, says Cathy. A wife in every port. And he had abused all the daughters. All of them. 'Not your actual *intercourse*,' drawled Cathy, nasally. 'I'm still virgo intacta, myself. But everything else you can think of. Pettings and pryings. *You* know.' Liz nodded, encouragingly, as though she knew. 'And then there was a showdown. My mum found out. Their mum found out. Mum wanted to shop him. Wanted to gaol him. But we girls refused. I mean, think of the publicity. Anyway, how could we? Stand up in court, and all? And anyway, my mum only wanted to shop him to spite Anthea. What good would it have done any of us? But it's ruined my sex life. I mean, I haven't *got* any sex life. What do you think I should do?'

The question seems so vast that Liz shakes her head to disown it. But Cathy pursues.

'I mean, orgasms,' she persists. 'There were orgasms.'

'You could try therapy,' suggests Liz, playing for time.

But she has struck the nail on the head.

'Yes, that's what I was thinking of,' says Cathy, in a matter-of-fact, pleased tone. 'That's exactly what I was thinking of. And when I realized who you were, I knew you could help. Tell me how to set about it. You will, won't you?'

'Of course,' says Liz. 'Come and see me, when we get back.'

'I mean,' says Cathy, 'what good would it do, putting him in gaol? You know what I mean? It's better to keep out of his way.'

'*My* father,' says Liz, 'used to expose himself. On street corners. He got had up for it.'

'Really?' asks Cathy.

But she is not interested. She cannot make connections or comparisons. She is interested only in herself. She has got what she wants out of Liz.

'*My* father,' she begins again, 'has got this *obsession* about clocking up lays, he's obsessed with the numbers game, he . . .'

But Liz groans, slightly. She cannot bear any more of this stuff. Her head aches. The hour is up. She wishes she had her secretary, to ring the bell, to show Cathy the door, to bring in the next patient. Her head aches, and she feels very hot. Cathy's voice drones on, but Liz ceases to listen. After a few minutes, her eyes shut. Eventually, Cathy notices and withdraws.

When Liz falls asleep, she enters the Bad Time of Dream Time. She is not getting better, she is getting worse. Her visitors have poisoned her.

For a long time, she drifts on the edge of consciousness, trying to wake out of the nightmares. And then she surrenders.

For two days, she moans and tosses. She dreams of firing squads and Roger Casement and the Belgian Congo and a tally of severed arms. She dreams of babies born without arms or eyes, victims of Agent Orange. She dreams atrocities. She dreams of spade on skull, of death in the clearing. She dreams of trenches and minefields and piles of skulls. She dreams of the Red Road and the sound of shells and an ox card heaped with the dead bodies of Chet's family.

She dreams of her old analyst, Karl, who appears before her robed in saffron carrying Stephen Cox's head upon a platter. She dreams she is back in Abercorn Avenue, cleaning her dead father's shoes. She dreams she is watching her sister Shirley making love to a Japanese photographer on the marble floor of an art gallery in Toronto, watched by admiring crowds. She dreams that she is making love to Gabriel Denham, watched by Edgar Lintot and Charles Headleand. She dreams that Simon Grunewald is gnawing and nibbling at the base of her neck, intent on devouring her marrow and her brains. She dreams of Stephen Cox, bald as an egg, with bones and metal plates exposed.

From time to time, she emerges from these troubled spaces and looks around her with interest and some alarm. Her hospital room has now taken on a more serious air. The frivolous orchids have retreated, and she seems to be on an intravenous drip. Her own blue and white striped Marks & Spencer nightdress has been exchanged for a white clinical robe. Trays and trolleys cluster around her. A screen bleeps. A nurse attends.

When she shuts her eyes, she immediately re-enters Dream Time. She has always been a good Dreamer, but never has she found Dream Time so accessible, so obedient, so near. It crosses her conscious mind that this is bad news, that she has gone too far through the permeable membrane ever to return. Whole dreams unfold, each detail clear and sharp and distinct. She is robed in a stiff long medieval robe, green embroidered in gold. Her body can feel each dry stitch, it can feel the rub of the cloth, the coarse knap. She is to be executed. She is receiving advice on how to meet her death with dignity. 'Take a step forward towards the block, as you fall,' she is told. She rehearses her own death. Again and again she steps forward, lays down her head for the axe. Where does this come from, whose life does she relive?

Now she is watching a small child, of eight or nine, shivering upon a gallows on a hill on a cold morning. Liz is in the crowd of spectators that has gathered. The child calls, 'Mummy! Mummy!' and Liz tries to call back, but she has no voice, she is frozen into a pillar of salt, she is condemned to watch helplessly as the noose is placed around the neck of the child. She cannot tell whether the child is a boy or a girl. Luckily, she wakes before the drop, but she wakes in terror.

Then these narrative dreams, these *tableaux vivants* of death from the dark places of history, begin to fade and dissolve and speed up and liquefy, as she is rushed and whirled through vast oriental landscapes, through lakes of purple lilies, along rivers, across deserts, through forests peopled with chattering beast-men with bird faces, pig faces, monkey faces. The creatures drop away, and she is whirled through unpeopled clouds and storms and surging phosphorescent seas. She is weightless, bodiless. Are these dreams her own, or are they urged upon her? She does not know these places, she has never known them, she has not the waking power to create them. She is tossed upon them, until at last the turbulence begins to settle and slow and solidify, and she finds herself gliding along an avenue of marble effigies and tombstones and urns, and there, at last, she finds Stephen waiting for her, not the bald and skeletal Stephen of nightmare, but Stephen as he had been in life. There he stands, white-suited, distinguished, the man of letters, smiling at her quizzically, holding out both his hands to her in welcome. He is standing on a black and white marble paved check floor, and light falls on him from above from a clerestory of arched ecclesiastical windows. The setting is solemn, but Stephen's face is not. He has his own smile, ironic, disarming, amused. He reaches out his hands, and, as she extends her own to take them, she hears him say, but oh so plausibly, so matter of factly, so reassuringly, so unceremoniously, 'You see, it's all right, it's quite all right!' She stretches out, but he recedes, smiling, from her sight and her grasp, and she wakes, and finds herself in a high hospital bed in Bangkok.

Tears of hot relief fill her eyes and overflow. So it is all right! This is the important message that Stephen has taken such trouble to bring her from the underworld. She weeps and weeps. The nurse crosses to her, pats her, smiles cheerfully, points proudly to the bleeping monitor. Liz is on the mend. She is getting better fast.

Liz shuts her eyes, to see if Stephen is still waiting there for her, but he has vanished. And when she opens them again, she finds Charles Headleand by her side.

*

She is delighted to see the old monster. He seems equally pleased to see her. He had flown out soonest when alerted by Alan to the possibility that she was not well. But now he finds her picking up fast. She has turned the corner. He has come to take her home.

Charles is impressed by Liz's entourage. He is particularly taken with Miss Porntip, and even manages to be courteous to Gabriel. Bit of luck, really, running into Gabriel in Saigon like that, he says, from time to time.

Charles brings her news from England. A lot has happened during her brief absence. A cabinet minister has resigned, Jonathan Headleand has been done for speeding on the M11, Nicola Stowell has been made a governor of the BBC, Aaron's play is to transfer to the Coronet, and the Lady Henrietta has mercifully announced her engagement to a merchant banker. The proprietor of the *Informer* has been exposed in a sex scandal, and Teddy Lazenby has been packed off to Northern Ireland. The road is still up outside Liz's home in St John's Wood. Sally Headleand has entertained her father Charles to a supper of vegetable curries, and Charles in return has offered to lend her the deposit on a new flat in Stockwell. Charles has dined with the Anthony Blands and lunched with the Queen.

Liz listens to this harmless gossip with rapture. How good to know that the Old Country still ticks over as it always did! She is particularly interested in the luncheon with the Queen. What did they eat, what did She say, what was the cutlery like? What was She wearing, who else was there? Charles cannot give an adequate reply to all these questions, although he remembers the menu quite well. Some kind of coddled egg, followed by pheasant, followed by an excellent crème brulée. And Her Majesty was wearing a red dress. What kind of red, Liz wants to know. Crimson, scarlet, magenta, Venetian, Indian, terracotta, puce? Oh, just *red*, says Charles, affably. You know. *Red* red. A sort of darkish *red* red.

Liz shows Charles her new ruby. He admires it. She has gone off the idea of charging him for it. Why the hell should she? She has got more than her money's worth out of Charles. He owes her nothing. It is decent of him to come all this way to rescue her. Not,

MARGARET DRABBLE

of course, that she needs rescuing. She has managed quite all right on her own. In fact, as she lies there convalescing from whatever affliction it may have been (doubt has now been cast on the TSS theory, other tropical diseases have been suggested) she finds herself able to congratulate herself, after a fashion, on the success of her expedition. She may not have penetrated Cambodia, and she may not have brought Stephen home alive, but she has unravelled a mystery. She has not done badly.

So Charles comes and goes, and he and Liz comfortably chatter of this and of that. Her flight home is confirmed. Only one delicate subject do they avoid, and that comes up on the aeroplane. As they settle into their seats and fasten their safety belts, Liz suddenly asks, 'And what is all this I hear about your son Aaron and Hattie Osborne?'

*

Well, I knew she wouldn't like it. Well, would you, in her place? But I must say she's let us off lightly. It could have been a lot worse. I think her adventures have given her something else to chew on. Just as well, from our point of view. I suppose you think it's a bit off, the way I keep on seeing things from my own point of view, what with Stephen dead and all. But what other POV can I see things from but my own? As Saint Joan said to the Inquisition, if I remember rightly.

I must say, Marcia Campbell has been a trump. Yes, that's the word for her. A trump. Pouring oil all over the troubled waters. She invited us all to supper, and gave us a good laugh. I like that black man of hers. In the old days, I might have felt obliged to give him the eye. Nice not to have to bother, isn't it?'

Anyway, me going into a decline won't help Stephen, will it? So that's the end of *that* story. Well, almost. I was *enraged* when I heard that crook Gabriel was trying to pinch my plot. I tried to ring him in Bangkok, to tell him that Stephen belonged to me and that he'd have to pay me good money if he wanted to use even so much as a shot of a jacket of a paperback novel, but he'd already buggered off back to Ho Chi Minh Ville with that ugly Australian battleaxe. And the telephones in Ho Chi Minh Ville don't seem to work too well. I tried to send a fax but it's probably still wandering round the airspace of the Indian Ocean. I don't understand that satellite business.

I didn't know quite what to do about Stephen's flat, to tell the truth. Aaron and I have been sort of boxing and coxing (oh God, that's not meant to be a *jeu de mots*, I assure you) between here and Chalk Farm, but really we need somewhere bigger and better and more salubrious. Both these pads are too small for a baby. On the other hand, I'm not sure I want to *live* with Aaron. I mean, I love him to death, and all that, but living with is another matter. He's an awful slob. So am I, but in a different *style*.

Good news about his play, though, isn't it? And he's getting on fine with the next. He's on a lucky streak, he says.

Anyway, I thought I'd better come clean and have a word with Stephen's landlord, Mr Goodfellow. So I asked him round for a drink. It turned out that he knew all along that Stephen had cleared off. He kept looking at my belly, and I said all right, I know, no cats, dogs or babies, I wasn't sure whether or not to tell him that Stephen is really dead. It hasn't been announced officially yet. No obits in *The Times* or the *Inde*. Everybody *knows*, but that's different. Something's being cleared with the Foreign Office, according to Charles Headleand. But I don't know if Mr Goodfellow knows. I was wondering whether to mention the subject when he suddenly said, what about moving into a nice large ground-floor flat in Hampstead Gardens? Three bedrooms, sole use of garden, no steps, nice quiet deaf old lady above. It sounds perfect. The rent is peanuts, by today's standards. Mr Goodfellow's rents are always peanuts. Even I could afford it. Well, I jumped at it. It seemed perfect. Aaron can keep on the Chalk Farm dive, and run away when the babe howls. Or when I howl.

So, this is my last week here. Poor Stephen. He really is being phased out. I miss him. But there you go, it was his choice, and I can't say it hasn't turned out well from my point of view. I wonder what will happen to the stuff he left here? Not that there's much of it. I'm afraid I polished off the wine, and I can't see anyone queueing up for a few old copies of the *Old Moxleian* or a bicycle pump.

Liz says we should have a Memorial Service. I suppose that's right. I don't much go for that kind of thing myself. Remember Charlie Bentwood's? Every jerk I'd ever worked with was there, and everybody talked about themselves all the time, when they were meant to be singing old Charlie's praises. And the hymns! Charlie would have hated it. 'Abide with me', forsooth. 'Fast falls the eventide'. Forget it!

Do you think Mr Goodfellow is a saint? I think he may be.

The baby's coming on brilliantly. You wouldn't think I was a very elderly *prima gravida*. Despite all the substances I've used and abused over the past twenty-five years, I'm as fit as a fiddle. I'm a really bad example. I always knew I was made of special stuff. I can feel the baby moving. Aaron knows what sex it is, but I don't want to know. I won't let them tell me.

My ankles feel a bit funny sometimes, but that's my only complaint. They look a bit funny too. A bit puffy. But I'm sure they'll go down. My heart is swollen too. And not only with pride and joy. Did you know that the heart *doubles its size* during pregnancy? No, I didn't either, and I'm not sure if I believe them. But they swear it's true.

They're quite pleased with me at the hospital. There's a really nice woman there at the check-in who makes us all laugh as we present her with our little bottles of urine.

The only fault they can find is in my placenta. (Or is it *its* placenta?!) Apparently it's a bit wizened and undersize. (Unlike my heart.) Oh dear, I say, what can I do about that? And they laugh, and say, think big, and eat more liver. I bet liver goes out of fashion soon. I bet you it's the next thing on the death list. But I'm eating liver, like a good girl. *Fegato alla salvia*. Delicious. Remember, that stuff we used to get at school, like anatomical cross-sections, full of tubing?

The new flat is just great.

I met Polly Piper again the other day. It was weird. It was in Sainsbury's again, by the Freshly Squeezed Orange Juice. I was better stocked this time and prouder of my purchases, I was also pretty keen to tell Polly what was up, and I went straight for it.

'Hi, Polly,' I said, 'do you remember asking me if I regretted not having children? Here, in this very shop?'

'Don't tell me,' said Polly. 'You're pregnant.'

'Well, yes, I am,' I said. 'As you see.'

As a matter of fact, she couldn't see, through my chunky curly winter coat. I'm not *that* big.

'I'd heard rumours,' said Polly. 'But I don't know whether to believe them.'

'Well, it's true,' I said.

'Congratulations,' she said. 'How are you feeling?'

'A million dollars,' I said. 'And how about yourself?'

At this a kind of smug secretive look came over her face, and she looked around her, to see if any of the old crones or young thugs were listening in, and bent towards me, and whispered, 'Well, don't *tell* anyone, but I'm being translated.'

'What?' I said.

'*You* know,' said Polly, mysteriously.

I don't know, but I had to pretend I did. I couldn't say 'What?' again, could I?

'Oh, great,' I said. 'Just great. Congratulations to yourself too, then.'

'I hesitated a lot,' she went on. 'I mean, it's a big change, and what about my principles? But then, I thought I'd be more useful there than here. So I said yes.'

'You did quite right,' I said. God knows what she was talking about.

Has she been adopted as Monster Raving Loony candidate for Stoke-on-Trent? Been made a dame or a baroness or an ambassador? Or first British female astronaut? Something like that, I suppose. Well, some people can't lose and Polly Piper is one of them.

'Keep it to yourself,' she said, as she moved graciously off towards the fish counter.

'I will, I will,' I promised.

And I have, so far. I've only told you, and you don't count. I haven't even told Aaron.

Rum business, really. Women's lives. Eggs, blood and the moon. Rumour has it that Liz Headleand nearly died of some gynaeco-logical disaster in Bangkok. Aaron says she says it was toxic shock. But I don't know if that's true. I'd have thought it unlikely, at her age. I should have mentioned it to Polly. She'd have been fascinated. Perhaps she's been offered the post of shadow minister for Women by the lads of Walworth.

*

A date has been fixed for the Memorial Service. The death is now official, and obituaries have mourned the untimely death of Stephen Cox. One or two of the more right-wing papers have insinuated that he got what was coming to him, and that even if he'd changed his mind about the virtues of Pol Pot, he'd done it too late in the day to be forgiven. (One of these prompted Brian Bowen to send an indignant protest: Stephen had never been an apologist for anything, wrote Brian, he had been a witness and an observer.) But even the right-wing papers had been respectful and regretful. A fine, if eccentric career, an individual voice lost.

A church has been chosen for the service, after much theological debate between Liz, Alix and Hattie, who have found themselves in charge of the proceedings. Nobody thinks Stephen would have wanted a church service, but where else is there? You can't hold a service in Sainsbury's or Bertorelli's, can you? And his brothers want the big deal. Mother is still alive, in her nineties. Mother, say the brothers, wants a church, though she is of course not fit to attend. Mother does not know what she wants. She is kept alive on mashed baby food, spooned in at intervals by hired village girls.

They have settled on St Martin Undershaft in Holborn. It is a church with literary connections. Andrew Marvell, Samuel Johnson and Christopher Smart are said to have worshipped there. It was founded by a granddaughter of a victim of Macbeth. It was once a leper hospital. It gave succour to the condemned on their way to Tyburn. These credentials seem appropriate. The vicar is said to be a reading man, and the black and white squares of the aisle remind Liz of the dream in which Stephen returned through the ivory gates to tell her that everything was all right.

So far, so good. Many decisions, however, remain. None of them knows much about organizing this kind of event. One should put a notice in the press, but which papers, and how long in advance? The date is still far off, in late June, but they know they have to plan ahead. It will, in fact, be Stephen's birthday. Had he lived to celebrate it, he would have been fifty-five.

Charles is in favour of placing the notice in the *Independent*, which has become, he claims, the new Journal of Record, although it had not even been founded when Stephen left England. Liz favours *The Times*, and Alix points out that if any of Stephen's far-flung friends are to spot it they had better include the *Telegraph*, which has much the best distribution, and is the only paper she and Brian can ever find on sale when they take their rare trips abroad.

Does one invite people to a Memorial? And if so, whom? Does one need to get cards printed, and what shall they say? May members of the public also attend? Should they add the rubric 'Friends and colleagues invited' or will that open the church door to all sorts of undesirable literary riff-raff, to drunken poets and stoned

417

reviewers and wild publicity girls from long defunct firms and well-meaning bores from quasi-governmental committees? (Melvyn Stacey will of course get his personal invitation: no problem there. He has behaved well.) Should there be refreshments? Who will choose the hymns?

So the living, with some attendant mirth, discuss the remembering of the dead. Most of these matters are now settled.

Alix and Liz sit in Liz's drawing room, going through their guest lists and discussing the catering. Hattie, large with child, has just departed, leaving behind her one or two sentimental items salvaged from Stephen's flat and a trail of exotic suggestions — Marlon Brando, she thinks, would like to be asked, and what about President Mitterrand?

Liz has forgiven Hattie. She has become almost fond of her. It can't *last*, she tells Alix, but no harm done, and Aaron seems happy enough. Anyway, none of my business, says Liz. Anyway, babies are nice, says Liz.

Alix has now told Liz about Brian's illness and his major operation and his alleged recovery. She tells Liz that he feels fine. Liz has offered reassuring statistics about chances of survival, has confirmed the hospital's official optimism. Alix wishes she had told Liz earlier, and can no longer be quite sure why she did not.

Liz has offered to hold the post-Memorial reception in St John's Wood. She has space enough, and with luck people will be able to go into the garden. The stragglers will get lost on the way from the church, but that is a good thing. She has asked Deirdre Kavanagh to do the catering, and Deirdre has accepted. Deirdre has reappeared in Liz's life, after a five-year silence, and had greeted the commission with unnerving alacrity. 'Do you remember that New Year's Party I did for you, Liz?' she had said, when Liz rang. 'In Harley Street? New Year's Eve 1979, wasn't it? Wow, that was some party! People haven't got the stamina for that kind of thing these days. And this is a Memorial Service, you say? A wake? Who's it for?'

But at the name of Stephen Cox, Liz reports to Alix, Deirdre had gone very quiet. 'Jesus,' she had murmured, softly, over the phone, and then again, 'Jesus. So Stephen's dead, is he? Well, I always said he'd go too far one day. Stephen dead. God forgive me. God forgive us all.'

Or something like that, reports Liz, from which Liz had rightly concluded that Stephen Cox and Deirdre Kavanagh had had a little fling at some point in history.

'I mean, I'd no idea,' protests Liz, pouring herself another drop of Pernod, and watching the added water cloud the smoky Gallic green. 'I'd no idea at all. I'd no idea they'd even met one another. Stephen was a dark horse, wasn't he? I asked if she minded doing the funeral baked meats for somebody she knew, and she said not at all, not at all, that was the way things were going these days.'

She is drinking the Pernod in Stephen's honour. It was a drink he enjoyed. Esther, who also likes it, had bought the bottle for her on her way back from a visit to the French sponsors of the Venice Biennale. Alix, who dislikes aniseed, is drinking white wine.

'Yes,' says Alix. 'Depressing how many people in our address books are dead, isn't it? I'm glad you didn't snuff it in Bangkok.'

'I hope Miss Porntip will come over for the service,' says Liz. 'I'd like to see Miss Porntip in an English church.'

Alix smiles indulgently. She does not really believe in Miss Porntip. The cat on her knee dozes and purrs. Death seems 10,000 miles away.

'Rum business, that, about the Doctor and the Colonel and Paul Whitmore's mother,' says Liz, meditatively, as she tilts her glass so that the yellow light of the lamp shines athwart its shifting convections.

'Yes,' says Alix, less comfortably. The most recent development in the Whitmore story has disturbed her, as it has disturbed many, although it has, as she and Liz have already agreed, a certain poetic justice. The Doctor and the Colonel, dog breeders and employers of Angela Whitmore Malkin, have been gaoled for four years each for keeping a disorderly house, for taking and publishing indecent photographs, and for assault. Angela has got off scot-free. Her name had not been mentioned in any of the reports that Alix has read. Nevertheless, Alix believes that it was her own telephone call to the RSPCA on behalf of battered dogs that had set this train of events in motion. An abusive letter from Angela, burned as soon as read, had confirmed this suspicion. 'You will pay for this,' Angela had threatened.

Police investigation had revealed at Hartley Bridge flogging equipment, devils' masks, whips, chains, pulleys and pornographic videos. Evidence in court had alleged beating, genital torture, homosexual group sex sessions, nipple piercings, nitrate sniffing. The defence had pleaded consent amongst adults and lack of profit motive. Unsuccessfully.

And they *were* consenting adults, Alix now repeats, as she and Liz chew over the affair. Does one have a right to enjoy being tortured, to enjoy torturing? To enjoy cruelty?

'I could tell it was a Bad Place,' says Alix. 'It wasn't just the dogs. There was something unnatural about the whole set-up. But I suppose they were hurting only themselves?'

Liz shakes her head. It is beyond her. Human nature is bizarre. Blood will have blood.

'Do you think,' she begins, then hesitates, then continues, 'do you think they *used* the dogs? In their so-called disgusting practices?'

Alix laughs, glad the suspicion is out in the open.

'Well, of course, that's what I've been wondering. The dogs didn't feature much in the evidence. But I can't see how they *can't* have been connected, can you?'

'The mind boggles. Either way, the mind boggles,' says Liz.

'My poor Bonzo,' says Alix. 'Rescued from a life of sexual abuse. I haven't noticed any deviant behaviour in poor Bonzo. Though he is a very nervy dog, poor dear. He trembles a lot in his sleep. He has bad dreams.'

'So do we all,' says Liz. 'I dream of men with monkey heads and pig heads. What do you think that means?'

They speak of dreams, and forget the Doctor and the Colonel.

Before Alix leaves, Liz tries to offload on her some of the junk left by Hattie. Perhaps Brian, she suggests, would like these old school magazines, or the gold-embossed copy of Palgrave's *Golden Treasury*, with its motto *Extremum Occupet Scabies*, awarded for Good Work in the Lower Sixth? Alix rejects the magazines but accepts, a little reluctantly, the Palgrave.

As she looks through it on the Rapide Coach to Northam, she comes across a lined page of paper torn from an exercise book with a passage in Stephen's hand, bearing his signature, and dated 28 June 1951. It reads:

The illusion that simplicity once existed is analogous to the myth of Paradise: it fosters the sense of exclusion and exile. But as for man there is no Paradise, so there is no simplicity of emotion; we imagine that we once experienced it, that we once felt directly and received simply the impact of the senses, but we are thereby excluding ourselves from a realm which never existed and which cannot exist. We were not there, for there is no such place; and not by a retrogression to simplicity will we achieve our freedom. For any simplicity is a superimposed blindness, an exclusion of truth, as any Paradise is an exclusion of our one reality of pain. Tempting though it may be to claim that we once possessed innocence, and that all we need to do to be free is to repent and recant, we cannot do it: for if innocence never existed, we cannot reach a state of grace by returning to it, and in the vain attempt we lose courage on what is inevitably the path of corruption and complexity, error and gracelessness.

Alix stares at these words. They seem vaguely familiar. Had Stephen copied them out, and if so, from whom?

In 1951, Stephen was seventeen years old. His last message is his first.

*

Konstantin Vassiliou rarely sees a copy of a British paper, and when he does, he devours it from cover to cover, eating up the print hungrily. This is a change in him, over the past six months. Before that, he had been avoiding words. But now, screwing up his eyes against the fierce light, he makes his way through politics and business news and book reviews and articles on cholesterol and salmonella, and comes at last upon the dreaded name of Stephen Cox, a name both feared and desired. 'A service will be held at St Martin Undershaft, Holborn, at eleven thirty a.m. on Tuesday, 28 June to celebrate the life and work of Stephen Cox, lost in Cambodia. Friends and colleagues welcome.'

Konstantin lets out a low groan. How long has he been waiting for this message, this invitation? He has been in darkness. May he at last emerge?

He reads and rereads the notice. What does that word 'lost' *mean*? What is known, of the death of Stephen Cox?

(Liz to Alix: 'I'm damned if I'm going to put *"dead"*. What if he's *not* dead? How *can* you be dead, without a body? What if he turns up? Let's put "lost", shall we? He'll know what we mean.')

Lost in Cambodia. No month, no date, no year.

Konstantin looks at the date of the yellow, sun-stained, coffee-stained *Telegraph*. He thinks today may be 20 June. Or somewhere round about there.

Konstantin buries his head in his hands and rubs his eyes. Then he looks up at the houses on stilts, the harbour, the pier, the bay, the sea, the fishing boat, the naked children at play. The paper must have been brought ashore by someone from one of the two larger boats at anchor. Is that a yacht flying a British flag? This is a nowhere place. This is the end of the world. This is Paradiso, on the

Island of Flores. There are no flights from the island. The nearest airport is several days' sail away.

The sun beats down. The exalted palm-trees shimmer. The little open-air refrigerator, exuding CFCs, hums. Konstantin sucks at his Coke. Maybe he should go home. Maybe he has been summoned. He remembers Stephen lying in the wooden hut on stilts, skeletal, balding, mumbling in French and in Russian. He stares at the rubric, ignoring the brown barefoot children who are as usual plucking at his shirt for attention. *Lost in Cambodia*. A year, two years, have passed, two years of exile. And what of Akira Tanaka? Where is he? Konstantin, doomed, replays the road block, head in hands. He rereads *The Book of the Dead*.

When he looks up, he sees a young man in batik shorts walking along the curve of the grey volcanic sand towards him and the cluster of little square tin collapsible tables. He has flaming red hair, and is deeply bronzed. He sports an earring with a dangling green feather. He smiles, when he sees Konstantin, and lifts a languid hand in salute.

'All right, mate?' he says, as he comes within range. He speaks in the tones of pure North London. Konstantin, born and bred in N22 in the shade of the Alexandra Palace, responds in kind.

'Not so bad,' he says, adjusting a chair for his new companion. 'What d'you want? Hey, Johnny, a drink for my friend!'

'Same as you, thanks,' says the red-haired sailor.

'This your paper?' asks Konstantin.

'Yeah, must be. Dropped it off last night. Bought it in Darwin. Got yourself up to date with Old Blighty, have you?'

The young man's smile is broad, engaging, friendly. He has brown eyes and a scar down one cheek, picked out by the sun. His freckles glow. He drinks his Coke through a straw, and belches pleasantly.

They chat of this and that, sounding one another out. The young man is crewing for a middle-aged British couple on their way round the world. They picked him up at Cairns. They've got a 46-foot sloop, the *Espérance*. He guesses he'll stick with them a few weeks more, but he knows he won't make it all the way back to Europe. It's a soft berth, but it has problems. And Konstantin, what is he doing? Oh, just hanging about, says Konstantin vaguely. He admits to being a photographer. His gear, he says, is in Jakarta.

They get on well, Konstantin and Matt. They pass the time and chew the fat. They talk of the Boston Arms at Tufnell Park, of the Railway at Southend Green, of the Ally Pally and Clissold Park. Matt had been to Woodberry Down Comprehensive, Konstantin had done a stretch at Acland Burghley. Konstantin knows Tracey Foster, Matt's first-ever girl. Matt had met Konstantin's sister Maria at some gig down the Lock. Matt is a Gunner, Konstantin a Yiddo. Matt fills Konstantin in with two years of football results. Matt's been working for a year in Australia, now he's sort of on his way home. And Konstantin, where's he off to?

'Depends what day it is,' says Konstantin, enigmatically.

'How come?' asks Matt.

'I might get back to England. If I can make it before the 28th,' says Konstantin.

He outlines his plan. He shows Matt the paper and the Memorial notice. Matt stares at it in a mesmerized way and scratches his arm. He does not usually read the gazette page. Matt says that today is 23 June, and that Bali and its international airport are about three days' sail away. Yes, the *Espérance* is heading that way. Why doesn't Konstantin come and have supper on board and have a word with the skipper? They've got a radio, they could try to speak to Singapore, book a flight?

Matt is into the idea. He admits to Konstantin, as they dislodge the naked children from the *Espérance*'s inflatable dinghy, that he is really pissed off with Bob and his wife Eva, would appreciate a bit of livelier company. Maybe he'll hop off in Bali too. Bob and Eva aren't a bad couple, he says, as he pulls out across the water

towards the limp Union Jack, I mean they're not *bad*, but he's a bit
of a racist bastard, he keeps getting his pistol out and asking me if
I'd shoot a pirate if I had to. I mean, hell, he thinks *all* the natives
are pirates. Am I imagining it, or is this thing punctured? Those
little bastards! Look at them laughing their fucking heads off! Never
mind, it's only a slow one, we'll make it. No, Bob's okay, I suppose,
and Eva means well, but you know, they're a bit on the ancient
side. They can't stand the way everyone craps on the beach. Well,
that's just the way it is out here, isn't it? Doesn't worry you,
doesn't worry me. But it worries them. They like crapping in the
toilet and pumping it out on to the beach. They call that hygiene.
They like the middle man. But yeah, I reckon they'll be happy to
take you. They're a bit aimless. It'd give 'em something to do.

'Look at that. Awesome, isn't it?'

They gaze back, as the steep green cone of the island rises higher
at each stroke of the oars. The children play upon the shore,
throwing stones at one another and laughing and darting and
shouting. The brightly painted wooden fishing boats ride gently on
the soft swell.

'Bob's a retired investment consultant,' says Matt. 'Made a packet
and packed it in. Always said he'd take Eva round the world if he
struck lucky, and now he's sticking to his word. Always been a
sailing freak, has Bob. Man of honour, our Bob. Can you cook,
mate? We could do with a bit of inspiration on board, foodwise. I
mean, canwise. You can get a bit tired of the old bean dip and
lambs' tongues and tuna. How long did you say since you saw
England? Getting on for three years? That's longer even than me.
They say that things are getting wild back home. Muggings galore.
Steaming on the tubes. Cardboard city. Tell you something. Better
not mention Mrs T in front of Bob and Eva. They think she's the
fucking greatest. They met her once at a garden party. They think
she's the fucking queen of the fucking universe.

'Good mate of yours, this guy, was he?'

Konstantin stares at the changing geometry of the skyline. Matt pulls evenly upon the oars.

'Yes,' says Konstantin. 'He was a good mate. I think I killed him.'

Matt's rhythm with the oars does not falter. He ploughs on, a slight frown puckering the cloudless goodwill of his brow. He does not want to lose his new chum. He does not want to rock the boat. Gently, he inquires.

'Oh yeah? How come?'

Konstantin, the words spoken, is released from his two-year nightmare. At once, instantly, he knows that it is not true. He did not kill Stephen Cox. He did not even abandon Stephen Cox. Stephen was ill and dying. Stephen Cox would not have responded to a rendering of the Bardo of the Moments of Death. And Stephen Cox had died. That is all. End of story. He would have died anyway. There was no need to run away. Konstantin can go home. The penance is finished.

'Well, it wasn't quite like that,' he says, trailing a hand in the warm salty soupy blood-heat spermy water.

'So what happened?' asks Matt, delicately. The South Seas are full of refugees from fate, of victims and criminals. Matt has heard many stories.

And he listens to the story of Konstantin, as, later, they keep watch in the cockpit through the vibrant night beneath the stars, as the *Espérance* obligingly makes way through the favourable tides towards Bali. On autopilot, their feet up, they recline to the heavy flapping of the sails, sharing a cigarette and a snack of Vegemite on stale toast. Konstantin tells the story he has kept too long to himself, and, priest-like, Matt listens, absorbs, absolves. 'Not your fault, mate,' he says, as he rises to check the compass, to adjust a rope, to sweep the horizon casually through his binoculars. 'No way was it your fault. These things happen. You did your best.'

They settle back, as candle-lit fishing boats and distant islands and a tanker vast and high like a terraced Italian hill town float past them. Matt tells mariner's tales, of dolphins and turtles, of flying fish that whizz out of the water and rattle over the waves, of an exhausted young thin-winged gull that travelled with the *Espérance* for three days, hunched in the rigging, revived on crumbs moistened with Longlife milk by motherly Eva. No boyhood sailfreak was Matt, he had never been on a yacht in his life before he struck up with Bob in a bar in Cairns. It's easy, mate, he murmurs, when Konstantin admires his expertise with the topping lift. Nothing to it. Mostly, it's just autopilot, and on you go.

Towards the end of the watch, as a hazy pink dawn begins to infuse the Eastern sky, as the day already begins to warm, Matt coughs modestly and politely into a sympathetic lull of companionable silence.

'I say, my friend,' he says, and falters, diffidently.

'Yeah?' says Konstantin, encouragingly, anticipating God knows what reciprocal tale of woe – drugs, family disaffection, crashed cars, petty theft, abandoned girlfriends, abortions, AIDS? Matt coughs again, and risks it.

'I say,' he pursues, with some embarrassment, 'you wouldn't have any books with you, would you? I'm not much of a reading man, but you kind of get driven to it, don't you? I've been right through Bob's set of *Swallows and Amazons*. You haven't got a spare paperback to see me on my way? I'd do you a swap. I've got a Graham Greene in the cabin. *The Tenth Man*. It's a bit short, but it's quite good.'

Konstantin, realizing why Matt had been eyeing his bag with such longing, admits to an Eric Ambler picked up in a café in Sarawak. Sure, Matt can have it.

Matt settles back and gazes at the lightening horizon, satisfied. 'Great,' he murmurs. 'Great.'

The sky floods with colour. The sun rises.

*

Konstantin's journey towards the congregation at St Martin Undershaft may be the most hazardous and the most uncertain, but it is not the longest. Helen Anstey comes from yet further afield, from Christchurch in New Zealand. Unlike Konstantin, she has received a proper invitation, forwarded to her from the United Nations Border Relief Operation in Thailand. It had pursued her, via Hong Kong, to the refugee resettlement project in Christchurch, as she happened to open it on the day before she was due to fly back to the UK for her mother's seventieth birthday. She remembers Stephen Cox. He had been taught by her father. Yes, she thinks she may go to the Memorial. He had spoken well of her father. Not many do.

Mrs Yukio Tanaka, presumed widow of Akira Tanaka, receives an invitation, and immediately throws it away. She has no intention of travelling from Tokyo to Holborn to mourn a man she has never met.

Mme Mourre, on the other hand, who happens to see the public announcement in the *Independent*, thinks that she may well fly over from Paris for the day. She makes a point of trying to attend the funerals of her lovers. She thinks it shows respect. She remembers swimming with Stephen in a lake. She remembers taking him to the races. She had read all his novels, even the pseudonymous ones, searching, not always in vain, for her own image. Yes, on balance she thinks she will go. It is time she had a day or two in London. She can go to the new Clore Gallery in the afternoon, to inspect the Turner dawns and sunsets.

Some commit themselves, others hesitate. Deirdre Kavanagh worries about numbers. Rose Vassiliou, courageously and politely, true to form, accepts. Her husband Christopher, true to form, declines.

The little yacht ploughs its sparkling furrow. Great flames blaze upon the night, and molten red oozes slowly from green cones.

*

It is coming up to ten o'clock in the morning on a grey weeping Tuesday in late June. Liz Headleand sits at her dressing table in St John's Wood and stares at herself. She is still in her underwear, for she cannot decide what clothes will be suitable for the occasion. She has renounced black as too portentous. It is a little tricky, holding a Memorial Serivce so long after the event, and without even a carton of ashes. What if Stephen were to walk through the door as the hymns rise to heaven? She hopes to God that he will approve of the selection.

She decides finally upon the short crimson skirt and the made-to-measure saffron Thai silk jacket in which in Saigon she had heard the news of his death. She had lost weight during her hospitalization in Bangkok, and through an effort of will in succeeding months has not regained it. The garments fit her better than they did.

She slips into the skirt. The digital radio clock informs her that it is nine fifty-eight. As she fastens the zip, the phone rings. It is her stepson Alan, checking to see how things are going. He has declined to attend, for, as he says, he never met Stephen, and he is busy marking exams. But he wants to wish her well. He has been protective, since he received her distress call from the Oriental. He takes some credit for her recovery, as he now informs her. He is himself off in a couple of weeks to deliver a paper at a conference in Singapore. He is very proud of this. She, in turn, tells him to remember his malaria pills, and to avoid drug-pushers. An Australian woman with a perambulator full of heroin has just been arrested in a department store in Bangkok. She faces a death sentence. Take care, Liz says.

As he rings off, she switches the radio back on, in time to hear that there has been a major accident on the M4 between Heathrow and Junction 3. A lorry has crossed the barrier, and cars have piled into it. Avoid, says the news bulletin.

She switches off, and applies pink lipstick. Downstairs, refreshments wait under cling film, and bottles cool in the refrigerator. She fears it will be too wet to go into the garden. The blown roses hang their heavy heads and the clematis drags and trails. The car will arrive at ten thirty, the service will begin at eleven thirty. Charles is coming in the car to collect her. Alix and Brian will make their own way. So will Aaron and the pregnant Hattie. Marlon Brando and President Mitterrand have not yet replied to their invitations. But, if they choose to arrive, she will be equal to them.

So when is Hattie's baby due? Any minute now, from the look of her. It is hard to think seriously of Stephen, when there is so much still going on. People dying on the M4, babies being born, Alan's career taking off. Liz hopes that Deirdre Kavanagh will keep cool. She is slightly worried to hear that her semi-estranged yuppie stepson Jonathan, who had long ago had an affair with Deirdre, is to attend the wake. He had never known Stephen, and unlike Alan had never even read him, so why this sudden interest, unless it be for Deirdre? He is, of course, like his father, a television man, so he may be bidding for Stephen's bones. But she doubts it. It is the Deirdre factor that she fears.

Deirdre has already confided to Liz that after Liz's party, the party that ushered in the 1980s, she had been on a two-year blinder with, of all people, that madman Giles, who had seen in the New Year while sprawled among the pot plants of Harley Street: a wild time we had of it, once we fell in together, Deirdre had said with relish as she skinned tomatoes and pounded at cod roe. And where was Giles now? In hospital, being dried out. For the third time. It's all done on the National Health, Deirdre had said, adding lemon juice.

Liz supposes that she could have predicted something like this. But she had not. Will any such dramas be set in motion today? Or are they all too sober and too old?

Her clock flicks to ten fourteen. She switches off the radio, assembles her new black patent-leather handbag, her keys, her

Memorial programme, a clean sprigged handkerchief with a pattern of corn and poppies.

It had been quite a party, that New Year's Eve party. They don't make parties like that these days, thinks Liz, or if they do, I don't bother to go to them. Wasn't it that evening that Charles had announced his intention to marry Lady Henrietta? Or am I mixing up my dates?

She slips on her new yellow shoes. She hopes the rain will not ruin them.

Quite a lot has happened, in the last eight and a half years. Charles has been divorced and remarried and divorced again. Her mother has died. Esther has married. She herself has met Stephen Cox, and failed to marry him, and now she is about to bury him. She has a step-grandchild, and another very much on the way. She has moved house. Alix has moved house. Her sister Shirley has been widowed, and has married a Canadian metallurgist and gone off to live in Alberta. Her daughter Sally has graduated and got a proper job with Southwark Council and bought a flat with her friend Jo on a double mortgage. Her daughter Stella — no, she cannot bear to think about her daughter Stella. Will Stella ever forgive her and come home?

The clock declares that it is ten twenty-two. She hears Charles at the door. He is letting himself in. He calls so often now that she has given him a key. He is eight minutes early. These days, he is always more than prompt.

*

Alix Bowen, contemplating herself in a tilted cheval glass in Polly Piper's well-appointed spare bedroom in Regent's Park Road, sees herself robed in a ceremonial black dress purchased from French Connection in Sheffield for her mother's funeral. It also did service at her father's. She is getting a lot of wear out of it. It was a good buy.

Alix has spent the last two days worrying about the attempted suicide of Paul Whitmore. He had bungled it, poor fool. He had tried to hang himself, using it is said, the strands of an unravelled woollen jersey. Now he lies in the prison hospital, more brain damaged than before. Will he be costing the state more or less, she wonders, in his new condition? Will she ever be called on to visit him again? Have the Doctor and the Colonel ended up in Porston with him, or are they eating prawn cocktails in some soft open gaol of the south?

It has been a relief to get away from Northam. Her friend Polly is in excellent spirits. She has been made a baroness and will sit in the House of Lords. Alix does not know what this means, exactly, but she feels it must be good news. Polly will lecture the old boys on VAT on sanitary wear and other women's issues and it will do them a power of good. Alix and Brian have congratulated Polly warmly, although in theory of course they do not approve of the House of Lords. But if we have to have a second chamber, let it be subverted by you, Brian had said to Polly over a Thai takeaway. It had been a jolly evening.

This has been a difficult year for Alix and Brian. But things are looking up. Alix will not be needing this black dress as widow's weeds. The operation on the large intestine has been, they are assured, successful.

Alix powders her nose and delves in her washbag for her mother's second-best pearls.

She is reprieved from what they had come to speak of as her Life without Brian. She will not turn into that old witch, that mad recluse, that inspired sibyl. Or not yet, not yet.

Alix had hated Brian's illness. She had hated her own fear. She had hated the old-fashioned nineteenth-century hospital, with its terrible carved tragi-comic legend over its Ionic portals, reading, in huge letters, for all the world to see ST ANTHONY'S FISTULA & C. She had hated Brian's feigned stoicism and feigned humility. She

432

had hated the indignity, the reductiveness of sickness. She had, to her shame, quarrelled with the specialist, who had struck her as a pompous condescending unfeeling little prat. She had lost faith in the National Health Service, and had weakly wished that Brian had taken out private medical insurance decades ago, so that he could now be spared the shabby ward, the communal lavatory, the colourless drained old men with stubble beards, the plastic bed curtains, the walking drips, the smells, the institutional cooking, the pert bossy little nurses. She had wished they could purchase respect with money. She had sulked and behaved badly. She had failed the test.

But now she is forgiven. She does not deserve it, but she is. Brian has a new lease of life. They have disembowelled him and stitched him up and remade him as good as new. He is back at work and enjoying it. Perry Blinkhorn has been a brick.

Alix gazes at herself, adjusts her belt and hem. Black suits her. Mourning becomes her. She will pull herself smartly to attention, and face the day. She will enjoy it, she suspects. She will see old friends, old acquaintances, gathered together. Why not enjoy?

The shadow has fallen, but she will ignore it, and look the other way, into the light. She will forget that premature insight into decline, helplessness, dependence, bed pans, and, worst of all, the indifferent contempt of the healthy young. She and Brian have decades ahead of them. And here he is, at the door, a mug of coffee in his hand, saying it is time they were thinking of moving, for the radio says the traffic is bad in town today. She smiles at him, through the mirror. In August, they are going on a month's holiday. A whole month, to France. A month in the sun.

*

The Garuda Boeing from Jakarta circles over Heathrow, stacked for its descent. The flying monster is early, though it will not admit it to its passengers, who look at their watches, synchronize with

Greenwich Mean Time, stow away their copies of *Time* magazine
and *Asia Weekly*, stretch their legs, replace their shoes, inspect their
complexions, yawn, check their landing cards, gaze out of the
window at the silver snake of the Thames, and plan their onward
journeys. So far, so good. They think they are doing well. They
have not yet been told about the accident on the M4.

*

Esther and Robert Oxenholme are already in Holborn. Alerted to
the day's heavy traffic by Robert's driver, they have been dropped
off at Cambridge Circus, and are now sitting in a backstreet sandwich bar, drinking black coffee from thick white cups and sharing a
cheese and pickle roll. What are they thinking about? From here, it
would be hard to say. Their heads incline seriously together, and
they are deep in conversation amidst the clientele of van drivers
and motorbike dispatch riders. Are they discussing the inflated
prices of British Impressionist paintings? Are they planning a trip to
the École Française d'Extrême-Orient, or to the Queen of Novara at
Pallanza? Are they speaking of Robert's ex-wife Lydia Wittering,
who has broken an arm playing polo? Are they speculating about
the rumoured arrival of Simon Grunewald? Are either or both of
them having an affair with the mysterious woman in white? Are
either or both of them thinking of Stephen Cox?

Whatever the text or the subtext of their conversation, here,
from this side of the smeared pane with its scribbled legends of
sandwich fillings, they seem united, intent. They look more married
than they did three months ago. Esther takes a nibble of the roll,
Robert picks up a crumb of cheese from the plate on his finger.
Suddenly they both laugh. Perhaps it *is* Simon Grunewald of whom
they speak? Or then again, perhaps not.

*

The sky is heavy with rain. Purple and grey clouds darkly lower over the skyscraper called Centrepoint, and dull light reflects from high windows. Grey compounds grey, relieved only by gleams of a chalky whiteness. Stephen Cox's middle brother, Jeremy, the delinquent ex-jailbird, cannot find his way into the church. He has arrived early, for fear of being late, and now he cannot get in. There is a garden behind the church, with worn, flaking table tombs, and dingy beds of roses. Humble purple weeds flourish. An old armchair lurks in the shrubbery. Cans of Carlsberg Special Brew lie beneath the tangled jasmine. Bedraggled pigeons strut and pick.

Jeremy Cox stares at them with distaste. He smells dossers, though he cannot yet see them. He wanders on, and spots their encampment. An ark of an upturned settee, covered in wet bedspreads, like a children's garden hideout. A sodden cardboard box. This is no weather for sleeping rough. Jeremy Cox has tried it, and he knows.

He kicks at the litter of ring pulls from beer cans, and reads the label on a wet crisp packet. Prawn Cocktail Flavour. Just what you need for a night in the open.

A white light beats back from the grey stone of the building. Tufts of grass sprout from a cracked cornice. Plane-trees toss in torment.

Jeremy dreads seeing his brothers. He has avoided them for years, but now is drawn into their presence. He thinks of Stephen, baby Stephen. He hardly knew him. He has never read his books. Dead, now, and Francis, Andrew and himself all in their sixties. It hardly seems possible. How has it all come to pass?

Shall he turn and make his escape? Where the hell is the entrance? Are these more funeral guests?

He follows Esther and Robert Oxenholme into the church, is handed a programme, finds himself a seat at the back.

Slowly the pews fill. People whisper and wave and smile, then look solemn. They peruse their programmes, inspect the choice of hymns, the texts of the readings. They shake drops of water from their umbrellas.

Liz had wanted to include the crumpled passage on communism from John Stuart Mill in the programme, but had been overruled. She has, however, been permitted to select some Rimbaud. She has chosen the 'Chanson de la plus haute tour', and it is to be sung in a setting by Vinteuil. Liz has never heard it, but Aaron, who recommended the counter-tenor, tells her it is just fine, and she believes him. And as the words are in French, no one will understand them, and no one will object.

Alix, atheist connoisseur of hymns, is responsible for the choice of Clifford Bax's 'Turn back, O man, forswear thy foolish ways'. She knows that Stephen liked it, for he told her so. And anyway, *she* likes it.

Hattie had frivolously suggested 'Remember all the people, Who live in far-off lands', but she had on persuasion relinquished it in favour of 'As pants the hart for cooling streams,' a piece that she has since early childhood found curiously erotic. She has also with some perseverance tracked down a more appropriate poem by a Paris-based Cambodian poet, called 'Requiem for a Generation'. It is to be read, in translation of course, by Hilda Stark.

As the congregation settles, the organ plays some muffled music, and Liz gazes around her at the fluted pillars picked out in dark blood-red and gold, at the black and white tiles of her dream, at the gaudy turquoise and lighter red scrolls and twirls and ornaments behind the altar, at the funerary tablets upon the wall. Two plump winged cherub-heads hover solidly in heavy ivory-yellow corpse-marble above a polished skill. An inscription records the Vertues of Samuel Winter, renowned for his mildness of temper and benignity of mind.

Is that one of Stephen's brothers over there, fussily arranging his rain coat on the pew? He looks *very* like Stephen. And there is Stephen's landlord, Mr Goodfellow, with his mild untidy well-meaning features, peering short-sightedly at his programme, and that old boy must be Stephen's one-time tutor, Lord Filey of Foley.

There are Robert and Esther, there is Pett Petrie, there is Gabriel Denham (who might, thinks, Liz have bothered to put on a tie). There, good Lord, is Simon Grunewald! So he has made it! And there is Dr Marianne Sanderson, and Jonathan Headleand, and there is John Geddes, who seems to have lost a lot of weight. There are Brian and Alix, there is that chap from the British Council whose name she can never remember, and there is Melvyn Stacey. But who on earth is that elegant ash-blonde woman in a dark blue tailored suit with dark blue seamed stockings and a hat? And is that pallid, silver-haired worried-looking woman in a grey coat by any chance Rose Vassiliou? And where the hell are Aaron and Hattie Osborne? And can that be the representative from Stephen's old school, Moxley Hall?

Aaron and Hattie are on the steps by the side entrance. They are both laughing, but there is a note of hysteria in Hattie's laughter. 'Oh *shit*,' she says, '*shit, shit, shit*.' And shit indeed it is. A pigeon in the straining, groaning broad-leaved plane-tree above them has shat upon Hattie, and her raincoat and her best blue maternity dress are spattered with tablespoonsful of grey–green khaki excrement. She dabs at it with a piece of kitchen roll from her pocket, Aaron scrapes at it with a dirty blue white-spotted handkerchief. 'Oh Jesus, I look a *freak*,' says Hattie, staring crossly upwards angrily through the coarse tossing green leaves. 'Filthy, filthy, pesky, disgusting birds!'

'Come on, Hat, we'll be late,' says Aaron, coaxingly. 'Anyway, it's lucky, so they say. It's good luck, bird shit.'

'Is it really?' Hattie brightens.

'Yes, it is,' lies Aaron. 'Come on, sweetheart. Listen, they're starting on the first hymn, come on, we don't want to make too much of an entrance.'

As the voices rise in uncertain unison, Alix watches a bird perched on the ledge just outside the nearest window. It is the most horrible bird she has ever seen. Its feathers stick out at all angles, it is grey and black and huddled, its beak is crooked, and its legs end in pink leprous stumps. It is disease and pollution and death.

> Turn back, O man, forswear thy foolish ways;
> Old now is earth, and none may count her days.

They sing, and Alix finds herself reaching in her coat pocket for her wad of paper tissue.

> Earth might be fair and all men glad and wise,
> Age after age their tragic empires rise,
> Built while they dream, and in that dreaming weep

Alix sobs. In vain has she tried to fix her attention upon the unpleasant Bird of III Omen: the music has made its way through to her, the familiar sonorous Old 124th pours through her, and in Pavlovian reflex she sniffs and sobs. She has always been a sucker for hymns, and this one goes straight to the heart. School assemblies of old stir and thicken in her memory, and she sees her young self, resilient, idealistic, standing bravely to attention to the brave words of Wandsworth-born Clifford Bax. Oh, the possibilities lost, the great expectations!

> Would *man* but *wake* from *out* his *haunted* sleep,
> Earth might be fair and all men glad and wise.

And so indeed it might have been, might be! Why *could* not man wake from his haunted sleep? Why must it go on for ever and ever, death and destruction, tragic empire after tragic empire, Tamburlaine, Hitler, Stalin, Pol Pot, and the Stars and Stripes planted upon Mars as the imperial contamination spreads like a cancer through interstellar space? Will the killing ever stop, will the Numbers Game ever be played out, will atrocities ever cease, will the choir and the congregation be able to rise to the crescendo? No, of course not.

Earth shall be fair, and all her people one!

No, of course not, these voices are not powerful enough, they are not unified, they strain but they cannot make it, they are earthbound, feeble, out of tune. They are *human*. And God will not step in to help his people, for God is Dead. Even Clifford Bax had seemed doubtful about God, and more certain of the Inner than the Outer Voice: and since Bax's death God himself has died, again and again and again. Alix believes she has utterly relinquished him, but the ache lingers on in the amputated limbs. For years after the Death of God, Alix had continued to pray to the habit of hope that God represented, and had found herself once more, in Brian's illness, thinking of the possibility of prayer: but how to pray, in a universe of black dwarfs and red giants? How to pray, in a universe made of string? When I became a woman, I put away childish things, thinks Alix: things such as hymns, prayers, God, hope. The music revives in her a craving for them, a longing for comfort, for sugar, for the sweets of security. Is it this she weeps for, this loss? The very smell of school assembly, the smell of childhood returns to her: polished wood, pollen, boys' trousers, dust, an institutional provincial Non-conformist smell subtly different from this old sacred church odour. What a package they had been sold, of high-minded devotion, of public service and self-sacrifice!

She thinks of Betty Sykes, in her own eccentric way still obedient to that high calling, that long indoctrination: she thinks of Brian who has never needed God but who has always loved his fellow-men; she thinks of Paul Whitmore, whom God had utterly abandoned; she thinks of Stephen Cox, who had loved nobody and hated nobody, dying alone in a foreign land.

She hopes that Stephen did not die in despair. She hopes that it is true that he died of malaria, not at the hands of his fellow-men. We all owe God a death, but we hope not to find ourselves cornered in a guesthouse bathroom staring down the barrel of a gun, or forced to dig our own grave by our own kind.

'Earth shall be fair, and all her folk be one!' conclude the choir and congregation, with a faltering unpractised note of heart-breaking optimism, extended equally to the toiling billions of China, to the Indian subcontinent, to the Americas, to the fragmenting empire of the Soviet Union, to the Iranians and the Inuit and the head-hunters of Irian Jaya and the whole stinking selfish murderous brutish greedy gazetteer of *National Geographic* folk colourful and colourless, rich and poor, oppressing and oppressed: in short to the whole four or five billion individuals that make up the population of the globe, of whom this ragged, tattered, fragmented, faithless gathering makes but a miserably inadequate representation. Alix feels a sudden, terrible impatience. What are they *doing* here, in a *church*, for God's sake, at this point in time? Why can't we get on with the *next* thing? She blows her nose firmly, and Hattie Osborne dabs at her stained dress, and jetlagged Helen Anstey yawns discreetly, and Lord Filey noisily unwraps a throat sweet, and Charles wonders if he will get a parking ticket. (Or, worse, a clamp.)

During the address that follows, in which Stephen's virtues are respectfully but wittily recalled by one of his many ex-publishers, Alix stares firmly at the pigeon. Brian's illness has shaken her more than she will admit. Mortality huddles and struts on the window ledge. Paul Whitmore has tried to hang himself. Stephen is dead. What becomes of all those soarings, those flights, those intimations? Does life thin out now until death, is one's best hope now to cease to feel? Must one now give up, at this late stage in the game? Alix half wishes she had not taken up reading popular scientific theory. Chaos and string have unhinged her mind, and it wanders off unbidden into outer space, where it has no business, and which it can never comprehend. While scientists in their decaying mortal frames fret, aggrieved, anthropocentric, after the Nobel, that other time extends for ever, and nothing comes back but a thin cosmic giggle. We got over Copernicus, we got over Galileo, we got over

Darwin, we have survived Einstein and the Death of God and the Death of the Family and the Death of the Novel, and what can we now do but laugh? Can the joke save us? Or has it too gone off? Alix is depressed by the publisher. He means well, but he has gone on for too long. She hopes he will not make a joke about the Booker Prize. But he does, he does.

The bird glowers at Alix. Its hard pink-rimmed eyes stare balefully. Is it the soul of Paul Whitmore, come to haunt her?

The publisher returns to his pew, and Aaron Headleand's counter-tenor protégé takes the stand. Alix's genial spirits lift.

This is more like it. He is a pale, Swinburnian young man, theatrically dressed in a suit of the palest grey, with a silver waistcoat embroidered with scarlet dragons. His hair is chestnut, and it is tossed back from his pale brow in romantic waves that contradict the formality of his garments. He wears gold-rimmed spectacles, and his buttonhole is a white rose. He arranges his music, and nods to the solitary female flautist who will accompany him. His voice rises through the unsatisfactory layers of architecture, above the urns and monuments, above the pulpit and the floral decorations, above the heads of the Headleands and the Bowens and the Coxes, above the whole assembly. It drifts with pure and unholy and unearthly yearning into the arched empyrean.

> *Oisive jeunesse*
> *À tout asservie,*
> *Par délicatesse*
> *J'ai perdu ma vie . . .*

Up and up, on and on, mounting in a single strand, a liquid melody of mourning, defiance, challenge, regret:

> *J'ai tant fait patience*
> *Qu'à jamais j'oublie;*
> *Craintes et souffrances*

Aux cieux sont parties,
Et la soif malsaine
Obscurcit mes veines . . .

Brian Bowen, listening, himself reprieved for a while from de-
generation and humiliation and death, sees the face of his friend at
the age of twenty: ardent, diffident, tenacious. Brian owes his career
and his education to Stephen Cox. He owes his life to Stephen Cox.
He will never have another such friend. He sees himself and Stephen,
lying in the long grass in Dorset, reading, chatting, smoking, in the
springtime of their days.

Ainsi la prairie
A l'oubli livrée,
Grandie, et fleurie
D'encens et d'ivraies
Au bourdon farouche
De cent sales mouches . . .

He sees Stephen lying sick in a field hospital on the far side of the
world, amidst the buzzing of the filthy flies. In a solitude chosen,
willed, intensified. The voice soars and planes, beyond and beyond,
in its own disembodied sphere. How can it issue from this strange
perverse young man? And here comes the reprise of the first verse,
melancholy and triumphant: and as it rises in its final leave-taking,
the double doors at the end of the aisle burst noisily open. The
cadence ebbs and dies, and heads turn.

The newcomer stands there, facing the singer, along the full
length of the black and white tiles. He has made it. The singer folds
his music, gives a prim little bow as it were of recognition, saluting
the timing of the intruder, and then a little bow of dismissal to the
congregation, as he resumes his seat in the front pew.

Heads turn and eyes fix themselves not upon the ghost of

Stephen Cox but upon a dishevelled young man ill-dressed for a sombre Memorial Service on a drenching day. He is sodden and unshaven, and his grey–white muddy training shoes squelch with water. He is out of breath, for he has run all the way from Leicester Square tube station. His white shirt sticks to his brown body. His fair hair is dark with sweat. He carries a plastic sports bag emblazoned with a crouching tiger. He wipes his streaming forehead with his arm, and gazes wildly around him at the questioning faces, searching for the one he knows and loves and fears. The organist halts, hesitates, and continues, as Konstantin Vassiliou makes his way to his mother's side.

The eyes of the curious remain fixed upon Rose and Konstantin Vassiliou as the tune of 'As pants the hart' fills the assembly. It is a strange reunion. His whole body is still heaving with effort, and her demeanour is torn between tears and laughter. He puts his arm around her, squeezes her, and randomly picks up a hymn book. Disapproval, relief, embarrassment and joy chase one another across her features. The prodigal son has returned. He slips his arm around her waist. She is ruffled, distraught. How can she settle back into the dim mood of a Memorial for a man she never knew? She allows him to hold her, but pulls away from him a little as disapprobation struggles with delight. How *can* he have done this to her? Has he done it all on purpose? How long ago was this fuse planted, this plot laid? Her heart beats wildly, as the organ wheezes its familiar tune. Konstantin smells amazing. He smells of all the nations and airports and seaways of the world. Rank human odours rise from him, triumphing over wet wool and dry rot and Brasso and furniture polish and the ancient British bone dust of lepers eight centuries dead.

Slowly, as the service proceeds, through poetry and pieties, to its conclusion, the rapid breathing of Konstantin is calmed, and his overstoked energy subsides. Rose wriggles free from his clasp, and gazes sternly ahead. Konstantin takes up a more subdued and penitent posture by her side. Rose summons her resources of maternal indignation and, as the last strain dies away she rounds upon Konstantin. As murmurs and whispers and greetings and partings break out around them, she hisses at him crossly.

'Where *do* you think you've been all this time? And did you *have* to make such an entrance?'

Konstantin tries to look innocent. 'Didn't you get my message?' he mutters back. 'We sent a radio message through Singapore. And you must have got my card from Ende. Didn't you get my card from Ende?'

'Which card are you speaking of?' asks Rose, tartly. 'This year's or last year's?'

But all around them there is movement, and their little intimate domestic drama is swamped in waves and ripples, in gestures and jostlings. A new drama is declared, as Hattie Osborne says she will not come to the Reception, she will go straight to the hospital to have her baby. She's booked in for the evening, but she thinks she will go now. Aaron tries to dissuade her, and succeeds. Well, she will come for five minutes, perhaps, to the party in St John's Wood.

Simon Grunewald is chatting up the smartly dressed Frenchwoman, who has dashingly opened the conversation by saying that she once pushed Stephen Cox out of a window into a rosebed. The counter-tenor is receiving compliments from Robert Oxenholme. Liz Headleand is being introduced to the Cox brothers. Gabriel Denham is looking for Konstantin Vassiliou, but Konstantin and Rose have already vanished, and are walking arm-in-arm down the Charing Cross Road, their heads bent closely together, as Konstantin tries in ten minutes to account for three years of his life. Will Rose forgive him? Will he be forgiven? And what has been his crime?

The pavement outside the church is slippery from the rain. The sky is clearer now and a bright blue beats above, with high white cumulus blown in towering bundles, but a thin film of grease, water and birdlime coats the surface of the uneven stones. Liz, releasing herself from Stephen's brothers, hastening towards Charles, his car and her catering responsibilities, slips, and quite heavily, falls. It is her ankle again. She does not think she has broken anything, she assures Charles, as he helps her through the dirty garbage-strewn little back lanes of the rookery behind the church to the building site where the car awaits. She hobbles, in her short skirt. The car has not been clamped or ticketed. Charles opens the door for her, and she clambers in. She sits there, nursing her ankle, rubbing at the marks on her yellow silk jacket. 'You okay?' says Charles.

'Fine, fine,' says Liz, irritably. 'Just generally cracking up and losing my grip, that's all.'

And off they go, weaving their way towards the funeral baked meats and their high priestess, Deirdre Kavanagh née Nora Molloy, who greets them in flowing olive and silver, armed with a tray of straw-sparkling Veuve du Vernay, with a Venetian glass necklace of pale green and yellow roses round her throat, and a spray of hellebore woven into her Titian hair.

*

Is this the grand finale? Is this the End of History? Or is it all a Godawful mistake?

Those guests who make a quick getaway from the leper church and arrive in St John's Wood before the traffic of London grinds to a halt are in lenient mood. As far as they are concerned, civilization is doing just fine. They sip and munch and chatter, and some, risking their summer shoes, venture on to the wet grass of the garden and peer with interest into the little lily pond and admire the weighty yellow and crimson roses which drop their curved petals on the lawn. This is a Good Time post-Memorial party, with excellent refreshments, pleasant décor, interesting company. And they are all, after all, still very much alive.

Stephen's name hovers over the gathering, but it sheds little melancholy. At first some speak of him, and some do not. The service is praised, the Rimbaud setting receiving particular commendation. Stephen would have approved of it, it is agreed. One guest ventures that Stephen had chosen it as one of his Desert Island Discs: or something very like it. Mr Goodfellow tells a Stephen anecdote which serves as a fitting epitaph. Stephen, he says to a listening circle, had once modestly deflected the compliment of being an exemplary and tidy tenant in these words: 'I'm not really tidy,' Stephen had said. 'It's just that I don't have many things.'

This remark does the rounds, relayed from one group to another. Heads nod. So it had been. Stephen had lived light, and travelled light, and lightly he had departed. His wisdom is praised by women who hang on to their handbags amongst the spoils of Liz Headleand, by men whose attention flicks from time to time to their office desks or their parked cars. Stephen has reinforced their identities. They hold out their glasses for more wine.

Other guests are not so fortunate, and their view of the day's events and the course of post-industrial capitalist civilization may not be quite so benign. For this is one of those days, long awaited and by some gleefully predicted, when it seems that the whole system will break down. (And if the traffic can, why not finance, why not money markets, why not the machinery of the whole world?) The accident on the M4, which had forced Konstantin on to the tube instead of into a taxi, has introduced some virus into the bloodstream of the city, and traffic lights have broken down sympathetically all over the west and the north. Charing Cross Road, Tottenham Court Road, Baker Street, Marylebone Road and Euston Road are immobilized. Queues stretch northwards way up the Finchley Road. Once in, there is no way out. In stationary vehicles angry mourners berate their partners for having chosen the wrong route. Some abandon taxis for the Underground, only to find that it too is infected, its platforms dangerously crowded, its announcements on the blink. Aaron, threading through back streets in his old

Fiat, glances nervously at Hattie's belly and wishes he had let her follow her own instincts. Even if they get to St John's Wood, how the hell is he going to get her back again to the delivery ward? By helicopter?

Dr Marianne Sanderson and Helen Anstey are sharing a taxi. They are distant acquaintances, colleagues of a kind, and their conversation had begun politely enough, but now they are engaged in an impassioned argument about Konstantin Vassiliou. Marianne had said how delighted and astonished she had been to see him walk into the church so unexpectedly, what a relief to see him looking so well after so long an absence: expecting, clearly the usual Konstantin fan-club response. But Helen had snorted with impatient disapproval, and declared that the young man was nothing but a poseur and a parasite and a play-actor. He'd done it all on purpose, according to Helen – the disappearance, the dramatic reappearance, the lot. A spoilt brat, a head-turner, a self-indulgent clown. Marianne, shocked by this character assassination, had sprung to his defence: she had found him a serious person, the soul of kindness, so thoughtful, such a good photographer! *Anyone* can take a photo, says Helen. Give me a camera, and *I* can take a photo. There's nothing to it. But ask him to do your job or mine – why, he's completely untrained. He's an amateur. He's a playboy. He thinks he's Errol Flynn.

Marianne is so annoyed by this that she thinks of getting out of the taxi and walking, but then thinks better of it, as she does not know the way. So she and Helen sit and glower at the expensive over-heating hardware around them in irritable silence.

'Anyway,' says Helen, as the taxi gradually begins to edge forward, groaning and straining: 'Anyway, Konstantin's gay.'

'What?' says Marianne.

'Gay. You know. Homosexual.'

'I don't see what that's got to do with it,' says Marianne, 'I don't think he is, but even if he is, why shouldn't he be? Perhaps you're gay. Perhaps I'm gay. So what?'

Jonathan Headleand also finds himself stuck in the traffic, but he is alone and has nobody to argue with, so he just sits there, listening to his tapes. He has no interest in Stephen Cox or Konstantin Vassiliou, but he is quite curious to see Deirdre Kavanagh again. That is why he is here. After a while he rings Liz's number on his car phone, but it is engaged. He changes his tape and switches off his engine. Maybe it's better if he doesn't get there, after all. Maybe this jam is meant.

Simon Grunewald ditches his taxi and walks. He is good at walking. He has not come halfway round the world to be stopped by this kind of stuff. He has a good sense of direction, and he walks at a steady pace, arriving in St John's Wood just as Liz is beginning to get worried by the obvious absence of some of her more serious guests – where are the Cox brothers, for example, and what has happened to Alix and Brian? She is trying to detach herself from the attentions of Pett Petrie when Simon arrives: Pett is sticking to the view that somewhere in a safe deposit in Bangkok or Saigon or Hanoi or Phnom Penh lingers the text of the novel to end all novels, the Great Adventure into Nowhere, Stephen Cox's ultimate masterpiece, and Liz, who has long ceased to believe anything of the sort, is trying to explain that this is not so. She is pleased to see Simon, who explains about the traffic, and hungrily shoves into his mouth a whole large handful of canapés. He eats like a savage, but nobody seems to mind.

Charles is pleased to make the acquaintance of the exotic Simon, but a little disappointed not to see Miss Porntip. Maybe she too will make a late entrance, maybe even now she speeds towards them in lover's executive jet, maybe even now she hovers over the traffic in lover's executive helicopter? But he does not really expect her. She would not convince, in St John's Wood.

Gradually, stranded figures straggle in to swell the throng, with tales of disaster overcome. There is one woman in a black suit and veiled hat whom nobody recognizes at all. She speaks to nobody, but eats and drinks almost as heartily as Simon Grunewald. The rumour circulates that she is a professional mourner who works the beat. Aaron thinks he saw her at Jacqueline du Pré's Memorial, and Pett Petrie says she may have been at Reggie Smith's. Liz's half-sister, the easygoing and friendly Marcia, tries to engage her in conversation, but reports that she has failed utterly: the woman had simply stared at her in astonishment, her crimson-lipped white doll face like a mask, and gone on munching a sandwich. The Nightmare Life-in-Death is she, murmurs Marcia to Hattie Osborne.

By the time Marianne and Helen reach Dresden Road, they are reconciled. They have buried the hatchet over the corpse of Eric Rosenberg. Now *he*, Helen had conceded, had been a good egg. He had been the Real Thing. She remembered his Jack Lemmon imita-tion with particular admiration. She'd never actually seen any Jack Lemmon movies, she wasn't much of a movie-goer, but Eric's version had been very entertaining. She'd been sorry to hear of the accident. Yes, she would like a glass of wine. Can that, she asks Marianne, really be Robert Oxenholme? And if so, what on earth is he doing in this set-up? His father, she says, had been one of the few people who had stood by her father, when the troubles began. She must go and say hello before the party is over.

Alix and Brian Bowen are amongst those stuck in the worst of the traffic. They had driven down from Northam, and had driven themselves from Regent's Park Road to Holborn, and are now paying the price by sitting motionless in Lisson Grove. They take this philosophically. This is the way things are, increasingly, in London. It would not surprise them if the whole city came to a perpetual halt. As they sit peacefully, amidst the dull growling of engines punctuated by the occasional hopeless hooting of a defiant horn, they think about the Green Party and global warming and the car industry, as they would. But Alix and Brian are not as green as one might expect. It was all very well, they agree, for Alix's parents to go green at the end of a long and fairly comfortable life, but what about the car workers of Dagenham? What about the poor of India, of China, of Africa? Shall they not have their refrigerators, their motorcars? Is it not their turn now?

Alix and Brian have a new and by their standards rather expensive car, purchased from the legacy from Alix's parents. They are pleased with it and enjoy driving it and sitting in it. The death of Alix's parents had brought them more than a 1930s tea set and an old wardrobe and an embroidered tablecloth and a string of pearls, it has also brought them a share of the sale of the Bowen bungalow which Dottie and Dolly had wisely purchased well in advance of their eviction from the tied Deputy Master's Lodge. It had not appreciated as spectacularly as the Bowen house in Wandsworth, but it had appreciated nevertheless, and Alix, John and Jenny had done well from the scrupulously fair three-way divide of the spoils. The Doddridges and the Bowens may not approve of the new property-owning democracy, and they may not think capitalism the dream system to end all systems, but they cannot help profiting. The shabby *fin de siècle* terrace house in Wandsworth, purchased for £9,000, is now said to be worth £300,000. Alix and Brian find this unlikely. But, of course, they do not sell.

'I *suppose*,' said Alix, dubiously, staring around her at unswept pavements, a de luxe fish and chip shop, a teenage mother wheeling two babies in a keeling balloon-topped double push chair, an old man with a Tesco plastic bag rifling through the contents of a garbage bin, and her wealthier fellow-citizens yawning or tapping angrily at their expensive car wheels, 'I *suppose* I'd rather be sitting here stuck in this car than sitting stuck on a bus or down the tube. I'm beginning to think public transport is a lost cause. Do you think the Labour government will be able to rescue it?'

'I doubt it,' says Brian, who has become more realistic of late, and who is not in the mood to discuss transport subsidies.

'I mean,' says Alix, 'in the old days, when the Northam buses were almost free, I suppose I used to go on them more often?'

Brian does not answer, and Alix lets the subject drop. She is not very interested in it either.

They inch forward. Ahead, the lights are dead. Lucky they are not in the old Renault, which would have overheated by now.

'Do you think,' says Alix, starting off on another track, 'that by the year 2000 they'll have settled the Cambodian question? Will we be able to go and scatter Stephen's ashes at Angkor Wat? That would be a good way of celebrating the millennium.'

'Stephen hasn't got any ashes,' says Brian.

'Well, we could scatter *something*,' says Alix, unperturbed. 'I'd quite like to see Angkor, wouldn't you?'

'Not much,' says Brian.

They both laugh.

'Now,' says Alix, 'you've got to promise to enjoy yourself, at Queyssac.'

'I promise,' says Brian. And he means it. The Dordogne, he can take.

Another six inches, another stoppage. Brian switches on their fine new radio-cassette and tunes in to Capital Radio, which helpfully tells him that a power failure and a series of accidents are paralysing West and North-west London. Stay at home, advises the radio, unless your journey is absolutely necessary. Brian twiddles the knob and finds a discussion on the World Service about Eastern Europe, in which various experts assure their listeners that, despite *glasnost* and *perestroika* in the Soviet Union, the Eastern European dictatorships will never be overthrown. The Berlin Wall will stand for ever.

Alix and Brian listen for a few minutes, trustingly. Why should they doubt it? They do not know what is in store for them. They do not know that the End of History will shortly be announced.

They listen, and then they get bored. Brian changes programmes, looking for music, finding Nilsson. A man on the other side of the road goes mad and drives his car on to the pavement. Alix fixes her

MARGARET DRABBLE

attention on a little scene just ahead of them. A pretty and petite young traffic warden with blonde hair peeping from beneath her cap and a high, fresh country complexion and glossy gaily painted lips is in altercation with a young man whose beaten-up old banger has been clamped. Alix cannot hear what they are saying, but she can read it from their body language. She, on her dignity, is protesting that the clamping is nothing to do with her, it is done by a different department. He is pointing to a message on his windscreen, no doubt protesting Breakdown or Meter Broken. She is telling him that this is nothing to do with her either, and neither is this (eloquent gesture) amazing snarl-up. The young man, tall, dark, with long hair and high Mexican cheekbones, wearing a leather jacket and jewellery, fancies himself, and in Alix's view rightly, for he is a good-looker. The traffic warden fancies herself too, also rightly. As Alix watches, the young man kicks one of his own flattish tyres, shrugs his shoulders, and turns away with some final defiant wisecrack. And, as Alix continues to watch, the traffic warden begins to laugh. The young man turns back towards her, caught by surprise. The warden laughs and laughs. He makes some comment, which drives her further into hilarity. She laughs from a full throat, she hits out at him in mirth with her little gloved hand. She gasps some riposte. Both of them collapse. He has to lean on the rusty battered flank of his incapacitated and insulted property. She tries to control herself, looks round to see if anyone is watching her betrayal of the dignity of her uniform, and again succumbs. It is a dumbshow, a scene from the *commedia dell'arte*. They are both as happy as can be, there on the dirty pavement in Lisson Grove.

An absurd lightness of heart fills Alix, as she watches this absurd encounter. She does not really mind if the traffic stops for ever, if she and Brian sit here for ever to the strains of Nielsen and the spectacle of the silent laughter beyond the screen. This is just fine, just fine. No doubt it will be prettier in Queyssac-les-Vignes, in their little rented farmhouse. It will be sunnier, more picturesque than here. Nicholas and Ilse and Sam and the new baby will visit, and they will feast upon cheeses and grapes and tomatoes and basil and *petit pain au chocolat* and wine, not upon fish and chips from newspaper parcels. She looks forward to it. But meanwhile, it is just fine right here, with the hoardings advertising Guinness and the Tory Party, with the council blocks with their smart new burglar-proof entry phones, with the Roman Catholic primary school and the tandoori takeaway and the new private hospital called after Florence Nightingale, and the Home of the Chesterfield and a shop full of doll's houses, and a slogan declaring PSYCHIATRY KILLS! This is Good Time, Good Place. In comparison with the Fistula Hospital, this is just dandy. And even the Fistula Hospital wasn't all *that* bad. As long as you didn't have to die in it.

Brian is not quite as resigned to immobility as Alix. He says he is getting hungry. The Thai dinner had been delicious but insubstantial, and Polly Piper was not a breakfast person. He reaches for a mint from the glove pocket. Alix tells him not to worry, Liz always over-caters, and indeed when they finally reach Dresden Road there are still plenty of snacks left, although many of the earlier guests are now a little drunk. Alix furnishes herself with a glass, and goes off in pursuit of Esther, whom she has not seen for more than a year, whom she has not seen since her marriage; and Brian, inevitably, finds himself listening politely as Melvyn Stacey tells him about the anomalies (and in his view iniquities) of the continuing representation of the Khmer Rouge at the United Nations. It is a subject of which Brian knows a little but not much. He is willing to listen. If he gets a chance to speak, he will respond with news of the Vietnamese resettlement project in Northam.

In the kitchen, Jonathan Headleand is kissing Deirdre Kavanagh. The chain of her necklace has broken, and little watery glass leaves and frosted fluted petals and bright white shiny painted stamens shower into the uplifted cups of her brassière and scatter on the cork-tiled floor.

On Liz Headleand's best spare bed, Hattie Osborne lies flat on her back and wiggles her toes as she stares at the plaster rose in the centre of the ceiling, as she holds both protective hands palm down upon the mound of her unborn baby and wonders not for the first time whether it would be bad form to call it Stephen or Stephanie. She is calmly nervous. What if it all goes wrong, what if she dies under the knife, what if there is great pain? What if Aaron abandons her? She sighs, and shuts her eyes for a moment. It does not matter if he does. If she survives this adventure, she will never be alone again. She has married into the Headleands. Aaron may desert her, but Liz and Charles and Marcia never will. She has a family. They will not disown her now.

In the garden, Gabriel Denham is cross-questioning Charles Headleand about Global International's prospects in Hong Kong, and Liz is restoring to the finger of Marianne Sanderson the Pailin ruby she had failed to deliver to Dr Chhi Beng Sam.

Esther and Alix, reunited by a bed of nicotine flowers, discover that they have not met since their mini-holiday in Italy more than a year ago: they speak of Alix's researches and the Queen of Novara. Cathy Upwood, plucking destructively at a climbing hydrangea, talks to a raffish old bird in a felt hat who says she is called Marjorie, and who claims that Stephen Cox spent his last night in London at her seventieth birthday party. Cathy thinks Marjorie is making it all up, but why not? Cathy is a terrible liar herself, she well understands liars. In the dining room, Simon Grunewald is entertaining a wide-eyed Hilda Stark with traveller's tales about the burial rituals in Irian Jaya and the efforts of Catholic missionaries to prevent the villagers from surrounding themselves with stinking platforms covered with decaying corpses, and Robert Oxenholme is talking about cricket to Oliver, the West Indian lover of Liz's half-sister and his own distant cousin Marcia Campbell. When they meet, Robert and Oliver always talk about cricket, a subject about which both are knowledgeable, though they suspect that there is another, more interesting topic that they might chance on one day if they pursue the metaphor faithfully enough, if they get to the end of their views of Wes Hall, Malcolm Marshall and intimidatory bowling.

In the downstairs lavatory, the professional mourner is repairing her vampire lips. At the foot of the stairs, inconveniently interrupting the free flow of guests, Stephen's respectable brothers are brazenly interrogating one of his several publishers about royalty statements and monies due. Can it be true, they want to know, that that woman who calls herself Harriet Osborne is Stephen's literary executor? What *is* a literary executor? In their view, this phrase has no status in law. Who was Stephen's solicitor? Where is his solicitor? Why have they not been better informed? They are, after all, they insist, the next of kin.

Half-in, half-out of the house, on the pretty latticed Edwardian back veranda, Sally Headleand (who has only come for the drinks and the snacks) finds herself engrossed in an intense soul-to-soul confessional with one of Stephen's loyal ex-copy-editors from long ago. Sally has already told Pansy about her mad dead grandmother, her aunt Shirley in Alberta, her cousin Celia who is stuck in Oxford for ever, her sister Stella who is taking the slow boat back from New Zealand with a stop-off in China on the way: and Pansy has reciprocated with details of her own grandmother's death in a hotel fire in Brazil, her unreciprocated passion for one of her less talented but sexier authors, her daughter's asthma, and her sister's marriage to a Saudi Arabian engineer. Sally and Pansy have been drawn together by their hairstyles, for both have gone for a short-sided, butch, erect, highly coloured format: Pansy's is ink black, Sally's henna red; Pansy has deliberate metallic little curls over her temples, and Sally has an intriguing soft vestigial pigtail at the nape of her neck.

Liz, her duty to Saint Marianne accomplished, moves through the gathering, checking fluid level, noise level, compatibility, mobility. She forces Stephen's brothers away from the foot of the stairs into the drawing room and brutally introduces them to Simon Grunewald. She whisks Hilda Stark off to speak to John Geddes, who is trying hard to enjoy the party, although (and this he tells nobody) his lover Indra had died two days earlier holding his hand in the London Lighthouse, and he himself is worried about loss of weight and appetite. Is it grief, is it infection, and which would he rather it were? John Geddes smiles gamely, as Hilda is pushed his way. 'Darling!' he cries. 'It's been an age! You read that poem *divinely*! How well you look! *What* a lovely blue. Is that Thai silk too? I see Thai silk is *the* funeral fabric. It's beautiful. I *say*' (lowering his voice, glancing after Liz, bravely confronting and challenging comment on the worst of his fears) 'isn't our friend Elizabeth looking well. She must have lost a stone at least! That illness did her a power of good . . .'

Charles has moved on from Gabriel Denham, and is now gazing into the little pond with Marcia Campbell at water boatmen, Canadian pondweed, a black-spotted water-lily leaf, and a small pale fish. He too is speaking about Liz. He is telling Marcia about the first time he met her, thirty-odd years ago, when she was the newly separated wife of Edgar Lintot. Dr Liz Lintot, house physician at St Michael's Hospital. He had met her at a noisy party in Greenwich, given by a bunch of young barristers and a journalist from the *Telegraph*. He had spent the evening telling Liz about the death of his wife, about his three little motherless boys. She had listened greedily, had nodded and prompted, had been fascinated by his tale of sorrow. 'She was a bloody good listener in those days,' says Charles, with a heavy sentimental sigh. 'With me, it was love at first sight.'

'Why don't you two get together again?' asks match-making Marcia, with mock-innocence.

'I've thought of it,' says Charles. 'I've thought of it. But you can't wind back the clock, can you? You can't make water flow uphill. No, I'm afraid we buggered that one up. Shame, really.'

'Yes,' echoes Marcia, 'it's a shame.'

Up on the best spare bed, Hattie is telling Aaron that she feels odd. Low back ache, might even be labour pains. How's the traffic, she wants to know. She doesn't fancy giving birth in the Fiat. On the other hand, what if her waters break all over Liz's smart white drawn threadwork fake-Victorian cotton counterpane? In the bathroom, the vampire is perfuming herself with Liz's Eau de l'Herbe Bleue. In the kitchen, Deirdre Kavanagh is gazing in dismay at the pieces of a gold coffee pot that she and Jonathan have in their passion dislodged: its fragments lie on the floor amongst the crushed Venetian glass roses.

In the study, the vicar is staring at the titles of Liz's books. He feels left out, neglected. Alone of the guests, he feels he is not getting the best out of this gathering. He has no complaints about the refreshments, no, they have been more than satisfactory: but he had hoped for a little serious conversation. He is a conscientious man, a professional, and in preparation for this event he had dutifully read his way through most of the *œuvre* of Stephen Cox. He had sat up until the small hours, reading an essay on Coleridge and the French Revolution. He had been expecting a higher tone, a more reverent remembering, from these literary types. He had been game to talk about the historical novel, about the French Commune, about the Goncourt brothers, even about post-modernism, if it should come to that. But hardly anybody he has met has even mentioned Stephen, let alone his *œuvre*. They are all absorbed in their own affairs. Chatter chatter, gossip wink and wave. Who *are* all these folk? What strange hairstyles the young affect, and how bizarre the shoes of the counter-tenor! He cannot work out who is married to whom, who divorced from whom. Is it possible that the vastly pregnant not-so-young woman can be Dr Headleand's daughter-in-law? Surely not. And who on earth was that shabby young man who had burst into the church so noisily in the middle of the service? What has happened to *him*?

'Yes,' continues Charles to his willing auditor, 'I proposed to her in a Chinese restaurant. In the middle of some party or other. She was making eyes at Gabriel Denham. We were all having dinner after a show. I'll put a stop to *that*, I thought to myself.'

'Very wise of you,' says Marcia. 'Why don't you ask her again?'

Liz, herding and rearranging, ringing an ambulance for Hattie, picking up fragments of Royal Worcester, encouraging Deirdre to make more coffee, wheedling the vicar out of the study and into conversation with Mr Goodfellow, looks around her with pride and satisfaction. It has all gone off very well. She should give parties more often, she decides, as the ambulance wails to a halt outside her front gate, as Hattie descends the stairs on Aaron's arm, as party-goers assemble on the path to wave and blow kisses and shout good luck, good luck, let us know how you get on! Another grandchild, what fun! Ah, life is amazingly exhilarating, thinks Liz, as she turns back to her house full of people. The vicar and Mr Goodfellow are talking about Confucius, Jesus Christ and worldly goods. They speak of the blessed life of the vagrant. 'Yes,' repeats Mr Goodfellow, 'Stephen didn't have many things.'

After Hattie's departure, the party ebbs, and guests begin to take their leave. There is a brief flurry of revived energy as an Express Delivery van arrives from Gatwick Airport bearing a large white oblong cardboard box as big as a tombstone containing a sheaf of yellow and wine-brown orchids and a message from Miss Porntip. It is greeted with admiration and disapproval. Deirdre fails in her attempt to find a vase large enough to contain the ostentatious blooms, and goes upstairs to have a little lie-down on the spare bed vacated by Hattie. She falls fast asleep. Jonathan, distracted, drives off to Norwich. Charles also drives off, saying he is going back to the office, but Liz suspects he is going for a little lie-down in Kentish Town. Robert Oxenholme's car arrives, but Esther says she will not accompany him: she will stay a little to help Liz tidy up. Brian nods off in the large chair in Liz's study. He tires easily these days.

458

And so it is that Esther, Alix and Liz, the Evader, the Widow Maker and the Wounded Healer, find themselves drinking tea in Liz's kitchen, and chewing over the day's events. Yes, they agree, it had all gone well. The service, the music, the readings. It had been a good turn-out, they had done Stephen proud, and Hattie's timing had been inspired. A death and a birth. Of course, says Liz, it wasn't entirely accidental, she had arranged it on purpose. Stage-managed it. A theatrical couple, Hattie and Aaron. In Liz's view, the baby will be a boy, but Aaron, although he knows, will not tell her. Hattie wants to be surprised, so Liz too will have to wait. Alix is also about to become a grandmother. Ilse is expecting a baby any day now. She knows it will be a girl. She will be called Maia. No, Alix does not know why: some private reason.

They have not met, these three, since their little Italian holiday in the lakes, which they now celebrate. They reminisce, and promise themselves that they should meet more often. Husbands and grand-children and illnesses and affairs of state must not be allowed to sunder them. Why do they not arrange to take another little holiday? This year is bespoken, but next year, why do they not take a break together? Why do they not go for a walk in the country, as they used to do in the old days? In the old days, they had talked of a walking holiday. They have never done it. If not now, when? And where should it be?

One can go on such holidays in France, in Italy, volunteers Esther. They book your hotels and carry your bags. Liz says she has had enough of abroad, why not try England? Because of the pissing awful weather, says Esther. I mean, look at it.

They gaze out of the window at the dark purple sky, the thunderous lilac, the ghastly battered hanging pallid grape-clusters of the wisteria. It is beginning to rain again, heavily. Thunder rumbles in the distance.

'Still, I do fancy England,' says Alix. 'There's nowhere quite so good for walking. We always used to say we'd do the Devon

Coast Path. Or the Ridgeway. Why don't you all come up and stay with me, and we'll redo the Pennine Way? Or we could do the Three Dales Walk. Ryedale, Dovedale and Glydale. It's wonderful country.'

The idea attracts them. Yes, they agree, they will pursue it.

'I mean,' says Liz, 'we're not getting any younger. We'll get out of practice, if we don't go soon. We'd better not leave it until we're seventy.'

She has forgotten all about her bad ankle. Despite her words, she has forgotten all about ageing and death. They have all forgotten. They may not be getting any younger, but they are not getting any older either. Time is an illusion, they can arrest it. Yes, they will defy the English climate, and make a plan. Their spirits rise.

As they sit there in a kitchen piled high with unwashed glasses and plates, they are not to know what the next year has in store.

They are not to know that the weather of England has changed utterly, and that the summer of '89 will bring them blue skies and unclouded sunshine, an unimagined and unchanging radiance. They will be rewarded, as they walk along the green ceiling of the limestone and by the singing river, with the glory of Paradise. It will beat down upon them and reprieve them from mortality, as they sit on the short starred sheep-cropped turf and eat their egg and anchovy sandwiches, as they greet a bent old man by a gate, as they drink from a mossy stone fountain in a village square, watched by a lonely young Oriental furnished with a rucksack and a pair of binoculars. He will watch them with envy, the three women, as they laugh by the fountain, and drink the ancient water. Is he a Japanese Brontë scholar, or a Korean ornithologist, or a palae-ontologist from Brandipura? Shall they invite him to join them? One might expect it to be Alix who will wish to take pity on his solitude, but in fact it will be Liz, who, briefly, will meet his eye and smile: for she will still be subconsciously searching, will indeed for ever search, for the lost Mitra Akrun.

But this is all in the future, unrevealed. Now, it rains. Yes, they will meet soon, they promise one another, as they stand in the stained-glass Edwardian portico, as Brian puts up his umbrella.

Liz waves them off, and returns to her emptied house. It had been, she considers, a triumph, of its kind. She wanders from room to room, surveying the damage. How soon will there be news of Hattie's baby? Who spilt that wine on the hall carpet? Where has her cat taken refuge?

Miss Porntip's alien blooms are still trapped in their box. As she releases them, she thinks suddenly of Rose and Konstantin Vassiliou. Why had they defected? Why had they failed her feast?

*

There is no way that Konstantin and Rose Vassiliou could have attended the reception in Dresden Road. They belong to a different world and a different density. They have wandered into this story from the old-fashioned, Freudian, psychological novel, and they cannot mix and mingle with the guests of Liz Headland. They should never have been invited.

There is not time for them here.

Konstantin and Rose sit in the café in Seven Dials, drinking cup after cup of coffee.

Is it Rose's fault that Konstantin is a sweet bird of death, a mourning dove, a destroyer, driven by childhood responsibilities to haunt battlefields and widows and orphans and starving children?

Is it Rose's fault that Stephen, whom she has never met, lies dead in an unmarked grave? Is it Rose's fault that Konstantin has been through the slough of despond and dwelt in the valley of the shadow? This is the language she gave him, these the images, and this the pain.

Is it Konstantin's fault that Rose Vassiliou looks old and worn, that her face is etched with little lines of sorrow, that her hair has turned grey? Is it Konstantin's fault that her nails are bitten to the quick like the nails of a schoolgirl?

We must leave them there, mother and son, to their own explanations, to their own reconciliations. We cannot overhear their conversation.

Nor can we see Mitra Akrun, as he strides through the forest, girded not with a camera but with a cartridge belt. Mitra Akrun has been much invoked, by his mother, by Konstantin Vassiliou, by Stephen Cox, by Liz Headleand, by the *Bangkok Post*, by the charitable agency that used his mother's image to raise funds for its own purposes. But he will not respond to the summons. He will not present himself at Site Ten, he will not reach the family embrace. He will not step back through the gates of horn. He will march on, armed, blooded, bloodied, a rusty Chinese rifle at his back. Many have died and many more will die in their attempt to maim and capture him. He grows and grows, he multiplies. Terribly, he smiles. He is legion. He has not been told that he is living at the end of history. He does not care whether his mother lives or dies. He marches on. He is multitudes.

Bibliography

Arendt, Hannah, *The Burden of Our Time* (Secker & Warburg, 1951)

Baker, Mark, *Nam* (Sphere, 1982)

Barnett, Anthony, 'Perennial Cambodia', *New Left Review*, March/April 1990

Becker, Elizabeth, *When the War was Over* (Simon & Schuster, New York, 1986)

Dalglish, Carol, *Refugees from Vietnam* (Macmillan, 1989)

Dimas, David D., *Missing in Action – Prisoner of War* (Orion Publications, La Mirada, California, 1987)

Gide, André, *Travels in the Congo* (Knopf, New York, 1929)

Fawcett, Brian, *Cambodia: A Book for Those Who Find Television Too Slow* (Talonbooks, Vancouver, 1986)

Fenton, James, *All the Wrong Places* (Viking, 1989)

Finlay, Rosalind and Reynolds, Jill, *Social Work and Refugees* (National Extension College, Cambridge, 1987)

Gorer, Geoffrey, *Bali and Angkor: Or, Looking at Life and Death* (Michael Joseph, 1936)

Heiser, Joseph M., *Vietnam Studies: Logistic Support* (Department of the Army, Washington, DC, 1974)

Herr, Michael, *Dispatches* (Hodder, 1989)

Isaacs, Arnold R., *Without Honour: Defeat in Vietnam and Cambodia* (Johns Hopkins University Press, Baltimore, Maryland, 1983)

Jacob, J. M., 'Pre-Angkor Cambodia: Evidence from Khmer Inscriptions' in Smith, R. B. and Watson, W., eds., *Early South East Asia* (OUP, 1979)

Kiernan, Ben, *How Pol Pot Came to Power* (Verso, 1985)

Lewinski, Jorge, *The Camera at War* (W. H. Allen, 1978)

MacAree, David, 'Letter from Phnom Penh', *Balliol College Annual Record*, Didcot, 1988

MacDonald, Malcolm, *Angkor and the Khmers* (Jonathan Cape, 1937)

Malraux, Clara, *Mémoires* (Grasset, Paris, 1963)

Myrdal, Jan and Kessle, Gun, *Angkor: An Essay on Art and Imperialism* (Chatto & Windus, 1971)

Mysliwiec, Eva, *Punishing the Door: The International Isolation of Cambodia* (Oxfam, Oxford, 1988)

Nguyen Khac Vien and Huu Ngoc, *Vietnamese Literature* (Foreign Languages Publishing House, Red River, Hanoi)

Phongpaichit, Pasuk, *From Peasant Girls to Bangkok Masseuses* (International Labour Office, Geneva, 1982)

Reynell, Josephine, *Political Pawns: Refugees on the Thai–Kampuchean Border* (Refugee Studies Programme, Oxford, 1989)

Schneebaum, Tobias, *Where the Spirits Dwell* (Weidenfeld, 1988)

Shawcross, William, *The Quality of Mercy* (André Deutsch, 1984)

Warren, William, *Jim Thompson: The Legendary American in Thailand* (Houghton Mifflin, Boston, 1970)

FOR THE BEST IN PAPERBACKS, LOOK FOR THE 🐧

In every corner of the world, on every subject under the sun, Penguin represents quality and variety – the very best in publishing today.

For complete information about books available from Penguin – including Puffins, Penguin Classics and Arkana – and how to order them, write to us at the appropriate address below. Please note that for copyright reasons the selection of books varies from country to country.

In the United Kingdom: Please write to *Dept JC, Penguin Books Ltd, FREEPOST, West Drayton, Middlesex, UB7 0BR.*

If you have any difficulty in obtaining a title, please send your order with the correct money, plus ten per cent for postage and packaging, to *PO Box No 11, West Drayton, Middlesex*

In the United States: Please write to *Dept BA, Penguin, 299 Murray Hill Parkway, East Rutherford, New Jersey 07073*

In Canada: Please write to *Penguin Books Canada Ltd, 2801 John Street, Markham, Ontario L3R 1B4*

In Australia: Please write to the *Marketing Department, Penguin Books Australia Ltd, P.O. Box 257, Ringwood, Victoria 3134*

In New Zealand: Please write to the *Marketing Department, Penguin Books (NZ) Ltd, Private Bag, Takapuna, Auckland 9*

In India: Please write to *Penguin Overseas Ltd, 706 Eros Apartments, 56 Nehru Place, New Delhi, 110019*

In the Netherlands: Please write to *Penguin Books Netherlands B.V., Postbus 3507, NL-1001 AH, Amsterdam*

In West Germany: Please write to *Penguin Books Ltd, Friedrichstrasse 10–12, D-6000 Frankfurt/Main 1*

In Spain: Please write to *Alhambra Longman S.A., Fernandez de la Hoz 9, E-28010 Madrid*

In Italy: Please write to *Penguin Italia s.r.l., Via Como 4, I-20096 Pioltello (Milano)*

In France: Please write to *Penguin France S.A., 17 rue Lejeune, F-31000 Toulouse*

In Japan: Please write to *Longman Penguin Japan Co Ltd, Yamaguchi Building, 2-12-9 Kanda Jimbocho, Chiyoda-Ku, Tokyo 101*

The first two novels in her acclaimed trilogy

The Radiant Way

Liz, Alix and Esther were among the most brilliant of their generation. To these three gifted and ambitious young women, fresh from Cambridge in the 1950s, the world offered its riches. On New Year's Eve 1979 they reunite to celebrate the birth of a new decade. What does the future now hold for Liz, assured Harley Street psychotherapist, wife, mother and stepmother; for relentlessly well-intentioned Alix, teaching English literature to young girl offenders; and for Esther, eccentric connoisseur of art, resolutely single and living at the wrong end of Ladbroke Grove? In exploring the lives of these three women and in telling of their loves and losses, their hopes and fears, Margaret Drabble creates an unforgettable panorama of our changing times.

A Natural Curiosity

Now in their fifties, Liz, Alix and Esther are more than ever disposed to question, to re-evaluate, to examine their motives and directions in the brutally prosperous, atrocity-hungry society of eighties Britain. In a narrative that moves effortlessly from black comedy to acute social observation, Margaret Drabble's *A Natural Curiosity* picks up some of the characters and stories of *The Radiant Way*, while adding others and shifting the scene to the North, in an engrossing continuation of her vivid panorama of the way we are today.

'This book, like its predecessor, is a remarkable mixture of rambling but compelling narrative, psychological insight, generous human portrayal, acute observation, humour, horror, beauty and disgust' – *The Times Literary Supplement*

BY THE SAME AUTHOR

The Ice-Age

Anthony Keating is middle-aged. His undoubted talents have brought him a dodgily prosperous living as a property developer, an estranged wife, a devoted mistress, several children and a heart attack.

The Realms of Gold

Frances Wingate is a very competent lady. A successful archaeologist with four healthy children, she is famous and, above all, independent. So, what is she searching for on her trips into the distant past of the desert or the nearer past of her family?

The Middle Ground

The middle years of Kate Armstrong are caught between parents and children and are free of neither. When Kate is forced to make a reconnaissance of the middle ground of her life, she makes some surprising discoveries.

The Millstone

Rosamund – independent, sophisticated, enviably clever – is terrified of true maturity. Then, ironically, her first sexual experience leaves her pregnant . . .

The Garrick Year

This novel takes the lid off a theatrical marriage; inside we find Emma, married to an egocentric actor playing a year's season at a provincial theatre festival, David, her husband – and Wyndham the producer. The mixture rapidly turns to acid.

Jerusalem the Golden

The girl from Northam was grateful to find herself accepted in London intellectual circles. She could become the golden girl and have real affairs with married men, just like in the novels.

and

A Summer Bird-Cage
The Waterfall
The Needle's Eye